KISS OF LIFE

KISS OF LIFE

Alicia Over

Book Guild Publishing
Sussex, England

First published in Great Britain in 2010 by
The Book Guild Ltd
Pavilion View
19 New Road
Brighton, BN1 1UF

Typesetting in Baskerville by
Nat-Type, Cheshire

Printed in Great Britain by
CPI Antony Rowe

A catalogue record for this book is available from
The British Library.

ISBN 978 1 84624 493 3

For my late husband, Alan

ACKNOWLEDGEMENTS

Anne Phipps for all her help and encouragement.

Jonathan and Isabel, my brother and sister-in-law, for their constant support.

Myra and Bryan Lillywhite, Maryrose Lacey and many other friends who kept me going.

PROLOGUE

1945

Doctor James Brandon was unaware that a new social order was afoot. This was largely due to the fact that his mind was mostly consumed by the practice of medicine. He was known to discuss a patient's urinary output, and worse, at dinner parties. This was inconsequential as he only mixed with other doctors and therefore these subjects would have been a normal topic.

James' preoccupation with his profession had paid off handsomely. He was, at forty-four, senior consultant physician at a large provincial hospital. He had written papers on lung disease and had treated and cured a local patient who had since become a Cabinet Minister. His star was in its ascendancy.

Good looks in James' case, however, counted for little. He was pedantic and formal and this prevented any female from seeing him as other than a rather arrogant and unapproachable figure. James himself gave no encouragement, even unthinkingly, in this area as he was a happily married man with two sons whom he hoped would follow him into his profession.

Having methodically cleared his desk on this early September evening, James, for once, was not thinking about his hospital commitments but more of getting home and taking his boys out on the lawn for cricket practice. He collected his bag and made his way to the front of the hospital where his car was standing in its assigned parking space. No one dared to place their vehicle on this hallowed

1

spot. James was not a man to cross. Placing himself, fussily, into the driver's seat, he pulled out the choke and started his car, then eased his way onto the empty road.

On the drive home he fleetingly thought how pleased he was with his new registrar, Andrew Galbraith, home from the war, keen, ambitious, thorough and, importantly, respectful towards him. With the addition of young Miles Templeton, his houseman, son of an old university friend, his patients were in safe hands and this left him free to enjoy the weekend with his family.

As he reached home, his sons, Christopher and Jonathan, were hiding in the bushes that flanked the short drive to the imposing stone house. As usual they chased after the car along with Jason and Hera, the yellow Labradors. The dogs were inseparable from the children. James feigned surprise at their presence which made the three of them laugh, and the dogs bark. After parking he beckoned the boys.

'I thought we'd have a bit of cricket practice,' he promised them with a suggestion of a smile, knowing what the response would be. The boys whooped with delight and raced to get the brown leather cricket bag from the back hall. It was deliberately left there for instant access during the summer. James entered the house by the kitchen door and approached his wife Susan, who was sorting seeds on the pine table. He walked straight to her and kissed her. It was a habitual kiss.

'I gather you're taking the children out for cricket,' she said and smiled.

'Yes, is that all right?' he queried.

'Of course – but I do need to talk to you,' she told him significantly as she continued with her seed sorting.

James hesitated. He sensed it was more important than a normal domestic issue. He kissed her again.

'You will have my undivided attention after supper,' he told her softly.

James left to change. Susan abandoned her seeds to start preparing supper for the family. Like James, she was efficient and practical and her gardening skills and animal husbandry during the recent war years had sustained not only her own family but others in the village. Susan was not beautiful and paid no heed to personal adornment, but she was elegant and refined in spite of her wild flaxen hair and gaunt frame. She had been noted for having one of the best pairs of legs in the hospital, when she worked there as an almoner, which had brought her to the attention of James.

Her husband returned, suitably clad and prepared to join the boys on the lawn.

'Where is Alex? We shall need her to field.' It was a command barked by James.

'Leave her be James,' Susan told him, 'you know she sends your blood pressure rocketing.'

James turned without comment to join his sons.

The two boys were jumping with excitement and urging their father to start. They were using the stumps in sword play and the ball as a discus. James did not curb their exuberance and viewed it all with an indulgent smile.

'We'll get Alex out to field,' he said, the kindly smile fading.

Silence fell. 'I think she's in the summer house – reading,' Jonathan said defensively, knowing how his sister irritated their father.

'She's always in there,' Christopher complained, relishing the thought of trouble.

The large square lawn was surrounded by pristine flower beds and a brick and stone wall. The summer house was in the far left-hand corner and the children spent much of their time in it. Jonathan walked across the grass to inform his sister that her presence was required. He then ran back to join his father and brother who were setting up the stumps. As James looked up, immediate irritation crossed his face as his daughter emerged from her retreat. She stood, belligerence written across her freckled face, framed by hair that looked like a sheaf of corn that had burst from its string.

'We want you to field,' James told her, stretching his arms ready for action and implying there was no room for argument.

'I want to bat and bowl as well,' she said without moving towards them.

Immediately Jonathan took the bat and offered it to her. 'You go first,' he said sympathetically.

Alex smiled at him and moved towards them. Bat in hand she stood at the crease. James took his time, not once looking at her. He stamped an imaginary clod, carefully re-tested the bails at the bowling end and again stretched his arms. Without warning he sent down a fast and accurate delivery. Alex was clean bowled.

'Out first ball!' James shouted. It was a silly and childish remark from a man of his standing. There was relief all round. Alex had made her point and the game was able to proceed in a reasonably convivial atmosphere until supper was called.

After supper the three children cleared the table and washed up; they took their time as bedtime for the boys succeeded this particular task. Alex had jobs like shutting up the hens and walking the dogs, and unless she had her mother to herself she would drift to her room, or back to the summer house to read.

The boys were going back to boarding school during the coming week. James was stretching himself financially to send his sons to his old school. Alex would miss them. She was a pupil at the local grammar school and it was one aspect of her life that suited her, particularly as she had now made the tennis team.

By the time she had completed her allotted tasks, James and Susan had retired to James' study with a tray of dandelion coffee and Alex knew that they did not like to be disturbed. She wondered what they did or talked about. It had come to her knowledge that married couples did things that were unimaginable, particularly if they happened to be your own parents. Biology lessons seemed to confirm this information; furthermore, there were one or two girls in her form at school whom she suspected of having personal knowledge. The boys, on the other hand, were coy about the subject, even embarrassed during biology lessons. They really preferred sport and to congregate with their own gender.

Alex had checked with her father's textbooks for additional clarification. Then, sure of her information she invited her two brothers to the summer house to give them a selective version of these basic facts. The boys were captivated, incredulous and even frightened about what she imparted, but she backed her information with smuggled medical textbooks from James' study. It earned her respect and admiration from her brothers who now regarded her as a fount of knowledge on worldly matters.

Meanwhile, James and Susan were now settled in the comfortable but well-worn armchairs in the study. Susan now had her husband's attention.

'About our dinner party next week,' she said.

'What about it?' he questioned.

'You have invited young Templeton and it makes us thirteen for dinner,' she stressed.

'What do you mean?' James was genuinely puzzled.

'It's unlucky to sit thirteen around a dinner table, and it's too late to ask anyone else,' she told him, somewhat impatiently.

'I didn't think you were superstitious,' he said with surprise.' I can't tell Templeton that it's off.'

'It's not just me being superstitious, some of our guests may well be,' Susan told him.

'Funny you should say that,' James said, gazing at the ceiling. 'Wilson-Jones cancelled a young female patient from his operating list the other day because one of the junior nurses inadvertently put her in what she thought was a pretty, frilly theatre gown – it was of course a shroud. The anaesthetist went wild and Wilson-Jones sent her back to the ward. He refused to operate.' James chuckled at the thought. 'Fortunately she was a routine list case and I think he did her the following week.'

Susan was not best pleased at the interruption, particularly as there was a serious suggestion to negotiate. 'To get back to our discussion about the dinner party.' She could see the hint of a smile on the face of her normally serious-minded husband. She knew it would be an uphill battle to gain her purpose.

'I have a solution. Alex is fourteen and it's about time she learned some social graces.'

Before she could elaborate further James exploded at the thought. 'She's a disaster, on no account is she to be included!' The smile had disappeared.

'She's a teenager, do try and be more tolerant towards her, she helps me a lot, she will know most of our guests and if she mixes with grown-ups a bit more maybe her attitude might improve – after all, you were the one that messed it up by inviting Dr Templeton.'

James realised that that the argument was lost. 'Her school results aren't startling, and I can't see anyone marrying her,' he muttered.

'Now, now,' Susan soothed. 'I will make her look suitable for the occasion and she can sit at the bottom of the table away from you; furthermore, Sonia always likes to chat to Alex. Anyway, what have school results and her marriage prospects to do with anything?'

'I don't want Sonia putting ideas into her head either,' James warned.

Susan did not need to reply. She had what she wanted.

Next morning after breakfast, when the boys had gone to start packing their trunks for school, Susan told Alex that she and James wanted her at the impending dinner party. Delight crossed Alex's face. 'Does Daddy really want me there?'

Susan nodded. 'I will put your hair in rags so you can have ringlets and you can wear that green velvet dress that cousin Anne sent, along with the green shoes.'

James came into the kitchen. Alex jumped and ran towards him but the smile died on her face as he turned away from her. Susan was not best pleased at his rejection of their daughter so she quickly moved the conversation on by saying, 'I'm going to need your help this coming week, what with the boys going back to school and the dinner party on Saturday.'

'Course I'll help,' Alex replied. To prove the point she scuttled off to do her routine jobs and when finished took herself to the summer house. It wasn't long before her brothers joined her.

'Anything to tell us?' Chris asked.

'Maybe,' she said, lying back in the deck chair and closing her eyes.

'Come on, tell us,' Jonathan coaxed.

She could contain the news no longer. 'I'm going to the dinner party.'

The boys were impressed. 'They'll all be talking about gall bladders and things, anyway why are Ma and Pa having this dinner do?' Christopher asked.

'Oh, to mark VJ Day, the end of the war, and to meet up with all the returning medical staff.'

'Why didn't Pa go to the war then?' Jonathan asked.

'Because he had tuberculosis in his hip, because Granny gave him lots of milk when he was a child, that's why he has that slight limp.'

'Ma makes us drink milk,' Jonathan said nervously.

'We can't get it now silly, all the milk is tuberculin tested.'

'You really know things, Alex.'

Her blue eyes glittered with excitement. 'Yes, and I intend to know more,' were her last words as they packed up for the night.

The following week dragged for Alex in spite of the frenzied activity in the household. Kath, who normally worked three mornings a week in a domestic capacity, was brought in to assist with the dinner party preparations and getting the boys back to school. When Saturday came, all seemed in hand.

True to her word Susan had put rags in Alex's hair and the 'corn sheaf' had been replaced by smooth ringlets. When the green dress and shoes were donned there was a trans-formation that even Alex herself could scarcely believe as she gazed at herself in the pockmarked mirror in her bedroom. The long, thin legs, and what looked like oversized feet, were cased in white lace stockings and the prettiest of green pumps. Her hair framed her pale face, but still those freckles were visible. She had secretly searched her mother's dressing table for cosmetics to conceal them, but had found none. Crayons and flower heads applied to the cheeks had only caused irritation and itching and proved to be a far worse option.

Descending to the kitchen area in her finery prior to the arrival of the guests, she saw her mother's astonished stare. 'Why Alex, you look wonderful!' she exclaimed.

James, who was opening bottles, turned. He froze. Susan sensed a derogatory remark and quickly told her daughter to take the wraps upstairs to the spare bedroom when the guests arrived.

'Who do you think will be the first to get here?' Alex asked, barely able to contain her excitement.

'Dr and Mrs Meadows,' Susan replied. 'Who do you think James?'

'Wilson-Jones, he always likes his operating lists to run to time.'

When the first guests did arrive it was neither of those but a cluster of six and they swamped the hall. Alex stepped back to admire the glamour of the wives and their dinner-jacketed husbands. The hardship of the war years had meant that dressing too formally for social reasons was insensitive, and clothing coupons were scarce. The dresses worn by the accompanying wives had a touch of yesteryear in spite of the sewing skills of their owners to adapt them. There was a whiff of naphthalene from the dinner jackets but it seemed the moths had not gone on a culinary spree during their incarceration in the back of the various wardrobes. Alex knew the women, all were local GP's wives. She marvelled at their transformation, particularly as it was accompanied by coquettish behaviour not normally associated with them. Even Susan was animated in her greetings. It boded well for the evening.

As it was warm, none of them had arrived with wraps so there was no requirement for Alex to whisk them away. None of the party spoke to her or gave her more than a cursory look. Susan greeted them and ushered them to the drawing room where James awaited with welcoming drinks and customary banter followed by guffawing and giggling, which receded as the guests were swallowed up in the throng.

Seconds later another couple arrived. Alex knew the husband to be Mr Travers, a consultant orthopaedic surgeon. Mrs Travers had been the ward sister on the orthopaedic ward.

'Is this Alex?' the kindly lady asked.

Alex nodded and found herself simpering.

'I shall have to keep my husband away from you I can see.'

Alex blushed. The inference excited her.

This time James came to take his guests into the now noisy drawing room.

9

Aunt Sonia then arrived with her man of the moment, Surgeon Commander Peter Gilbert. She was not married to him. Her husband of six weeks, Guy Bridges, a squadron leader in the RAF, had been killed in the Battle of Britain and it was recognised that she continued to grieve for him in spite of her whirlwind social life. She had been an erstwhile girl-friend of James until they both concluded there was no future in the relationship and she was more than happy when Susan supplanted her. A genuine friendship between them all remained.

James came to welcome them, giving Sonia a perfunctory kiss, was introduced to Peter Gilbert and then immediately broke into conversation with him and bore him off. This left Sonia free to retreat to the spare bedroom with the waiting Alex.

'You ravishing creature!' she told the girl as she held her at arms' length with disbelief.

'Mummy put my hair in rags,' the girl told her.

'The innocence,' Sonia sighed, almost with envy.

Again, Alex found herself simpering. She simply couldn't help it.

'Do you have any vanishing cream? Mummy doesn't use it.'

Sonia was puzzled. 'Why vanishing cream?'

'To make my freckles disappear.'

Sonia immediately opened her handbag and produced a small jar, followed by her powder compact, and offered it to Alex. 'Be subtle with it, only when you get to my age do you daub it on.'

Alex applied both cream and powder, Sonia then produced rouge and lipstick. 'I am probably going to be in deep trouble with your mother over this.'

Alex was ecstatic. 'No one will notice.'

Sonia's eyes widened. 'Oh yes they will, there are two or three lechers down there.'

Alex had heard this before from Aunt Sonia, so no

explanation was required. Difficult to imagine that any of those respectable looking doctors could be guilty of this label.

Fearful of leading her goddaughter astray, Sonia led the conversation on to safer topics and enquired about school and family life, then, making sure Alex had not been too generous with the cosmetics, she suggested they join the other guests.

Creeping down the staircase they made their way to the noisy drawing room. Sonia noted a young man talking to one of the more elderly wives. She swept herself and Alex towards them to make the introductions.

The young man was temporally taken aback. He stared at Alex. 'I was unaware that Dr Brandon had a daughter, I am his houseman, Miles Templeton.'

'Well you can see why he doesn't advertise the fact,' Sonia said quickly.

'Indeed I can.' Templeton's face lit up. He was having to tread carefully amongst such an august bunch of colleagues. One wrong remark to them or their wives could easily cost him future job prospects.

Just then dinner was called, James asking that each gentleman escort a lady to the dining room.

There was a rustle of activity as the men sought out a colleague's wife. Sonia was pounced upon by three or four admirers – her wonderful looks along with her vivacity made her irresistible. Almost invisibly she disappeared and Alex was left with the diffident Dr Templeton.

'Would you do me the honour of allowing me to accompany you, Miss Brandon?'

Alex could not remember a happier moment. To be referred to as 'Miss Brandon' was a new departure and reminded her of approaching adulthood. It was with trepidation that she put her arm on his and, with him, nervously followed the chattering guests into the dining room.

Once at the table she found herself seated near to Susan and diagonally opposite Dr Templeton. She was aware of his interest. Insecurity forced her to look in her father's direction – the 'rabbit and the headlights' syndrome – but he was too absorbed with his hosting to take notice of her. He was holding forth about how his sons would hopefully follow him into medicine.

'A dynastic medical family,' said a guest.

Alex was hurt – no mention of her future. At least she was secure in the fact that James' attention would not be focused in her direction. She leant back and took stock, thoughtfully letting her eyes linger over the animated company. Seated halfway along was the surgeon, Mr Wilson-Jones, who was smiling at her, but the smile had a lupine quality and it caused her to blush. Aunt Sonia, unknowingly, came to her rescue by suggesting that Wilson-Jones should carve the meat as he was bound to make a good job of it due to his skill in the operating theatre.

Alex quickly returned her attention to the safer ground occupied by Dr Templeton.

Relief at the conclusion of the war dominated the conversation, and there was much liveliness and happiness at the prospect of new and permanent careers ahead, and this, along with a plenitude of wine from the Brandon cellar was turning the gathering into a memorable evening for everyone. Alex felt the excitement – she had entered a grown-up world and it felt wonderful. Furthermore, she could see some admiring glances directed her way and each time she found herself simpering. She just couldn't help it, it was beyond her control and it certainly seemed to be having an effect on the roving eye of Wilson-Jones, even though the gorgeous Aunt Sonia was taking a lot of his attention. Eventually, when Sonia tired of him, he fixed her with a stare and called out.

'Well, young Alex, what do you intend to do when you leave school?'

Alex took a deep breath. She had no idea what would come out of her mouth. It had gone quiet. She looked at Templeton.

'I'm going to medical school, I'm going to read medicine.'

A voice boomed down from the head of the table, 'Oh no you are not, you won't have the necessary exam results.' It was James.

Alex blushed with shame, she felt the eyes upon her. She wanted to rush from the room.

'Stop it, James,' Susan hissed.

'Your mother said exactly the same about you, James,' Sonia told him, and waved her hand at him.

Wilson-Jones looked at her and Alex was reminded of Red Riding Hood. 'You can treat me anytime,' he told her softly.

She turned to Templeton and saw sympathy.

'All parents say it, you just *do* it, Miss Brandon, just do it,' he urged.

But it was not to Dr Templeton that Alex looked to for support. It was for Wilson-Jones that she twiddled with her ringlets and lowered her eyes.

1

Alexandra Rose Brandon qualified as a doctor the same year her father received his knighthood. Her success was overshadowed by this, indeed hardly noticed or commented on. Alex did not particularly mind as she had barely scraped through her finals and would not have done so except for her friendship with two other female medical students. Because they were committed they had kept Alex on course when she would rather have been out on the party scene. Magda in particular, a bright and eager student who was hungry, even greedy, for knowledge, had kept three noses to the grindstone and even tutored her two friends to keep them on track. Patricia, the other end of the triangle, was dogged and her perseverance was rewarded, and she constantly reminded Alex of this. The differing characters of the triumvirate bound them together, and their male counterparts, although constantly joking about female presence in a normally male bastion, held them in respect.

Now qualified, Alex found her attitude had profoundly changed. The charge that she had life and death decisions to make was weighing on her. Student pranks were over for ever and a new solemnity had taken hold. It came unbidden, and as Magda explained 'was part of the training'. Alex had secured the post of surgical houseman, but it was not what she really wanted. Jobs for women were difficult and she had a sneaking suspicion that her father's name had assisted in the appointment as there was a worthy crop of contenders.

Magda was now a casualty officer and Patricia had landed gynaecology and obstetrics. General apprehension assailed all three as they waited to join their respective 'firms' for their first day. They had collected in the doctors' dining room, able only to sip at their coffee. Consultants were renowned for humiliating their new appointees and expecting super-human stamina and expertise beyond their training; furthermore, Alex had been warned that her new boss, Mr Jarvis, was short on patience, and outspoken.

Magda roused them. They made their way to a large square area near the front entrance of the hospital, affectionately known as 'Concord'. Several corridors led into it and it was a collecting, trysting and information place as the walls were covered with noticeboards pertaining to all aspects of hospital, social and sporting life therein. It was buzzing with activity.

Magda squeezed Alex's hand before she abandoned her to the group headed by the dreaded Mr Jarvis. Three medical students were included and they looked reverentially at Alex, but Mr Jarvis soon dispelled this by saying, 'So you have decided to grace us with your presence, Dr Brandon.'

'Yes, sir,' Alex replied meekly.

'Well, let's not waste any more time.' And he turned abruptly and led the way to the surgical wards.

The rounds were terrifying, instructions were barked at her and the only helpful person was the ward sister who produced forms, X-rays and reports which eventually turned 'Mount' Jarvis from volcanic to quiescent. It was the start of a relentless and demoralising period and nothing that Alex could have imagined when she embarked on her medical career.

Not only did she have to attend to the patient needs on the wards but she was required in theatre as well. The following weeks were hectic but a routine was emerging, enabling her to have some spare time and connect again with Magda and Patricia who were faring no better with their consultants.

'Do you realise, every time we meet we talk "shop",' Magda commented as they had lunch in the dining room a few weeks later.

'Well, does anything else happen? If it does, it doesn't get through these walls,' Alex replied.

'This has really put me off having a baby.' Patricia sadly shook her head. 'The babies are fine but some of the mothers – '

Magda thumped the table. 'Stop feeling so sorry for yourselves, we'll have a night out. After all, we haven't spent any money since being in this hallowed Queensbridge Hospital.'

'Dinner at the Spencer?' Alex queried.

'You are such a snob, Alex, remember I'm just a common Liverpudlian, I was thinking of that fish place in the High Street.'

The three of them laughed and agreed.

Preparing for their first night out Alex felt almost guilty, soaking in the bath, washing her rampant hair and finally embellishing her face with little-used cosmetics. As she applied the lipstick she thought of Aunt Sonia and the dinner party that had shaped her life. It seemed so long ago. Here she was, qualified and independent with unlimited horizons. Tonight she felt particularly carefree and to make the point she added another layer of lipstick to her already reddened lips. Her reverie was interrupted by a banging on her door. She jumped up to let Magda and Patricia in. Both had taken the same care and trouble in their attire and were suppressing their eagerness to get going.

'You two look gorgeous,' Alex gasped.

'A white coat is not the most sexy garment,' Patricia commented. 'Hiding one's light, and all that.'

'Those black stockings and nurses' uniforms are a real threat,' Magda told them.

They were words that Alex would recall many months hence.

As they left their accommodation they met some of their male colleagues going to and fro from the hospital. It was obvious, even though well concealed, that their transformation was arousing interest. Even the jocular remarks were of a more flattering nature. As they sallied out into the Woodbridge Road the girls were in a mood they had not experienced since they passed their finals.

The small fish restaurant that Magda had designated was much trendier than she had led them to believe, in fact it was only recently opened. There were several couples and parties already there and ordering.

'A good choice,' Patricia said as she scanned the clientele and serving area.

Alex nodded. There were one or two extremely good-looking men that had caught her eye.

'They're all spoken for,' Magda told Alex, interpreting her thoughts.

'Surely there must be more where they came from,' Alex replied.

'We did cause a bit of a stir as we left the accommodation,' Magda said thoughtfully. 'I think we should highlight our personal attributes as we have tonight. There are plenty of good-looking, single men in the hospital. Here we are in our twenties with not a man between us.'

It was a good moment for the waiter to arrive and take their order.

When the food arrived it lived up to the delicious aroma that had preceded it. Alex was reminded of a post-war family camping holiday in France, and the lovely simple bistros where she and her brothers had been taken for special treats by their parents.

Magda had ordered wine for them. 'Men are like buses,' she told them philosophically, pausing with the wine glass in her hand. She took a sip. 'Not a single one, then three come along together.'

'I think Alex will be the first,' Patricia prophesied.

'Why me?' Alex asked.

'I just think married life and children are right for you,' Magda observed.

Alex shrugged, she didn't know whether it was a complimentary or derogatory remark.

'Your mother told me how wonderful you were with your two brothers, how you kept them entertained during the school holidays,' Magda continued.

Alex blushed as she thought of some of the facts that she imparted to Chris and Jon's receptive ears.

'Your younger brother told me he'd actually tested out some of the information you felt it was imperative that he should know and, the textbooks were particularly helpful.'

There was silence, then Magda and Patricia started to silently shake with laughter. Alex threw her napkin at Magda. 'That is the last time I invite you home!' But she joined in the laughter nonetheless.

The evening was a great success and they loitered on their way back, not anxious to end the rare and untroubled break from work.

'It's late, the proctors will be swinging into action,' Patricia remarked as she saw a scholar riding his bicycle at break-neck speed.

'Thank goodness those days are over for us.'

There were no time restrictions so they wandered in through the main entrance of the hospital. The night porter was there.

'Very quiet tonight, even casualty,' he told them.

It seemed to wind up what had been a wonderful evening and after parting from her friends and reaching her room

Alex went straight to bed where she slept deeply and dreamlessly. When she wakened the following morning she made a decision. From now on she would not be going on duty without serious cosmetic help.

This was the very morning to start. She was not due on until 11.30 a.m. Plenty of time to prepare. She went through the same ritual as for the previous night, even the same clothing, the only concession being flat shoes rather than high heels. Alex looked in the mirror. Her hair was now allowed to frame her pale face, the adolescent freckles long since gone. The lagoon-blue eyes were softly etched by black pencil, and further reddening of the lips and cheeks made her realise how the practice of medicine had sublimated her femininity. She wondered if anyone would notice or even consider why.

She made her way to the hospital. She was early but she did not want to incur the wrath of Mr Jarvis.

It was apparent that her colleagues did notice when they mustered. Even Mr Jarvis allowed his attention to linger two seconds longer. The registrar commented, 'Your day off seems to have done you some good,' and nodded approvingly.

Furthermore, there was a smidgen of politeness towards her.

'Look like a dogsbody and get treated like a dogsbody,' Alex summarised to herself.

She was in for a surprise when she discovered that Magda and Patricia had been struck with the same idea. Furthermore, the prediction that men were like buses – none, then three show up, became partially fulfilled. First, Richard. He was a senior houseman and an occasional nod as he passed their table in the dining room led on to a chance word of a jocular nature and then standing for a few minutes exchanging pleasantries. Since the cosmetic revolution he now sat with the girls, always of course implying that he was favouring them by reason of his superior status in the hospital, and masculine gender. He was, however, a welcome member to their group as he was a mine of information.

'Why does he grace us with his presence?' It was Magda who posed the question when Richard was absent.

'He has to fancy one of us,' Patricia volunteered.

'Not me,' Alex told her friends as they looked accusingly at her.

'That benign and avuncular appearance disguises a very sharp brain,' Magda told them thoughtfully. 'I wish I knew which one of us is the honey pot that brings him buzzing around.'

'He's overweight and has a red face,' Patricia said flatly.

'Maybe he has porphyria.' There was an acidic note in Magda's voice. 'Like King George.'

It had been her misfortune to have had a patient with this disease to examine and diagnose in the Bachelor of Medicine finals. And although she had correctly defined the symptoms she had not made the right diagnosis. It was an exceedingly sore point with her.

'He looks pretty healthy on the rugby field, I believe,' Alex told them. She knew Richard was not interested in her, but she agreed with Magda that female interest was the hidden agenda and all would be revealed in the fullness of time.

The next occurrence was obvious and required no threefold assessment. It occurred in theatre.

Alex, with her pencilled eyes and mascara, highlighted by her face mask, was aware that the anaesthetist was giving her a more attentive look than usual. She had noted him on other occasions but he was normally in a hurry and spared little time for conversation.

This particular day he was still disrobing in the surgeons' room. Alex, having sutured the final patient on the list, under the supervising eye of the registrar, made her way to similarly divest herself of the all encompassing theatre garb and ran into him. He put his hand out to introduce himself.

'I'm Douglas Ffrench, and you are Dick Jarvis's houseman.' As he ran his eyes over Alex he added, 'Or should I say housewoman.'

Alex blushed, but she felt excited. Dr Ffrench was an unbelievably attractive man and she had been noticed by him.

'Yes,' she said, confirming his remark. 'I'm Alexandra Brandon.' It came unbidden, the simper.

'I've been doing locum work here, working between four hospitals. Now I will be working here only.' He was watching her carefully. 'I hope I shall be seeing more of you in the future.' Again his eyes scanned her. Putting on his jacket and mustering his notes he smiled as he passed her, more closely than necessary, to exit the room.

Relaying the episode later to Magda and Patricia it got a mixed reception. Patricia was excited and giggly as Alex slightly exaggerated the encounter.

'The difference between him and those callow youths at medical school,' she sighed.

Magda shook her head. 'He sounds a bit too smooth if you ask me.'

'He is quite delicious, fair hair, blue eyes, movie-star looks.' Alex was not to be put off.

'So we have alpha and omega,' Magda said with resignation.

'What do you mean?' Patricia asked.

'Richard and Dr Ffrench – with two ffs of course.'

'Two of the buses have come along, at least it's a start,' Patricia said, seeking to diffuse the increasing tension that was developing.

Magda immediately changed the subject.

The next time Alex encountered Dr Ffrench was when she was scrubbing up. He emerged from the anaesthetic room, making his way into the theatre and as he passed he said,

'How sad that one so young should be sterile.' He was gone before an answer was possible.

It was a cryptic remark and Alex was not sure how it should be responded to. Within minutes she would be in theatre. She decided to ignore it.

During the list Dr Ffrench hardly appeared to notice her, but she was conscious of his presence. Magda was right as usual. One of the buses had reached its terminus. A terminus is not, however, a scrap yard, as Alex was to discover.

It took two or three weeks and as many encounters before Dr Ffrench re-ignited the contact between them. Again it was in the surgeons' changing room with just the two of them present. An exudation of charm preceded the conversation.

'I am so sorry not to have seen you, but circumstances have meant that my attention was concentrated on my moving into Queensbridge at the same time my mother was moving in Cheltenham. How I accomplished both, as well as my job, leads me to believe I must be superman.'

Alex was sure a 'double entendre' was intended in the last part of the remark.

'How about coming out for a drink tonight at the Spencer?'

For once Alex was relieved to say, 'I'm on call tonight.' It was all too sudden.

'Well, beautiful lady, when will you be available?'

Alex turned and looked behind her before asking, 'Where is this beautiful lady you wish to take out?'

Douglas Ffrench smiled. 'You know the beautiful lady is you, you must have been told thousands of times. Now answer my question – when.'

Alex was totally bowled over. She could not say 'no'. It was agreed they should meet the following night in Concord.

Imparting this news to Magda and Patricia, as Alex expected, had a mixed reception.

'Alex you must wear that blue suit of yours if you're going to the Spencer,' Patricia enthused.

'He wants to get you into bed,' was Magda's stark warning.

'Well he won't, but don't go putting ideas in my head,' Alex retorted.

'I have now seen him, and foreboding enters my soul,' Magda continued.

'Where did you see him then?' Alex was getting cross with Magda.

'Anaesthetists visit casualty, as it happens, I had a conversation with him.' Magda grabbed Alex's arm. 'Be careful our Alex!' A pseudo Liverpudlian tone made the warning sound kindly and well intentioned.

Alex smiled at Magda and Patricia; she wanted to dispel their worried looks. 'I know he's a charmer, but I do not intend to lose my virginity until I am married.'

Patricia and Magda clapped, but Alex couldn't wait for the Concord tryst.

She was so busy the next day that Alex gave little thought to her impending date. Two of yesterday's theatre cases were giving concern and had taken up her time and energy. As she handed over the reins to the registrar she felt a surge of vigour at the thought of the evening ahead with Douglas Ffrench.

Meeting at eight gave her plenty of time to prepare. There would be no interruption from her friends, as they were both on duty. Alex did not want to hear the 'gypsy's warning' again.

Slightly after the appointed time she made her way nervously to the front of the hospital. Nevertheless, her confidence was high. As she entered through the reception area and into Concord she could see him. He was looking at the noticeboards but turned as though aware of her presence. She could see the admiration in his eyes.

'Dr Brandon reporting to Dr Ffrench,' she told him playfully.

'I think you had better start calling me Douglas.' There

was a pause. 'After all, it sounds much more intimate my dear Alexandra.'

Again, the 'double entendre'.

'Then I insist you call me Alex, as all my friends do,' she replied, heavily stressing the word *friends.*

'It's a deal.' He knew it was also checkmate.

The evening was a great success now the goalposts had been set.

Alex became aware that the charm was a natural asset for Ffrench. He was easy to talk to, a good listener and an interesting conversationalist, and one or two ladies had cast admiring glances his way.

He told Alex about his family. His father had been an Army officer in the bomb disposal unit and five years previously had been killed doing his job. Douglas now felt responsibilities to his mother who was still grieving. He hoped her house move would assuage the hurt and encourage her to participate in society again.

Alex was impressed. *Admirable sentiments,* she thought. *Magda has seriously misunderstood this man.* She was careful when referring to her own family, stating that her father was a 'Midlands doctor'. Douglas did not seem overly interested in any event so there was no need to reveal more.

At the end of the evening he took her arm as he escorted her back to the accommodation. No hint of 'l'amour'. In fact he seemed serious.

'I've moved into doctors' quarters for the time being, I might rent a flat once I get settled in my job.'

'Do you plan to stay in anaesthetics?' Alex asked.

'I'm not sure, it's not so well paid as other branches of the profession. At the moment I'm quite happy, and I'll wait and see what opportunities present themselves. I'm only thirty-two.'

As the door of the accommodation appeared Alex turned and thanked Douglas. He made no move. 'I enjoyed this evening, we must do it again.' But he made no future arrangement between them.

Magda was in her room so Alex decided to pay her a late visit.

'I thought you might come back dishevelled,' she said as she greeted Alex.

'You have figured him out wrongly.'

Magda shook her head. 'I don't think so.'

'He was a perfect gentleman. Kind to his mother and that sort of thing,' Alex countered.

'History tells us that Attila the Hun was kind to his mother,' Magda told her with some sharpness, and then added, 'he may have figured out that you are no pushover and the stakes are high.'

'I've had enough of you, Magda, it seems to me you are jealous. I have had a super evening out and you just want to spoil it all.'

Magda was enraged. 'Don't you dare accuse me of jealousy! The number of times I've rescued you from scrapes, getting drunk and amorous, getting you off the hook with the proctors. All done in the name of friendship!'

'I don't need your protection, and you can keep your nose out of my business from now on!' And Alex flounced out, but when she got to her own room she slumped on the bed and sobbed. The sobbing continued until sleep overtook her and when she woke in the morning in her crumpled blue suit she felt a surge of remorse. She had no right to speak to Magda so cruelly. The one person who had believed in her, and encouraged her, she would never have achieved a medical degree without her. She owed Magda so much. There was only one thing for it – the grand apology and hope of forgiveness.

After preparing for work Alex went to Magda's room. She was not there. She must have been called out or decided to go on duty early.

It was unfortunate that the first person Alex ran into when making her way down the hospital corridor was Douglas. His smile turned to concern when he saw her.

'Are you all right?' He pulled her into a stairwell leading to one of the wards.

'Please Douglas, it's nothing to do with you or last night.'

'Work?'

'No.' She shook her head vehemently. Douglas wasn't going to give up until he had extracted an explanation.

'I have said hurtful things to someone and I need to put it right.'

A smirk crossed Douglas's face. 'I'd better let you get on with it, you can get me on my bleep if you need me.'

Alex remained in the stairwell for some minutes until it occurred to her. *He thinks I've dispatched a current boyfriend in favour of him, could he be that conceited?*

With this thought in mind Alex continued her pursuit of Magda, but it wasn't until lunchtime that she finally caught up with her. It wasn't the most convenient place either, staff were coming and going. Alex didn't care.

'I want to apologise to you, Magda, you are the best friend anyone could have. I want to retract every single thing I said to you last night.'

'Stop.' Magda pulled Alex into one of the wards and into sister's office. 'Could we borrow your office a minute, Sister, Dr Brandon is not well.'

Sister vacated her office and closed the door. Alex burst into tears and Magda put her arms round her and comforted her.

'No need to say anything more, Alex, too much water under the bridge.'

'Didn't mean to hurt "our Magda".'

'"Our Magda's" tough.'

Tough as she pretended to be, Magda was profoundly touched by her friend's contrition.

They shook hands and smiled at each other and vowed that no man would ever be allowed to penetrate their friendship again.

2

During the next few weeks Alex was disorientated by Douglas' behaviour. One minute he was declaring her importance to him, the next he seemed indifferent. He was also getting more persuasive with his affections even though Alex had made it clear that she had no intention of going to bed with him. Evenings together usually ended with a struggle as his hands roamed her body. He blamed her by saying, 'It's your fault, you shouldn't be so desirable.'

Alex was falling deeply in love with him in spite of this and she wondered how long she would be able to resist him.

She was now due for a job change. Surgery was not her forte. There was a post coming up in paediatrics and she desperately hoped to secure it. She had declared her intentions and as she had not 'blotted her copy book' with Mr Jarvis, she was hopeful.

Good fortune, like bad fortune, arrives in threes, as Alex was to find out.

The first was a telephone call from Douglas. He had just finished in theatre.

'Do you fancy having dinner at the Spencer tonight? I want to talk to you about something.'

It was on the tip of Alex's tongue to say she was unavailable. He had been particularly inattentive recently and she wondered if he was going to finish their liaison. To save her dignity she would assure him that the same thought had already occurred to her, but Alex knew she would be very hurt.

They met in Concord. Alex could see that Douglas was edgy. He did his best to conceal it, but she was now too conversant with his moods to be fooled.

He took her arm and led her out of the hospital.

'I feel quite hungry tonight,' she told him as they hastened their way to the Spencer.

'Good,' was all the response she received. He did however smile as he said it. If this was to be a 'last supper' at least she would bow out replete.

Once inside the hotel they were shown to their table. Before long a waiter appeared with a bottle of champagne and proceeded to open it. Alex was dumbstruck. Unable to ask the reason for the celebratory drink in front of the waiter, she looked at Douglas for an explanation. He was regarding her in a way she had never seen him do before.

'Promotion?' she asked while secretly thinking it was a ploy to lure her into bed.

He shook his head and continued to stare at her, and instead of tasting his champagne he placed his glass, rather unsteadily, on the table and then reached into his pocket and brought out a small box.

'Not promotion, I just want to ask you to marry me,' he said quietly and handed the small brown leather box to her.

Alex, with equal unsteadiness, placed her glass on the table and took the box. Inside there sparkled a solitaire engagement ring.

'What can I say?' she gasped.

'Yes would be the appropriate word.' He reached for her hand.

Alex was bereft of words. This had to be the most wondrous moment of her life.

'Don't tell me you are having to think about it,' he asked.

'Yes, yes, of course I'll marry you.'

Douglas leaned over, took the ring from the box and slid it onto her finger.

'It's beautiful,' Alex told him, although words were not coming easily.

'Just like you,' he replied, picking up his champagne glass and silently toasting her. 'The ring is Victorian and a family heirloom,' he told her, resuming the conversation.

Alex spread her left hand out for them both to admire the beauty of the stone.

'I shall treasure it. Oh Douglas, you are so adorable,' she said as they stared at each other with wonderment.

Mutual admiration was then interrupted by the appearance of the waiter. He presented the menu with a knowing look, aware that a romantic moment was taking place.

They chose their dinner at leisure.

'Snails,' Alex exclaimed. 'I had them with Aunt Sonia at some posh place in London when I was a medical student.'

Douglas nodded approval.

'What is steak tartare?' she asked him.

He described and recommended it, and though Alex had reservations about raw minced steak she reluctantly agreed with the choice.

'Look, Douglas, they have crêpes Suzette.'

'You like les crêpes Suzette, ma chère?' he responded with a pseudo French accent.

'Mais oui.' And the now little used simper came back.

'From now on I shall call you my crêpe Suzette!' His eyes glittered in the subdued hotel lighting. 'Flambé, I hope!'

'And soon to have an appropriate surname,' she reminded him.

Before Douglas could reply the waiter returned to take the order. With great coolness Douglas chose the forthcoming meal.

'I can't wait for you to be my wife in every sense of the word,' he whispered as the waiter departed.

'I can't wait for you to be my husband in the true meaning of the word,' Alex whispered back.

Similar little exchanges continued throughout the meal. After the dramatic finale of the crêpes Suzette followed by a leisurely coffee they wandered homeward. In the hospital grounds there was a bench shrouded by bushes. It was commonly used, even overused, for the same purpose that Douglas and Alex intended for it this evening. It was known in the hospital as the 'kissing seat' and had been donated by a grateful patient, though not intended for the purpose it was now notorious for.

The nearer they got to it the more their steps hastened and on reaching it they crashed down on the damp wooden slats. Tonight Alex did not restrain Douglas's enquiring hands but even he was not prepared to consummate their relationship on a hospital seat. Alex, however, got a taste of what their intimate married life had in store.

Passion spent, they talked for a while then kissed before making tracks for their separate accommodation.

Alex now felt she had reached the pinnacle of happiness.

Back in her room there was a note from Magda. It read: 'When you have finished your lustful, alcoholic nocturnal adventures could you contact Dr Peters about an interview for the paediatric post as soon as possible.' Alex kissed the note and flung herself on the bed. She was in raptures. How much more bliss could one person experience? She'd had to struggle for every bit of success and now it was dropping into her lap.

Surprisingly, that night she slept deeply and dreamlessly and waking in the morning she could still barely believe what had befallen her. She telephoned and spoke to her mother, telling her about the engagement. It was not the ordeal she had expected. Susan was calm and probably smug about getting a mid-twenties unmarried daughter off her hands. Enthusiastic congratulations were expressed along with the wish to meet this 'fabulous male'.

Alex also confirmed that she would be home that weekend when they could all enjoy an uninterrupted discussion to include all family members. She certainly did not want to hear cautionary words, especially from her father, and her mother was the best one to forestall this.

Then Alex re-read Magda's note about her job interview, and without delay dressed and headed for reception in the hospital. Running across the grounds clutching her white coat so that her stethoscope, torch and pen and patella hammer did not jump from her pocket she was reminded of her medical student days and being told by her tutor, 'Doctors only run in the event of fire, death or haemorrhage.' Silently she told herself, *and when they are madly in love and having an interview for the one job they really want.*

She arrived slightly breathless at reception and asked the receptionist to contact Dr Peters' secretary. Contact made, the receptionist handed Alex the telephone.

'Dr Brandon here,' she gasped.

You all right Dr Brandon?' A mature female voice enquired of her. 'You sound out of breath.'

'I've been running, but I've never felt better!' The breathlessness was abating, and the appointment for the interview was made for later that day, leaving time for Alex to meet Magda, Patricia and Richard over the coffee table and acquaint them of her news.

Once all four were assembled, without preamble, she blurted out, 'I'm engaged to be married to Douglas.'

Three pairs of eyes stared at her. It was Patricia who congratulated her first, with Richard jumping in quickly with humorous asides. Magda looked at her. Alex saw an almost pitying look in those wise chocolate eyes, but Magda uttered only good wishes for Alex's happiness.

Alex pulled the brown leather box from her pocket and showed them the engagement ring.

'I can't wear it because I'm going for an interview for the

paediatric post. If Dr Peters thinks I'm getting married I won't get the job, so please don't tell anyone for the time being,' she pleaded.

The trio examined the ring and admired the beauty of it. On handing it back they gave assurances that her secret was safe with them.

'Hippocratic oath, and all that,' Richard stressed.

It was time for Patricia, Richard and Magda to depart. Alex had time to kill. She had tried to contact Douglas to tell him about her interview; now she went in search of him. He was in the middle of pre-anaesthetic checks on the female surgical ward but he broke off to talk to her.

'Good luck, my darling,' he whispered when she told him the news. He had to return to his patient who was attached to the cuff of a sphygmomanometer. It was obvious the interruption was making her nervous and possibly affecting her blood pressure. Not an ideal prelude to surgery, but Douglas' soothing tone soon rectified the matter.

With still time to spare Alex decided to go to the doctors' common room, read the newspapers and think out her responses for the interview. Tricky questions were often asked and she did not want to be found lacking.

Eventually, when the time arrived, she tidied herself, taking extra care with the cosmetics because consultants were suspicious of overly made-up female interviewees. She made her way to the boardroom annexe. There were two other candidates waiting, and leaving no doubt of their obvious unease they looked at her with suspicion. One of them she knew vaguely, but he gave no sign of recognition so she took her seat and picked up a copy of the *British Medical Journal*. Her mind was too fraught to read, but she flicked through the pages to present a calmness that she did not feel.

After fifteen minutes, an interviewed candidate rushed from the boardroom red of face, and gave none of them a glance before departing.

Alex was surprised that she was the next to be called, as were the other two. They glared at her.

Dr Peters was a small man but had a pleasant countenance. He courteously introduced himself and then confirmed her identity from the sheaf of papers topped by her application form. Then, gesturing for Alex to be seated opposite, he informed her of his work and expectations from those assigned to him. She was delighted by the ease and straightforwardness of the questions he asked. Surely it couldn't be this easy? She remembered how insulting and devious Mr Jarvis had been at interview, but then he had offered her the job in spite of this. Was she being lulled into false sense of security?

Then it came.

'I believe you are the daughter of Sir James Brandon.'

'Yes, but – '

'Sir James and I were at a seminar,' Dr Peters continued, 'and we had a long discussion about fibrocystic disease, a very serious childhood condition, and of course Sir James is an authority on all lung disease so our meeting was fortuitous and helpful.'

'I trust this will not jeopardise my application,' Alex told him boldly.

'Of course not – '

'Or facilitate it.'

Dr Peters leant forward. 'It makes no difference whatsoever.' There was sternness now in his tone.

'I just wish to be employed on my own merits, Dr Peters.' Her tone was now conciliatory, she knew she had overstepped the mark. Always her father interfering, unknowingly in this case. It had soured the interview.

Surprisingly, Dr Peters smiled, a smile of understanding.

'I too had a distinguished father: Professor Peters, the haematologist. It is pretty tough, but you have to get used to it.'

He stood up and put his hand out to shake hers. Alex returned the courtesy.

'You will be informed whether your application has been successful,' he said without looking at her. She was dismissed.

Alex returned to the waiting area. The other two candidates looked at her, trying to gauge whether she had expectations of the job. She quickly left the now claustrophobic room. Once outside she moved a few feet away and then leant against the wall to calm herself.

I've scuppered my chances, she said to herself. She looked back towards the annexe to see the other two candidates emerge. They were agitated. She heard one of them say, 'Well, that was a waste of time.'

She walked away, her mind in turmoil.

Two days later it was no surprise to receive a letter informing her that her application with the Department of Paediatrics had been successful.

Douglas' view of the situation when Alex explained to him about her father's relationship with Dr Peters was, 'Who knows or cares? You got the job.'

Alex could see he was plainly bored with the subject, and furthermore the final days in her present post were difficult and demanding. She just wanted to complete her term without disaster striking. And yes, she wanted that paediatric job.

She had Douglas now. Wonderful, handsome, charming Douglas. He loved her, and she loved him. Nothing mattered as much as that.

Alex had now come to her final day on Mr Jarvis' surgical team. She had informed him that she had secured the paediatric post.

'I don't see you making a surgeon,' he told her, 'but I have no complaints and I wish you well in your career.' Coming from him it was praise, as it was the most pleasant remark he had ever made to her.

Deciding to make use of the few uncommitted hours before her weekend off and meeting Douglas, Alex headed to her accommodation for a big tidy up – white coats to the laundry and collecting any post from her pigeon hole. She was unused to such leisure. At first, she thought the letter was sticking out from the adjoining box when she went to the mail area. It looked official and was bulky, but it was for her. She stared at the typed envelope and decided to open it in her room lest it contain bad news.

In the privacy of her room she nervously, slit open the envelope and was horrified to see the name of a firm of solicitors on the heading. *Was a patient, or relative suing?* she thought.

She had to read it and face it, whatever.

Alex could not have been more surprised by the contents. A trust fund set up by her grandmother had now matured as she was over the age of twenty-five. She had inherited the vast sum of £11,600.

'We await your instructions,' the letter concluded.

She remembered Granny Brandon had set up these trusts for herself and her brothers before she died. Her father had taken control of them and she, Alex, had forgotten their existence. What better time for this to happen, just as she was about to be married?

She resolved that only Douglas would know about the inheritance. It would mean that they could afford to buy a house, furnish it and even purchase a car. What a way to start their life together!

Douglas managed to get off duty early because the operating list had been shortened. He came to her accommodation to tell her that he'd also managed to wangle the weekend off.

'What shall we do?' he asked.

Alex picked up the solicitors' letter and handed it to him. 'Read it,' she commanded without expression.

She saw apprehension on Douglas' face, then a look of incredulity as he digested the contents.

'So I am marrying an heiress now,' he said, shaking his head. 'Good job I asked you to marry me before you received this!' He moved towards her and kissed her.

'You smell of anaesthetic,' Alex told him, pushing him away.

'Deliberate,' he said, narrowing his eyes. 'I plan to anaesthetise you and have my evil way with you.'

'No flambé then,' Alex retorted.

'Yes, I definitely want that.' He paused. 'So what occupational therapy can we indulge in this weekend?'

'We could go home and you meet Ma and Pa. I was going for the day anyway because I thought you were working.'

Douglas grimaced. 'Well, I suppose we'd better get it over with,' he said reluctantly.

'I'll ring up tonight and ask Mother to meet us at the station.'

'Rubbish,' Douglas replied, 'I'll borrow Jeremy Carstairs' car. He doesn't mind, and I know he's working this weekend. In fact I had already hinted to him that I might need it.'

'I still need to phone Ma.'

When Alex dialled the Brandon home her mother answered. Susan was delighted by the proposed visit. It seemed that Aunt Sonia and Alex's brother Jonathan would also be there so it would make a family gathering.

By the time the weekend came Douglas had organised a car and arranged rendezvous and departure times for them. Alex was to be at the main entrance, where the car was parked, and was told, 'Don't be late.'

It took an hour for Alex to prepare herself. She was excited and was longing to show Douglas off to the family. *Wonder what Aunt Sonia will think of him?* she mused as she made her way to the front of the hospital.

Douglas was there already and was polishing a red sports

car. He was wearing a cap and tweed jacket. He looked magnificent.

Throwing the duster in the back of the car, he took her small Antler suitcase (a twenty-first birthday present from Aunt Sonia) and placed it along with his own in the boot. He then helped Alex into the confined space, running his hand along her leg as he tucked her in. He then ran round, jumped in beside her and started the car.

They were off on a very special weekend.

3

Douglas was an instant success with the Brandon family. He served a cocktail of deference and admiration to James; he listened attentively to Susan who bemoaned an invasion of rabbits in her vegetable garden; he assumed an air of male bonhomie with brother Jon and sweetened Sonia with the 'goddess' treatment.

He even patted the dogs.

Later, round the dining table, in spite of the presence of three doctors, James, for once, was not able to dominate the conversation with medical matters. The only reference was a pre-dinner toast to Alex regarding her paediatric appointment. Denied his lectern of seniority James could only listen. Aunt Sonia was her usual outrageous self, Jon regaled his family with anecdotes of London life – well laundered no doubt. References to the impending nuptials along with a plenitude of wine made for a convivial evening. Susan had excelled herself with the cuisine. It was simple – homemade soup accompanied by home-baked bread, followed by roast pheasant and vegetables – rejected by the rabbits – all polished off by her famous apple pie.

Pheasants had a magical way of appearing in the Brandon household, secretly delivered and no questions asked.

Douglas was in his element and Alex, too, felt she was now on a different level with her family. What a difference a husband was going to make.

Replete, and reluctant to leave the dining room, they all

nevertheless headed for the drawing room where Susan was serving coffee. Aunt Sonia flopped down on the shabby but comfortable sofa. Alex automatically helped her mother, attending first to Aunt Sonia, then to Douglas. Jon looked after James and himself.

Along with the coffee, Alex proffered a bowl of sweetmeats. Sonia helped herself but Douglas looked puzzled.

'Fudge?' he queried.

'No, it's called "tablet" and it's Scottish,' Susan told him.

'Delicious,' Sonia gurgled, her mouth rather full of it.

'I have Scottish roots, in fact most of my family live in Scotland,' Susan continued.

'That accounts for this magnificent repast we have all enjoyed this evening, Scots are noted for their hospitality,' Douglas told her.

'That is why I married her,' James added, enjoying the accolades his wife was receiving.

'And for her beauty, which she seems to have passed on to my future wife,' Douglas continued.

Alex shook her head. Douglas certainly knew how to smarm his way into popularity. No matter, it was a social occasion.

Soon it was clear that the gathering was flagging so Susan suggested retiring to bed. Douglas had been allocated Christopher's old bedroom. It was at the far end of the landing next to Jon's room and had what was called the 'nursery bathroom' nearby. The two boys had slept their childhood there. Evidence of this still remained, mostly by the hand of Susan rather than Chris and Jon's desire to hang on to a happy boyhood.

Douglas had already ensconced himself in his allocated room prior to dinner. Now reaching it by way of the shallow-stepped staircase he gave it a more thoughtful look. The door was ajar, and standing in the doorway was Alex. His attention immediately transferred to her.

'I've come to say goodnight,' she told him softly.

He drew her into the room but left the door open. His mouth and hands were on her.

'You've come to tease me,' he said, drawing away.

'I've come to praise Caesar, not to bury him,' she misquoted.

'Did I do all right?' Douglas asked, knowing the answer.

'You have them eating out of those "all pervasive" hands of yours, my darling,' she assured him. 'One last kiss and then I must go. I'm sharing with Aunt Sonia remember, so no sleepwalking.'

He pulled her to him again. 'I could really do with you tonight,' he said with resignation.

'I know, I can tell,' she whispered.

Just then Jon returned from the bathroom, and although he did not pass their door he knew what was going on.

'Pack it up you two, it's too late for all the anatomy and physiology stuff,' he called.

Alex and Douglas smiled and had one final kiss before Alex rejoined Aunt Sonia in the twin-bedded room at the front of the house and out of the way of temptation. Sonia was sitting up in bed, her long black hair cascading over her shoulders. Devoid of cosmetics she still exuded that air of glamour. It was part and parcel of her.

'I'm impressed,' she informed Alex. 'He is divine. Where did you find him?'

'We met in the surgeons' changing room – when he took his mask off.'

Sonia roared with laughter. 'Well done, my darling, I bet he's good in bed.'

'I don't know yet, but I have the strong suspicion that he most certainly is.'

'Then we must get you married with all haste so you can sample the delights of wedded bliss.'

Alex prepared for bed and they continued to discuss Douglas. Once tucked up and before the light was extinguished Sonia put her hand across the divide, and Alex reached out and took it in hers.

'Be happy, my darling Alex,' Sonia said before retracting her hand and turning on her side, and promptly falling asleep.

The next morning, after a leisurely breakfast, Alex went off to have a game of tennis with an old school chum. It was a good way of telling her friend about the engagement.

This meant that Douglas was left to the mercy of James.

'A constitutional round the garden,' he informed Douglas.

Douglas would have preferred something more leisurely but he had no intention of upsetting his future father-in-law. As it turned out the garden tour was merely the backdrop for an intensive grilling. Douglas, well used to imperious surgeons, weathered the situation with flying colours.

James, now satisfied with his future son-in-law's credentials, turned the conversation to Alex.

'Very headstrong, a very difficult child,' he said, shaking his head. 'Better now though, and I like that friend of hers, young Magda, she's good influence on Alex. I've never had a woman on my team but I would have Magda, very bright girl, very bright.'

They were heading for the summer house.

'The children used to spend hours in there during the school holidays,' James continued. 'Alex used to read a lot, in fact I imagined she would be a librarian or such, it never occurred to me she would read medicine. I always hoped my two sons would follow me into medicine, Chris, my elder son, whom you have yet to meet, is a lawyer. God knows what Jon does, but he earns more than the rest of us put together. Classes himself as a "managing director".' James shook his head sadly at the injustice of life.

The sound of a bell interrupted further conversation. It was Susan and she was beckoning from the house and indicating that coffee was being served. They strolled back across the lawn and took their seats on the terrace where a coffee pot exuded its inviting aroma. Susan had disappeared but soon returned with biscuits, probably more intended for the two sprawling dogs (more wayward than their forebears Jason and Hera) than the human element assembled.

Douglas jumped up and pulled a seat out for her.

Once seated, Susan turned to Douglas. 'About this wedding – '

Alex returned from tennis to find a beleaguered Douglas. He leapt up at the sight of her. Alex, only too aware of how cloying her parents could be, came to the rescue, taking his arm to pull him away. 'I've missed you,' she told him linking her arm through his.

'You look hot,' was Susan's comment.

'I'm definitely flambé,' she replied, giving Douglas a sidelong look.

He looked away. James and Susan were oblivious to the hidden intent of the remark. Susan suggested a bath.

'A freezing cold one, if you ask me,' Douglas muttered as she led him away. They ran into Aunt Sonia.

'I didn't hear you get up this morning,' she told Alex. 'Been playing tennis, have we?'

'I won several love games,' Alex told them, pretending innocence.

Sonia and Douglas exchanged looks.

'Good for you,' Sonia said. She did not know Douglas well enough to make a saucy retort.

'We will be returning to Queensbridge immediately after lunch,' Douglas informed Sonia. 'It has been a great pleasure to meet you. I gather you introduced Alex to the delights of snails.'

'Ah, yes, that gorgeous French restaurant – Madame something-or-other's, that was ages ago,' Sonia told Douglas, touching his arm. It was clear she was as impressed with him as were the rest of the family. 'Jon and I,' Sonia continued, 'are also heading back to London after lunch in that ostentatious vehicle of his. However I noted that jazzy number of yours Dr Ffrench. Very smart.'

'Yes it's very pleasurable to drive,' Douglas responded quickly, making no mention of the fact that the car did not belong to him.

Jon appeared. 'I've been told to round you up for lunch,' he told them.

Sonia took Douglas' arm as they headed for the dining room. Jon and Alex followed some steps behind and had time for a quiet conversation. They had always been good friends right from childhood.

'I am so happy for you, Alex, the family find him totally acceptable and we all wish you well,' Jon concluded as they reached the dining room.

Lunch was basic country fare, and the conversation was animated now that Douglas's position was established.

The weekend stay had been a great success.

Sonia and Jon tactfully bade them farewell inside the house, then hovered outside with Susan and James to see the lovebirds to the car.

Stowing their overnight belongings into the little eye-catching automobile and squeezing into it themselves, Douglas roared the engine and off they sped. Alex waved. It was a poignant moment, seeing her mother and father along with two dogs, left there together.

Douglas drove back in record time. There was hardly any traffic on the country roads.

'I have to get this car back to Carstairs. He needs it this evening,' he told Alex.

They unpacked the boot with speed, and Douglas left to re-unite his friend with his MG.

It was now required that Douglas and Alex should journey

to Cheltenham for Alex to meet her future mother-in-law. Alex was dreading it. The sooner the better it seemed, and afternoon tea, rather than a protracted visit, would soften the forthcoming ordeal. A free weekend within the next month was not possible so a midweek visit was planned and arranged within the confines of both their work schedules.

Jeremy once again obliged by lending his treasured MG to them and a few days later Alex and Douglas were on the road to Cheltenham.

'Your friend Jeremy is very good-natured to lend you his car the way he does,' Alex observed.

'I do things for him. It's not one-sided,' Douglas commented dryly.

Alex did not reply, instead she took in the lovely country-side as they sped to their destination.

Douglas' mother, Diana, lived in a Georgian apartment. It was on the ground floor surrounded by shrubs and very privately located.

Douglas rang the bell. It took a few minutes for Diana to open the door.

Alex disliked her on sight. The prefix 'over' could be applied to every area of her being. She was overweight, over-coiffured, over-dressed, over-beautified and, worst of all, over-effusive.

'Oh dearest, do come in,' she gushed. 'Bring – what is her name again? – as well.'

It was not an auspicious start. Alex did not like the smell in the apartment either: it reminded her of decay and stagnation.

Diana showed them into a large drawing room stuffed with zestfully polished reproduction furniture. Ornaments abounded on every spare surface.

'So you are Alex,' the lady said, her memory returning. She looked Alex up and down and then, smiling, bade them sit on the large sofa.

45

The conversation was stilted, Mrs Ffrench making frequent references to her dear departed husband and the ensuing difficulty his death had placed her in. Even Douglas was unable to divert the conversation into more current topics. In an effort to bring the reason for the visit to Diana Ffrench's attention Alex leaned forward and proffered her left hand.

'I expect you would like to see the engagement ring. I am honoured to wear it, particularly as it is a family piece.'

Diana barely looked at it. 'Very nice dear.'

Alex looked up at her. Diana was staring at Douglas who was sitting behind her. It seemed to be an awkward moment. Then Diana looked more closely at the ring and said, 'Very beautiful. Shall we have tea?'

Douglas was ordered to wheel in the trolley, Diana reclined in her chair as her son clattered around in the kitchen. Again the word 'over' seemed to apply. The trolley, when Douglas lumbered in with it, was groaning with sandwiches and cakes which he proceeded to hand to them.

'So when is the wedding, dearest?' When Diana used the word 'dearest' the question was directed to Douglas and Douglas alone.

'As soon as it can be arranged. Lady Brandon will naturally be dealing with it,' Douglas assured her.

'My mother will be contacting you about guest lists and numbers,' Alex intervened.

Diana rolled her eyes upwards. 'Oh dear, I shall have to be so careful, you know how weddings cause such trouble.'

'Knowing my future mother-in-law I'm sure everything will be done to perfection,' said Douglas.

'Even when it is done to perfection some odious relative, that one hasn't seen for dozens of years, feels he or she should have been invited,' Diana told her son.

With tea finished, Douglas dutifully cleared the cups, saucers and plates and returned the trolley to the kitchen. It seemed to Alex that it was a labour expected of him and he performed it without question. Diana Ffrench was going to be a very difficult lady, and there would be problems ahead. Alex, however, would cross those bridges as she came to them.

Polite and safe conversation followed, with Alex terrified that one wrong word could scupper her chances of happiness with Douglas.

As the stilted conversation petered out, Douglas, mercifully, leapt up, using the "on-call ace card" to conclude Alex's introductory meeting with her prospective mother-in-law.

Saying goodbye to Diana was a traumatic experience. She clung to Douglas, and there were tears. Alex stole away, having been the recipient of a perfunctory peck on the cheek.

When Douglas caught up he said very little, and was quiet as they drove back to the hospital.

The next day he was his old self again.

The lead-up to the wedding was a frantic blur for Alex. Magda and Patricia were to be bridesmaids. Brothers Chris and Jon, along with Richard, were to be ushers and Jeremy Carstairs would be Douglas' best man.

Douglas was sanguine about the flurry of arrangements, though enigmatic about the honeymoon programme. It seemed to Alex that somehow none of it involved her. Her brain had detached itself from this section of reality.

She did her best to fulfil the summonses from her mother. This usually meant wedding dress fittings, floral bouquets and timings being synchronised and she merely obeyed the calls. After all, the family were doing all the work and paying for it too.

Magda and Patricia were supportive during this period. The compulsory job changes that junior doctors had to make meant that she dared not ignore her future, particularly as she was a female. Consultants tended to view her gender as having a 'San Andreas' marriage and fertility fault line. She had managed to secure a two-week holiday at the end of her next changeover. Douglas had less difficulty with his vacation dates.

Another day was arranged with Alex's parents, this to meet the rector of Alex's home parish in order to get the banns called. Again, the good offices of Jeremy meant that it would only cost half a day of their heavily committed time. They made short work of it, had a quick lunch with Susan, then headed for the church.

Mr Evans, the rector, was middle-aged with an avuncular manner. He greeted them warmly and then reminded them of the happy family relationship the Brandons had with his church.

'I've known Alexandra since she was a little girl,' he said. 'Lady Brandon is a pillar of the church and the community, she organises the flowers and she visits the bereaved and helps anyone in need. You, Alex, came here to Sunday school, as did your brothers, so there is a happy association, and your wedding will be a pleasurable event for the village.'

Alex could sense that Douglas was getting restless. In spite of this he made his usual charming remarks to the rector when addressed.

'As both of you are doctors I will not unnecessarily harangue you on moral issues and obligations, only say that marriage is a desirable state for man and woman.' Then Mr Evans wound up the meeting by confirming the day of the nuptials and finally a short prayer.

Once outside the church, both Alex and Douglas heaved a sigh of relief.

'We must get back, Carstairs is getting a bit fed up with me borrowing the car,' Douglas said.

'I'm really not surprised,' Alex told him. It was then that

the idea came to her. 'I want to make a phone call before we leave.'

'Worrying about our patients, are we?' Douglas said, giving her a squeeze.

They walked the short distance back to the homestead. Douglas stopped at the bottom of the drive and examined an almost hidden name board.

'Westfield House,' he declared. 'I had no idea that was the name of your family home.'

'As we've lived here for twenty odd years, everyone knows the name of the place. I think Granny Brandon had it put up when she lived here.'

Douglas nodded approval.

Reaching the back door and making their way into the kitchen, Alex saw the tea tray ready for them. Susan appeared.

'Can I go into the study and make a phone call?' she asked her mother.

'Of course,' Susan replied and waved her hand.

Douglas shrugged, implying that he had no idea what the reason was.

'Are the family phone numbers in the usual place?' Alex asked.

Susan nodded, and poured tea for Douglas and herself.

Once in the privacy of the study Alex located her brother Jon's number and dialled.

Once pleasantries were exchanged Alex informed him of the reason for the call.

'How much does an MG cost?' was her question.

'About four hundred pounds,' he told her, barely able to keep the surprise from his reply.

'Could you get one for me? I want it for Douglas as a wedding present.'

There was a silence. 'Yes, of course I can, but what's wrong with the one he has at present?' Jon asked.

'It's not his, it belongs to a friend,' Alex told her brother.

'Ah.' Again a silence. 'Alex are you absolutely sure about this, it's a lot of money.'

'Yes, it would be for both of us, even though I don't drive. I want it delivered to Queensbridge before the wedding so we can go away in it on our honeymoon.'

'Anything for you, my dear sister, give me the instructions.'

'I will send you a cheque and directions. Please don't tell anyone,' she begged.

'Your secret is safe with me, but remember if you change your mind just let me know.'

'I won't change my mind, even though it would take me six months to earn that four hundred pounds. Douglas just makes me so happy, I want to make him happy.'

'I understand, and I assume the name on the log book will be his,' Jon queried, even though he knew the answer.

'Of course, of course,' Alex told him. 'I have to go.'

Making her way back to the kitchen she found Susan and Douglas in deep conversation. Susan had made the assumption that the recipient of Alex's call was Aunt Sonia, so little interest was shown.

'We have to go, regrettably,' Douglas said to both women. Alex gulped down a cup of tea before departure.

'I don't know how much longer I can keep borrowing this car,' Douglas told her again. 'I don't want to upset Carstairs.'

'We have done all our longish journeys now, we've no need to visit either parents and the wedding arrangements are all in hand, we can use the train if necessary,' Alex assured him, mentally proposing to speed up the delivery of the new car.

Back at the hospital Alex threw herself into her work. Her knowledge was increasing and she was thinking about in which direction she wanted to take her career. It had to accommodate the fact she would be married and have children. Magda was the one to ask.

'I see general practice for you,' was the answer when the question was raised.

'Mr Jarvis always used to say the GPs are the backbone of the NHS.' Alex told her friend.

'I would wait until you are married and then decide, but whatever happens don't let Douglas decide for you,' Magda warned.

Alex snorted. 'Come on Magda, you know I'm the Emmeline Pankhurst of the nineteen-fifties, you've said as much yourself.'

'Yes, but you are madly in love now.' It was said smugly.

'Douglas actually encourages me to make my own decisions. He's never once opposed any of my actions or ideas,' Alex said defensively.

'I think he's got you exactly where he wants you,' Magda said, immediately regretting the remark.

'He hasn't got me into bed, and he definitely wants that,' retorted Alex.

Magda tactfully changed the subject. 'By the way, Patricia is somewhat involved with Peter Phipps. It seems pretty serious.'

'What?' Alex exploded. 'Peter Phipps the psychiatrist?'

'None other,' Magda confirmed.

'But Patricia is the most normal person in the world,' Alex said incredulously, and she and Magda laughed together at the thought.

'What about you Magda?' Alex asked slyly.

'Don't bother that head of yours about me, I can look out for myself.' Magda blushed.

It was occurring to Alex that she was losing touch with her two friends and she knew it was due to Douglas. Perhaps when the wedding was over she would have more time for coffee sessions. She made up her mind that, whatever, Magda and Patricia would always be part of her life.

The next two weeks were uneventful until brother Jon

rang to say that he had the car. Alex decided that Douglas should have it as soon as possible. Jeremy Carstairs was making it patently clear that his car was not going to be available from now on and that Douglas was in a position to purchase one of his own.

Alex secretly arranged with her brother that Douglas' wedding present would be delivered to the front entrance of the hospital. Jon would bring a friend along who would follow in Jon's car so they had a vehicle for the return journey to London. Alex planned for herself and Douglas to be available in a certain location without alerting him.

On the appointed evening she suggested going for a drink at the local pub. She rushed to get ready, leaving plenty of time for the rendezvous. She was with Douglas when the landlord, well used to doctors on call, shouted her name and pointed to the telephone receiver he was brandishing over his head.

Alex rushed for the anticipated call and smiled as she digested the message and returned to her curious fiancé.

'Guess what, Jon is unexpectedly in Oxford and wants to see us for a few minutes,' Alex said innocently.

'Where is he?' Douglas asked. 'Maybe he'll come and have a drink with us.'

'He's at the front entrance. I doubt if he will have time to stay.'

They made their way across the road to the front of the hospital; Alex saw the bright red sports car standing neatly parked. Jon was nowhere to be seen.

'I say, look at that little number, I wonder who owns it?' Douglas hastened over to examine the car in detail. Alex followed and Jon appeared. They stood either side of Douglas and Jon produced an envelope and handed it to him.

'What's this?' Douglas asked.

'I think you had better ask your fiancé,' Jon told him and nodded in the direction of Alex.

'It's my wedding present to you Douglas,' she told him with a smile.

Douglas picked Alex up in his arms and held her, his head buried into her neck. When he released her he looked at her and said, 'What a wonderful girl you are, my darling Alex.'

Jon was now jangling the ignition keys at Douglas, anxious to be gone now the delivery had been completed and the romantic asides were in full flow. His friend had appeared and introductions made but it was plain that Douglas and Alex needed to be alone to celebrate their new acquisition.

Alex turned and kissed Jon. 'Thank you so much,' she whispered in his ear.

'No trouble at all,' he whispered back. 'I'll always be around if you need me.'

The men all shook hands and exchanged farewells. Then Jon and his friend walked across the car park and loaded themselves into a sleek Jaguar, and with a wave and a whoosh they were gone.

To say that Douglas was thrilled was the understatement of the century and the rest of the evening was spent extolling the virtues of his new toy. With Alex in the passenger seat they took a spin round Queensbridge.

Later that evening, when the initial excitement had abated, they went for the promised drink. On the way home they sat on the hospital bench. Douglas gently stroked her hair and caressed her cheek.

'I will be the proudest man in Christendom the day I marry you,' he told her softly.

Tears sprang in Alex's eyes; she leant over and put her mouth on his.

It was the first time in her life that anyone had ever associated her with the word 'proud'.

4

The weather augured well for the impending wedding. In spite of the immense task Susan had undertaken in its preparation, she still found time the afternoon before to collect Alex, Magda and Patricia from Queensbridge. Travelling back with the excited girls was somewhat of a relief because the next day it would all hinge on her. Susan was a born organiser and it never crossed anyone's mind that anything other than a happy and successful day would ensue.

Magda and Patricia were well acquainted with Westfield House, having spent weekends there when medical students. On their arrival they received the customary canine welcome followed by a casually dressed and relaxed looking James. Magda and Patricia bounded towards him and James pretended to fend them off, but he was more than delighted to see them and told them so.

He hugged his daughter more soberly but with tenderness. James always had difficulty displaying affection.

'I gather the male contingent relevant to tomorrow's event is now at the local hostelry?' he queried.

'Should be,' Magda replied. 'Douglas was going to be the pathfinder for Jeremy and Richard. A swarm of MGs in the village will cause some excitement.'

'Hardly a swarm,' James commented, his precise mind at work. No one was listening.

The girls unloaded the car and headed for their rooms.

Magda and Patricia were spending the night in the twin room, lately used by Alex and Aunt Sonia. Alex was back in her childhood bedroom, significantly changed, and so much smaller than she remembered. Peeping from her window to the side of the house she could see the marquee filling the lawn where those erstwhile games of cricket and tennis had been played all those years ago. Here she was now, about to be a married woman. A new era.

Not able to wait to catch up with her friends, Alex made her way across the landing and down the corridor. She heard them before she saw them. They were spinning around holding their bridesmaids' dresses against themselves. Alex leant against the wall and watched this girlish behaviour before reminding them that a rehearsal had been arranged at the church for seven o'clock.

'I wonder if Douglas and company have arrived, they're supposed to meet us at the west door,' Alex said.

'Let's walk up to the Red Lion and see if their cars are there, always a good starting point,' Magda suggested.

The inn was a short distance from the house, and they encountered a few of the villagers who regarded the little party with curiosity, but spoke kindly to everyone, and particularly to Alex. The wedding was a big event; a local girl from a respected family.

Walking round the side of the Red Lion they saw the two MGs parked side by side.

'Bingo,' Magda exclaimed.

'Shall we go in and find them?' Alex suggested.

'We don't need to,' Patricia told them, 'the mountain is coming to Mohammad.'

Hardly were the words spoken than Douglas appeared. He stretched his arms out and Alex ran into them. They exchanged a restrained kiss.

'Three women doctors,' Douglas mused. 'I wonder what the collective noun is.'

'Not a murder I hope,' Patricia ventured. 'Isn't that magpies or some such bird?'

'Crows,' Magda corrected.

Douglas grinned with pleasure at the thought he had provoked, but Magda was not amused by the conversation.

'I see you have your name up on the pub sign,' she told Douglas tartly.

'Something you will never find out, Magda,' he countered.

Alex stepped in. The conversation, although appearing to be flippant, had undertones.

'Are you happy with your accommodation?' she asked.

'Perfection. What could be better than a bedroom within reach of the bar?' Douglas told them.

'What about the other two? Magda enquired.

'Carstairs is still asleep because he had an exciting date last night. Richard is reading and waiting for opening time,' Douglas explained.

'You do remember that the three of you are invited back for supper after the church rehearsal?' Alex reminded Douglas. 'It's only buffet style.'

'We shall be more than happy,' was the answer.

The girls decided to leave the men to their own devices and slowly made their way back to Westfield House. There was much activity – contracted caterers scuttling round, and it reminded Alex of a beehive, there was almost a buzz in the air and everything seemed purposeful.

They had an hour before the church meeting.

'Let's go and have a drink,' Alex said quietly to her friends, even though there was no possibility of being overheard.

Raiding the vast sideboard in the dining room Alex found a bottle of wine and the necessary corkscrew.

'Will this be all right? It's becoming quite fashionable to drink this now,' she said, popping the cork.

'Do you remember our student days when we drank Merrydown cider?' Magda reminded them. They all nodded.

Alex filled the first glass and handed it to Magda, then slowly filled the next for Patricia before finally pouring her own. They then toasted each other.

'To a "gaggle" of women doctors,' Patricia proposed. 'Douglas wanted a collective noun, he's got one.'

'Yes, gaggle we women will. We are in the profession and we're here to stay,' Alex reinforced. They clinked their glasses together and then took their first taste of wine.

Alex now led the girls through to the drawing room where they could lounge in comfort. Laughter was coming easily as was clever conversation and the wine bottle was emptying fast.

Seven o'clock was looming and they would soon be required at the church. Alex realised that it was going to be necessary to conceal their indulgence.

'We can't turn up at the rehearsal reeking of alcohol,' she told her giggling companions. 'I'm going out to find a country remedy for us.' She left them lolling on the sofas. and made her way to the garden for mint and parsley. She grabbed handfuls of both and returned, determined to treat her friends even though they were grimacing at the thought.

Magda and Patricia looked suspiciously at the greenery being proffered.

'I bet those dogs have been over this,' Magda complained

'Eat it,' Alex ordered as she stuffed some into her own mouth.

The girls complied by pretending to be cows, chewing the cud, but they sobered up enough to creep out and make their way to the church. James had distanced himself, declaring he required no rehearsal in handing over a wayward daughter to an unsuspecting spouse.

Douglas, Jeremy and Richard were already there chatting to Mr Evans, the rector. Evans greeted Alex as she and the girls arrived, and the introductions were made.

'You've been drinking,' Douglas hissed.

Alex nodded. 'It's all right Douglas, I'm not going to dance on the pews, we are merely – relaxed.'

Mr Evans tactfully intervened and started the rehearsal. He rambled on and Alex found it difficult to concentrate in the proximity of her future husband. At last the verbiage stopped and action took over. Alex alerted herself.

Richard was delegated to stand in for James and walk Alex down the aisle. Amusing asides were quipped, mostly at the expense of the bride and groom. Then Richard, with an Elizabethan flourish, handed her to Douglas.

More verbiage from the rector and the rehearsal was over.

After thanking Mr Evans and promising to follow his instructions the following day they made their way to the west door, where Alex would enter the next day. Once outside the church they screwed up their eyes in the sunlight and stood chattering together. They then made their way back to the house in a leisurely manner.

Douglas pursued his verbal displeasure about the girls imbibing, but it was obvious that his irritation was more about the fact that the girls had stolen a march on him and his friends than the act itself.

Alex soothed him by putting her hand through his arm as they strolled homewards. By the time they reached the drawing room Douglas' good humour had returned, particularly as James was quick to serve pre-supper drinks, and by the time the buffet was ready there was a relaxed and convivial atmosphere accompanied by the clink of glasses and chink of cutlery.

Susan showed no sign of stress, though she frequently absented herself from the supper party to attend to the last minute details that were being brought to her attention by the caterers. She remained unflustered and seemed to deal with all the queries concisely and authoritatively.

At the end of the evening Douglas mustered his two companions to return to the inn. Alex saw them to the door.

Richard and Jeremy tactfully went on ahead to allow the bride and groom of tomorrow a last lingering kiss. As they parted Alex watched as Douglas slipped away into the night shadows to catch up with his companions.

When she returned inside it was to find Magda and Patricia clearing up in the dining room. Susan had other ideas. 'To bed with you all,' she commanded as she walked into the room.

They were all too tired to argue, and were secretly thankful to be dismissed. They made their way upstairs and bade goodnight to each other.

Once in her room Alex regarded herself in the mirror. Over the years she had both despaired and admired herself in its scarred surface. Tonight, like the mirror, she was in a reflective mood. She smiled at herself knowing that she was stepping into the unknown and wondered what her new life with the dashing Douglas had in store for her. She was exhausted – she knew she would require all her energy for the next day, so she tore herself away from the mirror and her musings, undressed and sank into bed. In spite of the pressures she was feeling, sleep came quickly and the first she knew was the sun bursting in through her bedroom window.

Susan, with perfect timing, appeared with tea.

'Must be a special day or something for you to do this,' she told her mother.

Susan placed the tea on the bedside cupboard and kissed her daughter.

'Good heavens, whatever is going on today?' Alex teased.

Susan sat on the edge of the bed and took her daughter's hand. 'Your father and I are so happy for you darling,' she told Alex softly. 'Douglas seems such a decent man.'

'He really loves me, Ma, and I love him,' Alex said, tears liquifying her blue eyes.

'I know, I know,' Susan soothed. 'Remember this will be the happiest day of your life, so no tears.'

After Susan departed Alex drank her tea, but her pre-bridal thoughts were interrupted by an ebullient Magda along with a contrite looking Patricia. Both were fully, but casually, dressed.

'She's a bit hung over,' Magda said, nodding in Patricia's direction.

'Obviously got into bad company last night,' Alex remarked as she got up from her bed and stretched.

'What about this stuff you tell everyone is hair?' Magda asked, lifting Alex's wayward locks. 'Hopefully someone is going to harvest it before you go before the public.'

'Ma has arranged for someone to do it for me,' Alex assured her friends. 'Anyway, I want to get dressed now so why don't you two go down and start breakfast and I'll join you in two minutes flat.'

Breakfast was in the dining room, as the kitchen was too much in use at present and the girls were pleased to be out of the way. It wasn't long before Alex joined them. They took their time choosing cereals accompanied by creamy milk along with bread rolls and Susan's homemade marmalade. A coffee pot exuded its aroma and seemed bottomless as they conversed together.

'I hope Pa won't bleat on about my childhood mis-demeanours when he makes his speech,' Alex said with alarm.

'You bet he will, and it won't necessarily be amusing,' Magda forecast, wagging her head.

'We know he has little sense of humour, it could be so boring,' Alex said with resignation.

'Carstairs and Douglas will have to save the day, because they can be incredibly amusing,' Patricia told them.

The conversation was interrupted by Susan. 'Could you go and have a bath?' she told Alex.

The three girls burst into laughter, and Magda sniffed suspiciously around Alex.

'A hairdresser is coming in from the village, I don't want you bathing after your hair is done,' Susan said, somewhat acidly. 'I don't have time to do it myself.' And she stalked off.

'Poor Lady Brandon, I think it's getting to her,' Patricia commented after Susan was out of earshot.

It was noticeable that the nearer it got to the wedding, the shorter tempers became. Civility was threatened, and the arrival of brothers Chris and Jon did nothing to assuage the mood. In fact they fanned the flames by their insensitive humour. Even Aunt Sonia, along with husband Peter, did little to bring calm to the increasingly volatile situation.

Alex, Patricia and Magda by now were upstairs getting ready, and mercifully unaware of the deteriorating conditions below.

Jenny had arrived with her hairdressing equipment which virtually blanketed the room. She and Alex repaired to the bathroom for the washing process. Alex, head encased in a towel, flitted back to her room, not wanting to be seen in this compromising situation. Jenny, like a lot of hairdressers, became a confidante. She listened patiently to Alex who exposed her fears and trepidations about the wedding – things that she would never have confided even to her nearest and dearest.

Jenny listened and comforted and sympathised as necessary and, best of all, did a good job with Alex's hair. She had secured the wayward locks with combs and given the finished product a trial run under the headdress.

The bridesmaids were wafting between the rooms in various stages of dress. When Susan and James came to change as well, they were careful to time their movements to avoid collisions on the landing.

Excitement was mounting. Magda and Patricia, now ready, crept along to help Alex with last minute details. They both looked wonderful. Magda's dark eyes sparkled, her short curly hair twined round her delicate ears. She looked as Alex had never seen her look before. The choice of cream coloured bridesmaid's dresses was an inspired one. Patricia, too, with her heather-like hair and grey eyes, had also been transformed. Alex, now in her plain white silk dress that followed her shape to perfection, was struggling with her emotions and temper.

'Does my abdomen stick out?' she asked irritably.

'No, of course not,' the girls echoed.

Alex was getting hysterical. 'I look awful. What if Douglas changes his mind?'

'Shut up,' Magda said authoritatively, 'or I'll call your father.'

Alex closed her eyes in resignation, a hint of a smile on her lips. One of the Labradors had entered the room and nudged her. Alex bent down and stroked him.

'Stand up,' Magda commanded, 'we don't want you going up the aisle smelling of dog.'

'Worse odours than that, as we know only too well,' Alex replied. As she stood up, Magda took the veil that was lying on the bed and reached up and placed it on Alex's head. 'Keep still,' she said impatiently as the headdress was arranged. Alex stood quietly as the girls secured the veil.

'Although the words stick in my throat,' Magda told the bride, 'you look wonderful.'

Patricia agreed. Time was fast approaching for them to leave for the church. They could hear Susan on the landing; Magda went to the door to beckon her in. When Susan entered all three girls stared at her. The transformation was unbelievable – the country wife was now chic and elegant. She was too preoccupied by her daughter and failed to notice the admiring looks.

Gathering up the bridesmaids and fussing over last minute details, Susan shooed them onto the landing, but not before gingerly giving her daughter a last minute kiss.

'Come now girls or we will be late. The cars are here.'

After the clatter down the staircase from Susan, Magda and Patricia it went deadly quiet. Alex poked her head round the bedroom door to find James waiting there – he too, looked handsome in his grey morning suit.

With his arm outstretched James beckoned Alex to him, and led her slowly down the staircase. Once in the hall he picked up the bouquet of white flowers sitting on the hall table – roses, lilies and ferns in enormous profusion. Almost ceremonially he handed them to his daughter.

'I'm a very proud man today,' he told her. From James, this was praise indeed.

Although the car ride to the church was a short distance the car was lavish and comfortable and allowed Alex to spread herself and the flowers. James held her hand, supporting her.

Arriving at the west door of the church Susan and the girls took charge; it was unnecessary fussing, but it was almost ritualistic. Alex endured it.

Finally, Susan was satisfied and handed her daughter back to James. Susan scuttled off to her pew, Mendelssohn's 'Wedding March' struck up, Magda and Patricia took up their posts behind her and James led her in to the church.

The first thing that Alex saw was shafts of sunlight stabbing through the haze onto the sea of feathers on the ladies' hats. It took her breath away. It was like some Impressionist painting. Father and daughter made their way slowly down the aisle. Alex saw Douglas turn with that look of love in his eyes. She wanted to shout, 'I do, I do, I do!'

As she reached her appointed spot, James released her, she turned and handed the bouquet to Magda.

Douglas took her hand and the ceremony started.

The reception was a blur. Alex remembered the smell of grass inside the large marquee more than precise events. Fragmentary episodes like Diana, over-plumaged, and overchampagned, bearing down on her like a feathered avalanche. Wilson-Jones, with his lupine familiarity whispering, 'Lucky man,' into her ear. Her brothers repeating childhood jokes slightly transformed into an adult genre. James starting his speech in the earnest hope that the residents of Queensbridge would be free of illness and accidents this day as most of the medical staff from the university hospital were over-indulging in Warwickshire. Aunt Sonia's velvet eyes welled with tears of happiness for her. And lastly the best man reading the telegrams, adding in slices of medical humour appreciated by the Brandon family and friends but somewhat lost on the Ffrench kith and kin, Douglas being the only doctor in their ranks.

Alex ate little, even though the food and champagne was liberally proffered and of such excellence as to be a constant subject of comment among the guests. Douglas was in his element as he chatted to all and sundry, unaware that his bride had picked at her food. He kept hold of her hand and gave it the odd reassuring squeeze. The day was being a great success.

The cake was now due to be cut. Silver and white, it stood with its three tiers topped by a plaster bride and groom. The waiter who had brought the cake to the table now carefully removed the little statue, promising to box it and keep it safe for them. The two top tiers were then removed and spirited away leaving Alex and Douglas poised with a large silver knife, which they plunged into the centre of the cake. One of the guests made a 'surgical' riposte which caused laughter amidst the clapping. The cake was then dispensed with further champagne after which the reception drew to its conclusion.

Susan suggested that Alex and Douglas retire to change into their going-away clothes. They slipped away and once in the privacy of her old bedroom with her husband, they both crashed on the bed side by side. Douglas then turned and kissed his bride,. He threw off her headdress and started to loosen the buttons on her wedding dress, then stopped.

'Not here, I think,' he said rolling away from her.

Alex sat up, her dress starting to roll down. She clutched it to contain her modesty. Douglas smiled. He stood up and exchanged his morning suit for a lounge suit. Alex sat up and watched and then she, too, slowly took off her dress and shoes. She needed help with the buttons; Douglas assisted but he took advantage of the close contact, running his hands across her flesh – it was a taste of things to come.

For now they had no alternative but to change quickly and return to the, now baying, crowd downstairs waiting for the honeymoon send-off. Alex peered out of the window.

'No one out here now, they're all waiting in the drive, I suspect,' she told Douglas and hastened her dressing.

With both now ready they made their way down to the front door, from where the buzz was emanating. A cheer went up as they emerged. Susan thrust the wedding bouquet into Alex's hands and signalled for her to throw it.

Goodbyes were exchanged and Alex scanned for her bridesmaids, tossing her bouquet in their direction. Patricia was the taller so she caught it.

The little red sports car had been embellished. Douglas picked Alex up and fed her into the passenger seat amid continued cheering. He then ran round, jumped in, started the car and roared away down the drive. Alex looked back and waved at the throng until they were out of sight, then turned back to her husband and nestled into him. Douglas stopped as soon as possible to de-slogan the vehicle and remove a number of dangling tin cans. He placed the latter in the boot, promising to return them with interest once back in Queensbridge.

It was a breathtaking drive to the Cotswolds, but Alex was apprehensive and excited about her wedding night. On reaching the hotel she was not disappointed. It was old and full of atmosphere and owned by a retired naval officer and his wife. Alex could imagine that the words 'shipshape' and 'deck swabbing' would figure frequently in these immaculate premises, and almost wondered why they hadn't been 'piped' on board.

The room the owner showed them to was large and contained a four-poster bed, and through another door was a large bathroom for their private use.

The naval officer, whose name was Jessop, having appraised them of the hotel amenities, informed them that dinner would be served in about half an hour, then discreetly departed.

'Let's go down to the bar and have some champers,' Douglas said, looking at his watch. 'Our luggage hasn't been sent up yet, and I could do with a drink.'

Alex went into the bathroom to tidy herself. Like the rest of the hotel it was quaint, beams in the walls and a large white bath tub with imposing taps and the wash basin made to last at least a thousand years.

'Hurry up, darling,' Douglas told her as he joined her in the bathroom and washed his hands. It was an intimate moment and confirmed to Alex that she was now well and truly sharing her life with this wonderful person.

They sauntered down to the bar and Douglas ordered a bottle of champagne. The waiter, with great ease, removed the cork and served the drink to them. Mr Jessop appeared with a menu, and as they chose their courses they discussed the wedding and the guests, until interrupted to be shown into the large candle-lit baronial hall where dining took place. 'The Admiral' (as they now referred to Mr Jessop) had allocated them a private area by a window, and although other diners were arriving they felt secluded but still part of the dining public. The views were outstanding, the village seemed to be caught in time, undamaged by the war, though some of the once beautiful garden had discreetly been converted to vegetable growing and had not yet returned to its former glory.

Alex looked at Douglas. Perhaps one day they could live like this, away from the disease and suffering that was part of their everyday life. She could not tell this to Douglas, not tonight, perhaps not any night.

The food arrived. Douglas had selected steak and kidney pie made by Mrs Jessop, and Alex chose chicken Maryland, again homemade. No crêpes Suzette however, so they settled for gooseberry fool.

Over coffee, Douglas once again took her hand and declared how much he loved her. 'Something I intend to prove in a few minutes' time,' he asserted.

Alex smiled.

Mr Jessop appeared and enquired whether they had enjoyed their meal.

'Perfectly delicious,' Douglas assured. Then, explaining to Mr Jessop that they had had a tiring day and needed an early night they headed to their room.

Douglas disappeared into the bathroom so Alex started to shed her clothes. He reappeared before she could put on her nightdress. He gazed at her as he hastily removed his clothing.

'You look like one of those Grecian statues,' he told her.

'Except I'm animate,' she told him softly.

All clothing removed he came towards her. 'Don't put that nightdress thing on,' he said, taking it from her and throwing it on the floor. Then he took her hair and loosened it so it hung over her face and shoulders before picking her up and taking her into bed.

'The best of marrying a doctor is that they know where all the anatomy is, and the physiology to complement it,' Alex thought.

She was about to find out that he had an honours degree.

Her expectations were more than met.

The next morning, when Alex woke, she was lying with her back to Douglas. She turned towards him. He was on his back, his eyes closed. She snuggled into him. 'You really are 'flambé,' he told her without opening his eyes. Alex nuzzled him. 'So are you, in fact, you have to be the god of fire, Vulcan himself,' she teased. Douglas smiled, he liked the analogy. He was about to turn to her when there was knock on the door. 'Your breakfast, Dr Ffrench,' said a female voice that turned out to be Mrs Jessop. Alex snuggled down under the bedclothes as Douglas called for her to enter. Mrs Jessop, along with a young girl, had brought the breakfast trays laden with food, which they placed on a bed table similar to those used in hospitals. Mrs Jessop tactfully avoided eye contact, but the young girl looked embarrassed, particularly when she espied Alex's discarded nightdress on the floor. The contents of the trays, along with a posy of flowers, were arranged on the bed table which was then placed by the bed for them before Mrs Jessop gathered her diffident helper and departed.

Alex emerged from hiding. The aroma was delicious. Douglas raised lids and declared the contents.

'Grapefruit, cornflakes, smoked salmon and scrambled eggs, bacon, sausages, fried bread, toast and so on.' He picked up morsels and fed them into her mouth, then they both started nibbling the food interspersed with kissing. It was a sensual experience. Alex could not imagine her parents rising to this. They were too old fashioned. She was a modern woman with the world at her feet. She felt her real life was now starting. The one she had always dreamed about. The one that included a career and a husband.

She had achieved Nirvana.

5

Alex and Douglas' accommodation seemed so dreary and cramped when they returned to work after their honeymoon. Alex was glad she'd decided to keep her old rooms on. Both she and Douglas needed the extra storage space for their joint belongings. Also, if Alex was on call and up most of the night she could return to her rooms to snatch some sleep without disturbing her husband, even though it was an infrequent occurrence.

She now found that she was seeing less of Magda, Patricia and Richard. On the few occasions they had coffee together Alex told them how happy she was, even under the restricted circumstances of hospital life. Outside her work Douglas dominated her thoughts.

Autumn was setting in, the nights getting darker. Douglas liked to wander over to the pub across the road from the hospital and insisted, when available, that Alex went too. It was not what she particularly wanted, but Douglas got his way by saying he wouldn't go without her. They only ever had one drink, but Douglas met colleagues and exchanged views before they returned to the doctors' quarters.

It was after one of these sessions that Alex decided to broach a subject that had been on her mind.

'Douglas,' she said, 'I have been thinking.'

'Leave the thinking to me,' he told as he grabbed her and pulled her to him.

She pushed him away.

'Douglas, listen to me,' she pleaded.

He released her. 'What does my little crêpe Suzette want?' he asked in his mock French accent.

She wished he would be serious.

'Douglas, why don't we buy a house here in Queensbridge, I have Granny's money, and we could easily afford one,' Alex wheedled.

Douglas shook his head. He was instantly serious. 'I don't think so, we don't know yet in which direction our futures lie. You are coming to the stage where you have to decide about further exams for your chosen speciality. If some heaven sent opportunity comes our way we don't want to be shackled by a house we cannot sell.'

Alex was disappointed, but she knew Douglas well enough now that pursuing the subject would make him even more stubborn about considering it.

'Don't complicate matters when everything is so perfect,' he whispered as he drew her to him.

Alex could not resist him but the thought did not go away, it would be raised again. For now though he was right. Everything was perfect.

Thinking carefully about her future, Alex felt that general practice was the area she should aim for. After all, she hoped that they would have children one day, and it might be easier to manage work and family in that discipline. She wondered what plans Douglas had at the moment but he seemed content with things.

A few days later Alex had a summons from Patricia. She made for the dining room as requested, and Magda and Richard were there too. Lunch was the order of the day, and it seemed something of portent was in the air.

'I'm engaged to be married to Peter Phipps,' Patricia announced, brandishing an engagement ring on the appropriate finger.

Gasps of happiness and congratulations from their table

forced other diners to look curiously at them, but such was their elation they did not notice.

'Two down, one to go,' Alex joked.

'Don't you worry about me,' Magda told them.

The mood was celebratory.

'Peter and I are having a lunch party at his old college,' Patricia told them. 'I will send you invitations, but it is a week on Saturday, so keep it free.'

'My weekend off, marvellous,' Alex told her friend.

The gathering was short lived as they all had work commitments. Alex felt exhilarated by the news and the impending party. Telling Douglas later, she was surprised by his look of consternation.

'That's the weekend I promised Mother we would visit,' he told Alex.

'Oh no,' Alex exclaimed. 'Patricia is a special friend, it's her engagement, a once in a lifetime event.'

'I know, but Mother is on her own, and she desperately wants to see us, I can't disappoint her,' Douglas persisted.

'Can't we compromise?' Alex begged. 'You go to Cheltenham, and I attend the engagement party.'

'Mother will be heartbroken if she doesn't see you. Really Alex, it would be cruel to abandon the visit, furthermore she would never let us forget it,' Douglas concluded. Alex was devastated, but she felt had no option but to concede.

As soon as she could she told Magda about the situation and how upset she was. Magda said little, except to point out that it was lax of Douglas not to have consulted her about the Cheltenham arrangement when he made it.

Alex felt guilty. She had yet to tell Patricia that she and Douglas could not attend the lunch party. Before doing so she decided to lessen the disappointment on both sides by accompanying the 'inability to attend due to a previous engagement' note with a gift. When she had some spare time she took herself to a little antique shop that had recently opened. A few of the hospital staff had mentioned interest in it and had described reasonable prices along with what they suspected would bring long-term financial benefit. Antique collecting was becoming fashionable.

The shop had a careless look inside, but Alex felt that was contrived, but with good effect. The owner was a pleasant lady, chatty and knowledgeable, and jewellery was her main selling point. Alex browsed, and then found a set of boxed silver coffee spoons, which were Victorian and in immaculate condition. The price was also more than acceptable, so she made the purchase.

As Alex reached into her purse for the money the owner commented on her engagement ring.

'It's an heirloom, from my husband's family. I feel quite honoured to be wearing it, and I shall treasure it,' she said, gazing proudly at it.

The woman smiled, and wrapped up the coffee spoons. When she handed the parcel to Alex she gave her a card.

'Do tell your friends about me. I am always interested in acquiring *objets d'art*, jewellery and so on and I pay good prices as well.'

Alex thanked her and headed back to the hospital, pleased with her buy.

It turned out to be a good move, as Patricia was delighted with the spoons and forgiving about the absence. Douglas, however, was not impressed by Alex's visit to the antique shop.

'Fancy giving them something second-hand,' was his comment.

Another move was due for Alex. Paediatrics had been less fraught than most of the other areas and looming was gynaecology and obstetrics. She had now implemented her name change with the necessary authorities so she would be going to her new job as Dr Ffrench. How strange it sounded.

She was apprehensive about starting, but the consultant

preferred to have a woman on his team so he treated her kindly on the first ward round. Alex knew that 'gynae' was not for her, even though she had extreme sympathy for the patients. How they worried about their families. The obstetric side she liked better, and though the midwives coped most of the time there were still the inevitable ward rounds, and visits to the unit.

Alex's life was changing significantly, becoming polarised. Troughs of unremitting work along with the delights of married life were sometimes disorientating, and intersected on occasions. When Douglas took her to the pub he always put his arm around her shoulder or waist. The possessive act implied that conversation directed to Douglas included her, along with proof of ownership. Alex would have liked to have joined in the chat on her own account, as they were all medical staff. If she suggested having an evening with Magda, leaving him to the pleasures of the drinking sprees, it was rejected with, 'I don't like going on my own, so I'll give it a miss.' Then Douglas would sulk.

Furthermore, it was becoming clear that Douglas did not like Magda.

'Bossy madam,' he told Alex.

'I won't hear a bad word about her, I would not be here today without her,' Alex said angrily. 'She got me out of serious scrapes when we were students, and helped me with my tutorials.'

'All right, all right,' Douglas conceded, raising his hands. 'Just keep her out of my hair.'

This meant that Alex saw less of her friend in spite of trying to maintain the relationship. She knew Magda understood the situation without her having to spell it out, and it did not dent the friendship.

Patricia was now largely unavailable.

'She's having a psychiatric assessment with her psychiatrist,' Magda would explain with a smirk.

Alex also noted that Richard was attentive towards Magda now that she and Patricia were spoken for. Richard was a kind person and Alex wondered if he was just being a good friend, but some of the looks that passed between the two of them Alex recognised as being of a more intimate nature. Both were clever, and it had always been taken for granted that there was a meeting of minds. Now it seemed there was more.

Douglas did not care much for Richard either. He found him enigmatic, and he was mercifully unaware of the Magda/Richard entente.

Alex persisted with her desire to have her own home, and even carefully picked her moments with Douglas to pursue her objective. However, even at his most vulnerable he would still not budge on the matter.

Another need was now making its presence felt. Alex, on her visits to the maternity unit, would hover around the infants and feel envious of the new mothers and their off-spring. She and Douglas had never even fleetingly broached the subject of a family, and as he was urging the GP course on her it was hardly the time to mention it. Another hurdle to overcome she felt, for he was the most obdurate of men. Furthermore, he was exceedingly careful about ensuring there could be no slip-ups in this area.

After a particularly pleasant evening at the local and Douglas had willingly coaxed into one more drink than usual, Alex decided to seize her chance, particularly as their drinking companions had been extolling the pleasures and virtues of family life. Walking home in the crisp night air and snuggling into her husband, she hastened him to the wooden bench and suggested they sit for a minute to re-live their courting days.

Douglas was only too happy to oblige.

Flopping down on it, and clutching at each other they kissed and cuddled.

'The best thing I ever did was to marry you,' he whispered in her ear as he nuzzled it.

'I love you too, my darling Douglas,' she replied, 'which is why I want to talk about us having a baby.'

She felt his body stiffen and sober up. 'Ah, so we're getting broody, are we?' It was not unkindly said.

'I would like living proof of our love, and I don't want to be an "elderly primip",' Alex pressed.

'An elderly primip,' Douglas laughed. 'Many women over twenty-six have first babies without a problem. There have been no maternal deaths in this hospital for seven years, remember.'

'What about it Douglas?' Alex persisted, now wishing she hadn't introduced the 'elderly primip' factor. It was side-tracking the debate.

'I don't rule it out,' Douglas told her. 'At the moment we have to decide about our futures, first and foremost. A baby would certainly restrict our options, you have to make the next career move in three months' time, and who knows what I could get offered.'

Alex realised these were the same excuses he had used regarding buying a house. She was disappointed.

'Please think about it, darling,' she begged.

'You're shivering, let's go,' Douglas said, holding her cold hands and neatly changing tack. He pulled her up from the bench, put his arm around her and marched them home.

Once back in the warmth of the accommodation he prepared for bed, telling her of his workload for the following day. He was letting her know the subject of a 'Ffrench heir' was firmly closed.

It was difficult for Alex to understand how Douglas could be so insensitive about her desire for a home of their own, and now he was avoiding plans for a family. One, of course, was not possible without the other.

In spite of this he was wonderfully loving and this

rendered Alex powerless in tackling him in a more assertive way. She decided to let things rest for the time being, in the hope he would have a change of heart, knowing how she felt. They had only been married six months, it was early days for these major decisions.

Douglas was undertaking more private work. It went well with his NHS commitments. It was rare for him to have a disturbed night, while Alex, on the other hand, was running herself ragged.

'I'm sick of putting up IV infusions,' she told her husband wearily.

'We must see about some more qualifications for you then, and get you on the next rung of the ladder,' he advised.

'I'll talk to Magda, she fancies ophthalmology which is why she is reading her FRCOphth, and Richard is doing his MRCP as he always intended being a physician. Patricia is –'

Douglas interrupted by taking hold of Alex's arm.

'I'm your husband, *we* talk about your future,' he told her firmly.

'Of course, my handsome Vulcan,' she told him apologetically. She knew he loved being called by that intimate name which she rarely used outside the confines of the bedroom. It had the desired effect.

Now mollified, Douglas proceeded to make practical suggestions and the acerbity in his manner was gone.

Alex was tired and it was with relief that Douglas suggested bed. He helped her undress and into bed, kissed her gently and let her sleep.

When she woke the following morning Douglas was shaved and all but dressed. Knowing she had a day off he had been hoping to vacate the rooms without disturbing her. He came to the bedside and kissed her.

'See you this evening, we'll go out for dinner,' he promised.

In spite of his sharp remarks of the previous evening Alex

felt a glow of happiness. He'd been right to remind her that it was his place to help and support her now. There was nothing Alex liked better than to dine out with her husband. Tonight over the dinner table maybe ideas would flow.

During the morning she telephoned her mother. Not much news to exchange, she could hear the dogs barking in the background and could visualise the scene. It seemed an eternity away from her present life. Again, it made her think how good it would be to have a home of her own. It was then she hatched her plan – she would tell Douglas that she wanted to get started with her GP training and get into a practice. She would have to have a home of her own, as GPs could not live in hospitals.

After attending to a few domestic needs, Alex went into town. Undergraduates were flying around on bicycles, their black gowns caught in the breeze, making them appear like large prehistoric birds. On the way back she decided to visit the museum and art gallery, shining like a temple in the sunlight. Although she'd visited it many times she'd always had to leave before enjoying all it had to offer. She climbed the steps to the entrance, wandered in and was immediately caught by the tranquillity and peace the place exuded. Ambling round, Alex was overwhelmed by the art and the artists who had left such a legacy to the world without enjoying the rewards.

Wrenching herself from this gentle world, and in sombre mood she walked back to the hospital where she was meeting Magda in Concord prior to lunch. Both arrived to time, and quickly made their way to the cafeteria and helped themselves from the counter, chattering as they did. Taking up their familiar seats in the dining room Magda's first question was, 'Everything all right?'

Alex nodded and smiled – what a perceptive character Magda was.

'Been out house-hunting?'

'No, we're just sorting out a few things before we commit to that,' Alex explained rather lamely.

'I'm surprised the powers-that-be allow you two to stay in hospital accommodation, it's only supposed to be for on-call staff,' Magda persisted.

'We pay for it, it's docked off our salaries,' Alex said defensively, brushing an imaginary crumb from the table.

'As you know, since we rented a flat off the Pinewood Road Patricia and I have a great life in spite of work and study. The social life more than makes up for life's little grievances,' Magda continued.

'I'm married now, and I'm sorting out what my future options are as well as those of Douglas. I think general practice for me,' Alex said, lowering her eyes.

'You need "our Magda" round you,' her friend told her, touching her hand.

Alex sharply withdrew her arm from the table.

'You aren't in-calf or anything are you?' Magda asked suspiciously.

'Definitely not,' Alex assured her friend.

'You look very pensive this morning,' Magda said, her brown eyes burrowing into Alex's.

'I've been in the art gallery, it always has a profound effect on me.'

Magda stared at her. She remembered Alex only visited the gallery when she thought she was going to fail her exams and a bleak future loomed. Magda stood up. 'I must go.'

Alex remained seated and felt Magda's hand on her shoulder.

'You have our telephone number.' There was a pause. 'Drop round for a drink anytime.'

Alex looked up at her friend. Understanding passed between them and there was nothing more to be said.

It seemed strange that Alex should find it difficult to occupy her day off when she was always complaining about her workload. If she had a home of her own she'd be kept busy and this would not happen.

Now on her way to the common room to read the newspapers, she felt restless. Douglas would not be free until five. As she passed through Concord she glanced at the notice boards. Pinned up in the sport section was a request for women tennis players and an obliging telephone number. Alex wrote it into her notebook. Going into the common room she picked up the wall phone and dialled the number.

The voice that answered turned out to be that of a physiotherapist called Alison and she sounded helpful and jolly.

'Yes, I can find someone today,' she said in answer to Alex's query. 'In fact there's a threesome looking for a fourth right now.'

Alex lost no time in heading back to her rooms, changing into her tennis kit and making for the courts. Sure enough three young women were in play. They were only too happy to stop and include her, and after basic introductions they started. All were good players and after two sets it was decided to call it a day.

Retiring to the wooden bench on the edge of the court, further introductions were made. Two of the girls were nurses and the other a physiotherapist. The latter explained that she worked with Alison, and that Alison should have been playing today but work had intervened.

'I'll give you a list of names and telephone numbers so when you want to play just give one of them a call. In the meantime I'll put your name on the list, in fact we'll probably be asking you to play in the Hospital League,' the physiotherapist warned.

Alex was thrilled to find herself once more involved with a sport she enjoyed along with the camaraderie of other players. She felt so fit and well after the exercise and to round it off she had dinner with Douglas tonight to look forward to.

Returning to her accommodation, all thoughts of newspaper reading were now gone from her mind. She started to prepare for the evening ahead. When Douglas arrived he was fraught. He threw down his briefcase, loosened his tie and flopped down on the bed.

'Seven hour abdomino-perineal resection,' was all he needed to say for Alex's immediate sympathy.

'Do you want to go out tonight?' Alex queried.

'More than anything,' Douglas told her, reviving slightly at the reminder.

Alex smiled and continued to dress. 'It's usually me complaining about the work load.'

'Well, we can forget the hospital and everything therein and just go out and enjoy ourselves,' Douglas told her as he rose from the bed and made his way to the bathroom.

Once showered and changed he was his old self again. Alex had taken special care with her appearance too, and it was not lost on her husband.

Douglas decided to take the car tonight even though the hotel he had booked was but a stone's throw away. He liked to be seen in the little red sports car, and it certainly got him noticed.

They drove into the small near empty car park as daylight faded. An inviting aroma wafted from an open window in the restaurant area. They hastened in and Douglas was welcomed by the receptionist and ushered into the lounge bar as Alex trailed behind. Douglas ordered drinks, then enquired about Alex's day.

'I played tennis today with a physio called Libby and two nurses called Jenny and Pam. We had a great game, in fact Libby wants me to play in the Hospital League,' she told him.

Her husband frowned. 'I hope that won't mean you flying off here there and everywhere. You know I can't live without you,' and he leaned over, took her hand and squeezed it.

Alex felt she had to explain. 'I felt so good today getting my tennis going again, particularly as there are plenty of people around – available and of similar standard, and all it takes is a phone call. I felt exhilarated after the exertion.' She took a deep breath, hoping it made the point.

'I must say you have quite a glow this evening, but I assumed it was me causing it,' Douglas said, leaning towards her. 'You do know I'm going to make mad passionate love to you when we get home tonight.'

Alex looked nervously around but there was no one within earshot.

'What's it like to have an adoring husband?' he continued.

'What's it like to have an adoring wife?' she countered.

Their mutual admiration was interrupted by a summons to the dining room. Taking their seats in the traditionally decorated room reeking of past splendours the arrival of the menu put a temporary halt on the conversation. Studying the choices, Douglas exclaimed, 'No crêpes Suzette!'

'Doesn't rule out flambé,' Alex told him with lowered eyes as she continued to study what was on offer.

Alex chose French onion soup, making a play on the word 'French'. Douglas decided on a prawn cocktail as well as a steak, and selected a bottle of *Nuits St Georges* from the extensive wine list. The waiter nodded approval when he took their order. They had not long to wait before their food arrived.

It was obvious that Douglas was strung-up after his difficult day. He drank more wine than usual and rambled on about the drawbacks of his job. She on the other hand was hungry after her exercise on the tennis court, so was content to let him vent his feelings as she munched away. They could always leave the car and walk home if he was too inebriated to drive.

At the conclusion of the meal and with the help of a bottomless pot of coffee he sobered up sufficiently to drive home. Alex wished she could learn to drive; perhaps she should do so now. However, Douglas was amenable to taking her out and about so there was no real requirement for her to pass her test.

The bedroom was warm when they finally reached it. Douglas, however was not, as the alcohol had caught up with him. He wrenched off his clothing and sank into bed and before Alex could join him he was snoring soundly.

As she slid under the bedclothes she gently stroked his cheek. 'No Vulcan and no flambé tonight,' she murmured as she put out the light.

The following morning Douglas made no reference to the previous evening. Alex was not sure whether it was embarrassment or amnesia, but she did not pursue it. She remembered from her student days how no one much liked being reminded of their night-before antics.

Pitching into work again forced Alex to think about her GP future. Douglas agreed with her plans so she must take positive action. Her present consultant, affectionately known as 'J.P.' could not be easier to work for and the team as a whole was pleasant and helpful, but she most certainly did not like gynaecology and obstetrics even though she was gaining in confidence.

Yet with all this in mind things continued to drift. Tennis on her days off, dining out with Douglas, catching up with Magda and Patricia, sporadic visits to her parents and the obligatory visit to Cheltenham gave her no incentive to make radical changes. Work was going well, too well. There seemed to be an upsurge of gynaecological problems presenting themselves, and a lot emanating from casualty. The theatre list got longer, there was pressure on the beds, and Friday nights were the worst of all. Alex was mostly on duty.

A feverish session on such a weekend eventually ended in tragedy, and when Alex finally got to her room at two in the morning she wakened Douglas, sank into his arms and sobbed.

'We lost a patient tonight,' she managed to tell him between gulps.

He was tousled and sleepy, but grasped the situation. 'Patients have died before, what goes with this one?'

'She was twenty-two and attempted to terminate her pregnancy,' Alex said, continuing to sob.

Douglas stroked her hair. 'You mustn't become emotionally involved, I know it's tough sometimes.'

Gulping between breaths Alex said, 'She was an undergrad, and so pretty. Her parents are distraught, fortunately J.P. dealt with them.'

Douglas pulled her into bed with him, ignoring her white coat or the attendant medical attachments contained in the overloaded pockets. He held her close.

'Why do such terrible things happen to people, why do some people have to suffer?' Alex railed. 'The whole team worked to save her, even when she was dead we still tried.'

'I can't answer that question,' Douglas told her. He was clearly moved by Alex's account, and the trauma of losing a patient that she was experiencing.

'I'll make us a cup of tea,' he said, trying to divert the sadness from Alex's mind.

'No, no, I have to go back, we have another patient in casualty,' she said urgently. 'J.P. sent me away for a few minutes.' Her tears were abating now. Douglas was drying them from her cheeks with the edge of the sheet. He gave her a kiss.

'Are you all right now? he asked, with a hint of a smile.

Alex nodded. 'Douglas, thank you, thank you for being there when I needed you so badly, I didn't mean to disturb you.'

'Happy to oblige.' He turned back the bedclothes for Alex to leave. She brushed herself down before departing. At the door she blew him a kiss.

Back in casualty things had quietened down. J.P. greeted her sympathetically.

'Did you manage to get a cup of tea?' he enquired.

Alex nodded even if it was untrue. The grieving parents had departed and another patient needed attention. It was exactly what she required to restore normality.

The following weekend there was an almost similar situation, but this time no tragic ending. It was three in the morning before Alex could get back to Douglas. She did not mean to waken him and he was not best pleased at being disturbed. He could not get back to sleep so was bad tempered the next morning.

'Shall I go and sleep in my own quarters in future, on the occasional time I am so late?' Alex suggested.

Douglas reluctantly agreed.

The next two occasions that her work took her into the early hours she was able to tell Douglas in advance. He then drifted over to the Admiral pub on his own, for a nightcap. Well used by medical staff, he did not drink alone for long.

Alex also benefited from the arrangement because after a hectic session in casualty, theatre or the gynae or obstetric wards sleep did not come easily, particularly as she could get summoned back by the clang of the telephone. In her own rooms she could take a shower and a quick cup of tea and get what sleep she could.

One benefit was that Douglas was more receptive to the GP proposition. He did not like going to the pub on his own and he certainly did not like sleeping on his own; furthermore he was not happy about the dark circles showing under Alex's eyes and the lack of attention she was giving her appearance.

'You look like a panda,' he quipped.

Alex burst into tears, signifying the stress she was under.

'Only a joke,' he told her brusquely. 'Why do women always have to cry?' He shook his head.

After this Alex did her best to cheer up and although Douglas did not say sorry for his tactless remarks she found a spray of flowers waiting for her on the bed with a loving message, after which he took her out for dinner. Normality was back.

Or so she thought.

It was a Friday. Alex was on call.

'We have a postpartum haemorrhage down here,' the casualty officer informed her over the phone. 'Probably another couple for you too, a query ectopic and a charming lady who urgently needs a few gallons of fluid removing from her abdomen, most likely from an ovarian source.'

The call forced Alex back into her recently removed white coat. She scribbled Douglas a note as he was out at one of the local nursing homes giving an anaesthetic and would not be back until late.

Abridging the communication from casualty she ended the note with, 'Will sleep in my own kennel tonight, see you in the morning,' and concluded with the usual endearments.

Again, casualty was at bursting point when she reached it. A cursory examination of the three patients made Alex realise she could not handle this on her own, so she called the registrar. In the meantime she checked on bed availability and found she was in luck. To her delight J.P. arrived with the registrar and the work was delegated. The casualty sister dealt with the relatives and had swiftly got consent forms signed. The postpartum haemorrhage was prepared for theatre, the ectopic was an acute appendix and referred to the surgeons and the registrar admitted the last of the three to be dealt with first thing in the morning. It was medicine at its best.

After assisting J.P. in theatre and knowing the patient would now be in safe hands with the nursing staff, Alex glanced at her watch. It was not yet midnight. She knew it was politic to have a cup of coffee with her boss and discuss the events of the evening along with his instructions regarding postoperative care of the patient. J.P. was not one to waste time. He was concise and after coffee changed, checked with casualty that there was nothing further brewing, and then went home.

Alex took a last look at the two patients, wrote up their medication and felt she could retire to bed.

Maybe not my bed, she thought, and smiled to herself. It was only 1 a.m. She'd go and surprise Douglas.

With mounting excitement she stole across to the accommodation. Quietly opening the squeaky doors she made her way down the corridor to Douglas' apartment. Alex checked to see if he had left the door open but he hadn't. Putting her key in the lock as carefully as possible she gently turned it, slid open the door and took a few steps into the bedroom.

Immediately she sensed something was wrong.

There was a rustling noise, she felt a sense of panic, and as her eyes accommodated to the darkness she could make out a figure. It was scrambling out of the far side of the bed, and it wasn't Douglas. It was female in form.

Alex's mind froze.

The sense of shock was terrible, she leant back against the wall trying to control her breathing; her heart and lungs wanted to explode from their housing.

Semi-dressed, the female form grabbed the rest of her clothing from the floor in order to make her escape past Alex. The shaft of light from the corridor made it possible for Alex to recognise the intruder as the staff nurse from the surgical ward before the girl fled away.

Douglas pulled himself up and switched on the bedside light.

Alex remained pressed to the wall, unable to comprehend the unfolding situation.

'Mea culpa,' was all the explanation that was forthcoming from Douglas as he raised his arms.

'What's going on?' was all that came from Alex's quivering voice.

'I promise you it meant nothing,' Douglas told her as he extracted himself from the bed and pulled on his trousers.

'It means something to me, I can't believe what I saw!' Alex told him, putting her hands on her head.

Douglas walked across to her, but she recoiled from him.

'How can it not mean anything, it's the ultimate sign of love,' she argued.

'Let me explain,' he told her calmly. 'We were saying goodbye, I was telling her about my wonderful wife and how much I love her.' Douglas hesitated before adding, 'Then one thing led to another.'

Alex was overwhelmed, but her training came to the fore. 'I can't discuss this tonight, I'm too upset,' she told him, turning to the door.

Douglas approached, then grabbed her. 'Please Alex forgive me, I promise it will never happen again.'

'You're right, it will never happen again,' she rasped.

The smell of alcohol on Douglas' breath disgusted her, she shook him off and fled through the doorway. She did not bother to close the door and as she escaped she heard him call, 'All this can be sorted out, I know it can.'

Once back in the sanctuary of her own rooms, she locked her door and sank down on the bed. The tears did not come, she was numb. Her mouth was dry so she went to the tap for a glass of water and leant over the small work surface as she took sips from the glass in her shaking hand.

Returning to the bed she lay down and tried to collect her thoughts. Her heart was still pounding.

She'd been betrayed. What action was she going to take?

There was no sleep that night for Alex. Her marriage and subsequent life were rotating in her mind and in conflict.

87

Next morning she bravely prepared for the day ahead, determined that no one would detect her anguish. She applied her lipstick and eyeliner with resolution and more generously than usual – she did not want sympathy or advice from any quarter. She, and she alone, would deal with the crisis.

Before going onto the ward she went to the dining room for a cup of coffee. One or two of the medical staff nodded a 'good morning' to her and appeared to see nothing unusual in her demeanour. She was pleased about this. She was over the first hurdle. As the day passed, she coped, the patients' needs superseding her own misery at times. Of Douglas, there was no sign.

Bolting back to the security of her own rooms, she locked herself in mentally as well as physically for the second night. Mercifully, the hospital was quiet, she was exhausted and calmness was enveloping her. It was not a calmness of acceptance however – she had reached a crossroads and decisions had to be made.

Not tonight. Slipping into her bed, her eyes heavy with weariness, the telephone jangled. Alex hesitated about responding to it, as she wasn't on call.

When she did pick up the receiver the voice said, 'Vulcan here.'

'Leave me alone, I'll talk to you when I'm good and ready,' she told her husband as she slapped the phone back on its base.

Alex had taken her first steps to the signposts on the crossroads.

6

It was an agonising time for Alex knowing she had to make the biggest decision of her life. Over the following weeks she shied away from social contacts, almost ashamed, in some strange way. She did her work, then retired to the peace and safety of her rooms. Although she had fleeting glimpses of Douglas they had spoken only once, at her request.

'Give me a week,' she had calmly asked.

He had eagerly agreed.

Her mien was such that not even Magda suspected there was anything untoward going on.

At the end of the week Alex wrote a note to her husband asking him to meet her in a recently opened coffee bar in the middle of Queensbridge. The choice of this venue was to prevent acrimony being loudly voiced.

Alex got there early, complete with notebook. She ordered a coffee and quietly went through her jottings.

When Douglas arrived she was shocked by his haggard and unkempt appearance. Alex immediately ordered a coffee for him. He took his seat opposite her and stretched his hand out to take hers. Alex withdrew from the contact.

'I've missed you so much,' he told her. 'Please say we can start again.'

Alex could see the pain in his eyes. All his self-assurance had gone, and she was tempted to say that all was forgiven and feel his arms around her again. Instead she placed her hands back onto the table along with the notebook.

'I suggested we meet here as we need to talk calmly about things,' she said as her eyes wandered round the half-empty room.

Douglas nodded vehemently.

'Shall I start?' she asked.

Douglas continued to nod.

Without reference to her notes Alex began by telling him how devastated she had been by his actions.

'I know, I know, it was the height of stupidity. Please just let us put it behind us, I love you so much and it was a meaningless act that I deeply regret,' he interrupted.

Alex closed her eyes, because seeing Douglas as a supplicant stiffened her resolve.

'Your "meaningless act" has changed everything,' she told him, widening her eyes and looking directly at him. 'I can't forgive you, I would always be wondering when you were late back just what you had been up to.'

'It will not happen again.' He had to say it quietly because of the surroundings.

'Douglas, I want to separate from you and that means divorce,' Alex told him firmly.

'What? Just one indiscretion and you bale out?' She could see incredulity written on his face. 'I won't agree,' he told her.

'I am going to consult a solicitor and I shall name your charming little staff nurse as co-respondent.'

Douglas was nonplussed, but a shred of decency came to the fore.

'You know what will happen to her if she is cited,' he pleaded.

Alex nodded. 'Indeed I do. Matron will dismiss her, she will get a damning reference and may have difficulty getting another job.'

Douglas stared at her, surprised by the vitriol of his once loving wife. He ran his hands through his tousled hair.

'I suggest you behave like a gentleman. Agree to a divorce admitting adultery with person or persons unknown and we make a clean break,' she spat at him. 'I will make no financial claims on you, you keep the car and you salvage your reputation.'

'You've thought this out, haven't you, sitting in that room of yours along with Madam Magda hatching this plan.' Douglas was now getting angry and thumped the table.

'No one else knows,' Alex retaliated, 'but I want you to think about what I have proposed and we'll meet here in a week's time.' She stood up, ready to depart. Douglas remained seated, sipping at his now cold coffee.

'Think about what I have said,' Alex reminded him as she departed.

The walk back to the hospital was agonising. How she wanted him still, in spite of everything, but she knew deep down that there could be no happiness with Douglas and the sooner they parted the better for both of them.

Back inside the hospital Alex sought out Magda. She was still working but ready for a coffee break. Once in the common room with snatched refreshment they found a reasonably secluded spot in which to talk.

'I'm leaving Douglas,' Alex informed her shocked friend.

'What's happened?' was all that Magda could choke out.

Alex explained, sparing no details except the name and status of the staff nurse.

'I'm shocked but not surprised,' was the reaction. 'Think carefully, Alex, before you do anything irreversible. It's only a week since it happened, just give it a bit more time.'

Alex nodded, but she'd made up her mind.

Her next task was to tell her parents. She was dreading it, but they had to be told, and before anyone else decided to do the job for her. Hospitals were minefields of gossip. Her day off was before the second scheduled meeting with her husband. She decided to go home to Westfield, take the bull by the horns and get it over and done with.

As usual her mother met her at the station on the chosen day.

'Married life obviously suits you,' Susan commented as she gave her a peck on the cheek.

Alex, not wanting to be drawn said, 'How's Pa?'

'He is so busy, writing papers, attending conferences and seminars, and his NHS consultant work, it never stops,' Susan told her with a hint of pride as they made their way to the car.

Alex said little on the way home, leaving her mother to prattle away with local news and gossip.

The dogs were waiting outside in the drive when they reached their destination. They barked with excitement when they sniffed who it was, but they were glad to settle down again, their arthritic hips rendering them no more than a vocal challenge nowadays. Alex stroked them affectionately until they quietened. She noted James' car parked round the corner and it made her feel nervous about the ordeal ahead.

She followed her mother into the kitchen, unchanged from her childhood, and was overcome with a great feeling of despondency. Alex fought back the tears because she had no intention of cracking now.

James appeared and greeted Alex warmly. 'Dear girl,' he told her as he kissed her and led her through to the drawing room. He made for the side table and poured them all a pre-luncheon drink. Susan, having checked the dining room, then joined them.

'Cheers,' James said, raising his glass to his wife and daughter.

Alex could bear it no longer.

'I have some news for you,' she blurted out.

Susan looked at her expectantly and said, 'I thought you had a suspicious look of radiance, I think I know what you are about to tell us.'

Alex shook her head, hating herself for being such a disappointment to her parents.

'No, it's bad news.' She was having trouble controlling her emotions.

'One of you ill?' was James' immediate concern.

'Douglas and I are parting company,' she told them.

James and Susan exchanged horrified glances.

Alex walked about the room with glass in hand, her parents' eyes following her every move.

'What has happened?' Susan was the first to ask.

'Douglas committed adultery,' Alex told them bluntly.

Susan recoiled in horror. James swallowed heavily before asking, 'Are you sure?'

'Oh yes, I caught him in the act.'

Susan averted her eyes and placed her glass somewhat shakily on the small table.

'Did he give you an explanation?' James enquired. He was standing by the marble fireplace, his elbow on the mantelpiece.

'An explanation?' Alex repeated, looking at James with incredulity. 'Like it was an *accident* – I thought it was *you* – she *tempted* me? Shall I go on?'

'Alex, please,' her mother remonstrated.

James turned his back and gazed into the fireplace.

'Are you – ' he hesitated, carefully choosing his words, 'being a good wife?'

Alex was furious, knowing exactly what her father was implying.

'If you mean am I denying him his conjugal rights, the answer is *no*.'

Susan was appalled by the candour of her daughter.

'Alex, will you please control your use of language in this house.'

'I've done nothing wrong and you are making me feel as though *I'm* the guilty one,' she retorted.

'Perhaps you should consider reconciliation,' James advised, turning back to face her. 'Douglas seemed a good egg to me.'

'He cheated on me, he is a rotten egg!' It was a childish thing to say but Alex was now boiling with rage.

'I thought I would get some sympathy here but obviously not. Sir James Brandon with a divorcée daughter, bringing shame on the family, and you mother, president of the Women's Institute, how are you going to explain it away, particularly when the word is *adultery*.'

There was silence, then Susan took command of the situation.

'I can see you're very hurt, and with good reason, Alex, but I think you should let things settle down for a while before taking any action you might regret.'

Alex shook her head in disbelief.

Hoping to diffuse the volatile situation Susan announced lunch was ready and led them through to the dining room.

It was a stilted and uncomfortable meal. Alex felt isolated while her parents were trying to absorb the unexpected thunderbolt their daughter had delivered.

After lunch Alex decided to return to Queensbridge earlier than planned, and Susan was only too glad to drive her to the station.

'I think your father might sort this problem out for you,' Susan told her on the platform, looking nervously around lest anyone should hear.

The train was in sight and puffing towards them.

'I want no interference, thank you Ma, I will deal with my life,' Alex stressed.

The train came to a halt. Alex opened the nearest carriage door and stepped in. There was no goodbye kiss from her mother.

Back at Westfield House James was contemplating how his well ordered life was now thrown into disarray. He was irritated by Alex and her behaviour and he foresaw trouble ahead. The more he thought about it the worse his fears became.

'Adultery,' he murmured to himself. 'There will be a scandal.'

Alex on the other hand found her spirits rising as she chuffed her way back to Queensbridge. Her resolve for a divorce was strengthening, and the sooner the better. As the train steamed into the station she jumped out quickly and walked briskly back to the hospital. She did not want to meet anyone familiar until she'd made a certain phone call in the privacy of her room. Her luck was in, the workforce was far too eager to get home towards the end of the day to notice her as she threaded her way through them.

Sitting on the bed, back in her accommodation, she consulted her notebook, and having found the number she wanted she dialled it.

It seemed an eternity before her call was answered.

'Hello?' It was the silky voice of Aunt Sonia on the other end.

'It's me, Alex,' she said, then launched in with the Douglas saga.

Aunt Sonia was not surprised by her revelations, or the quaint reaction of Susan and James.

'I think you need to see a lawyer,' she counselled.

'Do you know a good divorce lawyer?' Alex pleaded.

'I know a really sizzling one called Gideon Prentiss, an old friend of mine,' Aunt Sonia continued. 'He's in the City, and I'll ring him tomorrow.'

'Thank you, dear Aunt Sonia,' Alex told her obliging godmother before ending the call.

Alex was exuberant because Aunt Sonia had understood, and she smiled at Sonia's remark that Westfield House would now have to be fumigated after the word 'adultery' had been uttered in it.

Alex slept well that night having accomplished exactly what she wanted. True to her word Aunt Sonia telephoned the following evening. She'd made an appointment three weeks hence with the 'sizzling' Gideon Prentiss. Sonia also offered to accompany Alex to the meeting. The offer was gratefully accepted.

Another meeting was in the offing. It was the much dreaded task of seeing Douglas in Chico's Coffee Bar. Alex wondered if he would attend. She left a written reminder in his post box so there was no excuse.

She made her way to the arranged venue early, and ordered a coffee. Again, she chose a quiet spot, but the place was busier than before.

When Douglas finally arrived some fifteen minutes late Alex was amazed at the transformation. He was smart and no longer abject. And he launched in without preamble.

'I want you to come back with me now, this divorce nonsense has got to stop. We put the past behind us, and start again,' was his opening gambit.

Alex stared at him.

'Sit down Douglas,' she ordered. 'There is no going back.'

Douglas reluctantly took a seat opposite her.

'Are we going to throw away a lifetime of happiness for one indiscretion?' he continued.

'Pa has spoken to you, hasn't he?'

'Yes, he telephoned me and said we had to reconcile our differences,' Douglas told her.

Alex was furious. 'Pa has no right to interfere, I haven't changed my position since we last talked.'

The waitress appeared and Douglas ordered coffee.

'You've made up your mind. To be quite honest I'm sick of it all,' he said impatiently.

'Me too,' Alex replied. 'I have arranged to consult a solicitor, because I want to get out of this so-called marriage.'

'Does your father know about this solicitor?' Douglas asked with surprise.

'No, and it's none of his business.' Alex had to lower her voice as the waitress returned with the coffee.

'Well, I've given you your last chance. It seems you are determined to finish it all, no doubt egged on by Magda and company,' Douglas said with disgust.

'You just don't get it, do you? I make my own decisions and it's my decision and mine alone that we finish this charade. I am vulcanised, fireproof – understand that,' Alex told him, shaking her head.

Douglas' face contorted with rage. 'The feeling is mutual, I'm sick of you with your hoity-toity ways. Mother warned me you might be a handful and she was right.' He then took a quick slurp of coffee to control his feelings.

Alex fumbled in her bag and brought out a small box. Douglas stared at it.

'As there is nothing to be gained from further meetings, I am returning the engagement ring, simply because it belonged to a past member of your family. You may wish to use it again,' she added sarcastically as she slid it across the table to him.

Alex was surprised when Douglas pocketed it and laughed.

'Family heirloom it possibly was, but not my family, I bought the thing at that little shop where you got the coffee spoons.'

To Alex, it was like a knife going through her heart.

Douglas stood up. He was smiling contemptuously, almost leering at her. He knew he had scored a blow.

'Do your worst Alex, it couldn't be as bad as living with you.' And he turned and walked out, leaving her to pay for his coffee.

Alex gathered her things together and the waitress came over with the bill.

'He didn't seem very nice,' she told Alex as she cleared the table.

Alex rose and, fishing in her purse, gave the girl a hefty tip.

'That has to be the understatement of the year,' she muttered.

She left Chico's with mixed feelings. In spite of everything Douglas was still physically attractive to her and she knew how dangerous that could be.

It was an interminable wait for her appointment in London with Gideon Prentiss. Aunt Sonia was being particularly supportive and rang frequently to help keep Alex's spirits afloat. There was not one word from her parents. They were annoyed by her intransigence.

When the day of the London meeting finally came Alex prepared with great care.

'I want you to look innocent and sort of rural,' Aunt Sonia advised.

Always eager to oblige her godmother, Alex played down the cosmetics and wore flat shoes. Sonia was delighted by her appearance when they met at the appointed hotel for coffee and a briefing.

'Perfect,' she breathed in her goddaughter's ear as she hugged and kissed her.

Aunt Sonia always added a touch of humour to even the most serious matters. Never more needed than now, when discussing tactics. Alex felt uplifted.

They walked the short distance to the City. Alex felt the buzz that being in London creates.

'I feel a real country bumpkin,' Alex complained as she gazed with envy at the smart girls going about their business.

'Trust me,' Aunt Sonia told her with a smile. 'I told you to dress like that with good reason.'

They arrived at their destination with time to spare. The receptionist had obviously been alerted to the importance of the client. Sonia was taken to the boardroom with the promise of coffee and Alex was whisked upstairs, where, after a wait of minutes she was taken into the hallowed office of Gideon Prentiss. She almost felt she should genuflect as she walked through the doorway, such was the atmosphere.

'Sizzling Gideon' however dispelled reverence from the proceedings. He was a modern man in an ageing temple! Alex liked him, especially as, after cursory introductions, he told her to 'spell it out'.

Alex fumbled for her notebook, but even without it the events of her disastrous marriage poured from her.

Gideon interrupted only occasionally. The adultery factor seemed the least important to him.

'So he did not provide you with a home and you paid for your hospital accommodation yourself,' he said, shaking his head with disbelief.

'Yes, it will be on my payslips,' Alex confirmed.

'I find this case quite interesting. As long as you manage to wring the conditions from him, I see a reasonably quick and painless settlement. Even so, divorce is a protracted business.'

'Well, there are inducements which I think he will find irresistible – ' Alex shrugged.

Gideon smiled back at her. There was understanding in his eyes.

'All I need now is the name and address of his solicitor,' he said, almost to conclude their meeting.

Alex was not able to provide that information, so closing her notebook she stood up. Gideon did likewise, and they returned downstairs to join Aunt Sonia, who was sipping coffee and reading magazines. It was apparent that she and Gideon met frequently on the social scene as they hugged and kissed effusively.

'I will do my best to expedite matters,' he told them.

'Please Gideon, do your best for my darling Alex,' Sonia pleaded.

'I can't wait, believe me,' Gideon said with relish. 'Goodbye Mrs Ffrench,' he said directly to Alex, 'I'll be in touch as soon as I have news.' He then shook her hand and blew a kiss to Sonia.

Once outside the offices, Sonia suggested lunch. They chose a nearby restaurant full of the legal profession judging by their clothing and conversation. Finding a suitable table in one of the quieter areas they were able to discuss the morning's consultation.

'He was so very nice,' Alex reported.

'He can be the nastiest piece of garbage if he needs to be,' Aunt Sonia whispered, 'that's why I took you to him.'

After ordering, lunch was served speedily and Sonia was pleased.

'We both need to get going before the rush hour,' she warned, so she and Alex devoured their meal and wasted no time heading back to their respective stations. London had charged Alex's excitement but as she arrived back in Queensbridge her spirits sank. Plans were forming and she knew the distractions of implementing them would help with the trauma she was now experiencing.

Her top priority was to find a flat. It was imperative for her to leave the hospital accommodation. In spite of the doom and gloom Alex felt much comforted by the fact that someone believed she was a victim and was prepared to help her in putting things right. Meeting up with her friends again she told them about her London visit. They, too, were supportive and cheered at the thought that Douglas would be getting his just desserts.

It was Patricia who made the proposal.

'Alex, why don't you come and share the flat with us?' she asked tentatively. 'I know it's only a box room, but Magda, Richard and I don't think you should be on your own.'

Tears came to Alex's eyes. 'I don't care whether it is a box room, I gratefully accept the offer.'

There were smiles all round. It was the first hurdle, and Alex had flown over it. Another hurdle appeared however. It was the fact that it was now common knowledge in the hospital that she and Douglas were parting company. While she had unstated sympathy she also encountered tacit hostility. She was sure that the circumstances around the separation were embellished and distorted; she remembered the game of 'Chinese whispers' from her childhood.

Unexpectedly meeting Douglas in the hospital corridor she slowed him down to ask if she could remove her belongings from his rooms at a mutually convenient time.

'No,' he told her acidly, 'you should have thought of that before you rushed off.'

'You're welcome to my toothbrush and flannel,' she retaliated. 'My solicitor needs the name of your solicitor,' she called after his departing figure.

'Haven't decided yet,' Douglas shouted back at her.

Alex sighed. It was an inevitable reaction from him. Bringing differences into their working environment was another matter and she vowed not to approach him again. She could risk a reprimand for allowing personal interests to intrude into working time.

Arranging the move to the flat was fun. The box room was small, but Magda allocated hall cupboards for her use. Alex was too desperate to put the past behind her to worry about cramped conditions. It was heaven. She and her helpers drank copious amounts of wine as they shunted suitcases and other chattels, and then slept soundly that night after their exertions.

Alex was also pleased that she was now able to make private telephone calls, she'd always worried about conversations going through the hospital switchboard and vice-versa.

The call she made had to be discreet, it was to the 'sizzling Gideon'.

'My husband has declined to give me the name of his solicitor.'

Gideon was not impressed. 'He'll be screaming for one when I start on him,' he forecast.

Alex was thrilled to hear such a positive outlook. She was sure she could weather the storm with all the support she was receiving from those around her.

Stormy times there were over the next months. She saw nothing of Douglas, but two of his associates were less than friendly towards her. The impending divorce had reached 'cause célèbre' status in the hospital. Alex was determined not to fuel the gossip. A summons from Gideon with a required meeting aroused mixed feelings, bordering on fear. Douglas was so dangerous now. He was like a wounded animal. It was sometimes difficult to remember how loving and admiring he'd been in the first throes of their marriage.

Aunt Sonia did not hesitate to offer her chaperone services when Alex rang her about the date of the next legal meeting.

'You can gorgeous yourself up this time,' she advised her goddaughter.

Alex did not fail her.

Again, the royal welcome awaited them, though Gideon kept Alex waiting for half an hour.

'My apologies for keeping you waiting but I have some good news Mrs Ffrench, which is why I was late,' he told her. He then picked up a document. 'I think we might go for an annulment rather than a divorce.'

'What does that mean?' Alex enquired.

'Much better for you, quicker and cleaner,' Gideon shot at her.

'What are my husband's reactions?' Alex asked.

'Your husband is very money conscious, more or less accusing his solicitor of delaying tactics so he can charge more,' Gideon told her.

Alex nodded and smiled, it sounded just like Douglas.

Gideon then asked a few more questions, some of a personal nature, but seemed satisfied with all the information that Alex was able to give him.

'That's all, but please do not enter into any liaisons until this is in the bag. We don't want to give any grounds for cross-petitioning.'

Alex was ecstatic. 'Thank you so much Mr Prentiss,' she said.

'Let's go and find the lovely Sonia,' Gideon said, concluding the meeting. He rose from his desk and led Alex from his book-lined office down the stairs.

Aunt Sonia was waiting eagerly for the news which Alex breathlessly imparted under the watchful gaze of the solicitor. They all shook hands and Sonia and Alex kept their delight muted until out of the building.

Clasping each other round the waist, Sonia then proclaimed, 'We're going to have one marvellous celebratory lunch!' And she homed in on a restaurant that reflected their mood.

It was the climax to a successful day.

Alex now had to adjust to being a single woman again, even if the legal side was not finalised. There were times when the loneliness was unbearable. Magda and Patricia, along with Richard and Peter, included her as much as possible in their social arrangements. She was also playing tennis, but there was a horrible gap in her life.

Douglas resigned, and moved to a hospital in the North of England. He let it be known that it was promotion. The last straw for him had been when a colleague had laughingly referred to the details of his impending divorce as a 'Ffrench farce'. It was of considerable relief to Alex to know that she could not now accidentally run into him. Moving in with her two friends brought back memories of student days, but without the penury.

All she wanted was to hear that the annulment was finalised – until then she was in limbo.

Thinking about the future was not easy. Magda and Patricia were steaming ahead. Alex resolved that she would not be left behind. She applied for courses and discussed possibilities with her colleagues. She was approaching the next hurdle.

She kept herself busy. It was the antidote to the misery, and this particular morning she had given herself a larger than usual workload in spite of the fact she had arranged lunch with her two friends in the cafeteria.

She was running late and they were already seated and eating when she rushed to join them. Worse still, there was a queue ahead of her and three noisy males were in animated conversation, oblivious of the need to move forward. They were blocking the aisle. The one nearest to her had his back to Alex and was wearing a Harris tweed jacket with leather patches on the elbows along with corduroy trousers.

Alex had seen them before and someone had mentioned that they were 'boffins' from Knightsville, the long-standing rival of Queensbridge.

Without warning Mr 'corduroy trousers' stepped back onto Alex's foot. He immediately turned round, placed his hands on her upper arms and apologised. His hazel eyes twinkled at her. 'After what I have done I think I should let you pass and get your lunch first.'

The other two stepped aside, it was like Moses parting the Red Sea. Alex slipped past them, thanking them as she grabbed what she could from the counter.

Magda and Patricia were waiting and had watched the incident.

'What was that all about?' Magda asked.

Alex explained.

'The fair-haired one is Professor Curtis, he's one of ours,' Patricia informed them.

'The other two are Knightsville alumna, one presumes,' Magda said, rather disparagingly.

'What about the toe crusher?' Alex enquired.

'Yes, he's a Knightsville boffin, written all over him,' Patricia said, looking at Alex with surprise, implying that Alex was naïve in thinking he could emanate from any other university.

'Why are they here?' Alex said with her mouth full of food.

'It's that big building going up on the other side of the road, medical research, genetics, that sort of thing,' Patricia said vaguely.

Alex shrugged, it was of little interest to her, but she did feel resentful about the influx of Knightsville boffins, as she saw it, picking the brains of the Queensbridge hierarchy.

The conversation then reverted to more domestic matters, and the boffins forgotten.

7

Although the legal side of her parting with Douglas was going well, her job satisfactory and the accommodation comfortable, Alex was unsure of herself. Magda was heavily involved with Richard and Patricia, likewise, with Peter Phipps.

Patricia was getting married in a month's time and would vacate her bedroom. It meant Alex could move into it. There was a lot more space and it had a quieter aspect.

On her days off Alex had gone home to try and rectify the estrangement that had developed between herself and her parents. Things were better, but they were by no means right. James, in particular, let his displeasure show and no reference was made to the divorce.

Tennis was filling the social gaps more and more, but it wasn't enough. Alex had played a few matches and enjoyed, not only the play, but the camaraderie with the other players, but they were hospital staff talking about hospital topics, and Alex wanted to broaden her horizons.

Feeling very sorry for herself after a long stretch on duty and on the dreariest of days, she decided to walk into Queensbridge and treat herself to some new clothes. She could find nothing she liked, but that was more her mental state than the lack of choice. She had lunch out, treating herself to her favourite dish, macaroni cheese, but it was not like her mother made, and she couldn't finish it.

Walking slowly back to the flat she saw a hoarding

announcing an exhibition at the Classical and Contemporary Art Gallery. She had more than enough time to spare so on impulse she turned and headed for the temple-like building and walked up the stone steps into the hallowed atmosphere.

Being a weekday there weren't many visitors or tourists about. Alex took a catalogue and proceeded to view the exhibits. In general they were of no great interest to her. There were three or four other viewers in the room and she quickly caught up with one of them. He was studying his catalogue and referring to the exhibit. He looked familiar, but it wasn't until he turned his head to look at her that Alex realised it was the toe-trampling Knightsville boffin. He was dressed so differently. Today he was sporting a leather jacket and open-necked shirt.

He smiled when he saw her. 'Hello again,' he said cheerfully.

Alex smiled back.

'I can't say I'm overly impressed with this,' he said, waving his catalogue in the direction of the exhibits.

Alex agreed. 'I'm going upstairs to see the paintings,' she told him.

'Can anyone come?' he asked.

'Of course,' Alex replied.

As they made their way back to the staircase the boffin stopped. 'I think we ought to introduce ourselves,' he said, holding out his hand. 'I'm David Freer.'

Alex took his hand. 'I'm Alex Ffrench,' she told him. 'You are *Doctor* David Freer, I presume,' she queried.

He nodded. 'I know you are Doctor Alex Ffrench because I saw you "modus vivendi",' he told her.

'You trod on my toe,' she reminded him.

Suddenly he became serious. 'As if I could forget.'

Alex blushed, she didn't know why. She turned and led him up to the picture gallery. He was immediately impressed

107

and they started discussing the art and she found David Freer to be knowledgeable.

'What are your favourites?' she asked.

'The Pre-Raphaelites,' Dr Freer told her, his eyes on her face. 'In fact you have the look of a Pre-Raphaelite yourself.'

'*The Scapegoat*, no doubt,' Alex said disparagingly.

'Why do you say that? I was thinking more of Rossetti, not Holman Hunt,' Freer told her seriously.

'Maybe all junior doctors regard themselves as scapegoats,' Alex told him.

Dr Freer nodded. 'I must admit I'm glad those days are behind me.'

They wandered round chattering, the art secondary to their purpose. He was so easy to talk to and so humorous. Alex had not enjoyed an afternoon like it for a long time.

Dr Freer looked at his watch. 'What say we go and have tea at that little teashop down the road from here?' he suggested.

Alex was thrilled, she felt alive again: *afternoon tea with a Knightsville boffin, what would Magda say to that?*

The little teashop was busy but from the greeting David Freer must have been a frequent visitor to the place as they were shown to a specially cleared table by none other than the owner. Alex was introduced as a colleague.

They were handed a menu. 'I can recommend the scones,' whispered the hostess across the table.

Alex nodded agreement, and the order was placed.

'Away from the hospital, you can call me David, and I shall call you Alex,' Freer insisted. Alex was surprised by his informality.

'Aren't you from Knightsville?' she asked conversationally.

'Yes, I'm here as part of the research team. That new building that's going up is going to have some of the most sophisticated equipment in the world, along with some of the most enlightened scientists, and we're going into areas that will transform medicine.'

Alex listened. She could sense David's excitement emanating from him.

'It revolves around our friend the "monk" – Mendel.' David continued.

'Oh, messing around with the peas,' Alex interrupted.

David looked at her, not sure whether she was joking about his beloved subject.

'It's strange how the smallest thing can have the most profound effects,' Alex mused.

David was reassured when he saw the contemplative look in her eyes.

Tea arrived, and it was all David had promised. Enticing scones, homemade raspberry jam and cream exploding from its flowered basin. They continued to talk as they ate, but avoided matters medical.

Alex was careful not to reveal details about her father – as usual she referred to him as a 'Midlands doctor' when the conversation turned onto personal topics.

'My father's an accountant, so's my brother, I'm the only doctor in the family,' David said soberly. 'Finance and medicine are strange bedfellows, however in my case they seem to accommodate.'

Replete from the intake of their sumptuous tea and with conversation drying up, David looked at his watch.

'I have to go to work now.' He called for the bill and when it arrived scattered plentiful change over it and on the table, then stood up and helped Alex with her chair, and then her jacket.

Once outside he shook her hand and thanked her for a pleasant afternoon.

Alex watched as he strode purposefully away. He'd disturbed her. She thought about those hazel eyes with humour lurking in them, and the dark, overly long, curling hair. He wasn't good-looking but he was bursting with masculinity. Not the aggressive sort, but the type that knows it has nothing to prove.

Alex knew this was no romantic encounter. He'd been friendly, but had kept his distance and had not suggested meeting again. Maybe he was married – those scientific men usually had a wife and several children. Why was she even thinking about him when it had been nothing more than a chance meeting?

She returned to the flat and attended to a few domestic issues before Magda and Patricia chattered their way through the door. They were surprised to see her, but asked how she had occupied herself on her day off.

'I had tea with the Knightsville boffin,' she said smugly.

Magda reacted immediately. 'What do you mean?' she asked sharply.

Alex related the events of the afternoon.

'You do realise you have to stay celibate while this divorce is in the offing,' Magda reminded her.

Patricia sniggered.

'You always have to reduce everything to Freudian levels,' Alex retorted.

'He's after your body,' Magda remarked as she unpacked her shopping.

'Nonsense,' Alex said angrily. 'He just wanted a companion over a cup of tea.'

'Perhaps he was after intellectual stimulation then,' Magda said sarcastically and without looking at her.

Alex blushed. 'I wish I hadn't told you now,' she replied shaking her head.

Patricia then launched in. 'Alex, Magda's right, you really must not even be seen on your own with any male, Douglas would jump on any excuse, however innocent, to damage you.'

Deep down Alex knew her friends were right, but it was hard to take criticism when she felt none was deserved.

'Richard and I are taking you out to dinner tonight, so get dressed up,' Magda told Alex as she disappeared into her bedroom.

Patricia smiled. 'Come on Alex, we're on your side, you'll forget all your problems when you're having a great time with Magda and Richard tonight.'

Alex brightened up. The girls had done everything to keep her going since Douglas departed. She must make an effort too.

Rooting through the hall cupboard which was currently her wardrobe, Alex found one of her more expensive, 'Douglas era' buys. She decided to wear it even if it was more formal than required for the evening ahead. Fortunately, Magda had chosen to pour herself into one of her smarter outfits and when Richard arrived he was suitably impressed and only too eager to escort two fashionable women to dinner.

The restaurant was newly opened and its reputation unknown. When they reached it, it was well illuminated and inviting. Inside was expensively simple. They were shown to their previously booked table and handed a menu. Richard ordered drinks for them. A nearby table was set for what looked like a largish party, but there were only a few other diners there.

Magda put her hand on her chest, a look of concern on her face.

'Does anyone have a safety pin on them?' she asked.

'A Smith-Petersen pin did you say?' Richard joked.

Alex and Richard shook their heads.

Magda stood up. 'I have to go to the cloakroom, a minor technical dress problem,' she told them as she sped off.

As Richard and Alex sipped their drinks, the door burst open and in came a group of males, though Alex detected two less exuberant females in their midst. They were laughing noisily and bantering with each other. It was obvious that the party table was intended for them.

111

They seemed to overwhelm the restaurant with their presence. As Alex looked up at them as they passed, she noted that David Freer was one of the group. He did not acknowledge her.

She quickly turned her attention to Richard.

'Why don't you and Magda get married?' she asked, fixing her gaze on him.

'I keep asking her, on a weekly basis,' Richard said sadly. 'She doesn't say yes and she doesn't say no.'

Alex flicked a look across to the party table. David Freer was in the thick of it and seemingly as vociferous as the rest of the group. Alex knew he had spotted her and she was upset that he had not even nodded in her direction.

Magda reappeared, repairs completed with the help of female kitchen staff. They were ready to order.

Magda turned and looked across at the noisy new arrivals.

'Isn't that your boffin boyfriend over there?' she asked Alex.

Alex nodded. 'He walked straight past me without a word,' she told Magda.

'Did he indeed?' was the reply. Magda then instructed Richard to hold Alex's hand.

Richard obliged, looking at Alex with puzzlement.

'That's enough,' Magda said after a few seconds.

Alex smiled. What a tactician Magda was.

They ordered their meal, glad to do it before the 'Freer' party took the full attention of the waiters. It arrived promptly, and was up to their expectations. Once finished Magda decided that they would not stay for coffee but return to the flat for a nightcap. Richard settled the bill and ushered them out into the night air. They walked home. It wasn't late and there were plenty of undergrads, as usual, flying around on their bicycles.

Back at the flat Alex made the coffee for them all. She sat

and drank hers, then excused herself on the grounds she had some work to update and made for the box room. As she went through the nightly beauty routine she started to wonder why David Freer had ignored her. She had seen him glance in her direction a couple of times, so why not nod or wave? It confirmed her suspicions that the tea shop interlude was just a time-filling exercise for him.

Why was she even remotely concerned? It was nothing more than that to her.

Getting back to work was therapeutic. To be in a pioneering hospital was challenging and stimulating and enabled Alex to sideline the hurt in her personal life. The patients were so trusting and grateful. All this was having a restorative effect on her confidence.

Douglas was most certainly past tense now.

Good news too from Gideon. Progress was slow but sure.

David Freer had been absent from the hospital for some weeks. He was, no doubt, working back in Knightsville. However, Alex ran into him in the unlikely area of Concord when he surfaced again. She was looking at the tennis bulletins, and he was browsing through the social events.

'Dr Ffrench, I presume,' he quipped. The hazel eyes danced with humour.

'Oh, hello Dr Freer.' Alex tried to sound offhand.

They were interrupted by one of the physiotherapists rushing at Alex and breathlessly asking if she could play in a tennis match at University College Hospital the following week. Alex studied her notebook and sadly shook her head. The physiotherapist departed like a whirlwind, muttering names of likely replacements.

Dr Freer and Alex smiled at each other.

'So you add tennis to your accomplishments,' David said, gazing back at the noticeboard.

113

'My accomplishments are few and far between, I'm afraid,' Alex said resignedly.

Dr Freer turned at looked at her. 'You underestimate yourself,' he told her.

'Tennis and medicine, and not necessarily in that order, is about all I do,' she said, a hint of a smile playing on her face.

Dr Freer stubbed his finger on the noticeboard. 'Complimentary tickets for *The Mikado*, available at reception. Why not come and do a bit of local theatre with me, tonight?'

Alex hesitated. The offer was tempting, but she remembered how he had ignored her at the restaurant and didn't want to appear too eager. She delved into her white coat pocket and produced her notebook again.

'I suppose I could,' she said reluctantly, frowning as she flicked the pages.

'I'll go and get the tickets this very minute. Meet me here at seven,' and David turned away and was gone.

Alex felt a thrill, and her steps felt light as she made her way to the ward.

There was no way she could impart news of the date to her friends, but containing her excitement was difficult. She sneaked back to the flat and changed before Magda and Patricia came home. She left them a note and couched it in ambiguous terms, no lies, but rearranged truth.

David was waiting at their arranged meeting place. He was wearing a black suit and college tie. Alex wondered what it would be like to be kissed by him.

As they walked to the theatre they chatted, innocuous stuff, even the weather came under discussion.

The theatre was packed and they fought their way to the stalls. The seats were excellent. Alex loved the drama of the operetta, and the costumes were outstanding. During the interval, and over a drink, David continued the conversation by asking how she spent her free time. 'Do you have a boyfriend? he casually enquired.

Alex shook her head.

'I know you don't have a husband as there is no wedding ring.' He nodded at her finger folded round the wine glass.

'No, no husband,' Alex lied, then said quickly, 'Are you married?'

'No, I am not,' he said without hesitation.

There were one or two people from the hospital of nodding acquaintance; she hoped no one to tell Dr Freer about Douglas.

Making their way back they ran into a colleague of David's. A cursory introduction was made. Her name was Miriam and Alex recognised her as one of the two women at the boisterous restaurant party. David praised the practice of complimentary tickets for hospital staff.

'How did you manage to get tickets? The complimentary ones ran out within minutes. You must have been there as the notice went up at the hospital,' she said, somewhat aggrieved.

Dr Freer was taken aback. 'Just luck,' he shrugged.

He had to have bought the tickets to take me, Alex thought, but it only confused matters. Back in their seats and during the last act Alex was trying to work out why. Perhaps he was keen. Alex shot a glance at him, just as the mezzo soprano gave vent to the words 'We're very wide awake, the moon and I.' David Freer was already studying her and their eyes met.

Magda's supposition that he was hoping to lure her into his bed was beginning to stand up. However, the man was aloof, he had not even touched her, and the conversation had been on the most general of terms. The signals were mixed.

Maybe the walk home would reveal his intentions.

It was not to prove anything. Again, generalised and safe conversation and the conventional 'thank yous' for a pleasant evening. No future invitations out.

Magda and Patricia were lying in wait. 'Where have you been?' they asked suspiciously.

'I've been to see *The Mikado*, one of the physios had complimentary tickets,' Alex lied.

Magda and Patricia glanced at each other but relief crossed their faces.

'Your lipstick is intact so I believe you,' Magda told her.

Tucked up in her bed, Alex thought about Dr Freer. He was a complete enigma. Douglas had made his intentions known very early on, as had the medical students at university. David had trapped her into three lies, and she despised herself for it. She had disposed of Douglas for this reason. At least when caught out he told the truth. She decided to refuse his next approach but as it turned out he'd disappeared off the face of the earth and again he was gone for weeks.

Now Alex had another job change, her father's speciality, general medicine. The consultant, Dr Gerald Greaves, had certain similarities to James. He was a precise man, without humour but with a disagreeable wife. Alex had the misfortune to speak on the telephone to her on the first day of the change-over.

Dr Greaves, however, treated Alex well, knowing who her father was. It was never mentioned but Alex knew that she was immune from gratuitous criticism because of the connection.

All thoughts of Dr Freer were receding too. There was no one else on the horizon either. She was too dangerous a commodity while in the middle of a divorce.

The one bright light had been the wedding of Patricia and Peter Phipps. It was a small country affair which surprised those who attended, considering that Patricia's father was a High Court judge. Her mother had died some years ago and the judge had become reclusive.

'He can't stand a lot of fuss,' Patricia explained.

The bonus for Alex was that she now occupied Patricia's vacated bedroom and she had space to spare.

As suddenly as he had disappeared, Dr Freer reappeared. She encountered him in the dining room and this time she benefited from a smileless nod.

He was in the company of Professor Curtis and his group, and there was a seriousness about their conversations.

A few days later and he had disappeared again.

It now became clear that in order to revamp her life Alex needed to change hospitals. 'A new broom,' she mused. Patricia, now married, and Magda (as good as), denied Alex even female companionship. She'd work her period on medicine and then try fresh fields and pastures new.

There was no social life for her in Queensbridge, nothing to do now except go home, and even that was preferable to loafing around the town on her own.

Her mother was encouraging when Alex telephoned her, so a day together was planned. Meeting at the small and little frequented station, mother and daughter embraced. Susan was being particularly maternal, and brought Alex up to date on family news as they sped home.

'Your father will be home for lunch.' It was said as a warning rather than as an expected pleasurable event.

James, however, was in a good mood for once when he finally arrived. He refrained from asking Alex personal questions until they were in the dining room tucking into steak and kidney pie.

'So how is this divorce of yours going?' he enquired.

'Slow but sure. Douglas is, so far, giving no trouble. I shall be glad to be a free woman again.'

'Mmm, next time you had better be a bit more circumspect about your choice of husband,' James told her.

Alex was amazed. James had welcomed Douglas into the family with effusive praise. She didn't argue about it. She would soon be rid of the whole experience.

James returned to the hospital after lunch and a now necessary snooze. Alex and Susan took the dogs for a walk. It was then that Alex told her mother of her future plans. A move from Queensbridge, a fresh start, perhaps nearer home.

'Does that mean you would be working in the same hospital as your father?' Susan asked with concern.

'Not at all, no hospital big enough for both of us,' Alex chuckled.

Relief spread across Susan's face.

'I haven't decided yet,' Alex continued. 'It will be when this contract finishes or when the decree nisi or whatever it is arrives, so it's some time ahead.'

Alex knew this information would be fed back in a palatable form to her father. It would save her from the inevitable inquisition.

Having cleared the air with her mother, the day proved relaxing and she returned to Queensbridge feeling rejuvenated.

Making her way back from the lecture theatre some days later, Alex was astonished when David, with a hint of wizardry, reappeared. He looked fraught and distracted when they collided in the main corridor.

'*C'est moi,*' he said as he disentangled himself from the encounter.

Alex smiled. Douglas had always reverted to his limited French when at his most romantic.

'*C'est moi aussi,*' Alex replied.

'This collision is probably fortuitous,' David told her. 'I need help and an angel of mercy steps into my path.'

Alex was startled. 'What has happened? she asked as her eyes widened.

'I have finally transferred to Queensbridge. I have rented a flat, and have a van full of belongings parked by the main entrance. I need some assistance getting myself settled in. Any chance you could be available?'

'I'm on call, so not today,' she told him.

David looked crestfallen. 'I'm free tomorrow evening

though,' Alex said, hoping to imply that her social life was such that she might spare an hour or two to assist him.

'Absolutely marvellous,' David told her, relief spreading across his face. He arranged to pick her up as she came off duty.

'Fish and chip supper gets thrown in,' he said over his shoulder as he whisked off for a meeting.

The encounter charged Alex's batteries. She could barely wait for the following day. She decided to inform Magda about the situation. Again, her friend was sceptical.

'You collided in a twelve-foot wide main corridor?' Magda queried.

'We were both in a hurry,' Alex defended.

A look of understanding swept across Magda's face. 'Keep it under wraps, Patricia and I will always give you an alibi, but remember it's yours and his future at stake here.'

'He has not made one remark, neither has he touched me, to make me think this is leading anywhere,' Alex assured Magda.

'He's too smart, this man has an above average brain. He uses it in every aspect of his life, he is gently roping you in,' Magda stressed.

'He's promised a fish and chip supper,' Alex said rubbing her hands.

Magda could not resist laughing. 'Then you are safe for another night, he will not do the *coup de grâce* on a fish and chip supper.'

'It would make me look rather cheap, wouldn't it?' Alex conceded.

Both girls burst into peals of laughter. Nevertheless Magda had furthered Alex's hopes that David Freer might have an ulterior motive, even if it wasn't ready to come to fruition. She wondered about teasing him a little, but she was aware that deep down in him was an iron will. He would dictate the protocol.

The following evening Alex leant against the white van in the car park, the arranged meeting place. Minutes later David rushed from across the road, removing his tie as he greeted her.

He unlocked the ancient van and they both wriggled in amongst the clutter.

'I bought this heap, thought it would come in useful, people are always moving around in these university towns so I could always sell it when surplus to my requirements.'

Magda was right in her assessment of this man. He was clever about the smallest detail. Well, she was going to see if she could outsmart him. She was not going to fall for his advances if and when they presented themselves.

This evening David had nothing more on his mind than the disgorging of the van's contents into his new abode. The flat was only a short distance from the hospital and off the Queen Eleanor Road. The area was quiet, and consisted of large Victorian houses which had mostly been converted into student accommodation. David had rented the top floor and his landlord retained the two floors below.

Unlocking his private entrance it revealed the uncarpeted staircase. Returning to the vehicle David dug in and handed Alex some of his clothing while he grabbed a couple of boxes of books. He then led the way up the staircase and into the flat.

As Alex clattered up the staircase with the box of clothing she sniffed at it discreetly and could smell his aftershave. She'd had hints of it when she'd been out with him and wondered what brand he used.

She unceremoniously dumped his stuff on a bedroom chair.

Alex found the flat to be more spacious than it appeared from the outside and the eaves gave it character without denying it space. David left her to wander round and it was obvious he had already started transferring his belongings as there were boxes in each of the rooms. Alex removed her coat and prepared for work. She followed David back downstairs to the still well-loaded van.

'You are not to lift these boxes of books, women's bodies are not designed for heavy lifting,' he warned.

'What are they designed for?' Alex asked mischievously.

'We can discuss that later,' he replied, his arms full of boxes.

Alex scavenged through the loose array of David's property, gathered up armfuls and scooted up and down the stairs until the van was emptied.

The place was scantily furnished and obviously with reject items, unfashionable and well used. David closed the flat door; it was time to start unpacking and stowing away the chattels. Alex started in the kitchen, and was impressed when she unpacked a large Kenwood mixer.

'My mother insisted I had it,' David told her sheepishly.

Having allocated drawers and cupboards to reveal the pathetic range of china, cutlery and glassware, Alex made her way to the bedroom. She stared at the bed. It had an enormous dip in the middle of it. She started to laugh. It brought David into the room. Alex pointed to the bed. 'Just look at that, I would love to see you lying there in your pyjamas in that great trough.' She giggled uncontrollably.

David was not amused. 'That could probably be arranged at a later date,' he said acidly, 'except I don't wear pyjamas.' And he then turned and left.

Alex decided to leave well alone and continued with her task.

Two hours later and David's humour restored, they flopped down on the sagging sofa. Alex felt it tactful not to comment on the springing after the admonishment in the bedroom. David had his mind on other things anyway.

'I shall now go out and find fish and chips.' He produced a scruffy piece of paper with a few locations on it. 'This is the

Guid Bleu of Queensbridge fish and chip establishments,' he told Alex.

'More like *Guid Noir*,' she said as she fingered the blackened list. 'You are *Le maître de la poisson et pommes frites* I suppose, no end to your talents, Dr Freer.'

'Some of which you have not yet seen, or felt,' he warned.

The last two words of that sentence sent a small shiver of excitement through her. David jumped up and excavated his trouser pockets for his ignition keys. Alex knew they were on the draining board in the kitchen so she jumped up to go and retrieve them leaving a frantic David to continue his search. Returning to the sitting room she stood swinging the keys in the air. David walked across and snatched them from her.

'Weren't you at *Keys* College, Knightsville?' Alex teased.

'Different spelling. Anyway I was a Trinity man,' he retorted as he snatched the keys and departed on the fish and chip quest.

Alex looked round the sitting room where David had spent most of the evening stowing his books on the plentiful bookshelves. Amongst his scientific tomes were art and literary editions and even a few novels. Science was the thing that dominated his life, and he was ambitious. Alex knew that his transfer to Queensbridge would not have been offered to any average scientific brain – David had to be exceptional.

It was half an hour before he returned. Alex smelled the supper before David made his entrance.

'I hope it's wrapped in *The Times*,' Alex told him, and was surprised to find that it was, when he produced it from the bag.

'No cheapskate stuff here,' he told her as he handed the package over.

They sank down on the sofa to the twanging of the springs, unwrapped their fare and munched away. It tasted good straight out of the paper and what an appropriate way to wind the evening up.

After a cup of tea David, now weary, informed Alex that he would take her home.

'I can go home myself,' she replied.

'No,' David snapped. 'You do not wander the streets alone at night.'

'If you insist,' Alex said, pleased that she would have an escort home, but not so pleased when the tatty van was the means of transport.

David was effusive with his thanks for her help, but again there was no mention of a further encounter.

Two days later Alex was informed that there was an item for her to collect at reception. She strolled along to retrieve it and immediately felt the packaging contained a book.

'Where did this come from?' she asked the receptionist.

'The university bookshop, I think,' the girl told her.

Alex undid it nearby, thinking the parcel was not for her and she would need to hand it back again. When she opened it she knew there was no mistake. It was a book on the Pre-Raphaelites, beautifully illustrated. The front cover had a Rossetti woman on it, standing alone in a garden. There was an accompanying message: 'Thank you for all your help. David Freer.'

Alex stroked the cover. It was the most wonderful gift she had ever received. On the spur of the moment she decided to cross the road to the new building, hoping to seek out David and thank him for the fabulous gift; her excuse was that there were no telephones connected as yet. Alex had never visited the place and in fact hospital staff were discouraged from the facility by the hospital hierarchy. Also, security seemed to be important. Dr Freer had never suggested a visit, but she felt her white coat gave her enough credibility for infiltrating this 'holy of holies'.

The smell of drying concrete, paint and a suggestion of disinfection hung in the air, and the acoustics were enhanced by the sparseness of the surroundings. Alex almost crept her way into the central area where she was met by a woman not best pleased by her presence.

'Can I help?' she asked.

'I was looking for Dr Freer,' Alex said hesitantly.

'I'm afraid he's not here, I think he's over in the main hospital,' the woman said. 'Dr Galbraith is here if you would like to see him,' she told Alex, pointing to a male figure in an adjoining room.

'No, it was a personal matter,' Alex replied. After which she beat a hasty retreat. Her only recourse was to leave a letter of thanks at the reception desk in the main hospital and hope it reached him.

Checking two days later that the letter had reached its intended recipient, Alex was horrified to find it still unclaimed. Asking for it back she decided to have another foray into the new building, hoping that at least she could leave the letter there if Dr Freer was still unavailable.

This time Alex was more self-assured as she made her way in and down the now familiar corridor. Ahead of her was the same woman she met on her previous visit, but this time she was in conversation with a male colleague.

They both turned and stared at Alex.

'Oh, you again,' the woman said, somewhat impatiently.

'I'm sorry to bother you again, but could you kindly give this letter to Dr Freer?'

The man took the letter. 'I'll see Dr Freer gets it,' he said helpfully. 'And you are?'

'I'm Dr Ffrench, Dr Greaves' houseman,' Alex explained.

'I'm Dr Galbraith, and this is Dr Weston.' He nodded in the direction of the less than helpful female. He proffered his hand. The handshake was warm. Alex looked at him. He had a familiar look, but she couldn't recall where she had seen him before.

'Dr Galbraith is in overall charge here,' Dr Weston informed Alex, thawing out slightly.

'Thank you so much,' Alex told them as she backed away, deciding to beat a hasty retreat.

Dr Galbraith waved the letter in the air. 'I'll see he gets it!' And he and Dr Weston continued their interrupted conversation.

It was a week before David Freer made contact. He telephoned Alex at home and late at night. Apart from telling her he had had to go to London, his conversation was fairly inconsequential and Alex was at a loss to understand why he had contacted her. Like all people who phone, he left the reason for the call to the last.

'I'm having a house-warming,' he announced. 'I hope you can make it.'

Alex was thrilled by this prospect and raked around in her wardrobe for her smartest outfit. She wondered who else would be there, maybe some of the rowdies from the restaurant.

It was with some excitement that she prepared for the evening when it finally arrived. She was happy with the efforts she had made to enhance her appearance. She was hoping that extra mascara and lipstick plus a dousing of perfume might draw some response from the host.

Alex timed it so that she arrived a few minutes late. She let herself into the flat; it was quiet, no animated conversation. The smell of cooking hung in the air. She climbed the stairs and found David immersed in his cooking preparations.

'Where is everyone?' she asked.

'There's only you and me,' he said.

'Oh! I thought it was a party,' she said, removing her coat.

'So it is, just you and I,' David told her as he stirred a bubbling saucepan.

His attention was soon distracted as he looked at her. 'You look wonderful tonight,' he told her, 'but then you do every night.' He removed the pan from the stove and led her through to the sitting room where he poured drinks for them.

'To the new abode,' Alex said, raising her glass. She then fished in her handbag and produced a package and handed it to him. David opened it in a very deliberate way.

'This is some corkscrew,' he told her as he removed the gift from its box. 'Thank you. I see it has the staff of Hippocrates with the snake on it, I shall treasure it.'

He moved towards her and kissed her cheek. He stayed for some minutes stroking the object. It was obvious he was impressed with its significance.

'I got it from that little antique shop near the hospital,' Alex told him, pleased by his reaction. 'I know it will be much used too.'

This produced a smile from both of them. They finished their drinks, and Alex could see David was edgy, no doubt worried about the food he was preparing. This was confirmed by his next remark. 'I must get this supper dish on the table,' he said with some urgency, and retreated to the kitchen.

Alex did not offer to help and she noted that it did not come naturally to David to prepare and serve a meal. However, the proof of the pudding was most decidedly in the eating and he had excelled with goulash and olive bread.

After supper they talked until Alex looked at her watch and exclaimed about the lateness of the hour. She stood up, as did David. Moving to him she intended planting a thank-you kiss on his cheek but as she did so he slid his mouth onto hers. She made no effort to free herself, in fact she found herself pulling him nearer. When they parted they stared at each other.

'I've been wanting to do that for a long, long time,' he told her quietly, 'and I suspect you've wanted me to do it.'

Alex could only nod. They kissed again.

'Do you have to go home tonight?' David asked hopefully.

'Yes, yes, of course I do,' Alex said with a sense of panic.

David sensed her fear. 'Then I will take you, let me just get my jacket and find those elusive van keys,' he told her.

'I'll go downstairs and wait outside for you,' Alex told him.

She hastened down the stairs, her heart pounding. The cold night air calmed her as she stood outside for a few minutes.

Upstairs David found his jacket and located the keys to his van. He heard a noise from the staircase and turned. Alex was framed in the doorway. He walked across to her.

'Yes?' he whispered.

Alex nodded.

8

Once the affair was kindled it consumed them both – every moment they could, they spent together. It was difficult for Alex to suppress her new-found happiness but they both agreed that discretion was paramount and should they meet in the hospital or in the company of hospital staff they would address each other formally. This intrigue further fuelled the situation.

In the hospital dining room they ignored each other.

'If you think you're fooling anybody, think again,' Magda told Alex across the table over a cup of coffee just as this very situation had occurred.

'You and Richard are doing the same thing,' Alex retorted.

'Yes, but I don't have a husband, and Richard isn't on a prestigious genetics programme,' Magda told her friend tartly.

'I can't help myself, he has everything any woman could possibly want,' Alex pleaded as she leaned forward.

'I know, I know, Freud was so right when he asserted his theory about the most powerful motivator, but just be careful,' Magda warned.

With Magda's words still ringing in her ears hours later, Alex made her way to David's flat with some quickly purchased food, and let herself in. Entering the bedroom to throw her coat on the newly acquired bed caused her to smile. David's financial prudence had been swept aside when he ordered the divan, though he declared the basis for his extravagance was the amount of time spent in it.

Making her way back to the kitchen Alex set to. First she uncorked a bottle of wine, then prepared supper for them. She heard him enter below and rush up the stairs. They kissed, just as a married couple might, before he took off his tie and jacket and flung it on top of hers in the bedroom.

Joining her minutes later Alex could see David was abstracted.

'Everything all right?' It was meant to sound like a casual remark from Alex.

'No, we have some wretched VIP coming tomorrow, and Andrew is insisting on everything being tip-top, which it is anyway.'

'Andrew, who is Andrew?' Alex enquired.

'Andrew Galbraith, we're now on Christian-name terms,' David told her.

A terrible feeling swept over Alex. Andrew Galbraith, some years ago, had been her father's registrar. That was why he seemed familiar when she was introduced to him the other day in the new building. What worried her now was whether he had recognised her. She had been a young teenager, surely he wouldn't remember her from that, her whole appearance had changed. Furthermore, her name was Ffrench and he was probably no longer in touch with her father. She convinced herself the chances of discovery were remote.

In spite of this, the feeling of being discovered haunted her, and David's irritation at tomorrow's visit blighted an otherwise relaxed and pleasant evening, their last together for a few days. They made the most of it, before a Hollywood-style parting.

Alex was on call and would not be able to even see David. He too had 'the visit' and other pressing commitments likely to take up more than a working day, therefore she was surprised when she received a phone call from him the next afternoon asking her to meet him in the car park.

She could see he was angry before he reached her. He was pacing up and down in front of his van. As soon as she reached him he grabbed her arm.

'Are you the daughter of Sir James Brandon?' he demanded.

'Yes, why are you asking?' she asked him faintly. 'Who told you he was my father?' She suspected Andrew Galbraith was the informer.

'He was the VIP who came to the new building today. Andrew must have phoned him and told him about us, I had only to look into his eyes, the same blue eyes as yours, to know of the relationship,' David told her, more in despair than anger as he released his grip.

Alex was visibly shocked but not surprised.

'I was left alone with Sir James, showing him the laboratories and library and so on. He was exceedingly hostile, warning me about the dangers of mixing with married women,' David continued.

Alex turned away. She started to cry. It felt as though her life was now in ruins.

David took her arm again. 'Tell me, are you married?' he questioned.

'Legally, yes, but I'm waiting for my decree nisi any time now. My so-called husband disappeared off the scene months ago. He wants rid of me as much as I want rid of him.' The tears were coursing down her face. Alex was desperate to reassure him.

David swore. He was shaking his head with disbelief

Alex continued to sob. They had now taken refuge behind David's van and were sheltered by bushes as one or two people passed nearby.

Without warning David pulled her to him and stroked her hair. 'Don't cry, my darling. We need to talk, I haven't been completely honest with you either.'

Alex looked up at him. He was running his hand through his hair, desperation written on his face.

'What do you mean?' Alex asked, perplexed. 'Are you married?'

'No, no,' David said impatiently, 'it's complicated and we can't discuss it here. I will come back to the hospital tonight. We will work this out,' he told her. 'I promise.'

Alex suppressed her tears. She was on call so she hastily tidied herself before parting from David and walking back into the hospital. She was shocked and trembling and she desperately hoped that serious decisions would not be required of her during the next hours.

Fortunately the hospital was quiet, and Alex checked with the wards and casualty that there were no developing problems before retreating to her accommodation. This evening it smacked of the Douglas era, the same rooms, the same smells, and now the same disastrous ending of her hopes for love.

She was crying when David arrived. He looked haggard. They stood and looked at each other for some moments before Alex signalled for him to sit on the bed.

'I think we must be totally honest,' David sighed. He reached for Alex's hand in an effort to reassure her. As he started to talk he looked away from her and stared at the carpet.

Alex remained silent.

'The new building, as you know, is going to have some of the most advanced technology, and new studies are going well, we are really going to transform traditional medicine.'

Alex was puzzled. What had this to do with her and David's blossoming love affair?

'The Gruter-Denningbee Corporation has built and donated the premises across the road to the NHS to further this,' continued David. 'Sir Arthur Denningbee is the group chairman, and his wife had breast cancer and was treated and died in the university hospital. Her sister and grandmother had previously died of the same disease. When it was explained to the grieving Sir Arthur about the strong possibility of a genetic link, and that this is the route that prevention and cure will take in the future, he swore he would find some way of helping.'

Alex knew she had to be patient, somewhere a connection was going to be made, but at the moment she couldn't see where.

'My father is the financial director of the Gruter-Denningbee Corporation,' David continued. 'Sir Arthur and my father are not only business associates but firm friends. 'It was because Lady Denningbee's death had such a devastating effect, not only on her family but on ours, that I decided to pursue this area of medicine.' David stopped.

'It is a truly wonderful thing to do,' Alex gasped. Somehow the phrase 'moral obligation' filtered into her mind. She could see that the next piece of the story was going to be painful; she couldn't help him, he had to tell her in his own way.

David bowed his head, his words were barely audible. Alex had to strain to hear.

'Sir Arthur has a daughter, Ruth. She played and socialised with my brother and I as children and teenagers. Like me she got a place at Knightsville and read medicine and like me intends to devote her working life to genetics. She is coming to work at the new facility once it is officially opened.' David raised his head and looked at Alex. 'Sir Arthur takes it for granted that our futures are linked.'

Alex felt a cold chill, it felt like her blood had drained away.

'You mean it is assumed that you and she will marry?' Alex whispered.

David nodded. 'Not just Sir Arthur, even my parents drop unsubtle hints about the suitability of the match.'

Alex's spirits were now reviving from the shock. 'Have you given encouragement to this expectation?' she asked.

'No, of course not, Ruth is a splendid girl, and I suppose I just went along with things, it was convenient. Then I stepped on your toe and everything changed. I'll leave you to figure out the implications if I reject his beloved daughter,' he added, raising his head and looking into Alex's eyes.

Alex stared at him. She saw agony in his eyes.

'I want to marry you, I want you to be the mother of my children, and I promise you it will happen, it may take time, but it is going to happen,' David told her solemnly. 'You will have to trust me.'

Alex sighed. her heart was pounding. She believed his sentiments, but was unsure as to whether he could deliver the outcome.

'I was betrayed by my husband, he committed adultery,' she said bitterly. 'It broke my heart. I felt as though I, too, had failed, that is why I am waiting for my decree nisi.' Alex's voice was wavering, the tears were starting again. 'Trust is something I have a problem with now,' she said, looking at the bedraggled David.

He jumped up, pulling her with him. Clutching her he said, 'Alex, I never thought it was possible to love anyone like I love you. I hesitated telling you about my background, terrified I might lose you.'

Alex nodded, she had sympathy. She, too, had not been honest about her marital situation for the same reason.

'I think I need to know about this betrayal that has caused you so much pain,' David said gently. 'We did promise each other total honesty.'

Alex found it difficult at first to tell David about Douglas, her words were hesitant, but then she poured out the saga, omitting most of the more personal details, grateful that someone would listen without being judgemental.

'You were very brave,' David told her. 'You don't deserve what I have landed on you today.'

'I seem cursed, love comes with a colossal price tag,' Alex

told him. 'I see plump and plain women with adoring husbands and a pram full of beautiful babies and I envy them.'

'One day you will have an adoring husband, and children, I promise.' David picked up her hand and kissed it. 'No one gets four aces in this life,' he continued meditatively.

Alex detached herself from him. 'We can't even have a drink because we are both working, so I'll make some coffee,' she said, and made for the tiny kitchen and the kettle. 'What is the future for us?' she asked as she returned with the coffee and slumped down next to David.

'I have made a promise that I intend to keep,' he said, clenching his fist. His next words however belied his last statement. 'I think we had better not see each other for the time being. Andrew will be watching us like a hawk.'

Alex nodded. She needed Magda and her wise counsel, her mind was in disarray. Finishing his coffee David took his empty cup to the kitchen and then headed back to her. He put his arms out to kiss her goodbye, but Alex turned from him.

'Just go, David, we've said everything that needed to be said,' she told him.

'Not like this,' he pleaded.

'Just go,' she repeated. There was anger in her voice.

He headed for the door, and as he opened it he said, 'I will be back, and I will keep my promise.'

The quietness after his departure was sepulchral, but Alex did not cry. Her mind was hatching plans. They were plans of recovery, but first she had to get through tonight. Her night's sleep was not interrupted even though she was on call. Her plan of action had started to formulate.

The next morning Alex was surprised at how calm she had become. *Perhaps I'm well practised in rejection*, she mused. Discharging her medical duties her first action was to call home. Susan was surprised and suspicious by Alex's request to be

134

met at the station, but she agreed to be there. On the train Alex worked out her strategy. James was her target; he had precipitated the situation she now found herself in.

Only her mother was standing at the small country station when she alighted from the train. She knew her mother was aware why the unscheduled visit was taking place. The greeting was perfunctory and the conversation on the way home was stilted and dull. James was waiting, which surprised Alex, but she was more than ready to launch her attack.

'I would like to see you and mother in the study as I have something important to say,' Alex told them.

Susan glanced nervously at James, but her husband showed no emotion as he gestured them both into his room and pointed at the chairs.

Alex refused to be seated.

'Father,' she said formally, controlling her quavering voice, 'you came down to Queensbridge and made insinuations about me and David Freer, and you and Andrew Galbraith concocted a plan to sabotage what was a harmless and pleasant association between us. I am finding this very hard to forgive.'

James was watching her, drumming his fingers on the desk. His face showed no emotion. Susan was visibly shaken.

'I think you will find that Andrew Galbraith and myself have saved you and your boyfriend a good deal of trouble and embarrassment. I suspect Freer has taken the hint and severed connections,' James said with conviction.

'I daresay you threatened him. I do not want you interfering in my affairs. Ever since I can remember you have made my life a battleground. I was condemned by you for being female. Now it is going to stop, you and your two sons can forget this irritating creature that causes so much bother to you. I intend to make my way on my own from now on, and to spare you further embarrassment I won't even use the name Brandon.'

James and Susan were stunned by her diatribe but James quickly recovered his composure.

'We are upset by this behaviour of yours,' James started, in spite of an agonising look from his wife. 'I think you should consider carefully all the implications and let the dust settle. Your mother and I will always be available and will help,' he added.

'I am going to leave Queensbridge, and make a new start, somewhere where you cannot reach me. I am going back now, please do not try and contact me,' Alex spat at her parents. She then turned to her mother. 'I will go and get Mr Redman to drive me to the station.'

'No, no, no!' Susan was distraught. 'I will drive you there, now if you want me to.'

Alex shrugged. 'It will be the last service you will perform for me.' But she agreed.

She saw a nod pass between her parents.

Grabbing her handbag Alex led the way to the front of the house where her mother's car was parked. Susan was hard pressed to keep up with her but shuffled in beside her daughter. Not a word passed between them on the way to the station. Alex stepped from the car and slammed the door. She did not look back as Susan drove away.

Back at Westfield House James was sitting in his study, his head in his hands. He was devastated.

9

Walking back to her flat from the station, Alex had never felt so alone. *To dispose of the love of your life and your family in twenty-four hours was worthy of a fictional heroine,* she thought ruefully

Reaching her destination and calmed by the walk, she wondered if Magda would be at their shared home as she let herself in. Alex heard movement and then a cheery greeting from her flatmate.

'So what have you been up to today?' Magda enquired.

'I have dispensed with David, and told my family to get lost,' Alex told her friend.

'No, I meant have you done anything exciting today?' Magda asked waggishly.

It forced a smile from Alex.

Magda went to the cupboard and produced a bottle of wine. 'I think we need a drink,' she said, pouring herself and Alex a generous portion. Magda listened intently as Alex narrated the last days' events.

'I would have loved to have seen Sir James' face when you had your say,' Magda said, closing her eyes, trying to imagine the scene.

'He had it coming,' Alex said bitterly.

'I don't totally agree, but he hasn't treated you like an adult, that's for sure. But he and Dr Galbraith have probably spared you and the gay Lothario a lot of bad publicity,' Magda said, replenishing the fast-emptying glasses.

'Has David phoned here?' Alex asked hopefully.

Magda shook her head.

'What am I to do?' Alex said despairingly. 'I seem destined to have disastrous love affairs and marriage, what is wrong with me?'

Magda clutched Alex's arm. 'Alex, you could have any man you want, I've seen some of the looks you get from the opposite sex, they all lust after you.'

Alex was shocked by Magda's directness.

'Take Douglas for instance, he wanted you on his arm and in his bed so it enhanced his male standing amongst his colleagues; as for David Freer, I have to say Alex, he is out of your league, even Daddy Brandon can't compete there. You were in the recovery stage of your divorce and easy pickings for a smooth operator like him.'

Alex reluctantly nodded agreement.

'Give yourself some time, play loads of tennis and, yes, change jobs. I also think you ought to phone Aunt Sonia, she has given you such good advice in the past and she knows Sir James better than anyone,' Magda advised.

Again, Alex agreed. The wine and the companionship were lulling her into a more amenable state of mind.

Magda poured the remains of the wine into their two glasses and proposed a toast, 'To discovering the antidote to testosterone,' she said as she held her glass aloft.

Alex clinked her glass with her friend. 'I'll drink to that any day,' she giggled.

Alex felt comforted by Magda's solicitous handling of her situation when she finally went to bed. However, waking in the morning with the effects of wine, the thought of work and the possible parting with David reduced her back to the misery of her lot. Magda had already departed for the hospital and Alex slowly prepared herself for the day ahead. At some point she would take Magda's advice and talk to Aunt Sonia. It was lunchtime before this became possible.

The first time she tried, Aunt Sonia's phone was engaged.

Trying again later Alex was pleased to hear her godmother's voice.

'Hello, Aunt Sonia, it's Alex!' She tried to sound breezy.

'Oh, hello,' was the response. Alex detected a glacial note in the greeting. It wasn't like Aunt Sonia, she usually launched some chatter after the greeting. Instead, silence.

Alex started to explain her predicament, expecting a sympathetic ear but, for once, she was taken aback by Aunt Sonia's response.

'You had no right to speak to your parents the way you did, they are wonderful people, and have provided everything possible for their family. I want you to retract your threats of isolating yourself, and instead ask for their help. Do not involve me until you have done that.'

Alex was dumbfounded. Never before had she heard Aunt Sonia so cross.

She quickly replaced the receiver. Her hands were shaking. Making her way to the cloakroom to try and recover from the onslaught, she washed her face in cool water. Looking in the mirror there was no sign of the inner turmoil.

There was nothing for it but to get back to work.

Another surprise awaited Alex. Dr Greaves was looking for her and it was urgent. He found her before she found him. 'Dr Ffrench, I have some good news for you,' he said as he took her arm and led her to a more private area. 'You have been granted a two-week study leave, details of which have been posted to your address.'

Alex smelt a rat. *Was this a diplomatic way of dismissing her?* she wondered.

'Most junior doctors find this very beneficial,' Dr Gerrard continued. 'I remember doing it myself and it cleared the path, channelling me into general medicine.'

Alex could only nod and accept that she had no way of combating the forces now lined up against her. Not even a word of comfort from David.

She tidied up her notes and left everything accounted for to assist a smooth take-over for her replacement, then took herself back to the flat.

The door was unlocked but there was no sound as she mounted the stairs. Magda was given to a chirpy greeting so she was wary of the silence. Reaching the small hallway she hesitated before walking into the sitting room. Standing immediately before her was her father and beside him, sitting on the dilapidated sofa, was her mother.

Susan jumped up and rushed at her daughter. 'My darling girl, we can't see you suffer like this,' and she enveloped Alex in a bear-like hug. The kindness was too much and Alex broke down. James approached and Alex was passed to him. She sobbed into his coat.

'You're still Daddy's little girl, and we are taking you home for two weeks,' he said gently. 'We will help you sort things out.'

Alex clung to James. He let her cry it out. It was the first time in her memory that he had ever embraced her. He released her carefully, and looked at her bloated and reddened face. He produced a hanky from his pocket and wiped the tears away.

'I can't have my beautiful daughter looking like this,' he comforted.

His concern caused further tears from Alex. James continued to soothe, and Susan retired to the kitchen to make much-needed coffee for them. James led Alex to the sofa, and they sat down together, James still holding onto her. She was aware of his determination to help.

'What have I done wrong, Pa?' she asked.

'Absolutely nothing, we mainline trains often end up in a siding, and it needs combined help to get us back onto the main track again,' he replied.

Alex felt like a little girl again. She had been reared on metaphors. None so pertinent as today's.

Susan entered with the coffee and dished it out to them.

'Thanks Ma,' Alex said to her mother, noting a moistness around Susan's eyes.

'Now,' James said purposefully, 'you are coming home with us, all arranged with Gerald Greaves. You need time to sort things out, and best not in the highly charged atmosphere of a hospital.'

Alex smiled and reluctantly agreed.

'Your mother and I promise not to try and influence you. I think you should know that we had a severe reprimand from Sonia and were told in no uncertain terms to sort ourselves out and appreciate and assist our wonderful daughter.' James put his hand on Alex's.

Susan nodded, and started to cry.

'What sort of man makes his wife and daughter cry?' James asked. It was an attempt to lighten the situation. Humour was not his strong point, but for once it worked. Susan and Alex had the suggestion of a smile on their faces.

Looking at his watch James suggested Alex pack her bags and then they would head home.

Susan assisted her daughter, and once in the bedroom chatted as she folded the clothes into the suitcase. 'Take some smart outfits as we have been asked out to a few dinner parties,' she advised.

Alex was not impressed; socialising was not on the agenda, but she handed a couple of smart dresses over to her mother to avoid any argument.

James was on the telephone, she could hear him, but what he was saying was not audible. His tone suggested satisfaction. Calmness was beginning to seep in.

Before leaving Alex wrote a short note to Magda and left it propped on the kitchen surface.

Once packed, James carried the luggage to the waiting car, discreetly parked some way from the flat, and safely stowed it in the boot. Alex flopped into the rear seat of the roomy vehicle. James and Susan took their places more sedately, but there was no sedateness about the driving. James whisked them home in record time.

Alex had to admit to the overwhelming feeling of peace and safeness that Westfield House enveloped her with. Her room and the view from it reminded her more of happiness than the sadness she was currently experiencing. Making her way downstairs Alex could smell cooking. She forgot when she had last eaten and her appetite was whetted. The dogs were hovering around.

James was preparing drinks in the drawing room and Alex was more than glad to quaff down his offering.

'Magda contacted us, gave us access to your flat and even left coffee cups for our use,' James told Alex as he settled himself into a capacious armchair.

'Magda did that?' Alex asked incredulously from the depths of the old sofa.

'Indeed she did,' James continued as he got up to dispense another drink, adding another for Susan who had just joined them.

'Dinner in twenty minutes, we are early tonight as we have all missed out on lunch,' her mother told them.

James and Alex nodded.

'I had a rollicking from Aunt Sonia too,' Alex told her surprised parents.

James and Susan started to laugh.

'I think we should toast her,' Susan suggested, waving her now empty glass at her husband. It was so out of character for her mother to propose such a thing, but James had no problem obliging.

Again, Alex's glass was generously replenished, and love and admiration mooted for the absent Sonia, and additionally Magda.

By the time dinner was served, Alex was ravenous and relaxed by the alcohol. The conversation was carefully steered away from all things medical, whether pertaining to herself or James. All prearranged, Alex felt, but nevertheless she was grateful. By the time bedtime came she was only too ready, and finding a hot water bottle in her bed was the final touch to a momentous day.

She was wakened the following morning by Susan bearing a cup of tea and a biscuit.

'We have a visitor coming today,' Susan tried to sound mysterious.

'Aunt Sonia?' Alex asked.

Susan nodded. 'Coming for lunch,' she said as she exited the bedroom.

Alex relished the luxury of tea in bed, then got up and took her time dressing and making up. The blobs on the mirror forced her to move her head around. She kept thinking of David and wondering what he was doing, and whether he thinking about her. Finally satisfied with her appearance she made her way downstairs. The dogs showed interest. Both were new acquisitions and unfamiliar to Alex. She patted them and hoped they would accept her as one of the family.

Susan produced coffee. They sat at the kitchen table and drank it. Again the chatter was generalised, no mention of past events.

'Could you walk the dogs, darling?' Susan asked. 'Down Badgers Lane and round, it'll give me time to prepare lunch.'

Alex was only too happy to agree. The fresh air and moments alone, to think, were welcome.

'Take my raincoat and wellies if you like,' Susan continued as Alex rose from the table and pushed her chair in.

Garbed up in her mother's clothing Alex leashed the straining dogs and headed for the route advised by Susan. The air was cold and bracing. Once in the confines of the lane she released the leads from the collars and let the dogs run free. Their pleasure was obvious. Alex watched as they sported and played together, but again her thoughts were of David. She would ring Magda and ask if he had phoned or if she had seen him.

She continued her walk and had words with the villagers. All seemed pleased to see her. Coming to the end of the walk she encountered a telephone box. She dived into the pockets of the raincoat, but there was no money in them. She now knew where to make discreet calls without her family knowing.

Getting back to the house Alex saw Aunt Sonia's car in the drive. The dogs ran ahead, their interest taken. Mother and Aunt Sonia would know she was imminent and would modify their conversation.

Aunt Sonia came to the door to meet Alex as she struggled up the drive. She held her arms in the air in welcome. Alex puffed and accelerated her pace to reach her.

'Thank God, you're all right my pet,' she whispered in Alex's ear. As they pulled apart Alex noticed tears in Sonia's eyes. She buried her head in her aunt's coat and cried too.

'Come now, we must be brave,' Aunt Sonia ordered. 'General Brandon will be here in a minute and he doesn't like to see his troops being emotional.'

'General Brandon has been pretty marvellous,' Alex told Sonia as she dried her eyes.

'I told you, they are a wonderful couple, but you have to trust them, Alex.'

Susan appeared, looking for her family; Sonia was always spoken of as one of them.

'I think we could do with some drinkies,' Susan told them.

Alex was surprised. Her mother was becoming quite a sophisticate. Drinks evenings and lunch parties were now becoming commonplace. A little while ago, gardening and executive membership of the W.I. would have occupied her spare time. She wondered what had triggered this change.

After removing her outdoor clothing Alex made her way

144

to the drawing room, where Sonia and her mother were already imbibing. Sonia leant over, hooked a glass from the side table and passed it to Alex.

The cold white wine was refreshing, and the three women spent a relaxed half hour before lunch chattering. At no time was Alex's situation mentioned or even hinted at. Her thoughts, however, constantly strayed to David. Her emotions were on a switchback, the desperation she felt at losing the man she loved and the comfort from her family were playing havoc with her mind. It was like her nerve endings were stripped of their casings.

Over lunch Sonia told a few jokes and prattled on about various acquaintances. Alex felt like an adult. Up to now she had always felt like a child in an adult world when at home. She liked her new-found status, and she was seeing her parents in a different light. She had a feeling that they were seeing her in a different way too.

Susan, always the perfect hostess, shooed Sonia and Alex back to the comfort of the drawing room after coffee, but had no intention of ending her little lunch party. Sonia however had to depart before James arrived.

Alex and Susan saw her to the car.

'Keep in touch, darling,' Sonia breathed into Alex's ear before shoe-horning herself into her natty sports car.

Alex nodded then attached herself to Susan.

Sonia nodded approval and drove away.

'I'll take the dogs for another walk, I could do with some fresh air,' Alex told her mother.

Susan was only too happy, and obliged with the outdoor clothing once again. This time Alex took her purse with her and it was full of change. She walked along the lane, and this time there were no locals about and her pace was quite fast. She had an objective. When it appeared she called the dogs to heel, put their leads on and tied them to the nearby fence, much to their disgust. She heaved open the heavy red

145

door of the telephone box and once inside lost no time in dialling.

'It's Alex, Magda,' she whispered, when her call reached its intended ear.

'Speak up, I can hardly hear you,' her friend told her.

'How are things?' Alex asked.

'Absolutely fine, but what about you?' Magda asked.

'Well, pretty good, the parents are really trying their best, but it is a bit tame here. Mercifully Aunt Sonia came for the day and livened things up.' Alex hesitated before enquiring, 'Any sign of David, has he phoned?'

'No, nothing. He seems to have gone to ground, try and forget him Alex,' Magda advised.

'Have you heard something?' Alex was suspicious.

'I've told you the truth. Anyway I'm coming to see you the day after tomorrow. Your mother has invited me for lunch,' Magda said, wanting to finish the call. 'See you then.'

Alex replaced the receiver and stared at it thoughtfully. 'What is David up to?' she muttered.

Outside the telephone box she could see that the dogs were getting restless, so she pushed open the door, released them from their moorings and made her way home.

Susan had planned a shopping expedition for the next day. To Alex it was a better option than mooning round the house, particularly as it was at Rossington Spa, a town known for its elegance and architecture. It also involved a twenty-mile car journey through lovely countryside.

'Dress yourself up,' Susan ordered, 'and we'll have lunch at the Pump Rooms.'

The day went better than planned and Susan became quite girlish as she and Alex thumbed through the latest fashions in a prestigious department store, and wined and dined in the Spa Centre.

Returning home later in the afternoon Susan told Alex

they would be going back to Rossington the following week as they had all been invited to a dinner party.

'I didn't know you had friends there,' Alex said with an accusatory note in her voice.

'Roberta Stephensen,' Susan replied.

'Who on earth is she?' Alex said, following her mother into the kitchen.

'I met her at some charity event and our paths have crossed several times. Her husband was the British ambassador in one of those Scandinavian countries and he died prematurely, so she came to Rossington along with her son who is a consultant at Rossington Hospital.'

Alex brightened up. She did not relish listening to ambassadorial manipulations over a dinner table, but if doctors were around that would certainly liven things up. There was still Magda's visit to look forward to and on the intervening day Susan had arranged tennis.

Still David nagged at Alex's mind. She was wondering if she should return to Queensbridge with Magda. It would cause an enormous storm at home if she did.

The tennis was next on the social list. Playing with her old adversary was always a pleasure. The two girls whacked the ball around for three hours and retired exhausted to the small pavilion where they caught up on gossip and reviewed their lives. Alex made no mention of David, but was able to talk about Douglas and his ignominious departure. They arranged more tennis in the days ahead, before Alex wound her way home.

Alex hugged Susan as she made her way into the kitchen – it was a demonstration of appreciation. *No parent could be doing more to rescue their offspring,* she thought. The exercise, followed by a hot bath and a snack lunch, had now tired Alex into a state of inertia. Her restlessness too was temporarily curbed. She was only too glad to flop down on the sofa and wait for her father to arrive from the hospital.

James was in a genial mood when he joined Susan and Alex.

'Wilson-Jones has asked the three of us for dinner this weekend.' He rubbed his hands with expectation. Alex felt no desire to go. Wilson-Jones was a 'lech', albeit a harmless one, and she did not want an old and whiskered roué hovering in her vicinity, even with the protection of James nearby. Alex declined and James did not pursue the matter.

Things were certainly livening up and going back to Queensbridge with Magda the next day was no longer going to be an option.

The evening was relaxed. They watched television and played Scrabble after dinner and, finally retreating to her bedroom, sleep came easily to Alex and was, for once, dreamless.

Waking in the early morning the advent of Magda dominated her actions. She walked the dogs, made a few purchases at the local shop for her mother and was well prepared when her friend arrived by car.

Mutual pleasure was written across their faces as Alex led Magda into the kitchen where Susan was preparing lunch. Greetings exchanged, Magda dived into her roomy bag and produced a letter for Alex.

Alex's heart missed a beat, but it was typed, and not from David. She tore open the envelope, pulled out the correspondence and read it.

Susan and Magda looked at her expectantly.

'I'm finally rid of Douglas!' she told them, putting her hand over her mouth to contain her excitement. Then the thought, *has it come too late?*

Susan and Magda knew exactly what she was thinking.

'What about a glass of sherry?' It was not a question from Susan. It was an order.

The sherry produced and dispensed brought a toast to Alex's good news. Lunch was then served and lingered over,

148

after which Susan tactfully suggested that the girls walk the dogs.

It was what Alex wanted more than anything, to have Magda on her own and drag out information about David.

'There is no sign of him, not in the dining room or with his cronies or anywhere in the hospital,' Magda reiterated.

'No telephone calls?' Alex persisted.

Magda was becoming impatient. 'No, nothing, he has disappeared off the face of the earth.'

Alex was stunned.

'Men often pledge undying love and promise the earth, then amnesia sets in,' Magda reminded her. 'Particularly once they have achieved their objective.'

They were both puffing with the uphill gradient. The dogs were whirling round them.

'Revert to your plan,' Magda advised, 'change of job, get some more qualifications, you're a free woman now, you have the all-important decree nisi or whatever.'

Alex nodded. 'I know you're right Magda. I just wish it was that easy,' she pleaded.

'Stay here for your two weeks, and I promise to keep you informed about David Freer, whether it be good or bad,' Magda continued.

'Yes, I want to stay now, my parents are so different and life is so uncomplicated and gentle here,' Alex murmured as she threw a stick for the dogs to retrieve.

'Your stay should only last two weeks, you are too young to bury yourself away here,' Magda said, kicking a pebble from the lane.

They passed the telephone box and it was downhill back to the house. All had been said that needed to be said.

It was time for Magda to go back to Queensbridge.

10

The next few days passed uneventfully. It was getting towards the end of Alex's two-week 'study leave'. Magda had been unable to supply news regarding David, though it seemed there was much activity in the new building.

Alex still believed that David was sincere in spite of his actions indicating otherwise. She remembered the intensity of his looks and words. The odds were stacked against him being able to deliver his promises. There seemed only one conclusion.

Tonight it was the Rossington dinner party. It promised to be the grand finale of Alex's country stay. She intended to make a splash and it was to those ends that she prepared herself. No one at the dinner party would know about her romantic failures.

Alex heard the telephone ringing. She hoped her father was not being called away. Susan appeared at her bedroom door. 'Telephone call for you, it's Magda. Take it in the study.'

Alex fled downstairs and into the study. She picked up the receiver and spoke. She heard the 'click' as her mother replaced the upstairs handset.

'The new building is being opened on Sunday,' Magda said quietly. 'It's to be known as the Denningbee Centre, and a "Doctor Ruth" is coming with Sir Arthur to open it. The boffin will also be there. I thought you should know.'

'Thanks Magda,' Alex said sadly, tears pricking her eyes.

'I'm glad I know, particularly as I'm coming back on Sunday.'

'Yes, I didn't want you walking into it, forewarned is forearmed!' Magda told her.

They said their goodbyes and Alex gently laid down the phone. She dabbed her eyes and then resolutely returned upstairs to finish dressing.

Touching up her mascara, she looked at herself in the mirror. 'I wouldn't mind a bit of flirting tonight,' she told her reflection.

James, as always, was ready ahead of time. He waited patiently for his wife and daughter and visibly approved their appearance when they joined him in the drawing room. Locking up the house and leaving the dogs to guard it, James opened the car doors for each of them to wriggle in. Alex was wearing a black close-fitting dress. so movement was restricted, and her shoes had the highest and spikiest of heels. Susan had lent her a cape to cover her shoulders. She wore a similar one herself.

When they arrived at their destination James helped her out, fussing over her; it was obvious he couldn't wait to show her to the other guests.

The house was a lovely specimen of Regency architecture and it dwarfed the three of them as they rang the bell. The door was instantly opened by the hostess, Mrs Roberta Stephensen.

Alex liked her the moment she shook her hand. Roberta was welcoming, jolly and very attractive. She took their capes and then took them up a wide staircase into the most magnificent drawing room. It took Alex's breath away.

Recovering from the wonder of her surroundings, Alex turned to be introduced to the other guests. She could see every man gazing at her and she knew the look. It boded well for the evening. James was only too pleased to announce his relationship to her, and she assumed a demure look which had paid off handsomely in the past, and would, she hoped, in the future.

Roberta's son appeared with a tray of drinks. He whisked them round, then came and greeted the Brandons.

'This is my daughter, Alexandra, ' James told Christian Stephensen.

Christian took Alex's hand. 'I assume that means I don't have to be formal and call you Dr Brandon.'

'Alexandra is fine,' she simpered.

'Christian is a consultant obstetrician and gynaecologist at Rossington Hospital,' James interrupted.

'You look very young to have such an important position, Mr Stephensen,' Alex told him archly.

Christian smiled, pleased by the flattery. 'Let me get you a drink, later on I would like to talk to you about something,' he said, and he disappeared. One or two of the men started to drift Alex's way, their wives' eyes drilling into her.

Christian returned with a martini cocktail, and playfully advised Alex to use his Christian name.

He drew her into the room and introduced her. Not all the guests were from the medical profession. There was an author, an artist and a show-jumper among the eclectic group, and the conversation was animated and amusing and driven on by a very clever hostess.

Eventually dinner was called and they trouped downstairs to a large formal dining room. Alex was seated between two very attentive men. They anticipated her every wish, particularly with the wine glass. They plied her with questions about her profession and froze out anyone who dared to hone in on the conversation.

Alex was feeling exhilarated, and something else had happened, something significant. Everyone was calling her 'Alexandra'. She felt like a new person, a phoenix rising from the ashes.

Alex looked across at her father. He was heavily engrossed

in conversation; he loved dinner parties and tonight was no exception. She felt a great surge of love for him. If nothing else the David affair had reunited the family, with all the attendant benefits.

It was eleven o'clock before the meal was finished and they sloped upstairs to the drawing room. Christian then asked Alex if he could speak to her privately. Intrigued, Alex followed him to his study. It was immaculate, his *Gray's Anatomy* in pride of place, but Alex felt that Christian was well versed and the book was for show rather than reference.

'Please sit down, Alexandra.' He motioned to a chair.

Alex seated herself, allowing a little bit of leg to be exhibited. Christian did not seem to notice.

'Your father tells me you are seeking another post, is that right?' he asked.

'Yes, I would like to move away from Queensbridge and get some extra qualifications,' Alex said.

'I have a post coming up in a month's time for a senior house officer, would you be interested?' Christian said it tentatively.

Alex gasped. 'I certainly would. Thank you for considering me.'

'Send me all your details. I will have to go through the interview formula, you understand. That will be nearer the time however,' Christian told her, smiling with satisfaction.

Alex was ecstatic. Fate was taking a hand and it was being dished out on a plate. Returning to the drawing room Alex noted speculative glances from the other guests, relief from the other wives, and, least interested, Roberta and Alex's parents – suggesting they knew the purpose of the meeting between herself and Christian. The party was breaking up, baby-sitters had to be released from their onerous tasks and early starts forced most of the company to gather their belongings and bid goodnight. James decided that it was time to go for them as well, blaming their departure on Susan and Alex.

Roberta kissed Alex warmly and Christian shook her hand. The evening had been a great success.

On the way home and from the back of the car Alex told James and Susan about Christian raising the prospect of a job for her.

'I know you put a word in for me,' Alex said, stroking the back of James' head.

'Christian is such a nice young man,' Susan commented, turning her head towards Alex.

'Rowed for his university,' James told them.

'That accounts for those big shoulders,' Susan continued. 'He looks very Nordic with that fair hair and those pale blue eyes.'

'His father was half Scandinavian, hence the name,' James informed them.

'And the looks,' Alex added. She sank back into her seat and there was no further conversation about their recent host.

Alex was pleasantly tired, and when they reached home she soon scuttled off to bed. Tomorrow was going to be a busy day – she had to pack her belongings ready for the return to Queensbridge. She was dreading it. She wondered whether she would see David and possibly 'Dr Ruth' and how she would react.

After a leisurely breakfast, and an inquest on the previous night's jollity, Alex mustered her luggage by the front door. James was going to drive her back to her flat and he loaded the boot and then urged a start. Alex was tearful and clung to Susan, but her mother reminded her of good things to come and edged her into the passenger seat lest she, too, showed her emotions and concern.

The road was quiet and James made good time in reaching their destination. Alex looked up at the flat. It looked dingy and graceless. James helped her in with the baggage, then, without too much ado, he left.

Magda was not at home and there was a depressing air about the place. Alex mooched about, peering in the fridge before unpacking her belongings. She was pleased that her flatmate had 'provisioned' for a lengthy siege as she did not want to venture out and run into the 'Denningbee' contingent. A second-hand account from Magda would suffice.

Alex had to wait for this, as Magda did not appear until late evening.

'It was the usual business, all the "molecular" hierarchy were there, including the "boffin". He and Dr Ruth looking very cosy together,' Magda related as she cracked open a bottle of wine.

Alex sighed. 'I was prepared for this,' she told Magda. 'Every cloud has a silver lining however,' and Alex related her meeting with Christian.

Magda was impressed. 'The intervention of fate, commonly known as Aunt Sonia,' she announced as she poured a drink for them.

'He was smiling and holding her hand,' Magda told Alex, deeming it was now safe to elaborate on the Denningbee opening ceremony. 'The new building is to be known as the Denningbee Centre from now on. Dr Ruth cut the tape.'

'She probably cut my feelings for him too,' Alex said thoughtfully.

They spent the rest of the evening quaffing the wine and speculating about Alex's future. Magda always made things seem so reasonable and so resolvable. In spite of the calmness and probably due to the wine, Alex's dreams were like a silent movie, flickering, fast-moving and incomprehensible. She wakenened the following morning feeling tired and drained. She had a meeting at eight o'clock in the lecture room and was eager to be there on time and to show attentiveness to the case histories under discussion. Dr Greaves had been more than accommodating about the so-called study leave, and there was still the requirement of a reference from him.

Alex was welcomed back. Her colleagues were helpful and sympathetic. She learned later that Dr Greaves had told them she was off sick.

'I will do the on-call jobs,' she told them. 'It's only fair, and I want to get "au fait" with the patients again. I see there has been a big turnover while I've been away.'

Dr Greaves consented to her suggestion, and the rest nodded approval.

Once the first ward round was completed Alex was given the jobs of a liver biopsy, a lumbar puncture and finally a chest aspiration. These procedures wiped all other thoughts from her mind. The nurses sent the specimens off to the laboratory and were keeping the first two patients lying flat and immobile. Alex checked on them. No complaint of a headache from the young man having had the lumbar puncture and no obvious bleeding from the liver biopsy. The young woman who had had the chest aspiration was problematic, her high temperature had not lowered and the nurses had called Alex back. The patient looked poorly.

Alex ordered an emergency chest X-ray on the ward and a repeat dose of diamorphine. The chest X-ray was unchanged. Alex decided to ring Dr Greaves at home.

'Give the erythromycin time to work. Call me back in two hours if her temperature is still elevated,' he calmly advised.

The registrar appeared and Alex went back to the patient's bedside. 'The temperature is still 105,' the staff nurse told them. 'Pulse 140.'

The registrar advised Alex to go to the dining room and get some supper, while he further assessed the situation. Alex nodded, she had not eaten, or had a cup of coffee, since lunchtime because of the investigations and their follow-ups.

Alex had the dining room to herself and the food had been warmed up, but she didn't care. She was grateful just to sit quietly and think about her patient. Her first night back was proving to be a nightmare. She was convinced the girl was going to die.

After an hour Alex returned to the ward. The relatives were there, anxiety and stress taking its toll on them. The registrar had seen them and dealt with the agonising job of the likely outlook for their daughter.

The staff nurse took Alex to one side. 'The relatives are wondering about Extreme Unction, do you think we should call the Catholic priest?' she asked.

Alex nodded. 'Yes, I think so.' She and the staff nurse exchanged significant looks.

Alex joined forces with her colleague and they examined the patient again. Hope for her recovery was fading fast. Everything had been done. The consultant arrived and in spite of many options being mooted between them it seemed no other course was available.

'I was hoping the erythromycin into her chest would have worked,' Dr Greaves said resignedly.

The arrival of the priest made them retreat from the bedside proximity. Dr Greaves decided to depart and leave Alex to it, along with the registrar. The patient had been allocated a 'special nurse', and all was in place for maximum care and comfort of the dying patient.

Alex had other duties.

A last look at the two male patients would relieve the gloom, she needed to get away even for a few minutes because the night was going to be fraught. The male ward was some distance away but for once Alex didn't mind. The walk tempered the jumble of thoughts in her head. All was peace and quiet and after a quick resumé of the patients the nurse in charge offered Alex coffee which she gladly accepted. The hours ticked away, but Alex could not rest. Chatting in the office on the male ward, the telephone rang, its tone muffled to avoid waking the patients. The nurse picked up the receiver and listened. She immediately looked at Alex and handed her the phone. Alex was prepared for the news, but putting the receiver to her ear she heard the magic words.

'Rosie's temperature is ninety-seven,' the staff nurse told Alex. Alex leapt up and hurried down the corridor; this time the distance was interminable, her feet barely touched the ground.

Alex went straight to Rosie's bedside, and as the patient briefly opened her eyes Alex's stethoscope homed onto her chest. There was ear splitting noise, but Alex knew they had won the war. The registrar appeared; he was smiling, but the suggestion of stubble on his face indicated the gravity of the last nightmare hours.

After seeing the joyful but tearful parents and revising the orders, Alex spoke of her relief to her colleague. His delight was as unashamed as hers. A warm feeling engulfed her. A twenty-four-year-old had been given back her life. If only all medical intervention could be this good.

On the morning round Dr Greaves insisted that Alex should not be on call that night. Alex was more than pleased as she wanted to assemble the job application details to send to Christian. She knew her conduct from the previous night would stand her in good stead for a reference. She had to make sure she did not blot her copybook from now on.

In the late evening, back at the flat, and after a robust supper assisted by alcoholic refreshment, she and Magda mustered their paperwork. Magda was studying for her FRCS now; she was collecting qualifications like confetti. They shared the dining table together and the occasional sentence passed between them.

Alex decided to write Christian an obsequious letter. She showed it to Magda before encasing it in the envelope along with other paperwork.

'You grovelling creep,' was Magda's assessment. 'I daresay

you'll get the job though.' The girls giggled, and pressed on with their tasks until midnight.

Next morning Alex carefully posted her bundle to Christian and wondered what the outcome would be. She didn't have long to wait: an invitation to attend for interview arrived by return of post, and the letter started, 'Dear Alexandra'!

Magda made much of it with remarks like, 'Oh, so we are *Alexandra* now are we,' followed by a curtsey. This annoyed Alex, but she couldn't feel irritation for too long. Life was far better with Magda than without her.

Alex found she could get a train directly from Queensbridge to Rossington. It meant an early start as it was an 11 a.m. appointment, but her spirits were high when the day arrived for her to make the journey.

She dressed soberly, though she showed no discretion with her cosmetics. Christian was enigmatic and she wanted to see how vulnerable he was to heavy lipstick and panda-like mascara. Was he viewing her as a junior doctor or as a woman?

Chuffing through the countryside on the local railway line was soothing. There were few people on the train, mostly housewives out for their weekly shop. It was a fine day and when Alex arrived at her destination she decided to cover the short distance to the hospital on foot.

She arrived early and reported to the reception desk in the old Victorian building.

The receptionist was officious and dismissed Alex, waving her to a bench. Alex took her seat and watched the comings and goings of the hospital staff.

Christian arrived to time, pleasure written across his face. He was immaculately dressed in a grey suit and matching tie and the crispness of his shirt suggested Roberta had been extravagant with the starch.

'Alexandra,' he exclaimed, 'I hope you had a good journey.'

Alex stood up and they shook hands. Christian then swept her off to his office, seated her and then plied her with coffee.

The interview was informal. Christian shuffled through her application but she knew he had made up his mind.

'I rang Dr Greaves this morning regarding a reference and he described you as dedicated and hard working,' Christian told her, leaning across the desk that separated them. Alex flushed with pleasure; Rosie's miraculous recovery had no doubt contributed to the Greaves assessment.

'I am offering you the post of senior house officer on gynaecology and obstetrics,' Christian told her formally.

Alex was thrilled. She had a good feeling about the future. It was a drastic move, but it augured well.

'I am very happy to accept,' she replied, and they shook hands.

Christian then took Alex on a tour of the hospital. At the obstetric unit moans and groans and babies crying greeted them as they pushed through the door. There was frenetic activity from the staff so they beat a hasty retreat. The gynae ward was calm and Alex was taken to the sister's office where she was introduced to Isobel Stuart who ran the ward with military precision.

'We would just like to poke our heads into the ward so Dr Ffrench can get her bearings,' Christian asked in an overly polite way.

Sister Stuart led them through the main ward doors where they stood and looked around.

At the sight of Christian, Alex noted a smoothing of the bed sheet, an adjusting of the bed jacket, and a patting of the hair along with an air of expectation from the patients. It was obvious that Christian was revered. She and Sister Stuart were hardly noticed.

With the round of the hospital now concluded, Christian glanced at his watch. 'How about some lunch to celebrate?' he asked.

Alex nodded. It was quite an honour to be treated to lunch by one's consultant!

They went by car to a recently opened Italian restaurant. The owner was Italian and greeted them warmly. Alex was not sure whether this was because Christian was a frequent visitor or because the restaurant was nearly empty.

The food was excellent and was accompanied by soft drinks. After the meal and over numerous cups of coffee they chatted, but in spite of Alex using some of her female wiles Christian seemed impervious and treated her with an almost paternal air.

Looking at his watch, he decided it was time to finish the convivial lunch break. 'I will drive you to the station,' he volunteered. 'Then I need to get back to the hospital to collect some lab reports.'

Alex felt swamped in Christian's large car and several heads turned at the station when they turned up in it and she jumped out.

On the way back to Queensbridge, Alex's mind was in ferment. A new life beckoned, but she couldn't wipe out the memory of David's fervent look when he made his promise to her. But healing the rift with her parents was the big bonus out of it all and who could tell what Rossington would offer?

Magda was in when she reached the flat. She was eager to know what had transpired with regard to the job.

'He offered it to me,' Alex said after telling Magda about the day's events.

'This Christian fellow,' Magda pursued, 'does he fancy you?'

'Not at all, I tested him and there was no reaction.' Alex sniggered.

'Sounds like he's a mummy's boy,' Magda said as she went to the kitchen and returned with coffee.

'I don't care anyway, I have had enough of men,' Alex replied as Magda passed the sugar.

Magda smiled to herself and the subject was changed.

The last weeks at Queensbridge flew past for Alex. So much to do. With the help of Susan, and a fleeting visit to Rossington, a small flat had been rented near to the hospital. Alex decided it was perfect for her requirements and it eliminated any lasting doubts about her move.

In all this time there had not been one glimpse of David. He was like the invisible man, and Alex sometimes wondered if he had even existed, or was just a figment of her imagination. Deep down, however, she was certain that she could never, in a million years, have imagined what had transpired between them.

On Alex's final day Magda threw a party. People came and went and she was overwhelmed by the good wishes for her future. Susan's arrival towards the end signalled Alex's departure. The car was loaded by many willing hands and after embraces and tears Susan accelerated away, not wishing to prolong the agony.

The party continued for some hours after their departure.

On the way home Alex opened the letter that Magda had handed her as she left. It was reiterating that she was a free woman.

Douglas was history.

An era was over.

11

Rossington Spa was turning out to be better than Alex had hoped for. The town was elegant and still retained features of its past glories. Shops and facilities seemed excellent and the hospital was well run and busy. Christian was turning out to be a good boss. He was kind and reasonable and his patients worshipped him.

Alex's social life was sadly lacking, and she missed the friendship of Magda and to a lesser degree that of Patricia. To fill the gap she had embarked on driving lessons and had joined the local prestigious tennis club. Along with her parents, Roberta Stephensen had invited her to dinner on two occasions and likewise when Susan reciprocated, Alex was taken by Christian and Roberta to the Brandon family home.

Alex was always careful how she treated Christian on these occasions; she never took advantage of the family connection. After all, he was her boss.

Her rented flat was her sanctuary, no one could intrude; she dared to think there, no one could read her thoughts.

After Alex's three-month probation period Christian told her he had no reservations about putting her onto a permanent contract.

'What about us getting you going on your FRCOG?' he encouraged.

Alex shook her head. 'I really want general practice,' she added quickly.

Christian gave a nod of understanding.

Tucked away in her flat that evening, and with a face-pack glued on, the telephone rang. It was Roberta. After general enquiries she gave a future invitation to Alex to the Royal Shakespeare Theatre at Stratford with Christian and herself. Alex was delighted; it was on her 'intention list'.

'I would be delighted, but I have to check whether I'm on call,' she told Roberta.

'Don't worry on that score, Christian will fix that,' Roberta said dismissively.

The date was arranged for the following week and Alex anticipated it with relish. Christian did not mention it, neither did he give any indication that he knew about the forthcoming event, and it was Roberta who finalised the arrangements.

Alex was picked up from her flat and sank into the back seat of the car. It was Roberta who did all the chattering until they reached Stratford and parked. Alex was surprised by the austerity of the theatre, but the atmosphere countered it.

Roberta spoke to several people and nodded to others.

'Mother comes here a lot,' Christian explained.

Leaving the two women, Christian went off to get programmes and order drinks for the interval.

'Christian is such a good son, so considerate,' Roberta told Alex as her eyes roamed round the assembling crowd.

'He's considerate to everyone,' Alex replied, with the word 'Oedipus' hammering in her head.

'Well, if he's a good son, he'll most likely be a good husband one day,' Roberta continued.

Alex immediately wiped the word 'Oedipus' and wondered if Roberta had someone in mind. She hadn't noted Christian showing any interest in the opposite sex.

Christian returned and handed them a programme each. He then suggested that they should follow the crowd now dispersing into the auditorium. They found their seats with little difficulty, and they were some of the best in the house.

Christian sat between Alex and Roberta and after some fidgeting they settled in. Soon *The Merry Wives of Windsor* started.

Alex was enchanted. She loved the sauciness and the exuberance of the cast and clapped furiously at the end of the first act. Christian and Roberta were amused by her enthusiasm. Christian then suggested they go for their interval drinks. Alex struggled from her seat and mingled with the crowd, keeping her eye on Christian. They shuffled out to the bar, and Christian soon had the drinks delivered to them. Sipping them, their only conversation was of the play.

When the bell went, they waited for the crowd to dwindle and then hurried back just as the lights were dimming.

The second act started. Alex was absorbed, her hands were in her lap. Then she felt a large hand encompass hers. She froze. She did not dare to look at Christian. She did not know what to do. Suddenly he squeezed her hands, and she looked towards him. He was inclined her way and was smiling. Alex smiled back wanly; it was a terrible shock and she didn't know how to react. After all, Christian was her boss. Out of the corner of her eye, Alex observed Roberta. She seemed oblivious of the Shakespearean-like drama unfolding under her nose.

Alex decided that it was best to sit it out, but the enjoyment of the play was now marred. Supper in the theatre after the play was yet to come. Alex had to control her emotions.

Christian behaved as though nothing had happened, but the conversation was limited to discussing the play at the supper table. Roberta was tired so there was no lingering about once the meal was finished.

Roberta designated Alex to the front passenger seat on the way home. 'You can drop me off first before taking Alexandra to her flat,' she reasoned.

Alex was petrified, envisaging a battle on the doorstep; there was no way he was going to be invited in. She was working out her strategy on the drive home.

As it happened her fears were unfounded. After dropping

his mother off Christian drove back to her flat and turned off the ignition. He then turned towards her and gently took her hand.

'Dearest Alexandra, you will now be aware that I have feelings for you.' He hesitated before continuing. 'I am hoping that you feel the same.'

Alex was astonished. 'I don't know what to say,' she said nervously.

'Well, perhaps we should spend some time together, and get to know each other,' he said calmly.

Alex nodded. Anything to extract herself from the present desperate situation.

'When is your next free night? Perhaps we could go out for dinner,' he said, squeezing her hand.

'Tuesday,' she told him.

'Then I shall pick you up here, at seven, on Tuesday evening,' he said with satisfaction

Christian then picked up her hand and kissed her fingers. 'Thank you for making the evening so enjoyable, you are such a charming girl,' he told her. 'I must let you go now, we have a theatre list in the morning.'

Alex jumped from the claustrophobic atmosphere of the car into the refreshing night air. Turning back, she called her thanks through the car window and sped for the front door. Christian waited until she had let herself in and then drove off.

Inside the safety of her flat, Alex leaned on the sitting-room door and closed her eyes. This bolt from the blue had now precluded any hopes of a night's sleep, theatre list or no theatre list.

Why was she hesitating? Thousands of women would give their right arm to catch the attention of this decent, wholesome man, a consultant at forty, a rowing 'blue' and as far as she knew no background complications.

She made for her small bedroom, ripped off her clothes

and jumped into bed. She stared at the ceiling. She knew what was missing – love. David had destroyed her ability to love anyone else. She closed her eyes, and all she could think about was David and the overwhelming and ill-starred love they had shared.

Alex opened her eyes and fixed them on a mark on the ceiling. All she could do was see what Tuesday night would produce. Sleep did come eventually, though she felt jaded the following morning.

Christian acted as though the events of the previous night had not taken place. Alex had managed to write a 'thank-you' letter to Roberta and at the end of the theatre list she asked Christian to give it to her.

He smiled knowingly and promised to deliver it.

Tuesday evening did not turn out to be the much-feared occasion the Alex had worried about. Christian was gentlemanly, and although he had declared his intentions he did not take advantage of this, neither did he use his seniority in his advances towards her.

The dinner was a leisurely affair, and Alex found Christian easy to talk to and that they had much in common. Again, Christian took her home and kissed only the tips of her fingers. He did arrange a second meeting for that week. It was at another restaurant and Christian implied that it would be smarter than tonight's.

Alex was now feeling more relaxed about Christian's courtship. His behaviour was exemplary. As a doctor, too, he showed understanding and kindness even to the most difficult of patients.

Alex's next night off was Friday. She prepared herself carefully, and thought, *perhaps tonight a kiss on the lips?*

The restaurant was slightly out of town and was owned by a Frenchman. It was obvious that Christian was a respected customer as the owner, Gaston, immediately approached and knew Christian by name.

They were led through the tables and Alex noted the women glanced at her neck and hands as she passed, before turning an admiring look on her escort.

Once ensconced in a reserved table, they were issued with gargantuan menus. Alex hid behind hers as Christian ordered the wine. After deliberation and consultation they selected their menu and then settled down to talk.

'You look very beautiful, tonight,' Christian whispered across the table. Alex lowered her eyes; what bliss it was to be flattered and admired again.

The meal was exquisite and Alex was warming to her new-found admirer. His 'Foreign Office' upbringing was a great asset and Alex wondered why he wasn't besieged by predatory females. He was almost the perfect man.

As they came to the end of the gastronomic delights served by Gaston, and the restaurant was emptying, Christian leaned across the table and took Alex's hand.

'I can contain myself no longer,' he breathed. 'Alexandra, will you marry me?'

Alex gasped with surprise. 'Christian, I don't know what to say,' she told him, as she gently extracted her hand from his.

'You don't have to say anything now,' he told her soothingly. 'I want you to think about it, and then let me know. I realise you have just come through a very traumatic divorce, your father told me about it.'

'My father? What has he to do with this?' Alex enquired.

'Well, I did ring him to tell him that I was going to propose to you,' Christian said, mystified by Alex's response.

'What did he say?' Alex asked, regaining her composure.

'With his blessing,' Christian assured her.

It all seemed so quaint, but it made her feel tender towards him.

Christian signalled to the waiter for more coffee. Alex would rather have made tracks for home and sort out the chaotic thoughts going through her head.

'Does your mother know?' Alex enquired, knowing the answer.

Christian nodded. 'She approves too.'

The waiter arrived with the coffee and Alex sipped it as quickly as she dared.

'If you are worried about marriage affecting our working relationship, I can assure you, it would not. At least not until we decide to have a family.'

Alex blushed; having a family was one of her dreams. The dream did not include Christian, not until this moment.

He finished his coffee and then went to seek out Gaston, leaving Alex to finish hers.

Having discreetly paid the bill he came back and helped Alex from her seat and, holding her arm, led her to the car.

They said little as they drove home, but Alex sensed that Christian seemed confident that his marriage proposal would be accepted. Arriving back at her flat he made no effort to seal the night with anything other than his accustomed kiss of her hand and watched her safely in through her front door.

Things were moving fast, too fast. *Would life with Christian be bad?* she wondered as she undressed and fell into bed. David would never come back into her life, she was now in her thirties, she must give serious thought to marrying Christian. There was that one crucial ingredient missing – love. With that in mind she closed her eyes and passed the night in troubled sleep.

Christian gave no sign of the previous night's discussion as he led his team onto the ward the following morning. Alex was watching him closely. They stood at the ward door assembling notes and X-rays and Alex, again, noted the stir amongst his patients as they fixed 'goo-goo' eyes on him and waited expectantly for him to reach their bedsides. Christian again seemed oblivious, but Alex knew it was dangerous for him to make even a frivolous remark in the hearing of his patients.

He was as good as his word about not rushing a decision from Alex. She did not consult anyone, it would entail mixed messages and only confuse the issue. This was her future, hers alone, and she must make the decision.

She wrote a 'for and against' list, which, when filled in, weighed heavily to the 'for' column and only had one entry in the 'against' column. That one word against was 'love'. Mulling it over she wondered if time might change that and Christian could supplant David in her affections.

It took a week of deliberations before Alex finally made her decision. Telling this to Christian he asked where he could take her so they could discuss it.

'Gaston's, I think,' Alex told him.

Christian smiled. He knew what the reply to his proposal was going to be.

That night, Alex's 'on call' duty magically changed, and Christian whisked her off to Gaston's.

Again, the delightful continental touch which Gaston gave his restaurant came to the fore, and he delivered them into their special seats which tonight had a romantic air. Christian leant over to her. 'Am I to order champagne?' he enquired, touching her hand.

Alex nodded and smiled at him.

Gaston intuitively appeared and took the order, and within seconds the champagne was being uncorked and spurted into the glasses.

Christian held his glass to Alex and said, 'Dearest Alexandra, to my fiancée, you have made me a very happy man.'

Alex raised her glass. 'To you, Christian, I am happy too.'

Gaston reappeared. He had prepared a special menu for them. Alex was hungry, she had made her decision and relief wiped away all the tensions of the past week. Over the meal they loosely talked of wedding dates.

'The sooner the better, and a register office, with just

immediate family and friends,' Christian proposed. 'But first, I am going to take you to Framptons. I need to put an engagement ring on that left third finger of yours'

Alex was overwhelmed at the speed with which Christian was arranging the future. She needed to slow him down. She leant across the table and pressed his hand.   'Can I ask you a question?' she interrupted.

'Of course dearest,' Christian replied.

'When did you first decide you wanted to marry me?' Alex asked.

Christian leaned back in his chair and looked at her meditatively; it was a few moments before he answered. 'The night you and your parents came to dinner, the first night I met you.'

The waiter returned to clear their plates and asked about a dessert. 'Crêpes Suzette?' he offered.

Alex panicked, the past was coming back to haunt her.

'No dessert for me,' she said.

'Nor for me,' Christian agreed. The waiter departed.

They dispensed with coffee and made their way back to Alex's flat.

'Would you like to come in and see it?' Alex asked shyly.

Christian looked dubiously at his watch. 'I'd better not tonight, in fact I'm going back to the hospital, there are a couple of things I want to sort out,' he told her.

Alex was relieved. The next move was on impulse. She leaned over, put her arms around Christian's neck and planted a kiss on his lips. He kissed her back, but it was passionless, almost hesitant.

She released him and thanked him for the evening.

As she started to leave the car he took hold of her arm. 'Goodnight dearest, you are the sweetest girl any man could wish for.'

Letting herself in to her flat, Alex was thoughtful. Did she want to be the sweetest girl any man could wish for? Christian

171

hadn't responded to her kiss as she was sure he would. She wondered when he would unleash the physical side of his declared love. Was he a dark horse?

The next evening Christian arranged the Framptons trip. The jewellery shop was located in the best area of town and had a fifty-year history of impeccable dealings in high quality products. Old Mr Frampton was the son of the founder and when Christian and Alex were let into the shop Alex was dazzled by the display of jewels. There were armchairs prepared for them and a female assistant brought coffee as old Mr Frampton marshalled his wares.

'My wife will be sorry to have missed you,' old Mr Frampton said. 'She will always be grateful to you, Mr Stephensen,' and he coughed to imply that Christian's medical ministrations had been of a delicate nature.

'My fiancée is a doctor, and works on my firm,' Christian said, introducing Alex.

Mr Frampton bowed reverently as he shook her hand. With slowness, due to advancing years, he produced three trays of diamond rings.

They were breathtaking. Alex gazed with wonderment as they sparkled in the directed light.

'Try them on, dearest, and see which you like,' Christian urged her. Mr Frampton discreetly melted into the shadows.

Alex tried them on, while Christian watched patiently. Eventually she tried one on for the third time. It was a cluster of seven diamonds arranged in a floral-type setting. Alex extended her hand for Christian's inspection. 'I like it too,' he told her. 'Is that the one?'

Alex nodded, and Mr Frampton appeared from the shadows. Alex handed the ring to him. The business was then conducted between Mr Frampton and Christian. Alex was out of earshot.

'Would madam like to wear it, or would you prefer I placed

it in its box?' Mr Frampton asked courteously once the cheque had been written.

'I want to wear it,' Alex insisted, and the ring was placed back on her finger.

As they left the confines of the little shop Alex linked her arm through Christian's.

'I have a surprise for you, dearest, we're going back to mother's for dinner, there to formally announce our engagement,' Christian told her, giving her arm a squeeze.

'I will ring Ma tomorrow,' Alex affirmed. 'It's so exciting.'

When they arrived at Roberta's house, Alex could smell the tantalising whiff of food. It was quiet as they made their way upstairs to the drawing room. Standing in a group around the fireplace with drinks in their hands were James and Susan along with their hostess. Glasses were raised and a chant of 'congratulations' met them. Alex and Christian looked at each other before Alex ran to James and hugged him, then to Susan and finally Roberta.

It was apparent that the engagement met with parental approval all round, particularly when Alex displayed the engagement ring and described the buying of it. Everyone had a story to tell about the legendary old Mr Frampton, and when dinner was announced the convivial atmosphere continued.

Alex helped her future mother-in-law and Christian chatted to James and Susan in his usual impeccable way.

Christian brought up the wedding plans. 'Alexandra and I would like to discuss them with you,' he told the parents. He started by informing everyone of the sequence of events. It was as though he was talking about the diagnosis and cure of a medical condition. It sounded clinical.

The ceremony and reception arrangements he laid out in detail. He had meticulously planned for it to accommodate his consultancy work.

'To follow, a week's honeymoon in Scotland,' Christian concluded. He looked round the table for approbation.

The parents nodded, but looked at Alex.

'Sounds wonderful to me,' she told them. Her fate was sealed, why bring up anything to disturb the goodwill that now existed?

When the evening drew to its end James offered to take Alex back to her flat. Christian was about to say something but Roberta quickly jumped in saying, 'That is a good idea, I'm sure Susan and James would like a few words with Alexandra on their own.'

Christian backed off. It was obvious he now felt it was his duty to fetch and carry with regard to his fiancée. No arguing with Roberta, and he was in unknown territory.

Susan and James took up the offer of coffee at Alex's flat even though it was late and James had a heavy workload the following day. Once in the confines of her small sitting room they asked if she was happy about the future.

'I don't want anything from the past to come and haunt you,' James told his daughter.

'It can't and it won't,' Alex told him.

'Christian is a very decent young man, with an excellent background and promising future,' James continued.

'We just want your happiness,' Susan interrupted.

'Please, don't worry, I know I will be happy with Christian.' Alex assured her parents.

Alex could tell by the look in his eyes that James was not wholly convinced. Her father glanced at his watch. 'We must be going,' he told them.

As Susan kissed her daughter she whispered, 'If you need me to talk to, or anything else, just ring me,' and she patted Alex's back.

Alex watched as her parents departed and then took herself back into the flat. She sat down and thought about the evening and what the future held for her. Somehow or other she was determined she was going to forget David Freer.

12

The weeks to the wedding sped past. It was strange having to formally address her fiancée as 'Mr Stephensen' when working at the hospital. Christian had confidentially told Sister Stuart, and even though she would not have revealed the information, Alex knew the staff were aware of the impending nuptials. Experience had taught her that secrets about hospital staff had a habit of leaking, sometimes haemorrhaging, out into the public arena, the vortex being the hospital dining room.

Unlike her previous experience of being the subject of gossip over Douglas' infidelity, and being at the receiving end of accusatory or sympathetic looks, things were now different. She was being regarded with respect and admiration, and she liked the feeling. It seemed Christian was regarded as one of the most eligible bachelors in the hospital, and had resisted all attempts to lure him into wedlock.

Alex's contact with Magda and Patricia was scant at present. This was due to work commitments on all sides rather than a cooling of their friendship. Magda wanted to meet Christian before the wedding and arranged to come and spend a night at Alex's flat with her. When Alex told Christian that Magda was keen to meet him, he immediately offered to take them out for dinner at Gaston's. Alex was delighted.

Making the final arrangements with her friend, Alex advised Magda to bring something smart to wear.

On the appointed day Magda drove down to Rossington. She and Richard jointly owned a Morris Minor, though it seemed Magda had priority use. The girls were overjoyed to see each other and tongues did not stop wagging.

Magda liked the little flat when she mooched around it.

'So I shall meet this Adonis tonight,' she said as she poked into Alex's wardrobe.

'You certainly will,' Alex replied, as she made them a cup of tea.

They sat down and chattered some more. Magda was making it plain that any discussion about the new building or its staff in Queensbridge was not on the agenda. Any attempt of Alex's to steer the conversation in that direction was met with a rapid change of subject.

Leaving it as late as they dared before changing, and constantly interchanging in the bathroom, they finally looked at each other with amusement as the final touches were in place. Almost to the minute the front door knocker hammered its message.

Alex hastened and let Christian in.

Magda stood back and watched as Alex brought him into the sitting room.

'Christian, this is my dearest friend Magda.'

Christian approached and took Magda's hand.

'What a pleasure to meet you,' he told her. 'I have heard so much about you.'

Alex could see that Magda was impressed.

'I've heard a lot about you, too,' Magda replied. 'I want to congratulate you both, I think you will be very happy together.'

It was unlike Magda to be so gushing, but it was heartfelt, and Magda was one of the quickest detectors of character flaws, and not behind in letting it be known to the parties concerned.

Christian looked at his watch. 'I think we'd better push off to Gaston's,' he advised.

176

He led Magda into the little hallway, Alex opened the door and they spewed out into the little drive where Christian had parked. As Alex locked her front door, Christian was helping Magda into the back seat of the car. Once in and the car door firmly closed he came back for Alex and assisted her into the front seat.

It was inevitable that medical matters should dominate the conversation on the way to Gaston's and even once in the restaurant the theme continued. The careers of all present were deliberated on with both seriousness and humour.

Gaston himself was drawn to their table and his ministrations along with his beautiful French accent enthralled the Queensbridge visitor.

Replete in the food and wine area, Christian suggested taking the girls home to see Roberta and having a nightcap, a proposal welcomed by Magda and Alex. As far as they were concerned the night was still young. They piled into the car and returned speedily to Rossington.

Roberta was delighted to see them, and it seemed to Alex that she was not totally unprepared for the visit. Again, Magda was drawn into the family atmosphere and it was after midnight before Christian took them home.

'I am impressed,' Magda told Alex.' Your Adonis is something special,' she continued as she undressed for bed. 'That rock on your finger says it all.'

'Yes, the more I'm with him the more I like him,' Alex admitted as she laid out the camp bed for herself at the foot of Magda's bed.

Magda looked at her curiously, but Alex was too busy to notice the stare.

'So it wasn't the flash of light and Saul suddenly becoming Paul then?' Magda persisted.

Alex looked warily at Magda; she knew what she was inferring.

'Richard and I started out as friends, and now I couldn't

live without him, in fact I am going to marry him,' Magda confessed.

Alex jumped up from her chair and stumbled over the beds to give her friend a hug.

'He has agreed that my career has to feature in our marriage, I am not just wife and mother material,' Magda continued.

'I wouldn't mind being wife and mother material with a bit of doctoring in between,' Alex said dreamily.

'I think we are both going to achieve our objectives,' Magda said as she slipped into bed.

Alex was now ready to slide into the sleeping bag on the camp bed; she was happily tired.

'You will have to put the light out,' she told her friend.

Magda's eyes were closed, but she instinctively knew where the light switch was. The room was plunged into darkness and seconds later the girls were asleep.

The next morning both Alex and Magda had to prepare for work. Magda stowed her bag in the boot of her car; she was driving directly to the hospital.

'Love to Richard,' Alex reminded her friend.

Magda nodded. 'See you at the wedding!' she called as she reversed out of the small driveway and sped away.

Alex felt flat after the exuberance the visit had generated. But there was no time to dwell on it, Christian had been lenient about time off, but she must not abuse her position with him.

When she joined Christian and her colleagues at the hospital he gave her no more than a nod. It was business as usual.

The weeks leading to the wedding were not as fraught as Alex expected. Christian, Roberta and Susan took control. All she had to do was to buy her outfit, and for once she spared no expense over this.

She was looking forward to the day, she would be seeing

her brothers and Aunt Sonia and when it finally arrived she was not disappointed.

Going to the register office with her parents in her turquoise silk suit and matching pillbox hat Alex could barely contain her excitement. The register office was Victorian and had quite a sense of atmosphere. Christian was waiting for her. He was dressed in a grey suit with a blue tie. He looked magnificent. Alex shed her attending parents and hastened to him. Many of the hospital staff were there. The ceremony began.

Once the legal formalities were over Alex and Christian posed for the mandatory photographs which were being snapped from every direction, thence to Roberta's house for the reception. Roberta had employed caterers for a spectacular buffet. To Alex most of it was a gorgeous blur of events sliding into each other, fragments of conversation from unremembered sources and all the time Christian, her husband, at her side and the promise of the wonderful life that lay ahead.

In collusion with Roberta, Susan and James, Christian suggested to Alex that now was the time to slip away. Their luggage was already in the boot of Christian's car so it should have been easy for them to melt through the door and escape. The guests had other ideas, and although Alex and Christian made the front door, a chasing throng was in pursuit. Furthermore Christian's car now had embellishments of a noisy nature.

'Get in,' Christian ordered. 'We need to get away.'

Alex fumbled her way into the passenger seat as Christian revved the car and they shot out of the drive.

'We'll go round the corner and I'll get rid of the attachments,' Christian told Alex. It was not to be; there were chasing cars and Christian had to keep going, clanking his way through Rossington much to the delight of the pursuing guests. Eventually the chase was over and Christian was able to detach the bows, ribbons and saucepans along with the 'Just Married' placard and fling them on the back seat.

Traces of confetti on them were brushed off and before resuming their journey Christian leaned across to Alex. 'Well, Mrs Christian Stephensen, what about a kiss?'

Alex flung her arms around her new husband and planted her lips on his. Although he reciprocated, it was muted. He held her back and gazed at her, then, freeing one of his hands, he stroked her cheek.

'I can't believe I've been so lucky to have found you,' he told her tenderly. 'I love you very much, Alexandra, you have changed my life.'

Alex looked into his eyes. 'I love you too, Christian,' she replied, nestling into him to blot out any intrusive thoughts that might spoil the moment.

Christian had arranged for them to stay in the Lake District for their first night, and it was long journey. When they arrived at the rather splendid hotel Christian suggested they dump their luggage and head for the dining room for dinner. Alex, slipping in to the ladies' room, replenished her make-up and loosened her hair from captivity, hoping it might induce a response from her new husband. Christian liked his forward planning to go to time and the hoped-for embraces were not on his agenda.

Making their way to the large formal dining room and being seated by a large window with beautiful views, Christian ordered champagne and then browsed through the menu. Alex was not overly hungry but ordered salmon. There were many diners, but in spite of this the atmosphere was subdued.

Christian, having selected his fare from the menu, turned his attention to Alex.

'Dearest, I think you should increase your driving lessons, and take your test, as soon as possible,' he advised.

Alex was surprised. Nothing romantic in that statement.

'I'm not thinking of anything as mundane as that at the moment,' she replied.

Christian smiled, but before he could answer the waiter arrived with the champagne. Several of the diners looked at them with interest when the cork was popped and the sound reverberated round the dining room.

'Did you enjoy today?' Christian asked.

'It has all been wonderful, and the day is by no means over yet,' Alex reminded him.

'By no means,' Christian agreed as he sampled the champagne.

Alex looked at him. He was so enigmatical. Douglas had made his intentions crystal clear, but Christian was revealing nothing.

At the conclusion of the meal, they strolled round the ground floor of the hotel before walking up the grand staircase to their room. Christian had the key and opened the door, but gestured for Alex to precede him. The bed was turned back and a bedside light was giving a gentle glow to the room.

'And so to bed,' Christian told her as he started to undress.

Alex felt excitement mounting, her fingers felt like bananas as she tried to undo the buttons on her jacket.

'Let me help you,' Christian said gently. He moved towards her and carefully released her from the jacket and then her skirt. Alex started to undo his shirt, it was all in slow motion, but with deliberation and was most definitely heading them towards the nuptial bed.

Unclothed and enveloped in the luxurious sheets with Christian next to her Alex felt the moment of truth had arrived. There was a promising start, but Christian's lovemaking was dutiful and short lived and once achieved he turned from her, seemingly to recover.

Alex was devastated, and wondered if this was to be the normal pattern of their married life, or was he so hyped up that it had inhibited his abilities? Previous experience made her plump for the former and sincerely hope for the latter.

Christian himself was in no doubt that he had given a good and satisfactory account of himself. It was two nights later however before it was repeated.

The Scottish honeymoon gave Alex time to review the situation. She had married a man with an impaired libido. On the other hand he was kind, generous and appeared to genuinely love her. She loved him too, but could she live with a man who was not able to physically satisfy her?

Alex thought of David's axiom, 'No one gets the four aces in life.' Could she accept three?

She lay awake for some time. She knew by Christian's shallow breathing that he was asleep. He was already awake and up the next morning before she opened her eyes. He came and sat on her side of the bed and had a red velvet box in his hands.

'Dearest Alexandra, this is your wedding present from me.' And he slowly opened the box. Inside was a matching necklace and earrings.

Alex gasped. 'Are they amethysts?' she asked.

Christian shook his head. 'They are alexandrites, your namesake. They change colour, sometimes green, sometimes brown, but mostly, as you said, amethyst-coloured.'

'They are beautiful, Christian, thank you for such a thoughtful gift.'

'Nothing is too good for you,' he said. 'Let me put the necklace on you.' And he took it from the box and clipped it on her neck. In close proximity, Alex leaned and kissed him on the lips and he responded.

Alex knew from that moment she was going to content herself with 'three aces'.

The honeymoon was relaxed and they toured around Scotland enjoying the scenery, the people and the food. The week went quickly and soon it was time to head home.

It took most of the day, and they were both tired when they reached Rossington. Roberta was delighted to see them and had prepared a late supper. Alex had now to officially move in with them.

She could tell that Roberta was unaware of Christian's shortcomings in the bedroom; how could she know?

'Old Mr Frampton called and left this package for you,' Roberta said, handing a parcel to Alex.

Alex gingerly opened it, but she knew what the contents would be.

'He apologised about it being late, but mentioned something about the engraving,' Roberta continued.

Alex handed it to Christian. 'This is for you, your wedding present!'

Christian looked astonished, but he took the box and opened it to reveal gold cufflinks.

'I shall wear these today,' he told her as he raised them admiringly and also for Roberta to see. 'My initials on them too.'

Roberta clucked approval.

Christian's attention was now focused on work and he urged Alex to prepare for a gear change. He was right – the first day back was overwhelming. Charles Beattie, Christian's opposite number and the senior consultant, had valiantly held the fort in Christian's absence and emergency work had been at a higher rate than usual. Christian's team had not been found lacking either, but were relieved to see both of them back.

Christian treated Alex as one of his junior doctors. No concession to their relationship was made, but she did have his ear when complications occurred, thus making her work less stressful, if not less busy.

Settling in to her new life, Alex was happy enough. Roberta ran the household and prepared meals, but did not interfere, retreating to her apartment and only staying in the main house when specifically invited. Alex did invite her quite often as she was amusing and wise and she knew it pleased Christian.

Jogging along in this contented, if not desirable, state, Alex woke one morning feeling nauseous. She had partaken of quantities of wine the night before and thought little of it, but the nausea was repeated and Alex could scarcely believe that she was pregnant. She waited until she was sure before telling Christian.

He was delighted and immediately took charge of events.

'Charles Beattie will look after you, as I'm not allowed to, and I think you should give up work too,' he suggested.

Alex protested, she did not want to give up her job.

'Surely I can work until I'm sixteen weeks,' she argued, and Christian reluctantly agreed along with certain provisos.

Roberta and Alex's parents were equally delighted by the news, and Magda squeaked her pleasure over a lengthy telephone call and promised to relay the news where appropriate.

It was a lifeline for Alex, it sublimated her basic desires into this wonder of nature that was living inside her.

The pregnancy was uncomplicated and during the early stages Alex played tennis and passed her driving test. She reduced her working hours before finally giving way to being cumbersome and a liability.

Christian became more anxious than she herself as the final days approached. Even feeling the pangs that meant a new life was about to emerge, Alex was laconic and unconcerned as she was driven by an edgy and anticipatory Christian to the maternity unit. She was given a side ward to herself and Mr Beattie's team took over and sent Christian packing.

The next hours were painful and lengthy but a baby son entered the world just after midnight. Alex's joy knew no bounds at the sight of this seven-pound bundle that had squawked his way into the world.

Christian was soon at her bedside, more affectionate than she had ever known him, and in awe of his little son that he gazed upon with admiration.

Alex was recovering well and soon her room was awash with flowers and cards as news of the birth spread around. She had been visited by Roberta, Susan and James who had come to see her and marvel at the wonders of nature.

'What are we going to call him?' Christian enquired.

'Guy, I want him called Guy,' Alex told her husband.

'As you did all the hard work, and I happen to like the name too, I will get him registered as Guy,' Christian agreed.

'Guy Robert, in respect of your mother,' Alex continued. She could see the choice of the second name greatly pleased her husband.

The next day Christian arrived earlier than usual. He took his place by her bedside and produced another red velvet box. He handed it to Alex. Inside was an opal pendant and drop earrings.

'To say thank you for making me the proud father of Guy Robert Stephensen,' he told Alex softly.

Alex recoiled, she had heard that opals were unlucky, but she managed to smile at Christian and cover up her fears.

'I have to go,' he told her as he got up from the chair and kissed her.

Alex examined the jewellery. She would secrete it in a drawer when she got home, but it had blighted her day and she stuffed into her locker.

Feeling low after this episode, and also because of the hormonal upheaval, Alex was uplifted when Magda poked her head around the door and enquired if 'madam was receiving today'.

'Madam most certainly is, particularly to Queensbridge doctors,' Alex riposted.

After a perfunctory greeting to her friend, Magda eagerly took herself to the cot and scrutinised the contents.

'He looks as though he has dropped off the ceiling of the Sistine Chapel,' she summarised.

'It felt like it when he was born!' Alex giggled.

Magda stayed for two hours and they laughed and gossiped together. Alex had never mentioned Christian's inadequacies, even to Magda. It was her secret, and hers alone, and she loved Christian sufficiently not to betray him. He had given her the one thing she had always wanted – a child.

At the end of her week-long hospital stay, and with a clean bill of health for mother and child, Alex was discharged.

Christian took her home and left her in the care of an eager Roberta. It felt strange to be home again, and Alex felt weepy. She had heard the phrase 'broken night's sleep' bandied about by parents and had never realised how devastating it could be. It took Guy three months to realise that his mother required to sleep at night.

To enable her to get around, Christian bought Alex a Mini. She was thrilled with it. She could pop Guy on the back seat, in the carrycot, and breeze off and visit her parents and friends. Roberta also offered to baby-sit for short periods which meant Alex could snatch a game of tennis.

Guy's development was a source of wonderment to Alex. He was a loving baby, encouraged by a doting mother, and his every movement was mulled over with Roberta.

Christian was equally proud of his son, but his heavy workload stopped him seeing the finer points of his son's progress.

The first year of Guy's advent was a happy one, though Roberta was less inclined to baby-sit as he became more demanding. Alex was only too glad to haul him around and have him admired.

Christian was leaving early for work these days. He visited his private patients before starting his NHS day and he would stay late to work, at peace, in his office.

Alex found her role as wife and mother pleasant enough and she was too busy and too tired to dwell on the lacklustre bedroom scenario. Christian was kind and generous and provided for their every whim.

Feeding breakfast to Guy, perched in his high chair, Alex wondered why Roberta had not appeared. It was customary for the three of them to breakfast together after Christian's departure to the hospital. Alex finished feeding her little son and then, cleaning him up, corked him out of his chair, attached him to her hip and made her way to Roberta's annexe.

She knocked on the door and called out, and heard a faint reply from the bedroom. Pushing open the door, she found Roberta still in bed.

'Are you all right?' Alex asked.

'Not very well this morning, I'm afraid,' was the answer, and as Alex approached the bed she was horrified to see how blanched and papery Roberta's skin was without the concealment of cosmetics.

'What is the trouble?' Alex queried.

Roberta tapped her abdomen through the bed coverings. 'Bit bloated here,' she admitted.

'Can I have a look?' Alex suggested, placing Guy on the floor.

Roberta nodded reluctantly.

'I'll go and grab my stethoscope, could you keep an eye on Guy?' she said without expecting an answer. She sped back to the study and whipped a stethoscope from a hook and equally speedily returned to her mother-in-law's bedroom.

Roberta was talking to Guy as he sat on the floor.

'Right, let's be having a look,' Alex said as she placed the stethoscope round her neck and turned back the bedclothes. To her horror Roberta's abdomen was distended and as Alex placed her hand gently on it she realised it was full of fluid.

Used to concealing her thoughts from patients, Alex smiled at Roberta.

'I need to listen to your heart and lungs,' she said as Guy started to gurgle. Roberta and Alex laughed. Alex was grateful to her son for releasing the tension. A cursory examination and questioning confirmed Alex's fears that Roberta was seriously ill.

'I will have to go and ring Christian,' she said authoritatively.

'Surely there's no need to bother him,' Roberta tempered.

'Yes, I'm afraid there is, he would never forgive me if I didn't keep him posted.' Alex patted Roberta's arm, scooped Guy from the floor and wound her way back to the main house.

In the seclusion of the study she rang the hospital, knowing the best bet of getting a quick response was to be put through to Sister Stuart.

'I need to speak to my husband urgently,' she told the mainstay of the gynae ward.

Sister Stuart grasped the situation and assured Alex that Christian would be located and respond to her with alacrity.

Alex sat down and played gently with Guy until her call was returned.

'Are you and Guy all right, my darling?' was Christian's first question.

'We are, but Roberta isn't, you need to come home at once,' Alex said urgently.

'What has happened?' Christian asked her, she could hear the concern in his voice.

'Just come, please' Alex insisted, and she replaced the phone.

Returning to her mother-in-law's bedroom with Guy she tried to reassure Roberta.

'It's serious, isn't it?' Roberta stated, even though it was a question.

'Yes, if we don't get you treated soon,' Alex replied.

'I've had a good life, and your marriage to Christian and the birth of little Guy has made me so happy,' Roberta told her.

'Well you are the best mother-in-law a girl could have,' Alex responded with a widening smile. Just then she heard Christian's car pull into the drive. She grabbed Guy and sped back to the main hall and reached it just as Christian let himself in.

'What the hell's going on?' he asked.

Alex pulled him into the dining room and closed the door.

'Roberta has ascites, her abdomen is full of fluid,' Alex choked out.

'What?' Christian had a job to believe his ears.

'I have a nasty feeling it's your department,' Alex told him.

Christian sank down on one of the dining chairs. 'Please God, no,' he said, anguished.

Alex put her spare hand on his large shoulder, as she hitched Guy up on her hip.

'I will never be able to forgive myself if she has ovarian cancer,' Christian continued with his head in his hands.

'She has concealed it, and as we know diagnosis is often too late even when the first symptoms appear,' Alex said, comforting her husband.

Christian stood up and changed his attitude. 'I will go and see her now,' he told Alex calmly.

'*Courage, mon brave,*' Alex said as she reached up and planted a kiss on Christian's cheek.

It was half an hour before Christian reappeared, and Alex could tell by the look on his face that the news was not good. He went to the study and closed the door. Alex knew he was making telephone calls for her admission to hospital.

'Charles is going to arrange immediate admission, Sister Stuart has an available side ward. Mother will have to go by ambulance as she is far too ill for a car ride.' Christian was shaking his head with disbelief.

'I will go down and pack her suitcase and get her ready,' Alex said helpfully.

'I will come too, we won't leave her alone,' Christian replied. They both made their way back to Roberta's bedside and informed her of the plans they were laying for her recovery.

'Oh dear, I am such a nuisance,' she sighed.

'Anything but,' Alex said breezily, hoping to inspire confidence, and she set to and packed Roberta's bag. 'I expect you will want all this fancy face cream and lipstick and your French perfume?' Alex asked her mother-in-law as she waved at the pots and jars before stowing them in a pretty flowered bag.

Roberta nodded gratefully, and motioned to Guy who was now in his father's arms and signalling he preferred to be with his mother.

Once Alex had packed for Roberta, Christian handed the lively child back to her. Guy was immediately mollified and wriggled into Alex.

Stilted conversation took place until the ambulance arrived. It was a sad scene as Roberta was loaded into the rear of the vehicle. All three adults knew she would never return to her home again.

13

Roberta bore her terminal illness with great dignity and fortitude. Charles Beattie and Sister Stuart kept her as pain free and comfortable as possible. Close friends and relatives visited and plied the little side ward with a wealth of flowers and cards and Isobel Stuart relaxed the visiting hours as it did not conflict with the smooth running of her ward. Christian was badly traumatised by events; he preferred his private thoughts and was unable to communicate the deep hurt he was feeling. Even after the well attended funeral he remained withdrawn and shied away from comforting words, locking himself into a remote world which excluded Alex.

Hoping this to be a temporary state of affairs Alex complied with his request to be left alone to sort out his thoughts, but was alarmed when he told her he wished for them to have separate bedrooms.

'Darling, I want to be there for you,' she told him.

Christian shook his head. 'I want to be on my own at the moment, it will only be a temporary arrangement, and has nothing to do with my love for you. My feelings are all over the place at the moment and I need time and space to sort them out.'

Alex had no option but to agree. There had been no physical contact between them since Roberta's illness had presented and she was well aware that grief manifests itself in many ways.

After three months of living with this intolerable situation Alex decided a trip to Queensbridge and the company of Magda was necessary. She had recently resorted to employing an agency nanny when she required some free time from Guy. Christian was working even longer hours at the hospital, burying himself in work to assuage the terrible sorrow he was experiencing and was not fit, anyway, to look after Guy.

Linda, the agency nanny, had been a great success. Guy loved her, she was young and jolly and best of all reliable. Her remark to a departing Alex was always the same. 'It doesn't matter if you're late, I'll be here.'

Unusually, Alex decided to dress up a bit and dragged out a silk coat, a pillbox hat and some high heels. It was an age since she had done so. It lightened her spirits; Christian's depression was affecting her and she was fed up with the gloom and despondency that was now part of her life.

Linda arrived on time, and Alex set off for her pre-arranged lunch with Magda.

Richard and Magda now had a small Victorian house and it was there that Alex made her way. Magda was ready and waiting with coffee and immediately uplifted her forlorn friend with her ready wit. Over coffee, Alex recounted the last months of her existence with Christian.

'It's a temporary business, he will get over it in time, and will once again be your ardent lover,' Magda forecast.

Alex lowered her eyes. 'He's never been that, Magda, it's sheer luck we have Guy.'

Magda looked at Alex with horror. 'That magnificent being looks loaded with testosterone!' she exploded.

'He's a "once a week man" if I'm lucky, and it's over in seconds,' Alex confided.

Magda was mute, she stared with pity at her friend. Even she was lost for words of comfort.

'The saving grace is Guy, I'd go crazy if I didn't have him, and now there is no possibility whatsoever of further fertilisation,' Alex continued.

'I don't know what to say,' Magda said as she continued to stare at Alex.

It was the first time in their friendship that Alex had known Magda to be bereft of words.

'Let's not talk about it any more, I came here for enjoyment and I am not going to blight the day with my problems,' Alex reminded her friend.

'You look pretty gorgeous today, and we are going out to have a splendid lunch. Richard hopes to join us and he is good for the ego,' Magda chortled.

The restaurant that Magda had chosen was a new one, and there was a lively and welcoming atmosphere inside as they took their appointed table. Magda was quick to order a bottle of wine and get Alex into the party mood. It wasn't long before Richard joined them.

'You ravishing creature,' he told Alex as he planted a kiss on her cheek.

Alex smiled. It was so refreshing to have a flirtatious remark said to her again. The conversation continued to be humorous and light-hearted throughout the meal. Towards the end Alex enquired in a very general manner whether David Freer was still around.

Magda and Richard exchanged glances.

'He's married to Doctor Ruth and he's heading for a post in London, I believe,' Richard said casually. 'We don't have much contact with the new building or the Denningbee Centre as we are supposed to call it. All hush-hush stuff going on there.'

Magda interrupted. 'Why don't we go back to the house for tea?' she asked.

Richard shook his head. 'I have to get back to work, but I couldn't resist seeing you Alex.' And he departed hastily.

Alex looked at her watch. 'I think I'd better be pushing off, but I'll drive you back to your house,' she volunteered.

'No, I need to drop in to the hospital,' Magda said wearily.

As they parted the two of them made future plans and reaffirmed their friendship. Alex felt better for her day out.

Getting into her car and driving up the wide road she had an impulse to veer off and take a last look at David's flat, a place where she had experienced the happiest moments of her life.

The avenue looked smaller and deserted. She parked her car further along and walked back. It looked much the same as when he had lived there. He probably lived in some vast mansion with Doctor Ruth now. Alex thought about his words, and how meaningless they had turned out to be, and yet the intensity with which they had been said could not have been faked. His actions left no doubt that his ambitions were paramount and probably even Doctor Ruth was as much a stepping stone as she had been.

Alex turned her head as she became aware of a figure approaching, impossible to identify as yet. It stopped and then slowly came towards her.

It was David.

Alex felt her heart pounding with fear. He was staring with disbelief.

'Is this a mirage?' he asked softly as he approached her.

'David, I didn't know you still lived here,' Alex said nervously.

'I don't really, I just keep the place as a sleep-over when I'm working late in Queensbridge.' His eyes were like bottomless pools. 'It's wonderful to see you Alex, you look so well, and so prosperous,' he told her. 'Why have you come here today?' he asked suspiciously.

'It's my first time back in Queensbridge since I officially left.'

The conversation had the parry and thrust of a fencing duel. Where was the opponent's weakness?

'I heard you were married,' he told her.

'Yes, I have a son too.'

David nodded. 'I'm glad you are happy.' His eyes were searching her face.

'I hear you are married, to Doctor Ruth,' Alex rejoined.

David nodded. 'I'd ask you in for a cup of coffee, but – ' he hesitated. 'It might be a little dangerous.'

'I'm quite used to danger,' Alex retorted. She felt her heart-rate accelerating.

'If you're prepared to risk it, please be my guest.' David spread his hands to indicate hospitality.

She followed him up the short garden pathway. Unlocking the door she saw the uncarpeted staircase and again she clattered up behind him. Again, it all seemed so small. David put the kettle on and removed his jacket.

'Why did you leave me?' he asked reproachfully.

'It was you who left me,' Alex told him.

'I was sent to America, to Columbia University for three months. When I came back you had gone, then I found out you were marrying someone else, I couldn't believe it. I asked you to trust me. I loved you Alex, I still do,' David told her despairingly.

Alex shrank back against the wall. She could not believe what David was telling her.

'I left a letter for you with Andrew Galbraith, explaining everything,' he continued.

'I never received it, David, I did not receive that letter!' she screamed, tears filling her eyes. 'After you left, father came and took me to Rossington, a job already fixed for me.'

David hit the wall with his hand. 'We've been manipulated, Sir Arthur is behind all this!'

'Why?' Alex asked, baffled by why she and David had to be parted.

'His darling daughter gets what she wants, and I was

important to the programme,' David said. 'Neither applies now, as it happens.'

Alex moved towards him. 'Why does it not apply now?' she questioned.

'Having your wife as your superior, when her interests lie elsewhere, makes for an impossible working relationship which overflows into private life and I have been offered a very good opportunity in London now, which I hope to take up in a month's time.' David shrugged at the intolerable situation he was in. 'What of you? You would not be here today if everything in your back garden was rosy.'

Alex flushed. 'It is . . . all right,' she stammered. 'I have a good husband, but – '

'But what?' David moved even closer to her.

Alex put her head on his chest 'I don't want to talk about it.'

David gave Alex a kiss. It was an automatic gesture of comfort, but it rekindled Alex's present need for physical love and she clawed at him. For a moment he fended her off, but he could not control his feelings either.

Back they were in the bedroom, time was on hold and troubles forgotten.

'I love you Alex,' David told her yet again, once passion had abated.

'I love you too, David,' Alex said, stroking his cheek, 'but this has to be the last time we meet.' Tears welled in her eyes.

'Please don't say that,' David replied, kissing her forehead.

'I have a sick husband, he recently lost his much loved mother and his grief is terrible. If he found out about us God knows what it would do to him, and he's a kind and generous man,' Alex sighed. 'I also have a son.' The tears dripped from her eyes.

David brushed them away. 'I won't ever give up on us being together one day,' he told her. 'I don't care how long it takes, but I made you a promise, and I intend to keep it.'

Alex turned away, then pulled David's arm so she could look at his watch. 'I have to go, my darling David,' and she threw back the bedclothes and retrieved her hastily discarded clothing and dressed. David watched her. There was resignation and sadness in his eyes.

As Alex repaired her make-up, David eased himself from the bed and dressed too. He flattened his tousled hair, then walked round and put his arms around her.

Alex put her hands on his shoulders, then slowly moved from him, letting her hands slide down his arms. Sobs were choking her, she felt his hands tighten on hers but she wrenched them away and made for the staircase.

'Don't follow me!' she choked. 'Don't make it any harder than it already is,' she said, waving him away.

She clattered down the stairs and he watched, head in hands. He wanted to chase after her as she ran to her car. All he could do was watch as she drove away out of his life once more.

On the drive home Alex managed to calm herself. Although Christian would not be there she had to face Linda and she had no wish to arrive looking distraught. As she pulled into her drive she made a final tidy up before letting herself in.

'I'm so sorry I'm late,' she said breezily.

'I expect you met up with a lot of your old friends,' Linda remarked.

'Indeed I did, and the time just sped by,' Alex continued.

'I told you it didn't matter to me about time, I'm glad of the extra hours. Guy is all bathed and ready for bed, and he's had his supper,' Linda reported.

'Has my husband phoned?' Alex asked.

Linda shook her head. 'Someone phoned and I've left the message on the pad for you.'

Alex checked the message, it was merely about tennis, no immediate response required.

She picked Guy up and cuddled him as Linda departed. The child nestled into her, it was obvious he had missed her. Tears came into Alex's eyes as she looked at him, how trusting he was. Alex knew she could not betray that trust.

Reading Guy a story before settling him down normalised an abnormal day. Downstairs she tidied up and prepared a meal. Christian seldom ate supper at home, preferring to avail himself of hospital food, but Alex always had something on hand for the few occasions that he did come home. She was trying to suppress the guilt she was feeling.

She heard his key in the lock and footsteps on the stairs.

'Hello darling!' she greeted him, 'have you had a good day?'

'Not bad, not bad,' he conceded. 'Did you have a good day?'

'You can't have a bad day when Magda's around,' Alex replied chirpily.

'Indeed you can't,' Christian agreed. 'Are we having supper together tonight?'

'Of course,' Alex said jumping up, 'and a bottle of wine?'

Christian nodded and went off to wash his hands and shed his hospital clothing. Alex tore round and prepared supper in the study. She was nervous, she didn't want to give anything away.

Christian returned, opened the wine and poured it into their two glasses. As Alex went to sample hers, Christian raised his. 'Alexandra, my precious wife, I know I'm not the easiest husband to live with at the moment, but please be patient as I try to resolve my difficulties over mother's death. I still blame myself for not spotting her illness.'

Alex nodded and took a step towards him, but he took a step back.

Over the supper table Alex came up with an idea.

'Christian, how about if we had a dinner party for your

mother's friends who helped her so much when she was in hospital, a commemoration, not a morbid wake-type thing. After all, she loved giving and going to parties and it would be a fitting tribute to her and a thank you to those friends.'

Christian was thoughtful. 'Who did you have in mind?' he asked warily.

Alex listed a few. 'And Isobel Stuart, Charles Beattie and his wife,' she ended.

Christian ruminated on the proposal before saying, 'I think that is a lovely idea, go ahead and arrange it. What a sweet, thoughtful girl you are, Alexandra.'

Alex lowered her eyes, her guilt could not be wiped away by giving a party.

The party preparations did however distract her and Alex enjoyed the telephone chats when inviting the guests after clearing the date with her husband. She even went to the hospital to personally ask Sister Stuart.

'I do the off duty so the date is no problem,' Isobel confirmed.

The next couple of weeks flew past. Alex was determined to try and blot out her trip to Queensbridge, but it was at night in her lonely bed that her thoughts were of David and those thoughts would not go away.

With her dinner party now imminent Alex had spared no effort to decorate the table and had sought out Roberta's favourite dishes to serve to the guests. Even her dress reflected the occasion – it was dark grey and she embellished it with jet beads she had bought at the second-hand shop in Queensbridge many moons ago.

Christian also dressed in a grey suit with a black tie, but he seemed at peace for once, almost like his old self; but the remoteness was still there. Perhaps tonight it would be breached.

The guests arrived with huge bunches of flowers. The women had dressed mainly in black, though a purple and a grey outfit were present amongst the gathering. The men also dressed sombrely, but the atmosphere most certainly wasn't sombre. Alex had made it plain that a funereal air was not intended, and the guests complied.

Isobel Stuart was the star of the party. Being on her own the men fawned on her and the women extolled her virtues regarding her work. She was well known and respected in Rossington.

Alex was delighted with the success of her dinner, and even Christian was relaxed and laughing, but there was a disturbing and terrible thought lurking, and it wouldn't go away. The jollity of the guests put it to the back of Alex's mind and tonight she was enjoying herself. She would deal with it tomorrow.

Christian was full of praise for Alex's efforts and felt they should start going out socially again, but he balked at the suggestion that he should join her in the bedroom.

'Don't pressurise me,' he said defensively, 'I will come back, I promise.'

Why do men make promises that they have no intention of keeping? Alex fumed to herself.

That night in bed her mind was reeling, but she was tired and she fell asleep in spite of her agitation.

The next morning was the big clear-up. To reward herself for her heavy domestic effort Alex rang Linda to look after Guy so she could arrange a game of tennis. What a relief it was to out in the fresh air whacking a ball around and along with the friendliness of the other players it released the tension of her unsolvable home problem.

Another week passed and alarm bells were now seriously starting to ring.

Alex suspected she was pregnant.

I will give it another month, she decided, but in her heart of hearts she knew it to be true. The father could only be David.

It was a terrible dilemma. Christian, being an obstetrician, could not be fooled into questionable dates or an immaculate conception. How was she going to extricate herself without a full confession? The thought plagued her. Furthermore it was going to be obvious soon, and scandal would follow. She desperately wanted this child, it was tangible proof of her and David's love.

As the weeks passed it was becoming more difficult to conceal her condition. Christian's abstraction was a blessing as he hardly noticed her and Guy's existence so extensive was his workload. Workload it was, as Sister Stuart had spoken to Alex about her concerns over his punishing schedule.

Alex was now eighteen weeks pregnant. She sat at the kitchen table, her head in her hands. What could she do? Should she just let Christian find out and then make a clean breast of her Queensbridge afternoon of passion? She groaned. It would destroy him, and he did not deserve that.

Should she pack her bags and depart? But there was Guy. She would be deemed a bad mother and he would be taken from her and that she could not bear. A decision had to be taken soon.

Alex's depression was terrible, she stayed away from family and friends, fearful they would spot her condition. Guy so loved her and she clung to him, even bringing him into her bed at night for his human contact.

These thoughts constantly swirled through her head. Tending to Guy and dealing with her domestic responsibilities during the day was an automatic procedure and it was a surprise to her, cocooned away one day, to hear the door-knocker being hammered.

She quickly tidied herself and wrapped her blouse across her thickened body. Answering the door she was surprised to find the hospital administrator and her father on the doorstep.

'We need to come in,' her father said brusquely as he took her arm.

They know about my pregnancy! was Alex's first thought, as their faces were thunderous.

'What is it?' she ventured, fearing the worst.

'Let's go upstairs to the drawing room,' James said, still holding her arm and guiding her up the staircase.

'What has happened, please tell me!' Alex pleaded.

Once upstairs and in the drawing room, James motioned for Alex to sit down. He seated himself next to her and the administrator took a seat opposite them.

'Alex, I have some very bad news for you, my dear,' James began.

'What, what has happened?' she begged.

'Christian had a heart attack this morning, he died in spite of immediate and continued resuscitation,' James told her as he placed his arm around her.

'Oh no, my darling Christian, tell me it's not true, this is a dream I'm having!' Alex was raving.

James intensified his hold on her. 'Darling girl, it's true. Every effort was made to save him, he was surrounded by colleagues but there was nothing they could do.'

'I can't believe it,' Alex sobbed.

Mr Rathbone, the hospital administrator, and James exchanged worried glances. Guy continued to play with his toys on the floor. There was a surreal atmosphere.

'Your mother is on her way, I will stay until she arrives,' James comforted.

'My deepest sympathy, Mrs Stephensen,' Rathbone said. 'Your late husband was a truly wonderful man, revered by his patients and admired by his colleagues. He was a dedicated doctor and it appears a deeply committed family man.'

'Thank you,' Alex whimpered. She put her head in her hands, she was distraught, and it was like some terrible retribution was being heaped upon her. She felt her father supporting her, as waves of grief overtook her.

'Is Guy all right?' Alex said, turning her tear-stained face to her father.

'Yes, but I think we should call Linda, and relieve you of worry,' James advised.

Alex nodded. 'Her phone number is on the pad, by the telephone in the study.'

Mr Rathbone stood up, and James pointed him to make the call.

Alex clung to her father.

'I think we shall get you some medication, particularly in your condition, this will not do you or the baby any good.'

Alex gulped. 'I should have told you.'

'I expect you and Christian would have told us when appropriate,' James told her gently.

When Mr Rathbone returned he stood in the doorway. 'Linda is on her way, I have explained the circumstances to her,' he said carefully.

Alex nodded and the tears started again.

There was rapping on the door. Mr Rathbone took it upon himself to answer it. Susan had arrived and she rushed upstairs, discarding her coat and seating herself down on the other side of the sofa to James.

'Dearest Alex,' she breathed, and she drew her daughter away from James and enveloped her.

Alex transferred her arms to the softer and warmer comfort that only a mother can give.

'I can't believe this has happened,' Alex repeated.

After soothing words from her mother, James suggested coffee. Susan disentangled herself and passed Alex back to James, knowing it would help calm the charged atmosphere.

Mr Rathbone decided to make a discreet departure. Again he extolled the virtues of Christian and told Alex that she could count on him for help during the following difficult days.

Susan rattled up coffee in the downstairs kitchen in double quick time and bore it up to the drawing room. James rooted around in Christian's wine cupboard for brandy. He laced each cup with a generous splash and they sat quietly and drank their beverage.

'Who is your obstetrician?' James asked. 'He will need to see you, and make sure this shock has not affected your pregnancy.'

Alex hesitated, she looked at James, then back to her mother.

'Well, Christian was,' she lied. 'Everything was normal so –'

James was surprised. 'We had better get you fixed up with someone,' he said in his doctor voice.

'Charles Beattie,' Alex said quickly, 'he is the senior obstetrician at Rossington hospital.'

Susan replenished their empty coffee cups and as she did so the phone rang in the study.

James answered it, and Alex and Susan were aware of the sombre tones if not the content of the conversation.

Linda then arrived. Guy had become fretful, but Linda was tearful.

Alex stood up and embraced and comforted the shocked girl.

'He was such a wonderful man, I'm sorry to cry, Mrs Stephensen, but I can't help it.'

'Don't worry, a lot of tears will be shed today, Linda,' Alex prophesied.

Linda picked Guy up and buried her head in his jersey. He pulled her hair and called her name. Linda lifted her face to him and smiled.

'You little darling, we'll go and have a story.' And she whipped him off to the nursery.

James now seemed pinned to the study. Incoming telephone calls were coming thick and fast, and he was making outgoing calls as well. News of Christian's death was spreading rapidly. Alex sat in a trance-like state, clinging onto her mother.

Another knock on the door. James had now taken control of this area. To Alex's amazement it was the bishop. She had only met him briefly, but Christian knew him well, as did James. He crossed the room to the standing Alex and took hold of her hands.

'Dear Alexandra!' There was soothing piety in his voice as he offered his condolences and finished by saying, 'Your husband was appropriately named.' He then turned to James and offered to officiate at the funeral service.

After his departure Linda appeared. 'Would you like me to get lunch for you all?' she asked.

'Including yourself, yes, very much so,' Susan replied.

Alex sat down again with her mother. It was as though she was outside the scene that was taking place, looking in on it. Although there had been a recent bereavement in the family, Christian had dealt with everything. Roberta's death and funeral had been much more contained, and of course expected.

James disappeared, he had business at the hospital. Formal identification and a meeting with the pathologist. In his absence Susan fended off the telephone calls and Linda took over the household with Guy's help. Numerous welcome cups of tea appeared, though Alex was unable to eat in spite of a tempting biscuit being put her way. She now lay dry-eyed on the sofa as Susan and Linda bustled about and Guy presented himself for a cuddle. What she wanted most was to go to her room, be in her own bed and sort out her jumbled thoughts. That would not be possible until it was night time.

James returned from the hospital. 'I have spoken to Charles Beattie, and he will take over your care. He said Christian had given no hint of the pregnancy.'

'Christian was so busy, it probably slipped his mind,' Alex explained.

'Sister Stuart is going to drop in and see you on her way home this evening,' James informed them as he consulted his notebook.

Alex nodded approval. Isobel Stuart knew how to handle these situations and had been an important factor in Christian's life.

The day slipped by slowly in spite of the interruptions. True to her word Sister Stuart arrived late in the evening. She was composed and direct and brought a posy of flowers with her and stayed only a few minutes.

Susan took on the supper preparations and laid the study table for them. Normality was seeping in. Guy was tucked up in bed and Linda was staying the night as were James and Susan.

Alex was the first to ask for her bed.

'Are you sure?' Susan asked with concern.

'I just want to go to sleep now,' Alex told them.

'If you need me, you call, or come and get me,' Susan told her daughter.

Alex nodded, heaved herself from the sofa and dragged herself to her bedroom.

Linda followed her into the room. 'I slipped in and made up the bed in Mr Stephensen's room and gave it a quick tidy up for your parents,' she whispered.

'You wonderful girl, Linda.' Alex hugged her and planted a kiss on her cheek. Linda disappeared and Alex flung herself on the large Victorian bed and crawled in to it. It did not occur to her to undress.

With the light out and solitude taking over Alex started to assemble her thoughts. She was now 'off the hook' as far as the pregnancy was concerned, but in her own way Alex had loved Christian; she could never recall an unkind remark being uttered by him and his generosity had been overwhelming. A piece of jewellery from the Frampton emporium was the accustomed Christmas and birthday gift to her.

Her instinct told her not to dwell on the past, but to look to the future. She would have the responsibility of two children, and as yet she had no idea how her finances would pan out.

Contacting David was out of the question, he was married and Doctor Ruth would be an adversary who would out-manoeuvre her at every turn. Survival was the important factor and that she intended to do.

Sleep was ravaged by flickering dreams, and Alex was worn out when she wakened and lay staring at the ceiling and its ornate decoration. There was a tap on her door and Susan came in with a tray holding teapot and cups.

'How are you this morning?' her mother asked.

'So it's true then,' Alex said unnecessarily.

Susan nodded and the poured two cups of tea for them, and then sat on a nearby chair.

'Your father has arranged for Charles Beattie to take care of your pregnancy, and when you are ready there are other details needing your approval,' Susan told her gently.

Alex burst into tears.

'It will get better, I promise,' Susan continued.

'It can't be worse,' Alex sobbed. Her lips trembled on the teacup.

'Your father and I will help any way we can. He obviously has to go to the hospital during the day, but I will be here until you say otherwise.'

Alex nodded and wiped the tears from her face. After a second cup of tea she decided to get up and tend to her little son.

'Get in the bath, and put on fresh clothes. Dump those you are in and I'll wash them,' Susan said practically. 'Leave Guy to Linda.'

It seemed strange to Alex that such mundane things could

be interspersed with the terrible tragedy that had just occurred.

Her mother was right however. Alex felt ready to face the day once she had complied with Susan's advice. Linda had taken care of Guy and James had long since departed for the extended drive to his hospital.

Alex slumped on the sofa. Her energy had seeped away. Susan encouraged breakfast and Alex managed a few mouthfuls.

Towards the end of the morning the phone calls started. Susan fielded them, writing each message on a pad and relaying it to Alex as unemotionally as she could. Then the flowers started to arrive.

Alex buried her head in them and left Linda and her mother to place them in vases. Wonderful and inspiring messages accompanied the blooms and Alex realised she was not alone with her grief.

Feeling there was little to be gained by lolling on the sofa and indulging in the 'morbid widow' pose, Alex wandered down to the kitchen. Linda was sorting out the flowers and was crying. Alex put her hand on her back.

'I can't believe he's gone!' Linda whimpered. 'He was such a good man, he was always nice to me, and he'd give me ten shillings now and again, and he loved you and Guy so much.'

'I know,' Alex said gently to the distressed girl. 'Somehow we have to cope with the next few days as best we can, they are going to be difficult.'

'Anything I can do for you, Mrs Stephensen, just ask,' Linda said, wiping away her tears.

'Yes, well, can you work full time, say nine to five for the next fortnight?' Alex asked.

'Of course I can,' the girl said, almost gratefully.

Alex's bout of energy was deserting her, she had to go back upstairs to the sofa.

Susan in the meantime had busied herself between phone

calls tidying up and bringing order back to a disrupted household. A coffee break was due for the three women and attention was given to Guy who was behaving as though he knew a significant event was happening around him. Susan laced Alex's drink with brandy on the order of James. Alex felt as though she floating along on a superstructure of routine domesticity.

'Would you like me to phone Magda?' Susan asked.

'Definitely,' Alex called from the depths of the sofa.

Susan returned to the study and Alex heard the buzz of conversation.

'She wants to speak to you,' Susan said, returning to the doorway of the drawing room.

Alex leapt from the sofa. 'Of course.'

Magda was short and to the point. 'Do you want me to come up and see you?' she said sharply.

'Yes, I do,' Alex replied, equally sharply.

'Be with you tomorrow.' And she slapped the phone down.

Alex could not wait to see her friend. Magda had a great facility for making the abnormal seem normal.

Susan said she was pleased that Magda was visiting Alex, though wondered about the brevity of the conversation. 'I am going out to do some shopping, we need a few provisions,' she added, giving an imperceptible nod to Linda.

'I think they both need a nanny at the moment,' Linda responded.

The remark caused Alex and Susan to smile.

In spite of so much activity, the day dragged for Alex, perhaps because she was so anticipating Magda's visit. The night was fraught with questions buzzing in her mind again and sleep was fragmentary.

Magda arrived early, and somewhat out of character was carrying the most enormous bunch of varied flowers, which she pushed at Alex. Nonetheless she was visibly shaken, even though she was endeavouring to conceal it. They hugged each other. It was a perfunctory gesture rather than one of deeper intent.

Susan had prepared the study for them, taking the phone off the hook and placing a tray of coffee and biscuits on the round table. She discreetly closed the door so they could enjoy privacy.

'I'm putting it all in a letter, I don't want to cause you distress,' Magda started by saying. 'I didn't know you were pregnant, how many weeks?'

Alex hesitated. 'Oh, about sixteen, I think.' She tried to sound vague. She didn't want Magda working out that conception coincided with her Queensbridge trip.

'Richard and I will come for the funeral. I liked Christian the few times I met him, and what of little Guy?'

'I suppose I ought to tell him, he hasn't asked for Daddy yet,' Alex said, slowly shaking her head.

'There are difficult times ahead for you,' Magda said with intensity, 'but Alex you are a great survivor and you have great tenacity, and if anyone can rebuild their life, well, it's you.'

Alex put her hand on Magda's arm. 'With friends like you, I can achieve anything,' she promised.

The conversation took a lighter note and Magda was persuaded to stay for lunch. Her presence brightened the restrained atmosphere that was an inevitability.

Alex was giving mind to Magda's homily: yes, she was a survivor, and yes she was going to rebuild her life.

14

Christian Stephensen's funeral almost brought Rossington to a standstill. There was no doubt it would not have been a good day to have required emergency treatment at the hospital.

The church was packed and so was the churchyard. Alex steeled herself for the occasion. Her mother had ordered a black coat for her which disguised her pregnancy; she was in no mood to discuss a new baby.

The bishop conducted the service, and the eulogy was almost a declaration of sainthood for Christian. Throughout, Alex felt James' vice-like grip on her arm and she was in a virtual trance-like state at the conclusion of the service. Standing at the door of the church with her parents she had her hand pumped, her face kissed and her body encompassed in bear-like hugs, as other people's tears splattered her face. She wanted the ordeal to end, but a few close friends had been invited back for tea at the house and it would be a while before she could escape to the seclusion of her room.

Alex knew what was expected of her, and she would be judged on her demeanour in times to come. She did not want to be found lacking.

The tea party at the house was better than Alex expected. Susan and Linda hosted it perfectly and little Guy introduced a cheery note. Mercifully, no one lingered and Alex was able to escape to her bedroom and sort out her thoughts. The funeral was a milestone. Friends retreated back to their work and lives, their duty done. Alex had now to pick up the baton and run with it.

She had taken Guy with her into her *sanctum sanctorum*, she let him play with the dressing table fripperies and took him to the bed and held him.

'Mummy wants to tell you something,' she said, gazing into his grey eyes. Guy put his hands together and waited expectantly. 'Daddy has gone away to heaven, and he isn't coming back.' Alex stroked Guy's hair as she told him.

'I know, Linda said Daddy had gone away, doesn't he want to come back?' Guy asked.

'Well – ' Alex was astounded by the child's grasp of the situation. 'He didn't want to leave us, because he loved us, but he has gone to a lovely place, where good people go.'

'Can we go and see him?' Guy persisted.

'No, one day a long way off we might see him again, we might go there too.' Alex continued to explain.

'Have we got another baby coming to stay?' Guy asked innocently.

'Yes. A little brother or sister for you, so you don't feel lonely.' She hugged her little son. How wrong for him to be deprived of his father.

'Mummy wants to sleep, do you want to cuddle up with me?' Alex asked, exhaustion overtaking her.

The child leapt from the bed and ran to the door. 'I want Linda,' he called. Alex was forced to heave herself from the bed, open the door and shout for Linda. The nanny was there and plucked Guy from the doorway leaving Alex to have her sleep.

It was the first really deep sleep that Alex had experienced since Christian's death and when she woke she knew she had to take control of her life and Guy's. Although there was a lot of legal decision-making to do in the weeks that followed, James was exemplary with his knowledge and brother Chris ironed away the irritations that unexpectedly sprouted up.

Alex's main concern was her baby. She had to plan for the approaching birth. Susan and Linda were going to have Guy while Alex was in hospital.

It was tipping with rain when Alex felt her first pangs. She didn't worry too much, but put the 'Guy care' plan into operation. Once he was removed to safety she drove herself to the hospital and reported to the maternity department. The staff referred to her as 'Dr Stephensen', remembering her from her time as houseman. Once labour was in full swing, to hear, 'Push, Dr Stephensen!' was an amusing side to an unamusing situation. Labour was brief and uncomplicated and Alex was handed a six-pound daughter at the end of a textbook delivery.

An hour later and back in her room, Alex examined the little girl. She could see traces of David in the crinkled, piglet-like creature swaddled in the adjoining cot. Alex's visitors were kept strictly to visiting hours. There was no relaxation even though she was in a side ward by herself. The head midwife was a stickler for hygiene and viewed all visitors as the harbingers of infection destined to riddle her maternity unit with streptococci and staphylococci.

The week spent there was full of anxiety and indecision for Alex. When she was released with her tiny bundle into the care of her mother (James was considered to be a contaminant, and banned) she felt weepy and unsure.

'So have you decided on a name yet?' Susan asked on the way to Westfield where Alex would be spending her post-natal recovery period.

'Yes, I'm going to call her Polly,' Alex said as she smoothed the skin on the child's face.

Susan was astounded 'Polly?' she repeated.

'I bet you thought I'd give her some posh Russian or royal name, didn't you?' Alex laughed.

'I thought you'd give her a – ' Susan hesitated. 'A different name. Why Polly?'

Alex shrugged. 'I just like the name, no other reason.'

'It has an association with parrots, or putting kettles on,' Susan said querulously.

'Polly Stephensen sounds very nice,' Alex defended. 'Long surname, short Christian name, same as Guy.'

'Yes, three syllables, I can see what you mean,' Susan conceded.

Alex stayed longer than intended with her parents. Family and friends came and plonked themselves down for lunch, but bearing toys and clothes for Polly.

Magda and Richard visited, and Alex knew they were suspicious about Polly's begetter. Alex remembered that Magda had a theory that a sperm was like a dog chasing a bitch on heat. Height and distance were of little importance; it had to connect with that egg at all costs. Magda was frequently shouted down by being told she was mixing it up with the spirochaete, that could reputedly jump ten feet. That was according to a message on the wall of a hospital lavatory!

Linda and Guy were enjoying Granny's hospitality too, and Linda set to when Alex was too tired to cope with Polly, but reality had to be faced and Alex knew she must serve notice and take herself back to recommence her own and her children's life. It was now six weeks of being cosseted and helped, of having food put before her and Guy whisked off for walks with the dogs, and holding court to family and friends and displaying her new child. That had to cease and a return to basic living had to be faced up to.

Susan drove her back to Rossington. The house felt dreary and damp, but she made Susan get back in the car and head home, no lingering goodbyes and thank-you's. Then she sat down and cried. Guy came up to her and put his short arms round her.

'Don't cry mummy, Daddy might come home now,' he told her.

214

'No, no, Daddy will never come home, it's just the three of us, for ever,' Alex said, fighting back the tears.

'Daddy might want to come and see Polly,' Guy persisted.

'No, he won't because he didn't know she was coming,' Alex explained with as much patience as she muster.

'Somebody might have told Daddy,' Guy said perplexed.

Alex got tetchy. Guy's continued questioning was irritating her. 'Just shut up, Guy!' she snapped.

Guy slunk away to find his teddy bear.

It was not an auspicious start.

In spite of Guy and Polly and their noises, the house felt sepulchral, there was almost an echo to every sound they made, and Alex hated it.

She unpacked and sorted out the kitchen. Life was going to be very different with two children constantly in tow. She hoped there would be adequate finances to employ Linda. As yet she had not ascertained her monetary viability. Probate had yet to take place.

One welcome telephone call was from Aunt Sonia, who wanted to come and stay for about three nights. It was an arrangement they had loosely discussed at the funeral and Alex was only too pleased that Sonia had followed it up.

It was an emotional reunion when her aunt arrived. She came laden with goodies, and there was a clanking of glass as she plonked down a box in the hallway. Alex whipped up lunch and Sonia took the first of the bottles from the box and uncorked it with practised skill. A glass each was soon dispensed, and the two women nibbled away at their make-shift lunch.

'I understand what you're going through, I was devastated when my darling Guy was killed in action.'

'What did you do, Aunt Sonia? Is there a way to relieve this terrible feeling?'

'No, you have to stick it out, work and friends help, but at the end of the day it will be two years before you feel normal.'

'Two years?' Alex was incredulous. 'Only twenty two months to go.'

'That's the spirit,' Sonia told her as she replenished their glasses.

Little Guy trotted into the kitchen and Sonia put her arms out to him. Guy was never averse to a cuddle and he quickly made his way to her.

Alex sat back as the two of them chattered. She was amazed at how competent Aunt Sonia was with a small child considering she had never had one herself.

Clearing up the lunch things she left Sonia and Guy to explore the house. They all met in the drawing room some time later.

'He could have a great career with the National Trust, we had the grand tour round the Stephensen mansion,' Aunt Sonia explained.

'I hope he will follow his father and me into medicine,' Alex mused. 'And, of course, his grandfather.'

'Things seem very good between you and you parents now,' Aunt Sonia noted.

'They have been superb, and Ma has really helped me with Polly.'

At the mention of her name the baby started to cry. Alex raised her eyes to the ceiling.

'I'll feed her,' Aunt Sonia volunteered. Polly was heaved from her carrycot and Sonia nursed her until the bottle was ready and then it was like a magnet onto iron when the milk reached its destination and was gulped away. Sonia's eyes travelled over her little charge.

'Where does the dark hair come from?' she asked.

'I think Grandpa Brandon was dark-haired, it's a regressive gene,' Alex explained, hoping there would be no further questions about Polly's looks.

Aunt Sonia seemed satisfied with the explanation and continued the feed.

The interlude with Sonia was inspiring for Alex and she was sad when the three days passed and Sonia had to return to her husband. As Alex said goodbye, little Guy burst into tears and hung his head.

'He really loves you, Aunt Sonia,' Alex told her, bending low to speak into Sonia's ear as her aunt revved the car engine.

'Not the first time I've been loved by a Guy!' Aunt Sonia called as she drove away.

Alex stood for some seconds in the drive looking after the departing car and holding Guy's hand. He had stopped crying, but Alex was about to start.

'Polly's crying,' Guy told his mother with a certain amount of excitement. Alex led him by the hand back into the house, wiping away her tears. It was a sentence Guy would utter many times over the coming months.

Difficult times loomed. The first shock was probate. Christian had been a lavish spender as Alex well knew, being the frequent recipient of his generosity. With prudence she could make it through the first year or so of Polly's life before having to seek employment. Meeting with the bank, it was suggested that she move to a smaller house. Alex agreed with this. The present one was large and ornate and expensive to heat and maintain, and it would relieve her of worry if she raised some capital.

Selling and buying houses would be a project for her too. Houses were not selling well, but she hoped Roberta's lingering touches gave it a stylishness that would attract a discerning and well-heeled buyer.

Her brother Jon forced himself from his *domaine* in France to take on the selling of Christian's car. He and his French lady-friend, Gi-Gi, came and stayed the night, replenishing and then plundering Alex's wine stocks.

'I want you to search this car before I take it,' Jon told Alex. 'I don't want the embarrassment of a buyer finding gynaecological instruments in the pockets or under the seats.' He raised his hand to show it was a no-go area for him. Alex complied, finding only a duster, which she waved in front of his nose.

Jon was driving Christian's car back to London, followed by Gi-Gi driving his car. Alex suspected he already had a customer lined up. There were hugs and kisses all round before departure. Alex was left smiling as Jon always made a merry quip when a possible agonising situation could emerge. Jokes about monkeys never failed.

Magda was the next visitor to cheer Alex's cheerless life. Again it was only an overnight stay, but they set off to view a few properties that might be suitable for Alex and her family. After taking the brochures home, opening the wine and having a major debate over suitability Guy decided to crayon the rejects, making them look more saleable. Polly was content to fling the contents of her plate, and scored a few hits which delighted her brother.

After the food blitz Alex whisked Polly to the bath leaving Magda with the marvels of television. While Alex was embroiled with a squirming daughter, the telephone rang and Magda answered it.

'It's your brother Jon!' she called up the stairs to Alex.

'Take the call for me!' Alex shouted back.

Minutes later Magda appeared at the bathroom door. Alex was drying Polly.

'Jon said to tell you that he has sold your car for £500, the cheque is on its way, and also that one of the monkeys wasn't in the cage at the time.'

'What good news, I was worried about that monkey,' Alex told her friend.

Magda shook her head, Jon had repeated the joke to her.

'In return, I told him one of my parrot jokes,' Magda said with an air of triumphalism.

'Oh, no,' Alex said, closing her eyes as she deftly put nappy and pyjamas on the kicking baby.

Magda took charge of Polly while Alex started to prepare supper, and when sleep engulfed the baby they took her up and placed her in the cot.

A leisurely supper in the kitchen along with copious amounts of wine led the girls to reminiscing. 'Is David Freer still around?' Alex slipped into the conversation.

'Good heavens, no, he's cleared off to London, and left the "Queen Denningbee" as she is now known, to run the new building. I think there was a power struggle,' Magda said with a certain glee. 'So what are your plans?'

'Get my finances in order, move house, rear two children, get back to work, not sure what I'll do in my spare time though,' Alex replied as she refilled their glasses.

'Patricia and Peter want to come and stay,' Magda reminded her.

'He'll probably want to psychoanalyse me and tell me where I'm failing,' Alex said sadly as she tinkered with her wine glass.

'As psychiatrists go Peter is pretty normal, but he has had the odd patient turn up with a shotgun on his doorstep; frightened the life out of Patricia,' Magda said with amusement.

It was time to turn in. Alex was weary, but much cheered by Magda's visit. They wandered upstairs, checked on the sleeping children and then retired to their respective bedrooms. Alex was quickly asleep. These days she was so exhausted that even dreams were at a premium, and waking in the morning she was often as tired as when she went to bed.

This morning she did not feel this way; breakfast all round was followed by a resumption of property interest as the estate agent rang to say there was a viewer for Alex's property.

'Let's get it tidied up,' was Magda's immediate response and she started, leaving Alex to sort out the children, before she joined in with the great clean-up.

Alex reinstated some of Roberta's treasures about the

place. These had been placed in safe keeping when Guy had become mobile.

Magda departed for Queensbridge before the viewing. Swearing abounding friendship she waved a cheery farewell to Alex and cruised out of the drive in her smart red car.

Alex felt the departure keenly, it was quiet now she had gone. A great feeling of loneliness swept over her, and even a bellow from Guy did nothing to remove it. Later in the day a couple came to inspect the house. They were taciturn and wanted cupboards opened and Alex felt a sniff from them signified disapproval.

The forced smile and thanks gave the clue that the property was unsuitable for their purpose, but it gave Alex a lesson in house-selling.

At the weekend Isobel Stuart arrived with some toys for the children and chocolate for Alex. She was nattily dressed, and looked like the cat that had licked the cream.

'I have some news for you Alexandra,' she said after downing a cup of coffee.

'*Dites-moi!*' Alex exclaimed, not altogether surprised that some exciting issue was in the air.

'I'm getting married,' Isobel said shyly.

Alex jumped up with excitement. 'I'm so happy for you!' she squeaked. 'Is it anyone we know?' she asked, using the 'royal' plural.

'Oliver Michelson,' Isobel said, watching Alex's face carefully.

'That name rings a bell,' Alex said, scrunching up her eyes.

'He's a local GP, I nursed his wife a few years ago, she died unfortunately. Then we met again as we both belong to the Bach choir, I think it was Handel's *Messiah* that clinched the deal,' Isobel confided.

'You must stay for lunch, and we must have a celebratory drink,' Alex said, then she turned with seriousness to Isobel. 'You will be sadly missed at the hospital,' she reflected.

'The king is dead, long live the king,' Isobel replied. 'Though having said that, Christian has not been adequately replaced and Mr Beattie is retiring soon. I'm glad to be leaving in a way.'

'I haven't met Dr Michelson, but I've written to him, and he's written to me, so he's a sort of pen-friend,' Alex said, injecting a bit of light-heartedness into the serious turn of the conversation.

'It will be a quiet wedding, but we would both like you to be there,' Isobel continued.

'I would be honoured,' Alex assured her friend, and then she went and opened a bottle of wine and she and Isobel toasted the future for both of them.

Lunch was a leisurely affair, Isobel using her ward sister skills in tact and optimism to leave Alex feeling enthusiastic about the future at its conclusion. Promises were exchanged before Alex's guest left.

It seemed weddings were in the air. Alex's brother Chris announced his engagement to his BOAC air hostess girlfriend. The word 'hostess' had alarmed Susan until it was explained to her that the girl spoke two languages fluently and had been at a finishing school in Switzerland.

Lavinia, as she was called, was to be introduced to the family. First port of call was the Brandon household, thence to Rossington for an overnight stay with Alex. Preparation of the homestead was important and Alex decided to house the affianced pair in the annexe so sadly vacated by Roberta. There were two bedrooms along with a plush bathroom, and a large sitting room. Alex carefully prepared it for the visit. Prior to her brother's arrival she had an update on Susan's assessment of the daughter-in-law-to-be.

'Very quiet,' Susan told Alex over the telephone, and with some hesitation.

'Ah, do I detect a note of caution, or are you just being a mother-in-law?' Alex teased.

'I don't want to put ideas in your head, you must judge her for yourself,' Susan replied. The remark had a sanctimonious smack to it.

'So she's on trial, is she?' Alex said playfully.

'Don't be obtuse,' Susan snapped, and they closed the conversation.

Alex could hardly wait to make the acquaintance of Lavinia. When the couple arrived, Alex sped down the staircase at the first knock on the front door. Opening it with a flourish, she found Chris was unlocking the boot of the car as Lavinia stood apart, a jacket over her arm. Alex knew she was not going to like her new sister-in-law. Lavinia had a patronising air and gave the impression she was lowering her sights in visiting this widowed creature bogged down with two young children.

Chris made the introductions. Lavinia' handshake was cod-like. Susan's words reverberated in Alex's ears.

'Leave your baggage here,' Alex advised, pointing for her visitors to go in the front door and up the stairs. 'Come and have a cup of tea and then we'll sort out your belongings.'

Before closing the boot Chris reached in, produced a large bunch of flowers and handed them to his sister. Alex exclaimed her thanks to both him and Lavinia then took them upstairs to the drawing room. Lavinia picked her way meaningfully through the toys that were scattered about, nudging away one or two with the toe of her elegant shoe. Disapproval was written on her face. Brief appearances and requests from the children were ignored in a very deliberate way.

Once tea was served, Alex was better able to observe her sister-in-law-to-be. Lavinia was stunningly beautiful, a natural blonde with baby-blue eyes and the straightest of noses, all this supported on a swan-like neck. This when Alex was looking and feeling her most unkempt. Susan was right, Lavinia was quiet. She barely entered the conversation even when encouraged to do so.

After tea Alex directed her visitors to the annexe. Lavinia showed a spark of life when assigned to her room and realising it was out of bounds to the children. Showing Chris to his room, no comment was made. It was a private area and the sleeping arrangements were not Alex's province.

Guy and Polly were hurried to bed, but the lovebirds seemed content in the annexe and Alex was able to get on and produce supper for them.

Lavinia had changed into a flowing garment which accentuated her slimness and gave her an ethereal look when she and Chris slipped through the annexe door into the kitchen.

'All is ready regarding the food, so we will go up to the drawing room for drinks,' Alex told them, drying her hands on a towel. They trooped upstairs and Alex handed responsibility of the aperitifs to her brother.

Lavinia was quietly looking round the room, this time free of toys and tidied up. Chris's expertise with a martini cocktail loosened Lavinia's tongue, though her conversation did nothing to dispel Alex's first impressions of her.

'I shall continue flying until we get married,' she told Alex as she twiddled the cherry in her empty cocktail glass.

Chris immediately leapt up to refill it and then his sister's.

'You don't plan to keep working once you're married then?' It was a provocative remark from the hostess.

'Not allowed to, anyway I want to be at home with my husband,' Lavinia told Alex. There was a hint of possessiveness in her reply.

'What do you mean, *not allowed* to work when you're married?' Alex questioned, emboldened by the second martini cocktail.

'My sister is a strong advocate of women's rights,' Chris intervened, 'and she has proved it herself by competing in a largely male bastion.' He scrunched his face up to signify approval.

Lavinia was not pleased. Compliments were her domain. During their supper party and the imbibing of quantities of wine a more relaxed atmosphere started to prevail. Alex tried not to be controversial in her talk, but Lavinia was heavy going and Alex did wonder if she became animated in the bedroom, or whether Chris had even established that yet. There were no significant looks between the two lovers such as she and David had exchanged when others were around.

At the end of the meal they returned upstairs to the drawing room for coffee. Weariness came upon them all. Chris sank back in his chair and Lavinia stretched her elegant legs out and laid her head on the back of the sofa.

Alex was envious to see Lavinia's manicured hand lying across the cushion, and her untroubled face looking at her doting fiancé reminded Alex of just how far she had descended down the 'housefrau' path. Her meditations were stopped by Chris mooting that bedtime had come. Lavinia stood up and blinked open her eyes.

'Thank you for a delicious supper, Alex,' she said with the suggestion of a smile. It was the first time she had addressed Alex by name. Chris came over and kissed his sister, repeating the thanks and the two made off, hand in hand, to the privacy of the annexe. Alex flopped down on the sofa. Lavinia had brought home to her that she must not be complacent about her situation. She was existing at present. She wanted to live again.

15

Alex's haphazard life was to become more ordered by the intervention of events and other people. The first thing that happened was that she achieved a sale on her house. This meant an electric reaction in finding a replacement, which had gone into the *mañana* file.

Magda was summoned and a fraught weekend was spent in frantic incursions into people's most sacred areas. Magda lugged Polly, while Guy was repressed from home demolition by Alex.

The major search operation did in the end pay off. Magda and Alex found that little gem and they both realised it simultaneously.

'I can see you here,' whispered Magda as they toured the premises. Alex nodded. It was much smaller than her present home but there was something appealing about its cosiness, and Alex knew she could turn it into a home for her and the children.

Alex was a novice in house buying and selling but she quickly 'clued up'. The hospital notebook came to the fore and copious lists were made to expedite the transaction and to ensure that avoidable mistakes did not creep in to foul up the proceedings. Her doctoring organising abilities came to the rescue, an area that had always earned her high marks from the consultant when she was a working girl.

An auction house was invited to sell the many artefacts that Roberta had acquired over her lifetime. Alex had to steel herself to part with these treasures. She did, however, single out special things, particularly associated with Christian, to pass on to Guy. The sale attracted a lot of interest as antique collecting was becoming fashionable. Magda, Richard, Patricia and Peter all assembled to help on the day, Linda came and took control of the children and Susan arrived during the lulls with picnic baskets and flasks to keep the troops going.

The move was worthy of a notable military campaign. Richard had a bottle of champagne concealed in his car and he released it from its moorings and dispensed it to the exhausted gathering sagging around Alex's kitchen table.

The move revitalised Alex. She was able to use Linda more often now that funds were more plentiful. She even got to the tennis club for a game.

It was only a temporary reprieve, and now the children were bigger she had to think about working again and providing an income. Furthermore, she had to think about Polly's schooling. She was determined that her daughter would receive the same education as her beloved son.

Polly was an independent character. She rejected cuddles and loving gestures, unlike Guy, who was the most affectionate child imaginable. He would take every opportunity to nestle into Alex and she had taken advantage of his demonstrative nature in her moments of despair.

'Don't cry Mummy, you've got me,' he'd tell Alex as she wept on his little shoulder.

To Alex, Guy was special.

Settling into the new house, with Guy now at a local school, was another hill climbed. Alex could go on foot with him and she met other mothers at the school gate to chat to. One of these mothers had a daughter at a nearby school and expounded the virtues of its curriculum, and Alex decided to explore this as a possibility for Polly. There was a kindergarten which led into the mainstream school.

Alex liked the place as soon as she stepped over the threshold. The headmistress was stern, but seemed fair and the achievements displayed on various walls by pupils past and present were a testimony to the educational standard provided. Polly's name was placed on the register for admission.

Painting and decorating the house and sewing name tapes on school uniforms, over and above the mundane tasks of cooking and cleaning, meant Alex's free time was at a premium. Her new home was taking shape and the disposal of effects from the Stephensen home had yielded a wonderful financial bonus for the family. Alex pressed on until her home was comfortable and practical for a working mother and two children. During this process she lost a lot of weight; sparing time to eat was a luxury, when a domestic issue needed resolving. Her parents voiced their concerns, but were secretly glad she was full of energy and planning the future.

Visiting the bank Alex learned that her finances were not in a robust state. Christian and his mother had been big spenders. Christian had set up a trust fund for Guy's schooling but had spent heavily on cars and the like and her jewellery box bore testament to his extravagances. So disposing of treasures was a must.

Back to work was the order of the day and her first probe was at the hospital. Certain that her husband's reputation and her own unblemished record there would be a passport to work, Alex was shocked to find a lukewarm response. An interview was arranged, but she was not being taken seriously. It was a blow to her self-esteem. A conversation with Magda clarified things.

'They most likely assume that you are exceedingly well-off and don't need the money, and secondly if Guy gets earache you'll clear off home and leave them high and dry,' she told Alex.

'Both assumptions are wrong,' Alex said defensively.

'Are they?' Magda asked.

'Surely I don't have to justify my domestic arrangements?' Alex said weakly.

'Yes you do, what about school holidays?' Magda said, rubbing home the truth.

Alex shook her bent head over the telephone. 'I could possibly afford Linda to fill in,' she persisted.

'Linda isn't going to sit around for the odd shift you offer her when she could be working full time,' Magda said impatiently.

'You're right, you're right,' Alex said, desperation seeping into her voice.

'I know it's tough Alex, but there will be a job for you somewhere that will accommodate your hours. There's a shortage of doctors. Just keep trying.' And Magda concluded the call.

Armed with journals and vacancy lists, Alex spent the next days trawling through them but every application was either ignored or met with a polite but firm rejection. Keeping cheerful for the children was difficult and being trapped in a land where adult conversation did not exist was telling on Alex. She would lie in bed at night wondering if this was to be her fate for the next years, with poverty added into the equation.

Time drifted on. The children were now settled into school. Alex had sold some of her jewellery back to the bronchitic old Mr Frampton. The alexandrites she kept; she would never part with them, her wedding present from Christian. She thought of his kind and considerate nature, perfect in every way – bar one. Her marriage seemed a million miles away now.

The advert was minute. Why it caught her eye, Alex would never know, as it was an oil company recruitment agency who normally advertised for geologists or petroleum engineers. On this day, however, they were recruiting doctors.

Alex wrote down the telephone number. It was more a gesture of defiance against her deteriorating situation than hope that this could be of any use to her. She left the fragment of paper on the kitchen table and started on her daily tasks. When the post arrived there was a snowfall of bills. Alex wondered why the utility services ganged up with their timing. Paying these demands was something she had never had to face until Christian's death, and it was a shock.

Her bank account was seriously depleted and she wondered how she could juggle the payments. She made herself a cup of coffee and fingered through the bills, hoping that she had misread some of the numbers. On impulse she lifted the paperwork and searched for the advert, but it was nowhere to be found. She stood up and painstakingly started to shake out the envelopes and statements which now covered her kitchen table in disarray. The more she searched the more panic-stricken she became. Sitting down again she reminded herself that calmness and orderliness was needed. She took a deep breath and then very deliberately started to probe every corner of the offending demands. Her determination paid off – the tiny scrap of paper had attached itself to the electricity bill. Shaking with relief, and delighted with her accomplishment, Alex made the telephone call to London.

The voice that answered was friendly and encouraging. 'Kuwait Oil Company,' she told Alex.

'Could you put me through to your personnel department, please?' Alex asked breathlessly.

'Could you kindly hold on as I connect you,' the soothing female voice continued, as the mystical noises peculiar to the wonders of telephone technology transported her to the hub of a burgeoning business.

'Good morning, personnel department.' Again, nothing but encouragement in the dulcet tones of the female voice.

Alex quickly and concisely gave her details after introducing herself under the almost forgotten title of Doctor Stephensen.

The response was immediate. 'We are looking for doctors in our medical department in Kuwait, two-year contracts and family accommodation provided. Registrar status, two British trained Kuwaiti housemen working with you. Salary determined at interview.'

Alex was excited. So far, so good. Nothing to deter her from pursuing this job opportunity.

'Would you like me to send you an application form?' the voice continued.

'Yes, please,' Alex barked out, hardly before the question was asked.

'That will be done. By the way, we also require a photograph, passport-type thing, and if you are serious you might want to start that off now and then it won't delay your particulars reaching us. I am Rachel Briggs, and I am the medical personnel officer here should you wish to contact me in the future. Doctor Randall is the chief medical officer here in London. He, of course, conducts the interviews, and we pay all expenses.'

Alex's spirits were soaring. After the glacial reaction she had received from her forays into the local job world, this was handing her hope.

'Look forward to hearing from you, Dr Stephensen,' Rachel added as she laid down the phone.

Alex made her first priority the passport photograph. She headed into Rossington High Street where a photographer had a discreet studio. She equipped herself with a bag of cosmetics and relayed her needs to the youthful studio owner as he approached from behind a curtain in the cloistered interior.

For such a small request a lot of positioning and angling went on, and Alex was feeling somewhat impatient by the time the clicks and flashes went off.

'Ready tomorrow afternoon,' the photographer told her as he disembowelled his camera in the dark room. Alex picked up her bag and left.

The photos were excellent. When Alex collected them as instructed, she could see that the messing about had been worth it. Now all she needed was for the application form to reach her.

Rachel Briggs was as good as her word, even better. Two days later a large package was delivered to the house, too big even to go through the letter box. It contained a booklet on Kuwait (Alex was pleased about that as her information on the place was sketchy, and she had had to check her atlas to establish exactly where Kuwait was located). There was an Arabic/English dictionary, designed for courtesy use rather than for the scholar. Then there was the company brochure, which made the place seem like some millionaire's holiday island. Swimming pools, tennis courts, American cars, a lavish club house with a vast dining room and bar. It was a new and untried life to Alex and it was beckoning. In amongst the literature was the application form which she had to fill out. Alex gave it a cursory look; nothing intimidating about it on first inspection, but she would deal with that later after she had glutted on the attendant information.

She decided to keep all communications between herself and Rachel Briggs in her bedroom, away from the random glance of any household visitor. This was her secret, not even Magda or Aunt Sonia would be privy to her plans. Alex wanted no 'gypsy warnings' from well-meaning family and friends.

After the children were tucked up in bed Alex slid the application form from its cosy holding and laid it on the kitchen table. This was the place that Alex used as her administration centre now that she was denied the luxury of a study. The questionnaire was straightforward, but Alex was careful to pencil the answers on a pad before committing

231

them to the form. There were two slots for photographs, one for the employee and one for the wife. The last section dealt with dependant family and a request for the payment of school fees. Alex filled it in even though Guy and Polly were too young to be sent off on their own to boarding school. The company provided an international school and that was good enough.

The uplifting effect on Alex was noticeable, even Magda, in her most recent telephone conversation, commented on it.

'I bet you're up to something, or is there a man in your life?' she asked sharply.

'I assure you, after three mistakes with the opposite sex, I am definitely not going to make a fourth,' Alex said firmly.

Magda was not convinced, but did not pursue that line of conversation.

Linda was less suspicious and put the euphoria down to the house move. In the seclusion of her bedroom that night Alex laid out the Kuwait literature over her bed. *Health in Kuwait, Kuwaiti Arabic . . .* but it was the glossy brochure that took her attention and she browsed through it at length and then could not sleep for contained excitement. Alex replied to the accompanying letter and completed the application form, requesting an interview. She couched it in terms that did not imply the desperation she was feeling. Two days later there was a phone call from Rachel Briggs. An interview in London was fixed for the following week. Linda was contacted and Guy and Polly's safe keeping was arranged.

In anticipation of the importance of the interview Alex splashed out on a new outfit and when the day came she attended to her cosmetic use with restraint. The train journey to London seemed slow in spite of the express service and she summoned a cab to take her to Oxford Street behind which were the company offices.

She was early, so a bit of window shopping filled in the time to the interview. Entering the portals a few minutes before the appointed time she reported to the reception area.

Moments later Rachel Briggs appeared and after introductions she bore Alex upstairs into a waiting room. 'Would you like coffee after your long journey?' Rachel enquired. 'Doctor Randall won't keep you waiting too long,' she reassured.

The coffee, when it arrived, was life saving. It calmed Alex's jangling nerves. The ambience of the whole place was soothing as was Doctor Randall when he appeared and escorted her into his austere office.

Doctor Randall approached the interview as though Alex had already got the job.

'Yes, there is married accommodation,' he assured her. 'We have ayahs who live in, and an international school. You will have to wait for your married accommodation for a few weeks, but you get a "summerbride".'

'What is that?' Alex asked.

'You stay in a house that belongs to someone else who is on leave, while the housing department sort out your permanent accommodation,' he explained.

'Would I still be able to have my family there, in this summerbride?' Alex queried.

'No, not until your permanent housing is allocated, but it would only be a matter of two or three weeks,' Dr Randall told her.

Alex pushed it to the back of her mind; she would solve that problem, but not now.

The rest of the interview went well. The more Alex heard about Kuwait, the more she liked it, particularly as it had the added bonus of an active tennis club. Concluding the interview, Doctor Randall hinted that the job was hers. Alex knew she must not take that for granted, many a slip . . .

The return journey home gave her time to digest the information. The benefits were multitudinous, and the salary four times more than she could expect in the UK. It would give her a sporting chance of employment back here when her contract was completed. She mused on the fact that she had at no point been asked about a spouse. She was there in her own right. An Arab country, albeit a British protectorate, streets ahead of her own in its approach regarding the employment of professional women.

The worst aspect for Alex was that she could not divulge a single word to anyone about her exciting project.

Linda and the children greeted her enthusiastically. Alex looked at them and a question rang in her brain. *Am I being fair to them?* She shook her head, she had no alternative. There were many British children out in Kuwait, leading happy and healthy lives. She could not moulder away in Rossington, living in the shadow of her deified husband.

Alex's hands shook when the London postmarked envelope plopped on her doormat two days later. The contents felt like more than one page, which suggested success. She carried it into the kitchen, took the carving knife and slit it open.

'It is with great pleasure,' was the first page's opening line. Alex closed her eyes. The news was exquisite. The second page indicated a medical in Harley Street was required, another trip to London. Alex was not worried about her health, she knew that she would fly through that little hurdle. TAB and ATT inoculations along with a repeat smallpox vaccination were imperative. The momentum was building, and there was no turning back.

The medical, as predicted, went smoothly, although the doctor concerned gave her advice about the sun and her fair skin. Apart from tennis she had no interest in basking about in a deckchair in the sun's fierce rays.

The final draft came, her clean bill of health. Now her departure date was reality: 15 October.

There were many plans to be laid, and first and foremost

her children had to be provided and cared for, for the few weeks before they could join her. Linda was the best hope, but she was going to need her mother's help as well, and that was going to be tricky.

Taking the children to her parents' house on her weekly 'afternoon tea' visit, she cornered Susan after the usual salutations.

Her mother was dumbfounded at the news, and not sympathetic.

After a lengthy diatribe Alex asked if Linda and the children could stay at Westfield House until she could arrange for them to join her in Kuwait.

Susan had an attack of the vapours at the suggestion.

'You can't possibly mean it,' she ranted.

'Mother, I cannot get a job in England, I have tried and tried. The stumbling block is that I have two small children,' Alex patiently explained.

Susan continued shaking her head with disbelief. 'Can you not get a nanny?'

'I cannot afford one, we have no income, and I have to work,' Alex stressed.

'Perhaps we could help you out financially,' Susan said vaguely.

'I don't want charity, my children are my responsibility.'

Susan stood up and paced around. 'Surely Christian left you provided for,' she asked.

'He and Roberta were extravagant, there were debts. He set up a trust fund for Guy's education, and that's about it. I've even sold some of my jewellery to make ends meet.'

The impact of her pleas and revelations were having an effect. She could feel Susan softening towards her.

'How long did you say?' her mother asked.

'Maximum eight weeks, and you would have Linda here to look after them, and Guy could go to the local school.'

Susan started to weep. 'My poor Alex, what has happened to you?' she whispered.

'Nothing that can't be put right,' Alex stressed. 'I'm asking for help, please Ma.'

Susan capitulated. She loved her grandchildren too much to refuse.

James might protest, but Susan had ways of persuasion. He always backed down if she was determined. Alex was sure she had won the day. To cement everything she rang Aunt Sonia with the news and arrangements. Pressure from Sonia would do no harm. Confronting Linda was the next objective and the following day, having had no retraction from Westfield House, Alex put the proposition to her part-time nanny.

Linda was delighted, and readily agreed to the deal. Alex was slowly eating away at the difficulties close to home, but Magda and Patricia had to be informed and their reactions could be unpredictable. As it was they both realised Alex had little option but to take a chance and gave her their blessing.

Alex had been sent a 'kit allowance' of £120. It was for the purchase of cotton clothing for herself and she went out on a shopping spree, but spent it mostly on the children. Time was running away and her departure date was imminent.

Although excited at the thought of the new life ahead, Alex was heartbroken at leaving her children. Their tear-stained faces haunted her, but Linda and Susan swept them off to the zoo with the promise of an ice cream as Alex got into her taxi and headed for the airport.

It was a sober and thoughtful journey.

16

Landing in Kuwait was a revelation. The airport consisted of a cage, and the passengers emptied inside it as the onlookers clung to the wire, either for mere curiosity reasons or to claim a loved one. After a perfunctory passage through customs, Alex was grabbed by a man who introduced himself as the company representative and was called Geoff. He scooped up Alex's baggage and bore her and it to a pickup. It was sweltering hot.

They were some distance from Magwa where the hospital and the company accommodation was located and it was a straight drive through miles of desert on a road that merged into infinity. There were occasional sightings of Bedouin camps and Geoff gave a monologue on the terrain and the expected conduct of employees who worked there. Alex sat and listened and absorbed the scenery, dabbing her face and hands with a damp handkerchief. When they eventually arrived she was shown to her accommodation which was a studio flat and situated in the bachelor section.

Unloading the vehicle Geoff told her she would stay there until her permanent house was available

'You will find food in your fridge, and tomorrow you will be picked up at seven.' He departed almost before Alex could thank him.

The studio was spacious and cool due to a noisy air conditioning unit. She wandered into the kitchen area and opened the door of the fridge. It was stuffed with a mixture of bottled water, salad and fruit, along with the basic milk and bread. The cupboard above held a selection of tinned products so starvation was not the order of the day.

Alex unpacked, spreading her clothing over the double bed before assigning it to the copious cupboards. Then she poked her head into the bathroom, which was luxurious compared to hers at home. Here she disgorged the contents of her toilet bag (a gift from Aunt Sonia) onto the spacious shelving and took a quick look at herself in the mirror.

She looked haggard, but it had been a twenty-four hour flight, stopping at Rome, Athens and Beirut. Once more or less unpacked Alex decided to have a cup of tea. She sat on the small sofa and gazed around her new quarters with satisfaction. She had everything she needed, it was almost like being a medical student again, and a sense of freedom flooded over her. No children screaming their demands, but she quickly sublimated those thoughts. They were dangerous.

There was a knock at the door. Alex jumped with surprise and curiosity. When she unlocked and opened it, in front of her stood a young woman.

'I'm Jenny Turner,' she said putting out her hand for Alex to shake. 'My husband Bob is your consultant, and we would like you to come and have dinner with us tonight.' A large smile stretched across Jenny's face.

'Please come in,' Alex said as she disengaged her hand from the firm clasp of her new-found friend.

Jenny looked around at the studio when she stepped inside. 'What do you think of it?' she asked.

'Very nice indeed,' Alex assured her. 'I would love to have dinner with you and meet my new boss.'

'No time like the present,' Jenny continued, glancing at her jewelled watch.

Alex excused herself and fled to the bathroom to repair the damage the last two days had inflicted on her. Minutes later she was ready to be taken to her new acquaintances' home and enjoy an unsolicited evening out.

Bob Turner was every bit as pleasant as his wife. Their hospitality was outstanding and they tuned Alex in to what life in Kuwait was about.

'Single women are at a premium out here,' Jenny said with a hint of provocation. 'Nursing sisters and teachers are the only available supply. I was a nursing sister and I was married in six months,' she said proudly.

'I have no intentions in that direction,' Alex told them soberly. 'I have two children and they will be joining me as soon as accommodation is available.'

'We both hope you will be happy here,' Jenny continued, undeterred.

Alex could see the houseboy discreetly clearing the dining room and it reminded her.

'I need to get an ayah,' she said to her hostess.

'The housing department will fix you up,' she was told. The Turners were a mine of information, but Alex could feel weariness overtaking her and it was becoming an effort to sustain conversation and show enjoyment when it was so well deserved. Jenny could see her guest was flagging and suggested driving Alex back to her studio. It had been a relaxed and informative evening and Alex was grateful. She looked forward to working with Bob.

As they stepped outside to get in the car Jenny looked up at the crescent moon.

'It's the other way up in the UK,' she said lightly.

Alex looked up and sent a message to Guy and Polly, it was a childish gesture, but she felt she had somehow contacted them.

The 'induction course' was cut short. It should have lasted four days, but after two, Bob Turner needed Alex urgently. A case of severe burns had been admitted and resources were stretched.

Alex was appalled when she saw the patient. He was being nursed in a medical side ward to minimise the infection risk. She knew he would die within the next forty-eight hours, but as it happened he lasted a week. It was a tragic start to Alex's contract. However, in spite of this, the sense of exhilaration was tremendous: Alex was back doing what she wanted most, being a doctor!

Medicine practised here was very different to that at Queensbridge or the Rossington hospitals. That did not mean it was inferior, it was just different. Malarial parasites, schistosomiasis and amoebic dysentery were unknown in the UK, but commonplace here and to be excluded before delving into what had brought the patient to the hospital in the first place.

Time in Kuwait ran at breakneck speed. In one day, work, a visit to the *suk*, a drinks and supper party, all seemed to coalesce. It reminded Alex of the old silent movies when the screen flickered the action in seconds rather than the modern-day movie-maker with his or her protracted offering.

Alex had telephoned home. Speaking to her children was agonising, though they both sounded happy, and only once did Guy cry. There was no news on the housing issue, but she was offered a summerbride.

'No, I'll stay in my studio until my permanent house is available,' Alex told the housing officer. She thought it might chivvy him up into finding her a permanent abode. Another two or three weeks passed and she wondered how much longer she could keep her mother sweet with regard to the children.

Her next call to Westfield House did give her cause for alarm. There was a distinct coldness in the conversation, though nothing was complained about. Perhaps she should agree to a summerbride and insist her children should be included. It was a terrible worry.

Then her next call to Westfield House forced her to ask, 'Is everything all right?'

There was a momentary hesitation from her mother. 'Yes, yes all is well.'

Again there was a curious lack of warmth in the rejoinder, but when the children spoke to her they seemed happy enough. Maybe her mother was getting fed up with the situation.

The housing department was adamant that children were not allowed in a summerbride, and again Alex tried to pressurise the housing officer into finding the elusive house for her and her family.

The frantic speed of life, and the heat, pushed aside immediate concerns. The 'ostrich syndrome' was coming into play. Alex did not even phone the UK for the next two weeks. Then she got a phone call from her father.

After a terse greeting he launched in. 'We have some serious concerns about Polly.'

'Polly? What is wrong with Polly?' Alex's voice rose an octave.

'First of all we thought it was "failure to thrive" but then I had her tested for fibrocystic disease – '

Alex screamed. 'No! No, please God not that!' She was hysterical.

'No, not that, she does not have it,' James told her, trying to calm the situation. 'I think you should come home, she is undersized and underweight and needs further investigations. The paediatrician is referring her to London.'

Alex had her hand over her forehead, the news was devastating.

'I shall make arrangements to come home at once,' she said quietly.

'I think you should,' James agreed, before ringing off.

The next day Alex had to put into operation her intended departure. It was painful. Bob and Jenny were devastated, and hoped she would return, but the personnel department was not happy with her. She loved Kuwait and its people, the job suited and challenged her and the life was exciting; now she had to give it all up. Her responsibilities as a mother overrode all else. Polly was ill, and a mother's place is with her child at such a time.

Alex sleep-walked her way onto the plane. Nothing felt real, she was entering unknown territory; where it would lead, she could not imagine. She slept fitfully on the flight, and it was freezing cold in London when she disembarked. Susan was there to meet her. She had not brought the children lest the flight was delayed.

'This is a great pity,' her mother stated.

Alex was not sure whether it referred to Polly's health or her hurried departure from Kuwait.

'How is Polly?' Alex asked as she settled herself into the car.

'Well she isn't really ill, she eats and sleeps well, but she just isn't growing,' Susan said with a puzzled air.

'Maybe she's fretting for me. Having said that, Polly is the least affectionate child any parent could have.'

They were driving through a tunnel.

'Not like Guy,' Susan said, peering through the windscreen with a furrowed brow.

'Not like Guy,' Alex repeated.

Reaching her parents' home, Linda brought out the children and held onto them until Susan had parked the car. As Alex stepped out Linda released them.

'Mum-may!' Polly called as her little legs raced towards her mother. Bigger and burlier, Guy let his sister have the first embrace, but Alex pressed him to her and he buried his head in her coat. It was a touching scene.

Alex had presents for them, but they became shy and huddled back into Linda. James appeared. He welcomed Alex warmly and assured her that all would be well. They slowly made their way into the house. It seemed strange to Alex after the studio apartment in Kuwait.

Her parents were being amazingly tactful. No recriminations, no 'I told you so' and as Linda and Susan made off to prepare supper, Alex was left with James and the children.

'I took Polly to Rob Dixon, the paediatrician, and he agreed she was small for her age and did some investigations. She *is* producing the growth hormone,' James stressed, 'and she does *not* have fibrocystic disease.' There was a pause.

'So what could be the problem then, if there is one? Maybe she is just a slow grower.'

'Perhaps, but I have arranged an appointment in London with a geneticist, a Dr Franklin, and he will need to see Guy as well.' James smiled, and then turned to Polly. 'You are going to London with Mummy,' he told the child.

'Are you coming too, Grandpa?' Polly asked. It was obvious a rapport had sprung up between them.

'No, but Guy will be going with you on the train,' James said stretching his arms out to Polly. The child reached out to him and he lifted her onto his knee.

Alex could never remember her father ever doing that with her.

Polly chattered away, and Guy brought his book over to his grandfather for deciphering.

Alex felt excluded. She had only been absent a few weeks and yet her children were turning to their grandparents rather than to her.

James tactfully divested himself of their barnacle-like presence in order to get pre- supper drinks, but he continued to chaff and tease the little ones and it was obvious that he enjoyed having young fry around again.

Alex was tired and her energy didn't run to complicated child conversations this evening. Linda and the children had supper with James, Susan and Alex, then she discreetly led the tots away to bed, giving Alex and her parents time for more conversation on their own.

'So tell us about Kuwait,' Susan urged.

Alex gave a lengthy and glowing account. 'I was so happy to be working again, and it would have been a good life for us for a couple of years,' she said sadly. 'Thank you for being so helpful with the children.' And she raised her wine glass to her parents.

'We have enjoyed having them, and Linda is a pretty wonderful girl,' Susan told her daughter. 'Isn't that right James?'

Her father nodded and smiled. 'Young Guy made me laugh, playing with his aeroplanes, and Polly with her doll that had to be dressed and undressed several times a day.' He shook his head with disbelief.

'You are falling asleep Alex, darling,' her mother noticed. 'I have put a hot water bottle in your bed, so up you go.'

Alex needed no second bidding, and she scraped back her chair and left the dining room after wishing her parents goodnight.

Both children were asleep when she reached their room. She bent over and kissed them. They smelt fragrant, and lying there looked so innocent; how could she have left them? She clenched her fists and under her breath vowed she would never, ever leave them again.

Tumbling into her own bed minutes later, the room started to revolve and then Alex roared down a black tunnel and into a deep sleep.

The children, along with Susan, woke her the next morning with a cup of tea. Although the children were exuberant and Susan chatty, Alex had a feeling of anticlimax. Where did she go from here? First and foremost Polly's health concerns had to be dealt with, and that could well have a bearing on the future.

When the day of the appointment in London finally

arrived there was a frantic departure for the station. Guy was longing to board a train so he acquiesced with everything expected of him. Dr Franklin had specifically expressed in his letter that Guy should attend the appointment along with his sister.

Susan took them onto the platform and waited to see them safely into the carriage. She kissed them all and waved until the train went round the bend.

The journey was exciting, and they picked out landmarks and played I-spy. Reaching London filled Guy with awe, it was the vastness of the station and the people milling around with their luggage that left him standing in wonderment.

'Come darling, we must get a taxi,' Alex ordered, and mustering her little ones she began searching for the taxi rank. Time was not flush, they needed to get to the hospital with all speed for the late morning appointment. An obliging taxi driver appeared almost by magic and swept them off to their destination, and with a cheery wave left them at the main entrance.

It seemed strange to Alex, going into a hospital as a patient rather than as a doctor. She asked for Dr Franklin at the reception desk and was directed, by an unhelpful girl with acne, to the relevant department.

Guy began to cry. 'What is the matter?' Alex asked impatiently. He stood still and gazed with fear down the corridor stretching ahead, along with the ubiquitous smell of disinfectant. Alex relented and took to coaxing him, and he reluctantly followed her and Polly.

The department was Victorian, with highly polished floor boards which announced their coming. They reported to a nurse and were told to be seated in a conventional waiting room which was overly warm.

Alex was nervous, and it transmitted itself to the children. Polly sucked her thumb and gazed around the room, while Guy clung to his mother. They had not long to wait before being summoned into see Dr Franklin. It was a long room, probably two or three knocked into one. The walls were lined with well-stocked bookshelves which declared molecular sciences were of serious importance in this area of the prestigious hospital. There were two or three desks but the nurse led them to the furthest end of the room where Dr Franklin waited with a sheaf of notes. He stood up and shook hands with Alex and made playful remarks to Guy and Polly. Both children now clung to their mother, sensing danger.

Dr Franklin went over the investigations that had taken place.

'Polly is producing the growth hormone, no problem there, the wrist X-ray does suggest immaturity, but again no cause for concern,' he said, smiling comfortingly at Alex. She heaved a sigh of relief.

'What I would now like to do is to take blood for further analysis,' Dr Franklin continued. Before he could say more Alex heard the door at the top end of the room open and was aware that a figure had entered and taken its seat at the top desk near the window.

Dr Franklin seemed unconcerned at the intrusion, and whoever it was would be well out of earshot.

Alex squeezed Polly, and it wasn't until Dr Franklin produced the syringe that she started to whimper.

'As your husband is deceased,' Dr Franklin said delicately, 'I will need to take blood from your son for comparison as we need genetic material from the male side of the family.'

Terror struck Alex. She would have to tell Dr Franklin that Polly had a different father to Guy. She looked round. The figure at the top of the room was far to absorbed in his pile of notes to take any interest. She would have to reveal the secret or the tests were meaningless.

Guy started yelling at the prospect of a syringe entering his body.

'No, no it's all right darling,' Alex said, soothing her little son. She then turned to Dr Franklin and lowered her voice. 'Guy and Polly do not have the same father,' she admitted.

Dr Franklin did not bat an eyelid.

'Do we have access to Polly's biological father?' he asked, referring to the notes and avoiding her eye.

'No, I'm afraid not,' Alex blurted out.

Guy was still crying but Alex heard a movement behind her and turned. She was like 'Lot's wife' turned to a pillar of salt. The figure standing behind her, the same figure that had been present in the room, was David.

'Let me introduce you to Professor Freer,' Dr Franklin said, gesturing to David.

Unlike Lot's wife, Alex managed to gain control of her movements and nod at him.

Dr Franklin picked the distraught Guy up and assured him that no tests were required of him. He then produced a brightly coloured lollipop from a jar and Guy's tears turned instantly to smiles.

'I would very much like to see young Polly, and cast my eyes over the notes,' David Freer told his colleague.

Dr Franklin interpreted this as dismissal by a senior member of staff.

'Of course,' he said, and he wished Alex well with the investigation. Then he discreetly departed.

Once they had the room to themselves, David turned on Alex.

'She's my child, isn't she?' he said, narrowing his eyes.

Alex shrank away from him, his look was so menacing. She could not ignore the question.

'Yes,' she whispered without looking at him.

'Why didn't you tell me?' he asked in a more gentle tone.

Alex turned on him. 'So what would you have said or done?' she said sarcastically.

David moved towards her and picked Polly up. He gazed at her with wonderment and stroked her hair. He ignored Alex's remark.

'I will see my blood gets to the lab, so the investigation goes ahead,' he promised. Alex nodded, she was still reeling from the encounter.

'I want to see and take responsibility for my daughter,' David informed her, 'but for the moment let's get the medical side of things dealt with.'

Alex did not reply, but thoughts were buzzing in her head.

Polly was openly flirting with David. Alex felt a pang of jealousy as she saw her erstwhile lover succumb to the child's playfulness. She went over to David and snatched Polly from his arms.

'How did you know I was seeing Dr Franklin today?' Alex enquired.

'I go over all the outpatient notes as a matter of interest, and I saw the name Stephensen, spelt with the E, I worked out the date of conception from the date of birth. You provided the vital clue – Guy and Polly did not share the same father. The rest was easy.' David said.

'Do you have a family?' she asked watching his face.

'No, and I'm not likely to either in my present circumstances,' David told her bitterly.

'I would have thought that you and Dr Ruth would be living in some Cotswold mansion with a couple of kids and a nanny by now,' Alex said acidly.

David's eyes were like dark pools. 'How little you know.' It was said with sadness.

'We need to take Polly's blood,' David reminded her, and he produced the syringe left by Dr Franklin. Alex wound up Polly's sleeve and pulled the child's head away from the impending procedure. David had the needle in and the blood withdrawn in the twinkling of an eye, and Polly didn't even cry.

Guy was mesmerised, but David quickly assured him that he was not required to give likewise.

'I shall require blood from you too,' David told Alex.

'You've had your pound of flesh, and now you want blood,' Alex whipped at him as she drew her sleeve up.

David made no response to the remark but his face was stern.

'Thank you, Mrs Stephensen,' he eventually told her after sorting and labelling the specimens. 'I shall need to see you in a week's time,' he added.

'You or Dr Franklin?' Alex asked sourly.

'It will be me. In view of the paternity investigations, I'm sure you would wish me to handle the situation,' David said, fiddling with the notes on the desk. He pressed a bell and a few seconds later a nurse entered the room.

'Please take Mrs Stephensen and family down to reception and make an appointment for her, a week today. Accommodate her travelling arrangements as best you can.'

Alex felt as though she was a naughty fourth-former being dismissed from the headmistress's study.

On the way down to reception she was fuming. *How dare he treat her so! Well, she could certainly reciprocate when, in the future, he wanted access to Polly.*

Alex was thoughtful on the way home. The children were tired, and Polly stretched across the seat and was sleeping while Guy was rubbing figures on the steamy windows.

Back in her own home Alex rang her father and told him about the inconclusive nature of the investigations, and that further blood had been taken. It satisfied James. She referred to Dr Franklin as the doctor concerned. Mentioning David Freer in a professorial way at one of London's most reputable hospitals would have been like the proverbial 'red rag'.

The week dragged. Worrying about Polly and then having to face the one-time love of her life was making Alex's nerves jangle. She snapped at the children and was short with well meaning telephone-callers.

How she hated David Freer and his arrogant ways. She was powerless at the moment to bring him to heel, but she was determined that sooner or later she would get her revenge.

Trekking off to London again was easier this time. Guy had gone to school and Isobel would pick him up and give him tea, so she only had Polly to contend with on the journey. She reached the hospital in record time and they sauntered up to the waiting area.

Dr Franklin appeared and disappeared at intervals, then David arrived with Polly's notes and bade them enter the consulting room.

'I think you will be reasonably happy with the news,' David said, smiling at her and then at Polly. He whipped out a chromosome graph and ran his finger across it, explaining the significance. On the bottom line an X chromosome lacked a leg and David's finger stuck on the offending letter.

'This is it,' he explained.

'What does it mean?' Alex was frantic.

'Nothing more than she will not be a tall girl. Perfectly proportioned, I think she will be about five feet fully grown.'

Alex closed her eyes, the relief was enormous.

David put his arms out and Polly jumped into them. Alex was too weak to object to the encounter. David talked to the child and her response was artless. It was clear he was captivated by her. He drew back when she nestled into him and quickly handed her back to Alex.

'No more worries,' he said soothingly to Alex, and he shuffled the notes and returned them to their folder.

Alex stood up. 'Thank you, Professor Freer,' she said, mustering as much coldness as she could into the farewell.

David escorted them to the door and before turning the handle he said quietly, 'I will be in touch.' Then, opening the door, he ushered them out.

17

As good as his word, David Freer rang Alex a week later. His manner was completely different. After going through the social niceties he then asked if he could visit Alex and discuss his paternal responsibilities.

'No, I can't see you here.' Then, 'We could meet somewhere between here and London,' Alex said, relenting from her uncompromising position of denying him access to Polly.

'Name a place then.' David was being calm.

After some deliberation, Whipsnade Zoo was mooted and agreed upon. It was a good choice for Polly and accessible for both parents. Alex was curious about how David viewed his obligations and on neutral ground and amongst the general public it would discourage pressing behaviour.

It was an easy journey for Alex in her car, and Polly was in an excitable state about seeing the animals. David was already there when they arrived. He was leaning thoughtfully on a wall, peering into a pit, but his mind was not on the animals. A look of relief crossed his face when he saw them. He bent down and kissed Polly who was sitting in her pushchair, then turning to Alex he kissed her on the cheek.

'Shall we walk?' he asked when the greetings were over.

'Yes, of course,' Alex said, spinning the pushchair round towards the enclosures.

David took her arm. He was anxious to state his case.

'Alex, everything I have said to you has been the truth, and I still love you as much as ever. I am in the final stages of divorcing Ruth. Our marriage was a failure, it never stood a chance because of my feelings for you, and she knew it.'

Alex gazed into the distance. Could she trust him?

'Until I get my decree nisi I dare not compromise you, so our meetings must be discreet,' David told her.

'What do you mean, *our meetings must be discreet?*' Alex asked sharply.

'Ruth is vitriolic. If she gets a sniff of you and I meeting she will crucify you,' David said sadly. 'She has already crucified me.'

'Then I suggest we stay apart. I've had enough grief and anxiety in my life,' Alex replied, shaking her head.

David stopped in his tracks. 'Is that what you really want?' he asked.

Alex stopped too and faced him. 'I don't trust you, David, Polly is proof of that. I prefer to be on my own. I will allow you to see your daughter, but I'm doing that for Polly's sake not for yours.'

David hung his head. 'I deserved that, I know. I used to say that no one gets the four aces. Well, I'm not holding any at the moment.'

There was an open area ahead with a children's playground incorporated. Polly kicked her legs with excitement.

'Why don't you take "Tiddlywinks" here over to the swings and have a one-to-one time with her?' Alex raised Polly from the pushchair and handed her to David. His eyes were liquid with gratitude as he took her and gently lowered her. Together they ran for the slide.

Alex sat on a nearby bench and watched as father and daughter chased and jumped around, Polly's tinkling laughter carrying in the air. When both ran out of steam David lifted Polly high in the air and carried her back to Alex. The child was clinging round his neck like a limpet and did not want to return to her mother's arms. David pulled the vice-like limbs from his neck and Polly started to scream as he lowered her to the ground. Alex grasped her and shook her. 'Stop that noise!' she ordered, whereupon the child reduced her screech to a whimper.

'Shall we go and have a cup of coffee, and would you like an ice cream, Polly?' David said, trying to calm the tense atmosphere.

Polly shouted with delight and even Alex welcomed the refreshment.

Sitting at the table David produced an envelope from his inner pocket and handed it to Alex.

Alex took it gingerly. 'What is this?' she asked.

'I am going to pay towards Polly's upkeep, I shall give you fifty pounds a month in cash until my decree absolute.'

Alex threw the envelope down on the table. 'I don't want your charity,' she said, in spite of fifty pounds a month being more than welcome in her present straitened circumstances.

'Alex, I must support my daughter. If you refuse I shall go to your father and ask him to intervene.'

'You are despicable!' she answered, her lips quivering with rage.

David picked up the envelope and handed it once again to Alex. This time she accepted it. She did not thank him.

David then left in search of refreshment and came back with coffee, sandwiches and the promised ice cream, but the atmosphere was tense and the conversation clipped and curt. It was time for all to go home.

The meeting was food for thought for Alex in the coming days, and it wasn't long before David was on the phone requesting another session with Polly. Denying him would be dangerous. Alex had never divulged to a single person about David being the father of Polly, and it was something she wanted to be kept secret. He had to be kept at arm's length.

Alex decided that Rossington Park might be a good place to hand over Polly. It was well wooded and not much frequented on weekdays. David readily agreed, and on the appointed Wednesday afternoon Alex wheeled the push-chair with its contents down to the arranged meeting place. David was sitting on a bench waiting, and his face lit up at the sight of his daughter. Alex stopped the pushchair and out jumped the child and raced for her father. David engulfed Polly with his arms and her green eyes sparkled with excitement.

'Do you want me to bring her back to your house?' David enquired.

'No, I'll meet you back here in four hours,' Alex dictated. 'Any unavoidable delays and you ring me.'

David gave her a military salute acknowledging compliance, and returned his little charge to the pushchair and made off, promising her untold delights ahead.

Alex was disappointed that Polly was so bewitched by her male parent. It made her feel inadequate about her position as a solo mother. Even Guy didn't counterbalance that male presence in a household. Many war widows had had to do the same as her, and had reared well adjusted and un-complicated adults.

David's presence was unsettling and Alex knew that the secret would be out sooner or later if these visits continued. A second and welcome payment had again been produced, and Alex had a free afternoon when she was relieved of Polly; there were advantages in the arrangement.

It was a rainy day when a hint of trouble hit the organised and advantageous routine. Polly was fretful, and Alex was not in the mood for resorting to childish games. She was impatient with the child but became increasingly aware that something was seriously wrong. Alex gathered her diagnostic equipment and swept the grizzling child up to her bedroom. A cursory examination was alarming, but when Polly screamed when she looked into the light Alex's worst fears were confirmed.

Alex rang the hospital. 'I think my child has meningitis,'

she told the casualty department. A brief conversation and Alex was told to bring Polly in as an emergency. First she had to make arrangements for Guy, and the blessed Linda came to the rescue, as she always did.

Alex grabbed a few of Polly's belongings and bundled the sick child onto the back seat of the car and sped to the hospital.

It was 'action stations' once they arrived in casualty. Polly was deteriorating fast and the paediatricians were waiting. The child was swept away and Alex was left holding a teddy bear and being totally ignored in the *mêlée* that ensued. She sank down on a chair and wondered what was going to happen next, it was out of her control now. Half an hour passed and then a nurse appeared. 'It's Doctor Stephensen, isn't it?' she asked, opening up a folder.

Alex nodded. 'I need to take some more details,' the girl asked. Alex filled in the missing information and was then taken to the paediatric ward. Polly was in a side ward along with two doctors, and she was about to have a lumbar puncture. Alex started to cry. The sight of her darling child being subjected to massive investigation and medication was too much to bear. She felt a kindly hand on her shoulder, and the ward sister led her away to a waiting room and then ordered tea for her.

'What can I say to you, Dr Stephensen? You know what it's all about. All I can say is that we have many children like this and most of them hop, skip and jump their way home.'

Alex put her head in her hands as Sister poured the tea, recently produced by a scared looking junior nurse. A long period of time elapsed before the consultant paediatrician came to the waiting room. He was a recent appointee at the Rossington Hospital and had outstanding credentials, so Isobel had told Alex.

'Doctor Stephensen, my name is Jeremy Dinsdale.' He

rubbed his hands together before continuing. 'I am the paediatric consultant in charge of your daughter's care.'

The tears were coursing down Alex's cheeks, and as fast as she brushed them away more came.

'I can tell you we have initiated treatment, you got her here quickly. I'm sure this time tomorrow she will be asking for that teddy bear sitting next to you,' Doctor Dinsdale prophesied.

Alex shook her head; she knew, only too well, the dangers of meningitis. Her darling, her spirited little daughter, fighting for her life was almost more than she could bear.

'You can go back to her room, if you wish,' Dr Dinsdale told Alex. 'Is there anyone else coming to support you?'

Alex realised he was trying to be tactful, but she told him that she did not wish anyone else to be involved at this stage.

Dr Dinsdale recognised the sharpness in her tone and did not pursue the matter. Instead he patted her arm and escorted her down the corridor to Polly's isolation ward. Alex took her seat at the bedside. Polly was unconscious and flushed. Alex watched the infusion dripping its relentless way into Polly's vein. She bent forward and stroked the muddled dark ringlets that framed her face. Alex was never to know where she summoned the inner strength to control the turmoil and guilt going on in her mind. The priority was now medical and nothing else mattered.

Sitting, watching and waiting as the nurses buzzed in and out, as did the registrar and houseman, helped pass the hours, and as darkness came Alex did not relinquish her post.

Sister ordered refreshment, but all Alex could do was to gulp down the numerous cups of tea that appeared. Exiting to allow treatment and nursing care, Alex stretched her legs along the now gloomy corridor, waiting for that one sign of hope.

Returning to Polly's room, with its discreet lighting and immaculate layout, she took her seat and held the little hand on top of the snow-white sheet.

'Come on Polly, you're such a fighter, don't give up on this one,' Alex whispered. Her words were unheard, the child slumbered on.

Alex's vigil through the night continued. She felt no drowsiness so intent was she on seeing that first indication of recovery.

Hearing a movement behind her, Alex did not bother to look round; the nurses crept in and out all the time, trying not to disturb her. She was aware that someone was standing and watching the scene, and as she turned her head she saw the dark shadow and when her eyes adjusted she realised it was David.

Releasing Polly's hand, she stood up and moved towards him apprehensively.

'Why didn't you tell me?' he hissed.

Alex shook her head, she could not answer his question. Without warning he pulled her to him. 'You don't have to do this alone, I'm here now and we do it together.'

Alex pulled away from him just as the night nurse came through the door with a chair.

'Here you are, Professor Freer,' she said, placing the chair next to the bed. It squeaked as it contacted the floor and Polly reacted to the sound.

Alex and David turned to the bedside and hung over their child but there was no other sign of returning consciousness. The nurse departed and they both sat down. David touched his child, his mood grim, and with his other hand he took Alex's hand and squeezed it. Nothing was said. Both were thinking their thoughts, conversation impossible in the darkened and claustrophobic atmosphere.

As dawn approached, the night nurses appeared and tactfully asked Alex and David to leave while they attended to their little patient. Once out in the light corridor David led Alex away to a private area outside the hospital.

'We always seem to do our life-changing decisions in a car park,' he sighed.

Alex rounded on him. 'Nothing is going to change as far as I am concerned.'

'Oh yes, it is, but I am certainly not going to discuss it here,' David said, his eyes boring into her.

'Leave it, David. My child is desperately ill in there. That's all that matters to me!' Alex ranted, her distress overwhelming her.

'*Our* child, and I am here now,' David said, clutching her wrist.

'For how long?' Alex replied bitterly, but their argument was interrupted by the nurse coming to the doorway and beckoning them. Alex shrank back until she realised the nurse was smiling. David took her arm and they chased over to the doorway leading into the now familiar corridor.

They could hear conversation from Polly's room as they burst in. The registrar was there along with the night sister and they were leaning over the bed.

'We have got some slight improvement, her temperature is now ninety-seven, and she is responding to painful stimuli – ' the registrar started to tell them, but it was too much for Alex.

'My darling Polly!' she said, her voice rising in the charged atmosphere. Stepping to the bedside she bent over and kissed her daughter, almost with gratitude.

'I suggest you go home now,' the registrar said firmly. 'Have some breakfast and a rest and come back about eleven, after the ward round.'

David nodded his agreement. Alex was now in a quandary. She had vowed that David would never darken her door again and she knew how emotionally dangerous he could be, particularly under present circumstances.

They left and made their way back to the car park.

'May I come back with you?' David asked, almost over-politely. 'We have some things to talk about.'

Alex hesitated, but she was tired and confrontation was out of the question, and she didn't particularly want to be alone.

'Very well,' she answered, trying to sound as though she was bestowing a favour. 'You can follow me home in your own car.'

It was a short journey home, and Alex beckoned David into the short driveway behind her. She waited for him to step from his car before asking a question that had been troubling her.

'How did you find out about Polly?' she asked.

'I rang your home and spoke to Nanny Linda, who told me.'

'Why did you ring? Alex asked.

'I wanted to take Polly out, my visiting rights,' he reminded her.

Alex pursed her lips but turned and opened the front door to her house.

David followed her in. There were sounds from upstairs as Linda prepared Guy for school.

Alex called to Linda and she and Guy came leaping down the staircase for news of Polly. Delight spread across Linda's face at the news and then she excitedly shook David's hand as he thanked her for relaying the situation to him.

'I'll take Guy to school and wait for you to telephone when you want me,' Linda told them, putting an innocent look on her face.

Alex nodded and kissed Guy. Suddenly she and David were alone.

They went into the kitchen and Alex immediately started to prepare breakfast.

'We'll have something to eat, and then if you want a

shower and a rest I have a spare bedroom,' she told David pointedly.

Over the breakfast table David was very quiet; it was obvious there was something on his mind.

'I daresay you want to get back to Doctor Ruth.' It was a statement rather than a question.

David looked at her with puzzlement. 'Ruth and I parted company a long time ago.'

'What?' Alex said incredulously.

'The marriage didn't work, you got in the way.'

Alex blushed. 'What do you mean, I got in the way?'

'You know full well what I mean,' he said quietly. 'I will return to London after we've seen Polly and I intend returning tomorrow and having a serious talk with you. You will be here?'

'Maybe,' Alex replied. 'That is, unless I'm visiting Polly.'

David nodded, then changed the subject. 'Any possibility I could take you up on the shower and a siesta before we return to the hospital?'

Alex nodded and showed him upstairs to the spare room and adjoining bathroom.

'Take your time,' she advised. 'I have plenty to do downstairs.' And she turned on her heel and left him to it.

Clearing the breakfast table, her mind was in turmoil. What game was David playing? He was not going to worm his way back into her life, and the news about Doctor Ruth was shattering. If she, Alex, was the problem, why had he not sought her out and declared himself.

Fatigue was now overtaking Alex and she too needed to sleep. Mounting the stairs she saw David's bedroom door firmly closed. She moved quietly, had a shower and crept into her bedroom. Closing the door and pulling the curtains she scrambled into bed and closed her eyes. Sleep was instantaneous. She was wakened by David standing over her with a cup of tea in his hand. Alex clutched the sheet around her defensively.

'It's ten-thirty, I thought I should waken you. I've phoned the hospital, Polly is now conscious and taking fluids, reflexes normal and so is her temperature.'

Alex breathed a sigh of relief and sank back on the pillow.

'I'll go and wait downstairs,' David concluded, and turned and left her.

Alex sipped the tea, it was welcome, so was the news about Polly. Getting up from her bed was an exertion, the last hours had taken its toll on her. She flung on her clothes with little thought of fashion. All she wanted was to hug and kiss, and be hugged and kissed by, her daughter.

David was downstairs in the sitting room. He said little, but he insisted on driving her to the hospital. On reaching the children's ward they were greeted with smiles. Alex could not contain herself and rushed in to engulf Polly in a bear-hug. Polly objected; she was not an affectionate child and even in her weakened state she still let her dislike of these displays of emotion be known.

Alex looked at her daughter; the swollen eyelids and listlessness meant there was still a way to go with the illness.

Dr Dinsdale appeared and he and David shook hands and discussed the patient, after which he came over to Alex and gave her the same details. Alex thanked him warmly, and it made her realise how much she wanted to return to the profession and be able to restore health to those assailed by disease.

Alex and David stayed for an hour and then went back to the house, where David dropped Alex off before heading back to London.

After his departure Alex felt lonely and when the time came for her to pick Guy up from school she was glad to chat to the mothers waiting at the gate.

'Is Polly better?' were Guy's opening words when he ran out to meet her.

'Yes, I hope she can come home soon,' Alex said, soothing her son's concern.

'What did she do?' Guy persisted.

'Nothing, just caught some nasty bug,' Alex said, trying to finish the subject.

'You won't get it, will you?' Guy asked suspiciously.

'No, grown-ups don't catch things like that, only children,' Alex told him, allaying his fears.

Guy's face lit up with relief and he skipped off ahead.

Alex spent the evening helping Guy with his homework. David's impending visit the following day was on her mind and after putting her son to bed Alex, too, took to hers, but in spite of the tiredness, sleep was slow in coming. The next morning, after taking Guy to school and ringing the hospital, she prepared for David's visit. She did not want him to see her downtrodden and dull so she picked out a newish dress to wear and gave great care to her make-up, particularly her eyes.

David arrived promptly. Alex delayed answering the door too quickly, and exhibited surprise at his arrival when she greeted him.

David was not fooled by this as Alex ushered him into the sitting room. They spoke of generalities as Alex prepared a tray of coffee.

Sitting well apart David began by producing a sheaf of documents.

'You aren't going to try and take Polly away from me?' Alex asked with alarm.

'Anything but!' David reassured her. 'Alex, this is my decree absolute, I am a free man, and I want you to marry me – please.' His eyes were pleading.

Alex stood up. She was taken by surprise, and words stuck in her mouth.

David jumped up and stood by her. 'Please, darling.'

Alex wheeled away from him. 'You can't just come back into my life when it suits you!' she told him angrily.

'Alex, I've waited three wretched years to rid myself of the precious Ruth. Had I even contacted you she would have found out and cross-petitioned. I couldn't let you be dragged into a messy divorce. I've lived like a monk in order for us to be together. She would have destroyed you given half a chance.'

Alex sank down on the sofa. 'Let me think about it,' she begged.

David came and sat next to her. He put his arms around her, but she pushed him away.

'I don't know, you will have to give me time,' Alex said, shaking her head.

David looked at his watch. 'Five minutes, ten minutes?'

'Don't joke about such a serious matter,' she said, pouting.

'Kiss me, Alex, it might help you decide.'

'You come barging back into my life and expect me to kiss you,' she remonstrated.

'We scientific types always like to prove our theories. I think if you kissed me you would know for sure if you wanted to marry me.'

He was playing with her.

'I wouldn't marry you if you were the last man in the world,' she spluttered.

David took her arms and pinned them to her sides and then sank his lips over hers. She tried to bite him as she struggled to free herself, but the more she attempted to shake loose the more insistent he became. She was now frightened, her heart was pounding and he showed no sign of letting up. She ceased to struggle, more because she had run out of energy than because she wanted the experience to continue. David released her and stared at her.

'Go on, don't tell me you didn't enjoy that,' he told her.

'You come in my house and take advantage of me,' she said, lowering her eyes.

'How many times has the boot been on the other foot?'

'You are beastly,' Alex said, curling her bruised lips.

'You used to congratulate me for it,' David reminded her. 'Give me one last kiss and I will go away.'

'What about Polly?' Alex asked anxiously.

'I will provide for her.' It was casually said, and Alex was getting confused.

'In the unlikely event of my marrying you, I wouldn't want the marriage consummated until a wedding ceremony had taken place,' Alex said slowly.

'I agree to that.' David waved his hand as though the condition was unimportant. 'We both know what we are getting.' He leaned towards her. 'Does this mean a "yes"?'

'A *provisional* yes, but you have taken me unawares, I will confirm it after a night's sleep.'

'Do I get my kiss?' he asked again.

Alex was smiling now, she nodded and beckoned him to her, then like an insect she leant forward and snapped her lips over his. The magic hadn't gone. She knew before very long she would be Mrs David Freer.

18

The marriage ceremony was a quiet affair only attended by both sets of parents and the children, and was followed by a wedding breakfast.

David had laid the groundwork inasmuch as he had gone to see Sir James and inform him of their plans. Much to David's amazement, James had treated him with great civility, and the two men had reconciled their differences, much due to their obsession with medicine. James was a soft touch for a professorship and to claim one as a son-in-law was similar to him winning the football pools.

Alex was taken to the London home of David's parents where she was treated with great kindness, and when David's mother cornered her, it was to tell Alex how happy her son now was, and how unhappy he had been over the last few years.

The formalities over, they returned to Rossington for the weekend. David was currently living at home and he and Alex needed somewhere quiet to formulate their future plans. Furthermore they needed to re-engage with each other and Alex's house was the only place to provide this.

Susan had insisted on taking the children, along with Linda, back to Westfield House to enable the newly-weds to have peace and quiet before they were thrown back into the hurly-burly of work and family life.

It was a wonderful weekend. Alex felt the burdensome responsibility of rearing the children on frugal means ebbing away as David set out his intentions for their life ahead.

'We will have to go and live in London,' he said with a questioning look.

'Marvellous!' Alex told him over the breakfast table.

'I have the finances to buy a house for us, my old man is a genius where money is concerned, and he's been managing my affairs for a long time now.'

Alex squealed with excitement. 'A new chapter!' She placed her left hand on top of her right one and gazed at the broad gold wedding band. David leant across the table, took her hand and kissed it.

Although there was much to discuss David did not lose sight that this was a mini-honeymoon and they dined out, made love and shelved their prospects of cementing the late arrival of happiness with domestic issues. Each of them marvelled at being reunited and yet fearful that it might be taken away from them. The weekend came to a close with Susan's arrival with the children, she was tired and seemed glad to hand them back, and she didn't linger even for a proffered cup of tea.

Polly immediately attached herself to David and cavorted about him in an almost flirtatious way. David grabbed her and pulled her onto his knee.

'Polly, I am now your father, and I want to know what you want to call me.'

Polly stared at him for a few seconds. 'Can I call you Daddy? All the girls at my school have one except me.' It was plaintively said.

A look of pain crossed David's face, but he quickly hugged his daughter and agreed.

'I have to ask Guy now,' he told Polly, lifting her down onto the floor.

'I'll go and get him, he's playing with his train set.' And she skipped off to find her brother.

Alex put her arms around her husband. 'Well done, darling,' she whispered as she nuzzled his ear.

Polly returned with the objecting Guy.

David beckoned him over and Guy hung his head and shuffled towards him.

'He's going to be your father!' Polly shouted.

'Be quiet, Polly, mind your own business,' Alex reprimanded.

David lifted the heavier Guy onto his lap, but Guy was shy and couldn't look at his prospective parent.

'I'm your new father now. I am going to look after your mother, you and Polly from now onwards.' David stopped. Tears were welling in Guy's eyes.

'I look after Mummy,' Guy whispered, the large tears dripping on his knees.

'I know, and you have done a wonderful job,' David continued, visibly affected by the little boy's emotion.

Alex was fraught. Her darling son, so special, and how he had comforted her in those black moments. She wanted to rush and pick him up and hug him but she knew it was important for David to make the connection and she had to stifle the mother protection feeling that was pressing at her.

'I want to know what you would like to call me.' David said gently.

Guy thought about it. 'Nothing.' Again it was whispered and he continued to hang his head.

'Polly is going to call me Daddy,' David said, gazing into Guy's face.

There was no response from the child.

'I tell you what,' David said more authoritatively, 'you think about it, and when you have decided, you let me know.' And he let Guy slide down from his knee.

The little boy immediately ran to his mother and buried his head in her dress. Alex stroked his head, she and David exchanged anguished glances.

'I have Banbury cakes in the tin, would anyone like one?'

Alex knew they were Guy's favourite pastry. Immediately Guy's head emerged from its place of sanctuary, the tears were gone and expectation was written across his face.

'Would you like one, David?' Alex asked in an exaggerated way.

'No, thank you,' her husband responded in like.

'I wonder if Polly wants one?' Alex teased.

'I want one,' Guy said, looking up at his mother.

'Please, Mummy,' Alex reminded him.

'Please, Mummy,' the boy repeated.

Alex took the tin from the kitchen cupboard and brought a cake out.

'Seems you are the only one today,' she said, as she produced a plate and made him sit at the kitchen table.

Guy's enjoyment was obvious as he munched away, and the mood had changed. Alex and David returned to the sitting room where they hugged each other, pleased that they had averted a sensitive problem.

David had to return to London and would not be back until the following weekend, but Alex had plenty to occupy her. With David gone she chased off to the local estate agents and made the necessary house selling arrangements, and now Guy and Polly were at school it was possible to start a big tidy-up.

Released from the dreary routines of the pre-marriage period, Alex, with her new-found happiness, was now on the flight path to her beckoning London life, and it couldn't come quickly enough.

After jousting with the house-selling fraternity she made a sequence of phone calls to family and friends telling them of her plans. She had kept a tenuous link with them as she battled with her single status, resisting all their well intentioned invitations for socialising, preferring to struggle on without revealing her impecunious state and avoiding the inevitable questioning about Polly's paternity.

Great joy was expressed at the news, including immediate offers of help with the move, along with the unlimited provision of liquid refreshment! In between these frantic telephone conversations David managed to contact her.

'Miss you, darling,' was his opening remark, then Alex regaled him with the contents of the phone calls, and her visit to three estate agents.

'I have been in touch with a couple of agents myself about a dwelling for us. They were a bit vague, so I rang Mother and asked her to do something. She has that "Staffordshire bull terrier" mentality when given this sort of assignment,' David told his wife.

Alex sniggered, no estate agent would be vague with that *femme formidable.*

'I have to go.' Alex could hear the reluctance in his voice as he told her, and she wistfully replaced the receiver.

Whirlwind energy now took hold. She had to make the most of her house and clear the clutter that family life produced. She would start upstairs. Guy's room was not too untidy but his model aeroplanes were space-consuming, making the bedroom seem small. She picked them up and stacked them in his cupboard. Polly's room resembled a fire alarm escape route, everything channelled doorwards, including the bedding. Alex picked her way over it and restored tidiness, which she knew would cause a major disagreement later on that day. As they were the two worst rooms it was now easy. Her mind was consumed by David. She trembled as she thought of him. He had lived up to her every expectation, even exceeded it in some areas, particularly where the children were concerned. The sooner she could get to London the better. Rossington was stifling her. Only Isobel had understood and been her mentor and she was the only reason for Alex to feel sorry about leaving the town. Only bad memories now.

Tidying up the honeymoon suite, Alex picked up David's

discarded clothing. She held it tenderly, then raised it to her face and sniffed it. That old familiar aroma of his was like an aphrodisiac, but today was Monday and he wasn't home until Friday. Busying herself was the only answer now, and if there were gaps in her time schedule she would go and have tea with Isobel or make the twenty-mile trip to her parents.

Polly was particularly irritating over the next few days, demanding and non-placatory, and Alex was glad that she was safely away at school when the estate agents called to inspect and value the house. Polly's presence could easily affect the price and possibly sabotage a sale. The agents seemed pleased with the property and gave Alex a better than imagined price guide. She told David the good news over the phone and then enquired if the 'Staffordshire bull terrier' had delivered.

'She has indeed, I have a sheaf of "possibles" for us to browse over this coming weekend, in between other activities,' David said in a low voice.

'David, I miss you so much!' There was a tremor in Alex's voice.

'I miss you too, my darling,' he comforted her. 'We won't be apart for much longer, I promise.'

'We have only spent four days of our married life together,' Alex wailed.

'We've only been married six days,' David reminded her.

Putting the phone down Alex felt miserable. It was going to take weeks for them to buy and sell a property. All she wanted was to be with her husband. The week dragged and when David arrived on Friday evening he looked tired. Alex uncorked wine for them and he soon relaxed.

With the children tucked up in bed and supper consumed, David and Alex relaxed on the sofa together.

'Is it half term next week? he asked.

'Yes, and those two will drive me mad,' Alex replied, nodding her head towards the upstairs.

'Why don't the three of you come back to London with me and stay with Mother?'

'Really?' Alex said with interest.

'We could have a week together and go and look at properties,' David said, stroking her hair.

'Are you sure she wouldn't mind?'

'She suggested it,' David confirmed.

'Then I say "yes, please!"' Alex could not think of a better solution.

'I will ring her now.' And David disentangled himself from his wife and went to the hall and phoned his mother.

Although Alex could hear his voice she could not tell what he was saying, but the beaming countenance told her what she wanted to hear when he entered the sitting room.

'Any time except Wimbledon fortnight,' David said laughing.

Over breakfast the following morning David relayed the news to the children. They were excited at the prospect and departed to their rooms to pack their suitcases. With breakfast cleared away and Guy and Polly gainfully employed, David produced his sheaf of estate agents' details and spread them across the table.

'These properties are huge and expensive,' Alex told David, her eyes widening with disbelief.

'I know, but I want us to have plenty of space, the children to have a playroom, me to have a study where little fingers can't intrude and a big dining room so we can entertain.'

'Five bedrooms, what do we need with five bedrooms?' Alex said, waving the house details at David.

'You need five bedrooms to get the necessary downstairs accommodation, my darling,' he pointed out.

Foraging around among the brochures was turning into a game of Pelmanism, but gradually they started to select a few out from the rest.

'This one looks really nice,' Alex said. 'It's about the third time I've picked it up, it has a garage and a drive plus a garden with lovely stone steps leading down to it.'

David took the details from her and read them. 'Islington, good place, a lot of doctors and their families live in that area.'

'I'm a doctor too,' Alex reminded her spouse with a bit of sharpness in her voice. 'I hope to be able to practice again soon.'

David appeared not to hear as he gave no answer.

The telephone jangled urgently. Alex jumped up, spraying house details over the floor as she ran to snatch the receiver from its moorings. It was the estate agent, could Mr and Mrs Rankin view the house in an hour's time?

'Yes, of course,' she agreed, and relayed the news to her husband.

A quick rush to tidy up and to muster and corral the children, but when the knock on the door came the place was in apple pie order.

David let them in and after a handshake and a climate discussion Alex took them round for a viewing. Mrs Rankin had a habit of sniffing as she gazed about, as though to imply dissatisfaction, while Mr Rankin addressed all his remarks to David. Alex knew that no sale would transpire from the encounter. It was such a deflating business selling a property.

London beckoned, and her spirits revived. Frenetic activity to pack and prepare for departure on Sunday. David was making headway with the children, though Guy was still shy and mistrustful, and Polly continued to display vampish behaviour towards her father.

'Practising on me so she has perfected her feminine wiles when the boyfriends come along,' David remarked wearily.

Alex shrugged. Polly's behaviour was a constant source of irritation to her.

Departure the next day had a carnival atmosphere, with Polly singing 'Lord of the Dance' and Guy clutching his model plane in the back of the car, and with Alex winding her legs round bags full of clanking jars and bottles and advising the small fry not to distract their father when he was driving, all boded well. Arriving at the Freer (senior) household did not disappoint. The 'bull terrier' appeared, behaving more like a Labrador as she enveloped them all in embraces. It wouldn't have surprised Alex if she had gone round and licked them all in her exuberance. It was a lovely welcome, and a vast calorific tea awaited them in the dining room.

Grandma Freer then showed them to their bedrooms; the children would be sharing one. It was large and she had put a pink counterpane on Polly's bed and a blue one on Guy's.

The newly-weds had been given a room at the back of the house which overlooked the immaculate garden. It was quiet and peaceful and more thought had gone into the placement than first appeared. Alex was warming to her mother-in-law.

Father-in-law was a more serious man ('money has that effect' David had once told Alex). Grandfather Freer was kindly and seemed unworldly, but Alex knew it concealed a razor sharp brain, particularly relating to finance.

A new world was opening up, one that was exciting and was going to bring her within range of her old friends and Aunt Sonia. She would be able to see them in person rather than have fragmentary telephone conversations with them at some ungodly hour.

Settling in for the five-day stay took place after David left for work. Alex unpacked and Grandma made off with the children. David phoned during the course of the morning to say he had booked viewings on possible houses, two for that very evening. Meanwhile Alex contacted Patricia about their move to London. Aunt Sonia was next on the list and a lunch was arranged for Thursday. Communication with Magda was only possible after six in the evening, but Alex rated it as a successful start to her London life.

In the afternoon Alex took the children to a nearby park where there were swings and slides, a useful place to escape to, giving Grandma Freer breathing space and Alex freedom to assemble her whirling thoughts. As there were other children around, Guy and Polly could play with them and not bother their mother too much.

David came home early. He was bristling with anticipation over the viewings. Grandma took the children and Alex and David made off in the car. David was pretty expert at navigating around London and soon the first property hove into sight. They sat in the car and discussed the details, eyed up the outside of the property, and then approached the front door which opened almost miraculously as they reached it.

Alex did not like the house, it was scruffy and the woman was over-eager to sell. They cut short their visit as politely as they could and sped off to the next port of call. This was no better, but for different reasons. Alex was deflated, but David was more practical and insisted that their search would eventually pay off.

Grandma Freer had supper waiting for them all. Alex was amazed at the transformation in Grandpa Freer's appearance. His Sunday grey cardigan had been replaced by a natty business suit and it made him look years younger. He spoke little but listened carefully, particularly when the house viewings were under discussion. He referred to David as 'my boy' rather than by name, and he added an 'A' to the end of Alex's name but it was affectionately meant. Polly had her grandfather lined up. She engaged him in conversation and behaved coquettishly as she did so.

'Not content with vamping you, she now has her grandfather in her sights. We are going to have some trouble when she's a teenager,' Alex told David, with annoyance, later that night and in the seclusion of their bedroom.

David laughed. 'I wonder where that "vamping gene" has

come from.' And he grabbed Alex round the waist and steered her towards the bed.

The conversation about Polly's behaviour ended there.

A routine was emerging now: David flying off to work, the park with the children, and evening viewings of property. Again, there was disappointment with the latter. By the time Thursday came Alex was glad to break the pattern and make off to central London with Polly and Guy and have lunch with Aunt Sonia.

They chose a restaurant that tolerated children and Aunt Sonia exclaimed at how big Guy was now. Alex quickly changed the subject when Polly looked thoughtfully at them both. The child was painfully aware of her diminutive stature and it was accentuated by the above-average physique of her brother.

The lunch was a happy affair and Alex returned to the Freer household with her batteries charged.

Again an abortive evening on the housing front. Even Alex was beginning to realise that finding a house was not going to be that easy, but on Friday lunchtime David rang to say he would pick her up shortly so they could go and inspect another house. Grandma again obliged with the children and off the pair sped, not hopeful that their journey would yield their future home.

'This is a property I quite liked the look of,' Alex said, browsing through the details. It was the lovely garden and that flight of steps down to it that caught my attention.'

'Right area of London for us,' David told her. 'Let's hope.'

First impressions were favourable. There was adequate parking for two cars and a garage. Stepping into the hall Alex felt an immediate liking for the Victorian house. Prowling around with the owner who dispensed facts in a laconic manner gave her and David a chance to imagine themselves living there. It boasted five bedrooms and the requisite study so needed by David, and by the time they reached the garden they both knew this was the house for the family Freer.

Alex stood at the top of the stone steps she had so admired in the details. A small stone wall flanked either side culminating in two small pillars with stone balls resting on them. She looked at her husband and he gave her a quick nod, then suggested they leave. They thanked the owner, giving no hint of their interest, and departed.

On the way back they excitedly discussed the next move to secure the property.

'Do we really need five bedrooms?' Alex questioned.

'I want all the children to have their own bedroom, their own private domain.' David told her firmly.

'With our family and a spare, we really only need four,' Alex persisted.

'Always use the fifth as a box room,' her husband reasoned.

'Yes, better too much space than not enough, but the house is dearer than the others by a thousand pounds,' Alex continued.

'Leave that to me, do you or don't you want it?'

'Of course I do!' Alex hugged herself with delight in anticipation.

'I will drop you off at Mother's, go and tidy my desk, and then come back and we'll get off to Rossington,' David said, glancing at his watch.

When the car pulled up, Alex kissed her husband and leapt from the car and in through the gates. She could hear Polly singing as her grandma prepared tea.

'We are leaving as soon as David gets back,' Alex told her mother-in-law.

A look of disappointment crossed the older woman's face. 'You won't have any food in the house, stay and eat here.'

'No, we need to push off, and we'll get fish and chips for tonight,' Alex assured Mrs Freer.

'Any luck today?'

'Maybe. You did a splendid job getting all those estate agent details. You saved us hours of plodding around.'

Mrs Freer was mollified and she served tea to the impatient children.

Alex started to assemble all their possessions in the hallway ready for departure and it wasn't long before David arrived and transferred them into the boot of the car. There was a sense of urgency now.

An hour later saw them speeding homewards to Rossington.

19

Living in London met every need for Alex. It was near to David's work, schooling for the children was straightforward, furniture from the Rossington house fitted in well, and Alex was only a mile away from her friend Patricia.

The house itself was better than imagined, and Alex looked forward to turning it into a home. Over the next weeks she did just that and to cap everything she sold her Rossington property.

It was turning out to be one of the most blissful periods of her life. Her husband was turning out to be the main source of her happiness. He was working hard, and often home late, but Alex wasn't lonely. She had too much to occupy her and was fast making friends. Comfort was the theme she aimed for in the home and it was being achieved by prudent buying from sprouting local antique shops, of which there were many in the area. David's office had every wall lined with shelves to house his vast collection of books and to prevent certain small persons' curiosity about the human body a firm lock was placed on the door.

With the final stage of refurbishment complete David and Alex gave a house-warming party. Heavily medically orientated, conversations were inevitably restricted to the alleviation of disease along with astonishing finds in and around the body. Aunt Sonia had moved around in these circles so long that she had no problem understanding the drift of these conversations. Her husband, Peter, was a little more squeamish, particularly when the word 'nausea' cropped up as he was helping himself from the buffet. A replenishment of his wine glass smoothed the irritation, and an 'incident' had been averted. Magda was in good form – she had gained a little weight, and her two daughters with their saucer-brown eyes followed her about nervously. Richard was regaling a group of fellow consultants with a humorous anecdote and bass-toned laughter met the conclusion of his tale. Alex had little time to engage anyone in conversation, in spite of having a waitress service which seriously under-estimated the speed the medical profession could empty a wine glass. Alex had to supplement the top-up service.

The party was a roaring success and when the final guest had departed Alex and David sank down on the floppy sofa, tired but satisfied.

'You wonderful girl, where did you learn to throw a party?'

'Ma, she's a member of the Women's Institute, and do they ever know how to put on an event, even in wartime they could muster up mouth-watering food,' Alex told her husband.

'You did us proud, my colleagues are very impressed, and they liked the food too,' David joked.

'It was so good to be amongst medical staff again, to hear the jargon. I shall be so glad to return and do my GP training.' Alex said stretching her arms above her head.

David looked away and didn't answer.

'I'll get on and apply this coming week now everything is settled.'

David turned to her and leaned across. 'I want to ask you something, my darling.' His mood seemed serious and it worried Alex.

'What is it?' she asked, putting her hands on his shoulders. She was losing her balance and fell against him.

David tightened his grip on her and looked into her eyes.

'I would like us to have another child.'

Alex struggled to get away from him. She was appalled.

'David, we have two children, one of each, and one is yours, why another?'

David kept his grip on her. 'Please Alex, consider it at least.'

'No, no!' She was almost hysterical. 'Why do you want another?'

'I want us to have a child together, I want to be there when it's born, I want to see it cut its first tooth, take its first steps, say dada, mama for the first time, smile for the first time.'

'No, David, I can't do it, you don't know what it's like, no sleep for a year, heaving a carrycot in and out of the car, being vomited over, washing nappies, no,' Alex told him.

'You can have help, we can get a nanny and I'll be there too, you don't have to do this on your own this time.'

'I want to start my career again, I'm not particularly young any more and Guy and Polly are at school and off my hands so I'm free at last from the chains of motherhood.'

David was angry. 'You will never be free from the constraints of motherhood!' He pushed her away.

Alex was frightened. She had never seen him so intense. It was their first disagreement since being married.

He stood up and left the room. Alex continued to sit on the sofa and think about what he had said. She was upset, and he had blighted a spectacularly happy day.

Minutes later David returned carrying a tray of tea. He placed it on the small side table by the sofa and then took her hand.

'How could I be so crass?' he asked quietly. 'My beloved wife.' And he pulled her to him and kissed her face. It was an act of contrition.

Alex held onto him, but she knew the topic needed to be aired.

Releasing her, David then handed her a mug of tea.

'We need to discuss this, don't we?' Alex said gently as she sipped her tea.

He nodded.

'Polly won't be back for another hour, so perhaps now is a good time,' Alex continued, taking control of the situation. 'You tell me what you want,' she coaxed.

'Everything I said is what I want more than anything else and only you can deliver it.' David spread his hands out almost in supplication.

'Everything I said is what I meant, and I want to make you happy too, David, but the thought of another pregnancy is just too much at the moment. Will you let me think about it?'

'Of course. If you agree, you will not be on your own, you will have me, and I shall get the best possible care for you.'

'My career is important to me, I want you to understand that, just like your career is important to you, and the fact I won't achieve the lofty regions of medicine that you have doesn't lessen those same desires.'

David nodded. Alex knew he was desperately trying to understand.

A week passed. Alex struggled to find a solution to the impasse. As in the past she found David difficult to resist and it was dawning on her that she would acquiesce to his pleas. He was right, he had been denied those first years of Polly's life, and for Alex it would not be so arduous having another child with a husband around.

Nothing more was said until she prepared a special meal for herself and David. Polly was tucked up in bed, having been pandered to in an effort to get her there early. David was also on cue. 'Something smells good,' he said, discarding his jacket as he came through the front door.

'It's that French perfume you brought me when you went to that seminar in Paris,' Alex teased.

David smiled reluctantly, and for once was lost for an answer.

He followed his wife into the kitchen, stood behind her and placed his hands round her waist. He gnawed at her neck.

'I was hoping you would dispense some wine,' she said, enjoying the contact.

'Special occasion?' he asked, still gnawing at her.

Alex wheeled round and looked directly at him. 'Could be,' she said archly.

'Every occasion is special with you,' he replied, then stopped, the significance of her remark sinking in.

David released her and searched for the wine and corkscrew. There was urgency in his movements as he popped the cork. Handing Alex a glass, he picked another up for himself and clinked the glasses and tasted it. Alex sipped hers and leant against the kitchen table.

'So come on, tell me what this special occasion is,' he urged.

Alex playfully pushed him away and made off round the table. David put his drink down and gave chase. When he caught her he whispered in her ear, 'How long do we have before supper is ready?'

'Not long enough.'

Releasing her he returned to his wine. He watched his wife as she served up the supper. Once seated opposite each other and beginning their meal Alex picked up her glass of wine.

'I will agree to us having another baby,' she told David. He leant over and grabbed her free hand. She could see the delight written on his face and in his eyes. 'There are certain conditions, though.'

'Go on,' David urged.

'I do not want any more children after this one and I want to return to work as soon as possible.' Alex leaned back, slipping her hand from his, and noted his reaction.

'I agree to both those conditions, and we will get help of a domestic nature for you as well. Darling Alex you have made me so happy.' He picked up his wine and toasted her.

It was several weeks before Alex was sure she was pregnant, and in spite of her age she was little troubled by her condition. David was particularly solicitous and true to his word arranged a gardening service and one day a week domestic help from a lady who had a colleague's recommendation.

Continuing to play tennis with Patricia, without mentioning it to David, caused a major dispute when he found out.

'I forbid you to play,' he said angrily.

'You can't forbid me to do anything!' she shouted back at him. 'This is the nineteen-sixties, not the eighteen-sixties.'

David backed down; he was on dangerous ground.

'I worry about you and the baby, I don't want any harm to come to either of you,' he pleaded.

Alex took advantage of the situation. 'What if we had a dog? The children have often asked if we could have one, and I could walk it in the park, getting exercise, now that I'm giving up tennis.'

David nodded. 'It will have to be a soft-mouthed one,' he said, having been taken by surprise at the request. 'The children have never mentioned it to me.'

'When we were at Granny Brandon's house they used to play with the Labradors and then ask if we could have one. I was brought up with dogs always around, and I would like our children to enjoy the experience of having an animal and behaving responsibly towards it,' Alex persisted.

'I'm not anti-dog, it's just that we live in London and it's not the ideal canine habitat,' David replied, knowing he had lost the argument.

'We have a lovely big garden and a nearby park. Please darling,' Alex asked, turning her mouth down.

'We choose it together,' he insisted.

'Well, I know where there is a year-old spaniel, his owner plays tennis and is going abroad and wants to find a good home for him.'

David closed his eyes, he had fallen into the trap.

'We could have the dog on trial for a few days,' Alex said, continuing to wheedle her way into an unconditional acceptance from her husband.

David knew he was beaten. He was certain Guy and Polly would join forces with Alex, and he couldn't oppose them all.

The dog's arrival in the Freer household coincided with Guy's exeat weekend. Alex planned it that way. Disbelief and joy were displayed when Alex's tennis-playing friend brought the dog round. Polly and Guy were ecstatic and chased the poor animal around in an effort to stroke and cuddle him. The dog misinterpreted their actions to start with, but biscuits and other snacks finally lulled the animal into the realisation that they would exhaust him before he would exhaust them.

He was a gentle creature, and seemed to say 'thank you' with his eyes every time he looked at them. David was quickly won over and accepted that 'Bramble' was now a member of the Freer family.

Alex now made the most of her decreasing days of freedom. She lunched with erstwhile friends, shopped in the West End, mooched around art galleries and museums and sniffed out antique markets. It was a relaxed and happy time for her.

Visits to the antenatal clinic were uncomplicated, and as she approached the latter stages of pregnancy, the calmer Alex became the more apprehensive David was. He had never experienced having a pregnant wife before and his concerns grew.

They were unfounded. Alex, as with the other two children, gave birth with relative ease.

David was excited and emotional as he was handed his son to hold and he gazed at him with incredulity before handing him back to Alex.

'I just want a cup of tea,' she told her husband. 'Bung him back in his cot.'

David took back the infant and started to rock him in his arms.

'He's only just an hour old,' Alex reminded.

'He's my son,' David told her.

The nurse entered the room and intimated that David should depart as certain procedures now had to take place for mother and child. David reluctantly handed the baby to the nurse, gave Alex a perfunctory kiss and a promise to return that evening, and rapidly departed.

The nurse attended to the baby as Alex changed back into her own nightdress. She was tired. A tray of tea arrived and after lying back and sipping the warming beverage Alex fell into a deep sleep. Later that evening she roused herself for David's impending visit and combed her wild hair. She added a little lipstick and waited for him.

He entered the room quietly, but his eyes were on the cot, and he walked round and stared at the little creature. Alex coughed, but her husband was too engrossed and full of admiration for the contents of the cot.

'He's beautiful,' he muttered.

Alex lifted herself up on her elbow to face the cot and said, 'He looks like a piglet, his feet are like trotters, he has bristles on his head, and he's all pink and squashed, and look at his snout.'

David recoiled with disbelief. 'He's nothing of the sort! He's wonderful, nearly every newborn has bristles on its head.'

Alex lay back on the pillow. Her husband walked round the bed and took her in his arms. Alex lay motionless as he kissed her.

The nurse entered. She had a huge vase containing red roses.

'Here you are, Professor Freer, I've put them in water for you.' She placed them on Alex's locker.

It was a shock, and the tears filled Alex's eyes.

'What can I say to you, my darling wonderful wife? You have made me such a happy man today, I'm beginning to think you *can* have four aces in this life.'

Alex put her fingers gently over his mouth. 'Don't tempt fate,' she advised.

David nodded and then changed the subject. 'What are we going to name him?' he asked.

Although a name had formerly been discussed, no decision had been taken.

'We need to decide as I will have to register him.' David told his wife.

'I'm quite happy with your suggestion, Thomas,' Alex said.

'Thomas James?' David asked.

Alex agreed, leant over and looked at her son. 'Hello Tom, it's Mummy here, and Daddy too.' Then turning back to her husband she commented, 'He doesn't look quite so piglety tonight.'

David shook his head. 'I don't want you telling him at his twenty-first birthday party that he looked porcine when he was born.'

'Oh, he'll no doubt be dashing and irresistible, just like his father,' Alex said, stroking David's cheek.

'I was going to say that he looked like you until you raised the piglet thing. I think I see the Brandon trademark in him, so he'll be wonderfully exciting and innovative,' David said, leaning over her and half closing his eyes.

'You are not supposed to sit on the bed, cross-infection, remember?' Alex reprimanded her husband, pushing him away.

David jumped up and returned to his seat, casting an eye in the direction of the cot.

'Polly has been well behaved, in fact leaning over backwards to be helpful, offered to buy me an ice cream,' David said, laughing at the thought.

'Just happened to buy one for herself at the same time, I suppose,' Alex said, shaking her head. She was well versed with Polly's manipulations. 'What about Guy? He has half term just after I get home, so he can see his new brother, and I can see him.'

'Our children are not going to boarding school, and I wish Guy didn't have to, but Christian left instructions in his will, and the necessary provision, so we have to honour that,' David said sadly. 'He can't call me Dad, yet, either.'

'Be patient darling, he was my everything until you came along, and it's difficult for him.'

'I love him as my own son,' David told Alex, gesturing with an extended hand.

'He's away at school having to stand on his own two feet, and he's such a sensitive boy, I worry about him,' Alex confided.

'We'll be seeing him soon, and we must line some treats up for him,' David reminded her. 'A new baby is a very distracting business and people feel left out.'

'He loves Banbury cakes, we must get him a Banbury cake, I always get one for him as his half-term treat.'

'Do I have to go to Banbury to get them?' David asked dubiously.

'No, no, there's a little shop that has them, near Patricia. I found it quite by accident, so whenever half term looms I get a couple.'

'I'll go and get some, don't worry. Guy will have his Banbury cake.'

The Banbury cake discussion at an end, David looked at his watch.

'I reluctantly have to go, the babysitter has to be home by ten o'clock tonight.' He stood up and stretched. Alex could tell he was tired.

'If you don't want to come tomorrow, Tom and I will be all right. Have an early night, because I shall be home the day after, and sleep will be at a premium from then onwards,' Alex warned.

'I shall be here tomorrow,' David told her softly as he made his way round the bed to say goodnight to his little son. Then, kissing Alex, he crept out.

Alex was longing to leave the maternity unit. She was bored. Her baby was thriving and she wanted to be back in her own environment with the family. Wandering about the following day she noticed the midwives flying around along with doctors rushing to emergencies. She wanted to be part of that again, along with having a husband and family to return to at the end of the day. Any chances of achieving in the higher echelons of medicine were gone for ever, and perhaps they were never there. Magda had managed it, married and the mother of two daughters, she was now a consultant in the research department. Patricia, on the other hand, worked part-time in family planning. She and Peter had two children also, so it was possible to combine motherhood and work. Not yet for Alex, and the years were passing.

She was solemn when David arrived that evening.

'I want to come home,' she greeted him.

'And I want you home,' he said as he pawed over little Tom. 'The house is like an empty shell, there is almost an echo when there is a noise, even Bramble is subdued.'

There was a shortage of news, so David discussed his work and some of the frustrations he was encountering. Alex listened patiently but with little interest; his work complex and breaking new frontiers, and beyond her competence. The stranglehold of motherhood was too powerful, nappies and baby-food dominated. Even David would have to take a back seat while she sorted out the priorities.

She realised she was not bonding well with her new son

and that was why she wanted to get home. On a one-to-one basis with Tom, maybe her motherly feelings would engage.

David was oblivious of her inner turmoil. Alex suspected he, too, was suffering. Their lives were disjointed and since being married they had not spent a night apart since the first week.

As usual he gave her a farewell kiss and stroked the infant before flying off. Alex did not sleep well that night. Tom was restless and snuffly, but he was feeding greedily and Alex was sure their discharge would not be hampered.

David arrived on time and belongings were packed and ready. They made their way to the car, parked conveniently near to the unit. Alex slid into the passenger seat with her new charge as David, with the help of a porter, loaded the boot. She shivered, it was cold after the overly-warm room she had occupied. The traffic was light but David was driving cautiously on the way home making Alex impatient.

Barking from Bramble met them as they entered the house. His exuberance knew no bounds, and he took a cursory sniff at the carry-cot and quickly established that none of his material needs would be forthcoming from that area so turned his affections back to Alex. Everywhere was neat and tidy and David unloaded the car. Alex put Tom in a ready-prepared pram and set about unpacking.

'Do we have plenty of food in the house?' she enquired.

'Absolutely stacks,' David reassured her. 'I cleaned Sainsbury's out of baked beans.' David hugged Alex. 'Welcome home, darling,' he whispered.

Alex clung to him. He disengaged himself and told her he had to go back to work, but would be home again in a couple of hours.

Left alone with her new baby, Alex felt tired and depressed. Tom had lost his neonatal look and had so far shown no signs of irritability, so Alex hoped his time-clock synchronised with hers.

She wandered round the house and lovingly touched

familiar objects. Three children now, she thought, any chance of a career was receding fast, but she had David and she knew she would sacrifice anything for him.

There was a stack of cards on the hall table. Alex glanced through them without opening them until she saw the childish hand of Guy on an envelope.

'To Mummy and Thomas, lots and lots of love from Guy'; two kisses followed. Alex clasped it to her heart and closed her eyes. Her beloved Guy, even so young he always said and did the right thing.

During the day Alex slowly started to impose her authority on the household again and when David returned she had unpacked and slotted Tom into his allotted place in the family circle.

The next weeks proved that David had kept his word – he had arranged plenty of nursery and domestic help and his attention to his wife was exemplary. Alex lacked for nothing, and as a proud father David was fast becoming a conversational bore: even Alex was fed up with him extolling the virtues of his children.

Little Tom was proving to be a good baby, and Alex started to take up a number of new interests as well as rediscovering some old ones. David had procured pre-course work for GP training, Alex had initiated occasional games of tennis with Patricia and involvement with charity events opened up a stimulating lifestyle, without compromising family commitments. She was also making new friends. It was a period of great contentment, and Alex was now forced to take stock. Her waning desire to practise medicine and the pleasurable replacements streaming in troubled her, in her reflective moments. It wasn't what she had quite planned for herself when she rushed off, with high ideals, to medical school.

Then, she had not met David Freer. He had changed everything and given her everything she ever wanted.

That was now her world.

20

Contentment with her lot was brought to a halt, and it happened after a particularly jolly supper party with some local friends. Alex was nauseated and eventually vomited the evening's intake of food and wine.

'Did we imbibe a little too freely?' David enquired with amusement.

Alex nodded, but blamed an allergy for her condition.

David roared with laughter.

Although she slept, Alex was still nauseated the following morning. She didn't mention it to David before he left for work. She ate some toast but the feeling persisted and over the next few days she had occasional bouts of sickness. Another symptom appeared, and with it came fear, dread and panic.

It was necessary to make certain of her diagnosis and to initiate certain procedures before breaking the news to David. She guessed what his reaction would be and she wanted her course of action to be cast iron, no room for negotiation. Fait accompli. The right moment also had to be chosen. It would be no good informing him as he walked through the door from work on a Friday evening.

It was Tuesday, and she prepared a supper to his liking and uncorked his favourite wine, but waited until he had finished supper and the children were tucked up in bed before she launched her bombshell.

'David, I think I'm pregnant,' she blurted.

'Oh!' was all he could muster.

'Is that all you have to say?' Alex said, trying to control her emotions.

'Well, it's a big surprise, and I'm attempting to arrange my thoughts here,' he answered.

'I am not happy, you promised me there would be no more after Tom.'

'I know, but darling we can rear and love another child,' he pleaded.

'No, we are *not* having any more children,' Alex insisted.

'Bit late to say that, anyway temptation was put my way,' David told her, trying to lighten the mood. 'Can't do much about it now.'

'Oh, but I can do something about it now. I can now, legally, have a termination.'

David sat back on his chair, horror on his face. 'I hope you're not serious.'

'I am deadly serious,' Alex told him, 'and you can't stop me.'

David calmed himself. He could see trouble looming. 'Whatever you want, Alex, I will back you. I am so sorry, I should have had more understanding,' he said, playing for time.

'I have already started the ball rolling, the sooner the better. I am fed up with this nausea and not feeling well.'

Alex could see shock on David's face. He was struggling with his emotions.

'I don't know what to say, except whatever you decide I am a hundred per cent behind you,' he told her softly.

'That's it then.' Alex stood up and started to clear the table.

David walked round her and stood behind her, putting his arms around her waist. 'Whatever we do we are in it together,' he whispered.

Alex made coffee and they retired to the sitting room and

further discussed the problem. There was muted accord between them and a plan of action was drawn up. Alex lost no time in getting the legal side sorted; it was not difficult, and when the obligatory green form was duly completed and signed David kept the pressure on to 'think again'. He was desperately unhappy about her decision. Tetchiness and coolness had seeped into their idyllic marriage, but both were entrenched in their solution to the problem. Alex was furthermore becoming sick. She was barely able to keep food down and needed to rest throughout the day. David realised that he must not only agree with her stance but whole-heartedly support it. She was thin, pale and listless and it broke his heart to see her suffering so, particularly as he was half responsible for the problem. He was also aware that it needed to be dealt with sooner rather than later.

David made this known to her and reconciliation took place. Alex booked herself into a reputable clinic.

Arrangements having been made for care of the children, David gave all the time needed to support Alex through the next difficult hours. Taking her to the clinic was nerve wracking and once there the receptionist asked them to sit down and wait for the nurse to come and take details.

David held Alex's hand, and continued to do so even when the nurse put in an appearance. Basic notes were set up, nothing more than name and address and next of kin and then Alex was led away. David stood and watched and when they reached the swing doors she turned and looked at him. He looked so forlorn, Alex stopped. 'I've changed my mind,' she told the nurse.

The girl nodded. 'That's all right,' she said reassuringly. 'You are free to do so right up to the theatre doors.'

Alex looked back at her husband. He was frowning, and couldn't hear what was being said. She walked back to him, and their eyes locked together. 'I've changed my mind,' she reiterated.

'Then I'd better take you home and look after you,' was his only comment.

Back at the house, babysitter Kirsty, hired for Alex's short stay in hospital, was relieved of Tom's care, but David asked if she would return and help Alex until her health improved. The girl eagerly accepted.

Alex resigned herself to the morning sickness. She knew that by sixteen weeks it would disappear, but it was a nuisance, and it was making her short-tempered.

Sunday was the one day of the week that David liked to sleep in, but Alex woke early. She felt particularly queasy this morning, so she slid from the bed, grabbing her silk dressing gown without disturbing David and made her way downstairs to the cloakroom out of earshot. She was perspiring and the retching was persistent. Eventually she controlled it by deep breathing and then stumbled into the kitchen, where she received a rapturous welcome from Bramble. Still clammy, Alex unlocked the glass doors to the terrace and gulped down the early morning air. Bramble raced down the stone steps into the garden. Alex then turned back into the kitchen, switched on the kettle and made herself a mug of tea.

The tea was doing little to relieve the nausea, but she sipped it anyway, walking out onto the terrace and starting down the stone steps. Bramble came racing towards her from the bottom of the garden. She could see him coming at breakneck speed, and as she took her next step to intercept him her foot trod on the dressing gown and she toppled forward.

The last thing she remembered was heading for the dog as he reached the base of the steps.

Alex was unaware how long she had lain crumpled on the grass. When she opened her eyes the sky was revolving and her head was buzzing and Bramble was standing sentinel by her. Closing her eyes to blot out these visual abnormalities she gingerly opened them again, hoping to stop the revolutions and the buzzing. Normality was returning. To establish how much damage she had done to herself she first moved her head. There was no pain. Then, one by one, she tested her limbs; again, there was no pain or displacement. Heaving herself up, she sat gasping, the effort had been enormous. Bramble stood by, clearly on guard and wondering what he should do.

Alex gave herself a few minutes before making the final push to stand up, but it wasn't as bad as she had feared. Her head was now starting to ache, and it was necessary to get inside and inspect herself with the help of a mirror.

Her dressing gown and hands were covered with grass stains and the bottom of her nightdress was ripped, she knew not how, but she held onto the low stone wall that flanked the steps and feebly made her way back into the kitchen where she slumped down on the nearest chair. Giving herself a few minutes before getting to the cloakroom where there was a large mirror and means of getting cleaned up, she patted the vigilant Bramble who refused to be parted from her, but she was recovering quickly now, no obvious trauma, and a clean-up would finish the clumsy incident once and for all.

Alex's face was dirty, particularly her nose. She sloshed warm soap and water over it and scrubbed the remaining green from her hands. She could hear David coming downstairs.

'Are you all right? he called.

'In here,' Alex replied.

David was appalled when he saw her. 'What has happened?' he said, looking at the grass stains.

'I fell down the steps,' Alex told him resignedly. 'But I'm all right.'

'Did you hit your head?' her husband persisted.

'Yes, I think so, I don't remember,' Alex said, feeling confused.

'So you were unconscious?'

Alex nodded.

David pushed her down onto the lavatory seat. 'Sit there and I'll get my torch and stethoscope.'

When he returned he examined her eyes with his torch. 'You know how dangerous head injuries are, how long were you unconscious?'

'I don't know, seconds,' she said, as he then put the auriscope to her ears.

Next he stood her up again. 'Take off your nightdress,' he ordered.

Alex shrank away from him and crossed her arms along her chest.

'What's the matter?' he barked, 'I want to examine you.'

Alex looked down at the floor.

'I don't believe this,' David told her impatiently.

Alex pulled up the nightdress and showed him her legs. Her knees were covered in cement and grass stains. David gently cleaned them and then moved them around. Satisfied there was no apparent damage he then examined her arms and shoulders. 'Bruising will occur in a few days, but all seems well. I am going to be watching you with regard to that head injury,' he warned.

'I'm all right,' Alex confirmed, 'in fact it's cured my nausea.'

David helped her up, she was stiff, but she could hear Tom crying and the day had to begin.

Once Alex washed and dressed it was like any other Sunday. David cooked lunch followed by a leisurely afternoon with the children. Because it was fine, Alex and David took them to the nearby park where Polly ran off her excess energy and played on the swings and slides and Tom staggered on his little legs trying to follow her example. David put them to bed after reading to them and then joined Alex, but tonight there was no pre-supper drink. The possibility of concussion was still in David's mind.

An early night was proposed. David had an early start and Alex had to book herself in for antenatal appointments the next day.

Alex was soon asleep. The day had been busy, and fraught. David, too, lapsed into a heavy sleep. In the early hours of the morning Alex experienced terrible abdominal pain. She clutched herself and shuffled from the bed, making her way to the bathroom. The pain was intense and she was feeling dizzy. She grabbed the wash basin before dropping to the floor with an almighty crash. Through the clouds of semi-consciousness she saw her husband's face and she could hear him shouting, 'Hang on, I'm going back to the bedroom to call an ambulance!' He placed a towel under her head, and when he came back he brought his blood pressure machine and took a reading. She could feel him tending to her, she knew not why. Time was telescoping and then there were ambulance-men lifting her and quickly and unceremoniously loading her onto a stretcher. She heard David instruct the ambulance crew, and the word 'incomplete' mentioned. Alex knew, even through the haze, that she had lost the baby.

'I can't accompany my wife as I have three children in the house,' David told the two men who were carrying her downstairs. 'Just get her to Mr Fergusson as soon as possible.'

The ride was bumpy but speedy, with barely any traffic on the roads. Arriving at casualty Alex was whisked in and then taken into a lift, from which she arrived at what she presumed was the gynaecological ward. Brief details were asked for, and she was asked to sign the consent form. Capable hands took care of the rest. She was past caring what they did to her anyway, the pain was so bad.

Being trundled to theatre by a bevy of green gowned beings, Alex could not wait to lose consciousness, and with wonderful suddenness it came.

Opening her eyes hours later, she found herself back in

bed, presumably on a ward. David was sitting by her side, his hand on her arm.

'What has happened?' she asked through her crusted mouth.

'D and C, and everything is all right. But you lost the baby,' David informed her.

'So I got my wish,' Alex said sadly.

'All I care about is you, Alex. What has happened, has happened, *and* we have three beautiful children,' he reminded her.

'Who is looking after them?' Alex said, concern in her voice.

'Kirsty is looking after them, and she is living-in for the time being.'

'When can I come home?' Alex asked, trying to lift herself, and looking for that absent glass of water.

'Probably tomorrow,' David said, and stroked her arm.

A nurse pulled back the screen and asked if all was well.

'Could my wife have some water please?' David asked.

A few minutes later the nurse returned with a jug and glass and checked that Alex was recovering satisfactorily. 'Only sips,' she ordered her patient as she filled the glass with water.

Once the girl had departed Alex disobeyed orders and gulped down the fluid.

'Tut, tut,' David said, smiling for the first time. Then he looked at his watch. 'I think I'd better go home now and come back later when you have divested yourself of this unglamorous theatre gown. I have taken a week off work to be with you and I have given my students enough work to keep them out of the local hostelry until my return. Nothing vital is going on elsewhere that can't wait.'

He stood up and kissed Alex and their hands gently slid away from each other as he headed out between the screens.

Alex's recovery was straightforward and she was

discharged the following day. Guy being home from school immediately clung to his mother. Polly on the other hand barely acknowledged her. Tom was only interested in a food source and that was coming from Kirsty. Alex doubted that he'd even noticed her absence. As for Bramble, he was beside himself with joy at her return, probably hoping that the children's mauling would be diverted away from him now his mistress was home.

David was exemplary with his help and support, but Alex was haunted by the chain of events that had ended so dramatically.

After David returned to work and Alex's physical health was improving, doubts started to play on her mind. Was the loss of the baby some divine retribution for considering termination? She was a doctor, committed to preserving and restoring life. So constant were the thoughts that she telephoned Magda and told her how she felt. Little sympathy came from that quarter.

'For goodness' sake, Alex, the fall was accidental, you have three children, and you're always bleating on about getting back to work. I should say it's all worked out for the best.'

Magda was now a senior consultant and head of department and reasoned that if she could do it anyone could do it.

'Have you told David how you feel?' she enquired, with a note of irritation in her voice.

'No, he has enough on his plate at present,' Alex replied.

'Don't come snivelling to me, tell your husband,' Magda concluded before hanging up.

It was a typical Magda reaction, but as usual she was right. David had to be told, and soon.

With the two younger children in bed and Guy glued to television, Alex felt that the conclusion of supper was the time to drop it out, but David pre-empted the confession.

'Are you feeling all right? he enquired as he poured them

299

an extra glass of wine. 'You seem very distracted since you came out of hospital.'

Alex dropped her head and stared at the table. 'I just feel so guilty,' she told her husband.

'What on earth about?' There was no hint of sympathy in his voice.

'Well, thinking about having a termination and then falling down those steps, it felt like a curse on me.'

'I don't believe what I'm hearing. I accept a few hormones are charging around your system but this is ridiculous.' David was staring at her bent head. 'Look at me,' he ordered. She slowly raised her head and looked at him.

'I know that there is no … contact … between us at present and that is normal,' he said, leaning heavily on the word *contact*, 'but you must not blame yourself for something that was out of your control.'

Alex shook her head. 'I know you're right, but the feeling is there the whole time and I can't shake it off,' she admitted.

'Then we tackle this together.' He reached across the table and took her hand. He did not, however, reveal how this would take place.

The following Sunday, David invited Patricia, Peter and their two children for lunch. It was a lovely day and it was decided that eating on the terrace would please the small fry and eliminate a dining-room mess.

Patricia was in good form, and the children all raced off together round the flower beds. Lunch was leisurely and once over Peter suggested a walk round the garden with Alex. She took his arm as he requested. Plant identification started the conversation off. At the bottom of the garden in the more leafy area, Peter turned and stopped.

'How are you feeling, Alex?' he asked gently.

'David's spoken to you hasn't he?' Alex asked him.

'Yes, he has, and he is worried about you. I want you to tell me exactly what is bothering you.'

Alex took a deep breath and related her anxieties as they slowly patrolled the garden. They ignored David and Patricia sitting at the table in deep conversation and the children occupied with finding a frog in the undergrowth. Bramble was sitting, lion-like, watching the scene, blinking occasionally in the sunlight and ignoring the activity going on around him, almost rising above it.

'I think you are suffering with depression,' Peter informed her, 'reactive depression.'

'When you feel like this you can't figure it out. Of course. I'm suffering from depression,' Alex agreed.

'If David had told you, would you have believed him?' Peter asked.

'Of course not,' Alex smiled wryly. 'I'm making his life hell at the moment,' she said, shaking her head.

Peter watched her carefully, then said, 'I'm not going to prescribe any treatment because I think you will handle this, it may last a few more weeks but it will pass.'

'Can you make David understand that I love him, and I will do my best to get over this?' Alex asked.

'He knows that,' Peter said, kicking a stone from the lawn.

'The more I tell myself how lucky I am to have a husband and family and a wonderful standard of living the worse it makes me feel.' She looked imploringly at Peter.

'You have to find a device for switching off these intrusive and destructive thoughts,' her mentor warned.

Bramble came loping towards them followed by the children. They were surrounded by clamour so the conversation was brought to a close, though not the ideas it had promoted.

The next two weeks brought little change in spite of Alex diverting her metal processes into physical actions. Her garden was overly attended, which led to exhaustion and tearfulness – it seemed she couldn't win.

A Monday morning telephone call from Patricia had the hallmarks of a chat, but towards the end of it she casually suggested tennis.

'I have plenty of help in the household so the answer is yes, but I haven't played for ages so don't expect too much,' Alex told her friend.

'I'll pick you up at ten tomorrow,' Patricia finished.

The next morning Alex put on her whites. She had lost weight and they hung on her. She tied up her hair, knowing how oxygen-fed it was once on the court. Although apprehensive, there was a tingle of excitement and she greeted Patricia effusively when she came to pick her up.

Patricia's local club was fairly prestigious and well financed and this morning one or two of the female members were sitting around with cold drinks having just come off the court. There was a full view of play from this vantage point too. Patricia made a couple of introductions, and it all had a friendly ring.

Patricia wasted no time in getting down to play, but Alex was feeble and Patricia relentless. It was a situation that Alex was not used to and when a loose ball came over she ran at it and whacked back at Patricia's feet. Suddenly the game came to life and her shots started to come together. Patricia was well prepared and stepped up the game until she eventually took two sets off Alex.

Leaving the court Alex was tired but she felt exhilarated and sat down with the other women while Patricia went and collected drinks for them.

Conversation was tennis orientated, but only in general terms, and the experience was comfortable.

When David arrived home that night Alex told him about the morning's events.

'Good, good,' he enthused, 'join the club, get yourself up there.'

'Well, it is rather expensive, but I thought that we should

have family membership, then you and the children could get up there.'

'Probably not me, I haven't played for years, but certainly the children. I presume there is provision for them?'

'Yes, there's coaching on Saturday mornings for the juniors,' Alex said.

David moved towards her, but Alex put her hands out, fending him off, and she abruptly changed the subject.

Over the next weeks Alex continued to play and her game was improving rapidly, to the extent that she and Patricia were being invited to play doubles with the top lady players, and were certainly giving a good account of themselves. As a result the summer fled by.

Patricia arranged a lunch party in her garden, now the warm weather was coming to an end and the clocks would be changing soon. The children were back at school and less boisterous and it was the most perfect day for such an activity.

Arriving at the Phipps homestead, Alex noted another car in the drive.

'I wonder who else is going to be here?' she asked her husband.

David smiled and shrugged. Alex had an idea that he knew something she didn't.

Peter opened the door and greeted them, leading them out to the garden. To Alex's amazement Magda and Richard were standing on the lawn drinking. Alex was flabbergasted, but her face was soon wreathed in smiles as she and Magda embraced each other.

'Do I get a kiss?' Richard asked, and held out his arms.

Disengaging herself from Magda Alex flung herself onto Richard, but she quickly pulled away and glanced at David. She had not been in his arms since her discharge from hospital, and it was about time that she displayed her love and need for him again. His patience must be wearing thin.

Contact with Richard, brief as it was, reminded her of that intangible need between husband and wife.

Magda was in good form and had lost none of her sharp observational skills in spite of her now lofty position in medicine. She looked every inch the successful professional woman that Alex had always dreamed of being and had never achieved. Alex looked enviously at her friend.

Magda and Richard's two daughters looked more like twins in spite of an eighteen-month age gap. They were quiet and well behaved and stayed together throughout the luncheon.

Towards the end of the afternoon Peter grabbed Alex. 'Let's go and talk botany,' he said, indicating the leafy reaches of the garden.

'As long as it's not biology,' they heard Magda quip as they headed for a wooden bench at the far end of the garden.

'I suppose you are to ask me how I am? Alex started.

'Yes, I want the truth,' Peter said, staring at her.

'I feel loads better, in fact normal, almost.'

'Why is that do you think?' Peter asked, still continuing to stare at her.

'Tennis. When I started playing again, I felt better,' Alex said. 'QED.'

Peter shook his head. 'Patricia once told me about you, Alex, that she had to beat you at tennis as you never conceded a single point. That told me everything I needed to know about you.'

'That's only at tennis,' Alex said, wondering why it was so important.

'No, 'Peter said as he stood up. 'It's about how you approach your whole life.'

'Rubbish, I wanted to be a doctor, and I end up being a wife and mother.'

Peter sat down again beside her, his intensity unsettled her.

304

'You could have been as successful as Magda if you had really wanted to be.'

'I don't have the brains that she has,' Alex remonstrated.

'You chose your path, you married Douglas Ffrench and then divorced him because he wouldn't provide a home or family. You could have surged ahead with your career but no, you meet David, then when that didn't work out you marry Stephensen.'

Alex recoiled, it was all true.

'Alex you are a wonderful wife and mother, which is a career in itself, and you chose it too,' he reminded her.

This time Alex stood up and looked down at the ground, and then she turned her eyes on Peter.

'I know you're right, and I love my husband and children more than anything.' She sank down on the bench again facing him. They looked at each other, tacit understanding between them.

'You don't need me any more,' Peter said, finally breaking the silence.

Alex nodded agreement.

'There is something I must put right as soon as possible,' she said thoughtfully.

21

Peter's words rang in Alex's ears. He had said what she could not accept, faced her with it and rationalised it. She must now mend her fences with David.

Easier said than done it seemed. A loving approach was ignored and he retreated to his study claiming urgent work needed completing for the following day. Alex was puzzled by his indifference and speculative thoughts intruded which she quickly dismissed. His excuse was 'pressure of work', and Alex knew this to be true. He continued to address her by the same endearments but she wondered if that was just an automatic response. She had to give him a strong signal, now.

Strategy was all important, no good jumping on his lap, or making his favourite meal; a clear and unequivocal message had to be delivered.

It was several days before a preposterous idea entered her head and it was due to a rummage in her wardrobe. The box dropped out on the floor in front of her, she opened it and found the nightdress and negligee given to her by her mother-in-law when she married David. Alex pulled back the tissue paper and the feathers on the negligee fluttered. She smiled. How she had hated the gift when given it. She had never worn it, but now, maybe, it would be instrumental in saving her marriage. A plan was formulating and it needed the right set of circumstances for it to be successful.

A week later, the opportunity presented itself.

'I shall be late home tonight, probably eightish, I have

a tutorial to give,' David informed her over the breakfast table.

Alex smiled. *Perfect,* she thought to herself.

David glanced at her. 'You're looking so well now, my darling.' But he did not allow his eyes to linger on her as he had done in the past.

'I'm feeling well,' Alex rejoined.

David gathered his papers, kissed her on the cheek and departed.

Alex was in a state of excitement during the day. When Kirsty arrived she locked herself in the bedroom and tried on the lilac nightwear. It fitted well and Alex tried out various hairstyles to complement the outfit, but finally decided to leave her locks to hang free, David's favourite arrangement. Finally she searched in her dressing-table drawer and produced an unopened bottle of perfume, a present from David. 'I give you this because its name is what you bring me every day of my life,' he had told her.

Alex looked at the label: 'JOY' it declared, by Jean Patou, Paris. A tear filled her eye but Alex brushed it away – no time for sentimentality.

At lunch she dashed out to the local wine merchant and purchased a bottle of champagne, which she concealed in a shopping bag. Kirsty had sharp eyes and it was best she didn't see such things on a Wednesday morning.

The day was interminably long. The children were hustled to bed, Polly being particularly irritating by demanding an extra bedtime story, but it still left Alex time to set the scene for tonight's romantic interlude.

With Kirsty gone and the children asleep Alex made her preparations for the evening. After bathing she slipped into the night garb and preened about in front of the mirror. In spite of the vampish nature of her apparel she was circumspect with her make-up and finally, before descending downstairs, she doused herself in perfume.

307

Time was moving on fast now, only ten minutes, and she made her way into the kitchen and placed the chilled champagne on a tray along with two glasses and took it through to the sitting room, placing it on a side table. Then she switched on one of the lamps, giving the room a cosy atmosphere. The stage was set. All she needed to do was to recline in her inviting nightwear, and wait.

David was a few minutes late. As soon as he entered the house he called her name.

'In here darling, in the sitting room,' she cooed.

She heard a slight scuffle in the hallway and then the door opened and David entered – followed by his student.

The shock was terrible. David looked angry. He turned and pushed the young man back and withdrew from the room.

Alex covered her face with her hands, she was shattered. She had brought shame to her husband, he would now be the laughing stock of the hospital and university, her plan had gone disastrously wrong.

Shaking with emotion she rose from the sofa and made her way to the door. Silently opening it she crept out and up the stairs into the bedroom, then wrenched off the offending nightwear and flung it on the floor. She was choking, she had to get away, she had brought disrepute on her family. Dressing in her everyday clothes she stole back down the stairs. She could hear the murmur of voices from the study. She took her raincoat and handbag from the hall stand and then let herself out through the front door and ran out into the night.

David concluded his tutorial by giving some books and papers to his student. Although anxious to have him gone, he showed the young man into the hallway and expressed his good wishes for his future.

'Thank you so much Professor Freer, my whole future now looks rosy because of you. I shall remember all you have taught me, and dismiss all that is irrelevant,' he said pointedly.

As soon as David closed the front door he quickly charged into the sitting room. The light was still on and the champagne and glasses reposed on the table. David put his head in his hands as he turned and started to search the house, calling his wife's name, first quietly, then more urgently as it became apparent that she was no longer there. In their bedroom he noted the discarded nightwear. Picking up the nightdress he put it to his face. 'My lovely Alex, where are you?' he muttered. Downstairs again he noted her raincoat along with her shoulder bag were missing, and this caused him to open the front door and check whether her car was still there. It was, but he didn't know if that was good or bad news.

He was powerless. The children were upstairs, he couldn't leave them and go out and search for Alex. It was a terrible situation. In desperation he phoned Peter Phipps. 'Sorry it's so late but Alex is missing,' he said, trying to control his despair. Acquainting his friend of the details, Peter quickly took charge of the situation.

'I'll be over, don't worry, she has panicked and when reason returns, so will she.'

'I can't go out and look for her because I have the children,' David explained.

'It just happens my mother is staying with us, she can baby-sit for us, so both Patricia and I will come over.'

While David awaited his friends' arrival he searched the back garden along with the dog, but he knew Alex was not there, he could feel her absence.

Patricia and Peter were at the front door within minutes of him entering the house again. David related the entire sequence of events to his friends, sparing no details.

'You and I have to go out and look for her and we take the dog,' Peter decided. 'She wants to be found, she planned a surprise and it all went horribly wrong.'

'We have all had that happen,' Patricia reminded her husband.

He nodded, obviously knowing what his wife was alluding to.

'Ring me every half hour, in case she turns up here,' Patricia insisted as she followed the two men and Bramble out to the car. She watched as they swung out of the drive on their mission.

'She will go to familiar haunts, any ideas?' Peter asked as they scanned their surroundings.

'The park, but it closes at ten,' David said hopelessly.

'We'll go to the gates, and let the dog have a sniff,' Peter replied.

The park keeper was at the park entrance with his keys. They enquired about the likelihood of anyone still being inside.

'No, I've had a good look, no one in there, sir.' And he looked suspiciously at the dog, no doubt wondering if the two occupants of the car were looking for an effortless final night's exercise for the animal.

Peter drove slowly round the neighbourhood. 'I can just see the headlines in the local rag, "Professor and psychiatrist kerb crawling in north London"' he commented.

David allowed a smile but followed it with, 'Where the *hell* is she?'

They stopped at the nearby phone box and rang Patricia but there was no news.

David was now feeling the pressure. 'If anything happens to her it will be the end of me too,' he said desperately.

'*Courage, mon brave*,' Peter told him as they widened their circle of search.

Alex was now sitting in a coffee bar. There were but a few other people there, and the owner was glancing at his watch indicating that closing time was imminent. She was contemplating her future and it did not look good. She would by now have damaged her husband's reputation as well as her own and she was well aware of the cruel jokes that went around about senior teaching staff, often without foundation. And there was nothing that she could do to repair the damage.

The coffee bar was emptying fast so Alex settled her bill and slunk out. The night air was sharp. She pulled the collar of her raincoat around her neck, more as camouflage than for the temperature. She wandered aimlessly and it was accidental rather than planned when she found herself on the Embankment. Going to the wall she peered into the blackness of the lapping water of the river below, but it brought no answers, so she sauntered along until she found a bench. Perhaps here she could sort out her thoughts, the key one being, *Would David forgive her?* This was quickly followed by, *What would she do if he didn't?* The children, too, occupied her mind. There had to be a solution.

The same questions were bedevilling David as he and Peter continued to look for Alex.

'I think we're heading for Battersea Bridge,' Peter told his friend. 'Let's park the car and go for a stroll.' And he veered off into a parking area.

Putting Bramble on the lead they sprang from the vehicle and started to walk, eventually going down the steps to the riverside.

'Please God, not this,' David muttered.

'No, no, but it is a great area for troubled contemplation, so my patients tell me,' Peter replied.

David let Bramble off the lead, but he wasn't keen to lose sight of them and circled around, sniffing the unfamiliar territory. The search seemed fruitless and as time dragged on David's concerns grew.

Peter continued to bolster his flagging conviction about the conclusion to their efforts and enquiries, but the conversation was interrupted by Bramble, who stood without moving then raced off ahead. David and Peter gave chase. In the dim light they saw the dog sitting in front of a figure, and David knew without any doubt who it was. He stood for a moment to collect his wits and watched as a familiar hand was placed over Bramble's head.

'You go, I'll wait back here,' Peter said, conserving his words.

David slowly walked forward. Alex did not look up until he was standing in front of her, obliterating the light. She knew it was him.

Alex looked up into his face. David was shocked by her ravaged appearance. He sat down beside her and put his arms around her, he was choking with emotion.

'I'm so sorry, so sorry,' she whispered.

'For what?' David asked. 'You weren't to know I was going to bring home a student, but it doesn't matter, I love you and I don't care if the whole world knows.'

Tears were rising in Alex's eyes. David brushed them away.

'In fact I'm going to tell the world!' And David stood up and walked to the wall, where he started shouting. 'I love Alexandra Freer, my wonderful beautiful wife, I love her!'

Alex heard clapping and looked to see Peter walking towards them. She was now laughing and crying at the same time. She jumped up and ran the few paces to her husband and enveloped him.

'Come on then, Cathy and Heathcliff,' Peter said, lightening the atmosphere. He grabbed the dog and attached the lead, emotionally affected by the reunion. David and Alex trundled behind, arms still entwined. Peter urged them into the back of the car and they sped home.

Patricia was ecstatic on their arrival, and David insisted that the champagne was opened to celebrate what he referred to as a 'happy ending'.

The Phipps didn't hang around and, after quaffing the champagne, discreetly departed.

'Tennis on Tuesday,' was Patricia's parting shot as she slithered into the car.

On their own for the first time, David pulled Alex to him, and looking at the clock he remarked, 'Yesterday is past tense, no inquests and no apologies, promise?'

Alex nodded. To rake up all the emotions would be disastrous, better to bury it all and start afresh.

Together they did their nightly prowl of the children. Both were sleeping. When all the lights were switched off, they slipped into their bedroom.

Alex noted the offending nightdress on the bed, David picked it up.

'Put it on,' he ordered.

Alex gulped. His eyes were liquid in the dim light. 'Why?'

'I want the pleasure of taking it off,' David told her, leaning forward.

Alex could feel her heart pounding, it seemed a good idea to her.

The next few days were a blur as Alex slowly reverted to her pre-accident life. Guy was due home from boarding school, Polly was less waspish and little Tom was developing rapidly. Her husband was her husband again.

She thought carefully about Peter's homilies and advice and her two friends and their fulfilled ambitions. Magda, highly successful, two daughters and a husband who had put her career before his – he was her consort. Patricia, two children and a part-time job in family planning and an achieving husband. Herself, wife, mother and a high-achieving husband.

All three as medical students could never have envisaged that they would all take different paths to personal happiness.

Alex wasn't finished yet. She would, one day, do her GP

course, but when the children were settled. For the time being she wanted to love and care for her family: Guy with his aeroplanes, diminutive Polly and her feminine wiles, and little Tom struggling with his vocabulary. Although it was mental descent for her she realised that childhood is fleeting in the grand scheme of things and the bonus was David.

Back in the routine she was surprised when he suggested dining out mid-week; there was no anniversary or celebratory reason for it and the idea did not seem optional.

'Anyone else joining us?' Alex enquired.

'No, just thee and me,' was the answer.

The restaurant chosen was one that Alex had not visited before and it smacked of understatement and expense. The other women diners looked at her with interest as she walked through the dining room. As Alex was only wearing her crystal beads along with her wedding ring she knew she would be socially marked down.

The waiter showed them to their table and seated Alex.

'Phipps told me about this place,' David whispered, excusing himself from the decision to dine there. 'I believe the food is good.'

The menu, when produced, was enormous and all scrolled in French.

'*Farci*, isn't that stuffed?' Alex asked her husband as she peered round the menu.

'Behave yourself,' David told her as the waiter approached.

They ordered their fare along with a suitable wine. The overpowering menu sheets were removed and Alex and David could once again see and talk to each other.

'Bramble has worms, I will have to take him to the vet,' Alex informed her husband.

He leaned across the table. 'This is supposed to be a romantic night out.'

'Every night is romantic with you,' Alex said, with a pretence of shyness.

The waiter then reappeared with the wine, which he proceeded to open with lavish gestures. David tasted the sample poured into his glass and nodded approval and a following glug, glug signalled the start of a particularly good meal. The pudding was delicious and calorific and Alex was more than replete.

'*Farci!*' she whispered, and David shook his head, though he was amused.

The coffee arrived with a small tray of bonbons. David started to rummage in his pocket. Alex saw him pull a small object out. He put it on the table and slid it over to her. It was a little red box and Alex gazed at it. 'What is this?' she asked.

'Open it,' David ordered.

Alex picked it up and clicked it open. Inside, winking at her, was a diamond eternity ring. She picked it from its slot and slid it over her finger, joining it up with her wedding ring. Then she put her hand across the table to show her husband. He picked up her hand and smiled, then let his eyes drift back up to look at her.

'It's absolutely beautiful, thank you, my darling,' Alex gasped.

'I was going to buy you an overdue engagement ring, but the message seemed more relevant from an eternity ring,' he explained.

Alex could hardly take her eyes off the gift. David was not given to plying her with jewellery, and it was the first piece, apart from her wedding ring, that he had ever given her.

After settling the bill, they sauntered out and once in the car they kissed and cuddled.

'Do you remember that old van of yours?' Alex reminisced.

David leaned back in his seat and looked at the car roof. 'They were wonderful times, but nothing compared to what we have now.' He leaned over and kissed her again.

EPILOGUE

Christmas 1990

Alex decided to have a family party this year, in spite of the country being involved in a war. It was of particular concern to her as she had worked, albeit briefly, in the now beleaguered state of Kuwait. Furthermore her beloved Guy was in the RAF and could possibly be sent out there. She tried to dismiss it from her mind and didn't even mention her fears to David.

News from the Gulf dominated the television screens and specialist advisers appeared from the woodwork pontificating about strategy and outcome.

Alex remembered how happy she had been there, the young Kuwaiti housemen eager to learn and to please, the British community sociable and helpful and the drama of the undulating desert underlying it all. She was sad for the predicament the country now found itself in and relieved that help could be on hand.

Christmas was now her main priority. Sorting out the bedrooms was going to be complicated. She had had a difference of opinion, on the telephone, with Guy on this matter. He was bringing his girlfriend and had requested they share a room.

'Really, Guy, there are going to be children in the house,' she had admonished.

'Come on Ma, you can't tell me you and David didn't cohabit out of wedlock.'

'I will have to ask your father before I say yes,' Alex said frigidly.

316

She could hear her son chortling away on the other end of the phone as they said goodbye.

David's reaction, when she approached him, surprised Alex.

'Of course he can, no problem,' he said with brevity.

'But Polly's children will be here,' Alex persisted.

'I want no argument about it, they share a room.' And David walked away, denying any more discussion.

The decision helped the distribution of accommodation, in spite of Alex not being happy about it.

Magda, Richard and family along with the Phipps ménage were coming for a Boxing night party so the Freer household was awash with food and there was frenetic activity to give the house a warm and welcoming ambience for the large influx of humanity that was to descend on it. The two yellow Labradors, Jason and Topaz, fell in with the mood by following Alex and David around, trying to source where the delicious food smells were emanating from, hoping their owners might be distracted sufficiently to give them a sporting chance at a quick snatch.

It started on Christmas Eve. Polly, her husband Nick and their two small children were the first to arrive, and they were loaded with baskets and bottles as well as mysterious parcels. For once Polly was amiable and the children wide-eyed when they saw the Christmas tree. All four would be sharing the large double bedroom, the children in two camp beds which they tested for durability as soon as they entered the room.

Guy, and current girlfriend, Jo, were next on the scene, arriving at the same time as David.

Alex heard their animated conversation and dashed into the hall to greet them. Guy looked so handsome, so like Christian with his broad shoulders and authoritative air. Now a Squadron Leader in the RAF, he had attained his childhood dream of flying, dismissing 'medicine' in spite Alex's hopes in that direction. David escorted him and Jo to their room, sparing Alex the embarrassment.

317

Tom and his wife Alicia did not arrive until late. Tom had been on duty as surgical houseman and was tired, but his spirits revived as he mixed with his family. Alex was busy keeping them plied with food. As for alcohol they seemed able to keep themselves supplied from the more than adequate store that David had squirreled away. It was midnight before they all finally drifted to bed and Alex had laid out the itinerary for the following day.

'Breakfast at nine, present opening round the tree at eleven,' she informed them.

Guy was already up when Alex descended to the kitchen the next morning at seven-thirty.

'Happy Christmas, Ma,' he said, raising his coffee cup to her.

Alex moved towards him and clasped him to her. 'And to you, my darling son,' she told him, attempting to plant a kiss on his cheek. She could feel the tension in him as he pulled away from her, waving the coffee cup in the air. 'Everything all right, dearest?' she asked, puzzled by his attitude.

'Absolutely fine, looking forward to today.' But he turned and left the kitchen.

Alex knew it was unlike Guy to reject her affection. Maybe his girlfriend Jo had something to do with it. Pressure of work did not allow Alex to dwell on it and as the family appeared and excitement mounted. Alex put it down to an 'early in the morning after a surfeit of alcohol' reaction.

Breakfast was a cafeteria-type affair, but it was over and done with by eleven, when there was mustering in the sitting room. Alex's little granddaughters were barely able to control their excitement and, dressed in their velvet party frocks with big bows in their hair, they sat cross-legged at the base of the tree, gazing in wonder at the decorations and the mountain of parcels at its base. Jason and Topaz circled round, stopping for a stroke and a pat given automatically from the assembled throng.

David was popping champagne corks and distributing the

filled glasses around. Polly then took charge. She dived into the parcels and, reading the labels, passed them to the appropriate recipient, making sure her two girls were the first to have theirs. Shouts of delight and laughter rang in the air as each and all unwrapped their gifts – all but Guy. He was in earnest conversation with David. Alex saw David nod in her direction and Guy came her way, no smile on his face. He was clutching hers and David's present to him.

'Thank you Ma, for this gold key ring, I see it has a St Christopher tag on it.'

'To keep you safe, my darling, when you're scorching around the skies,' Alex said, smiling at him and patting his hand.

'It'll be in my pocket at all times,' he assured her, and kissed her cheek. Again, he was tense and unsmiling.

Alex had to depart for the kitchen and check that all was proceeding well with the turkey, but David followed her and lent a hand.

'Guy seems a bit sombre, is he all right?' Alex asked as she basted the bird.

'He's perfectly OK. Probably too much to drink last night,' David told her, then changed the subject.

'Can you go and put that Christmas tape on, I forgot in the excitement,' Alex asked.

David immediately departed and soon the sound of carols and seasonal music gently rang in the air.

Polly appeared. 'I've come to help,' she said, her green eyes sparkling with anticipation.

'It's almost ready, so go back and enjoy yourself, and I'll come too, in a few minutes,' Alex said, waving her daughter away.

Polly was only too happy to be dismissed. Alex was joined by the dogs and they gazed expectantly as the turkey was removed from the oven, not fooled by the foil covering hiding the bird.

David, on cue, arrived to do the carving.

'You haven't opened your presents yet,' he reminded her.

'I'll do that after lunch,' Alex replied as she stirred the gravy.

David looked at her with concern. 'Do you want me to call Polly?'

'No, I can manage, it's just about ready,' she told him. David made short work of the carving as Alex placed all the dishes on the sideboard in the dining room. All was in place.

'Go and tell them it's ready,' Alex ordered, as the animation in the sitting room was reaching crescendo point.

The dining room looked so festive. Holly and ivy decorated the long table along with crackers, and she had put place names around, putting her beloved Guy next to her. She could hear the family making their way in, and they soon helped themselves to the food and took their places. The dogs settled themselves near to the grandchildren on the premise they would have more difficulty getting food from the plate to their mouth so the chances of a morsel or two coming their way ranked high on probability.

Lunch went well. The family chaffed and teased one another, Alex and David sat back and listened as childhood anecdotes were resurrected, and in most cases embellished.

Alex had never felt so proud and happy with her family as she did today.

Coffee was now being served. The grandchildren had been excused from the table and had taken the dogs with them to further peruse Christmas presents.

Guy suddenly stood up. 'I want to say a few words,' he started.

A few 'oos' and 'aahs' met his opening remark.

He beckoned them down, intimating the serious nature of what he had to say.

'I would like us to remember "absent friends",' he said with seriousness. It immediately brought the family to attention.

'My father Christian Stephensen, who I do not remember, but Ma and Aunt Isobel tell me he was a pretty wonderful man.' The family raised their glasses.

'Then our fantastic grandparents, who we pestered, and plagued, and the fabulous Aunt Sonia, how we miss them and remember them with great love and respect.'

Alex gulped down her emotion, she had not expected Guy to do this. Again the family raised their glasses, and the mood was now sombre.

'As the old guard leaves us, a new guard moves in, and we welcome Nick, Polly's husband, like her, a lawyer. He is a company lawyer, I believe. He should have done family law, being married to my sister.' Everyone laughed, even Polly herself.

'Alicia, Tom's wife, a medical student, so instantly acceptable to her mother-in-law.' Again more laughter. 'Then my dear friend Jo, works for a publishing house so if there are any aspiring writers here today, please do not take advantage of the connection.' This produced clapping as well as mirth. Guy took a drink before saying, 'In conclusion – ' a barrage of further clapping started. He shushed them down, and Polly put her elbows on the table and cupped her head in her hands.

' – I want to propose a toast to Ma and to Dad, the best parents in the world.' He finished and the company stood up and raised their glasses, repeating, 'Ma and Dad'.

Alex was shocked, she put her hands across her face and stared at David. It was the first time Guy had ever referred to him as 'Dad'. She was amazed at how David contained his composure. As Guy sat down, David rose, glass in hand.

The family waited expectantly. They all knew the importance of Guy's last remark.

'This is the only time I would dare to say the words, "On behalf of your mother" – ' There was uproar, and feet pounded on the floor. As the noise subsided David continued. 'On behalf of your mother and myself I want to thank you for the love and joy that you have brought us over the years, not forgetting our two lovely grandchildren, and may all your hopes and aspirations be met, as ours were.' David sank down on his seat.

Alex got up from the table and walked round to her husband. She put her arms round him and kissed him. David squeezed her arm.

'Let's leave these two to smooch,' Polly called, and ushered the rest of the party from the dining room.

Left alone, David pulled Alex onto his knee. 'I think we will remember this Christmas for many a year.'

'I'm so proud of Guy today,' Alex said, hugging herself. A shadow crossed David's face.

Alex wondered if her praise was too fulsome, Polly was always hinting about 'Oedipus' with regard to her mother and brother.

Changing the subject, Alex told David to return to the sitting room with the family while she cleared up, but he refused, saying he wanted to spend Christmas with her rather than with that noisy lot in the sitting room.

It took two hours to bring order back in the kitchen area and Alex was tired, but it was the tiredness of satisfaction. David decided to take the dogs for a walk to pep himself up and before daylight finally departed. After he had gone Alex sauntered quietly along the hallway and was surprised to hear raised voices from the study.

She opened the door to find Polly and Guy obviously having a heated exchange.

'What on earth is going on?' Alex demanded.

'Remember what I said,' Polly spat at Guy as she flounced out of the room, barging into her mother as she passed.

Alex was astonished. 'I want to know what that was about.'

Guy shrugged, but did not look her in the eye. 'You know what Polly is like, she imagines slights and insults, it was

322

nothing more than an alcohol-inspired brother and sister ding-dong.'

'I sincerely hope so, I don't want anything spoiling this day,' Alex informed her son.

Guy moved towards her and put his hands on her arms. 'I promise you, Ma, nothing is going to spoil this Christmas.'

Alex disengaged herself, then patted his hand. 'Good, so we'll say no more about it.'

Guy then propelled her back to the sitting room and asked her to open her presents. The family gathered round as Guy handed her a package. The presents were thoughtful and useful. Then Guy handed her a small box. Undoing the ribbon and label holding it together she opened it to find a gold brooch in the shape of RAF wings. She picked it from the box and immediately pinned it on the collar of her blouse, then kissed her son.

Polly stormed from the room. There was an immediate gathering round, the family trying to diffuse a potentially flammable situation.

Alex, seething inside, continued to act as normal but intended to confront her daughter over her behaviour.

David returned, his cheeks were cold but he seemed invigorated by the walk. Attention now back on her husband, Alex sneaked up to Guy. 'I think your sister is jealous, and I'm going to have it out with her,' Alex told him quietly.

'No, Ma, please do not, you have misread the situation,' Guy pleaded.

'She is not going to flounce around like some prima donna, I won't have it.'

Alex waited until Guy was occupied elsewhere before she slipped from the room and up the staircase to her daughter's room. She knocked on the door and heard a disgruntled tone to enter.

Polly was lying on the bed crying.

Alex went to her and put her arms about her. 'What is it Polly? What is troubling you?'

Polly turned her anguished face to her mother. Her green eyes, highlighted by tears, blinked.

'Oh, Ma, it's not fair,' and she shook her head from side to side.

'If you think I love Guy more than you, you are totally wrong,' Alex told the girl. 'I love you just the same, but in a different way. You are my only daughter.' And she smoothed Polly's rumpled hair.

Polly looked at her mother with surprise; her crying had stopped. She looked into Alex's face and started blubbering again.

'Everything is all right, I promise, just forget it,' she sobbed, and turned her face into the pillow.

Alex had no option but to leave Polly to it, but once downstairs she made an excuse to lure David to the kitchen where she related the disturbing events to him.

He was impassive, but said he would go and talk to Polly.

Alex returned to the sitting room and flopped into a comfortable chair and watched her family for any signs of conflict, but all seemed to be good-natured, though Guy was more reflective than usual, obviously upset by his sister's behaviour.

Alex went to the kitchen to make tea. *They could all come in here and get it*, she thought to herself. Assembling cake and mince pies she heard David enter. He closed the door behind him, then came and stood behind her. Alex leaned back against him.

'I've spoken to Polly, I think she is just overwhelmed with Christmas, nothing more, so there is nothing for you to worry about,' he whispered in her ear.

Alex turned and looked him in the face. 'You promise me there is nothing wrong?' she said suspiciously.

'Nothing. No one is ill, her marriage is fine they have no debts, she is just overwrought.'

'Why attack Guy, of all people?' Alex said, shaking her head.

'Fair game, he's so equable and understanding,' David explained.

With tea now on the go and everyone, even the dogs, replete, a mood of quietness descended, including the odd snooze. By the time evening arrived there was little interest for party games and nothing more than a snack was of interest. Polly appeared and she seemed recovered from her display of temperament. Christmas Day had passed.

Boxing morning produced an interest in activity, dog walking, the park playground for the children and a visit to some of London's enticing sights. Alex was pleased to have the house to herself, as she had to prepare for her other guests. David was much occupied by television news of the Gulf situation and sneaked off to his study to keep abreast of the situation.

As the day wore on and preparations were in place for the evening, a mass disappearance took place. Alex knew the family were in the house but not a single noise emanated from any quarter.

As the guests were expected by seven, the family filtered out from their rooms, dressed to the hilt, and a few corks started to pop as they awaited the arrival of Magda and family and Patricia and Peter with their progeny.

When the doorbell rang David went to answer it. The sound of laughter preceded the arrivals into the sitting room. Introductions over, the party started with a swing. The younger age group severed itself from the parents, and the years slipped away as Alex and her contemporaries talked of their past exploits and acquaintances. The buffet went down well in the midst of this and time rolled away. Before the end David summoned Alex out into the kitchen. Guy was standing with a suitcase at his feet and was staring at her.

'I'm sorry Ma, but I have to go.'

'That's a shame,' Alex replied. David was holding her.

'My squadron is leaving for Bahrain.' Alex felt David's hold tighten. She looked at Guy, then at David, bewilderment on her face.

'What does that mean?' she asked, knowing what the answer would be.

'It means we have to say our goodbyes now. Because of security, I won't be able to ring you.'

'No, Guy, please!' and Alex lurched at him.

Guy gently removed her clinging arms, and David controlled her.

Alex started to cry uncontrollably.

'I'll be home again soon. This skirmish will be over in a couple of weeks,' Guy insisted.

Alex wheeled round on David. 'You knew about this!' she accused.

'Yes, I did,' he confirmed.

'I made him promise not to tell you,' Guy told her. 'That is what the row was about between Polly and I. She wanted me to tell you, but I knew it would upset you.' He sighed, moved towards Alex and embraced her. 'Please Ma, don't cry any more. When I get back we'll go to some posh London restaurant and celebrate. I've already said my farewells to Tom and Polly, now I have to say them to you and Dad.'

Alex clung to him. 'Take care, my darling son, come back to me safe and sound,' she sobbed.

'I promise,' he whispered, disengaging her. Alex stood back as David briefly embraced him.

'Take care of Ma, please Dad.' And he and David shook hands.

Outside in the hall, Polly and Tom were talking to Jo. All three looked serious, but forced a smile when Guy, Alex and David appeared.

Alex was now controlling her feelings. Guy picked up Jo's bag and carried it along with his own, stowing them in the boot of his car.

Without hesitating he helped Jo into the passenger seat, then raced round and jumped in himself, started the engine, and was gone.

Back in the hall, Polly fell into her father's arms, tears and conversation muddled up. David led her into the study and calmed her, and Alex and Tom followed.

'Go to the sitting room and get some brandy,' Alex ordered her son as she and David laid the swooning Polly on a chair. Alex cradled her daughter in her arms. Tom made off and quickly returned with a bottle and glasses.

Alex poured the liquid into a glass and put it to Polly's lips. The girl sucked it down, her eyes rolling. She was cold, so Alex sent Tom to get a blanket. It was one that belonged to the dogs, but it did not matter.

'Tom, go to the sitting room and keep our guests happy,' Alex ordered.

Polly was showing signs of recovery; her cheeks were flushed and she was gazing at her parents.

Alex poured another two brandies, passed one to David and kept one for herself. They sipped them as they watched their daughter regain normalcy.

'Can I go up to bed?' she begged.

'Of course, I will carry you up,' David told her, and he picked the slight five-foot frame of his daughter up and effortlessly carried her to her room.

Alex tidied herself up and then made her way to the sitting room. She knew Magda was not fooled by her absence, neither were the Phipps, but they gave no indication that there was anything unusual in the air.

The next two hours was an effort for Alex, to keep the party mood going, and to do justice to the seasonal celebration, but somehow she pressed on and found reserves of strength previously unknown to her.

'He'll be all right,' Magda whispered in Alex's ear as they kissed goodbye. There were extra squeezes from the Phipps as they departed, and this gave Alex a determination to keep the family on course during the next weeks.

Once the front door was closed, the first priority was Polly. Nick had been sneaking off to look after her during the party and reported that she was still upset by Guy's departure. David and Alex charged upstairs and found their daughter sobbing quietly into her pillow.

The girl turned and put her arms out to David. 'Daddy, please, why did Guy have to go?'

David soothed his daughter, holding her in his arms. Polly hadn't called her father 'Daddy' for years and it made Alex realise how deep the bond was between them.

They had to keep their voices low as the children were sleeping in the same room. Alex and Nick left them to it, silently withdrawing without father and daughter realising.

Alex had to clear up after the party but to her surprise Tom and Alicia had already made great inroads into the task. Alex felt guilty – poor Tom, she had given him so little attention and he was leaving first thing in the morning.

David eventually rejoined them, more or less as the clearing up was done. He said little but Alex could see he, too, was affected by the evening's events.

It was decided that bedtime was overdue so they all said goodnight and departed to their respective rooms.

Tired as she was, sleep did not come to Alex. She lay with her mind racing in various directions but always returning to Guy.

After what seemed an interminable time she whispered into the air, 'Are you awake?'

'Yes,' her husband responded.

Alex sat up and put the bedside light on.

David was lying looking at the ceiling, his hand on his head.

'There will be lots of parents experiencing the same feelings as us tonight. We have to get on with our lives. After all, Guy was saying they anticipate very little opposition, particularly in the air.'

'It won't stop me worrying, but you are right, life has to go on,' Alex agreed. She switched off the light and they snuggled down together and managed to sleep.

The morning was dark and activity was coming from all quarters as the remains of the family prepared to return home. Alex groped around in the kitchen, getting breakfast. The grandchildren were bleary-eyed, but Polly seemed her old self again, probably helped by Nick. Tom and Alicia, both used to 'snacking on the hoof' disposed of their muesli and coffee and were ready for the off, after a few medical exchanges. Polly, Nick and the children were not far behind and once gone David and Alex sank down on the sofa with a mug of tea each.

'I shall remember this Christmas,' Alex mused, 'for all the wrong reasons.'

David ignored the remark and took the conversation in another direction.

'Back to work, I have a seminar looming up in January, what about you?'

'Much the same. I enjoy my GP sessions and the Wednesday antenatal clinic. The midwives do such a good job. Working two days a week works well for me and I'll stick it out for another year, when I will be sixty.' Alex screamed at the idea.

'I think we should actively pursue our plans of retiring to a cottage in an Oxfordshire village this coming year,' David said thoughtfully. 'Easy access to London and for the family to visit.'

Alex nodded. 'This house is too large now, but I must have a garden.'

'Let's do it this summer, say nothing to the children,' David said, rubbing his hands at the thought. Their hopes and plans were interrupted by the telephone jangling. It was the start of many calls that morning and signalled the conclusion of Christmas and the approach of 1991.

Alex was glad to be back at work. The practice was a small one but run on traditional lines, and even as a part- timer she was included in decision-making and her opinion was frequently sought.

She thought of Guy all the time and wondered what he was doing. The news from Kuwait was not good. Television now played a significant role in bringing the war into the family home, and Alex avidly watched the news as never before.

David was away at his seminar during the second week of January. Alex missed him badly, especially as it seemed the liberation of Kuwait was imminent. It was dark and cold and she had no inclination to go out, other than to work.

Arriving back home, David was pleased with his week away. All had gone to plan and more research of significant value was coming to the fore. He had reams of paper that he stowed in his study to read at a later date.

By the end of January, things had changed.

The RAF was now involved in bombing runs over Iraq. Alex was now in a high state of fear for Guy and all David's carefully chosen words did nothing to allay it. She avidly watched the news bulletins and it seemed opposition was there in spite of the optimistic assessments by would-be experts.

One item of information that caught her imagination was that small gifts could be sent to Bahrain via RAF HQ. As well as her daily letters she desperately wanted to do it and an idea formed in her head, one that she could not possibly divulge.

Alex went shopping to a nearby patisserie and made her purchase.

The next morning the two Banbury cakes on the kitchen table were creating a divide of Grand Canyon proportions between Alex and her husband.

'I *am* sending these to Bahrain,' she insisted

'The RAF supply every type of cake imaginable, and particularly those on active service like Guy will get whatever they want,' David reasoned.

'When he was a little boy his half-term treat was a Banbury cake – when he is strapped into that Tornado cockpit risking his life over Iraq, he needs to know I am thinking of him.'

Her husband softened. 'Of course, send them.'

'Guy is not coming back to us.' The agony in Alex's eyes along with the statement confirmed David's own worst fears.

Every mother says that when her son goes to war. Alex knew she was only one of many feeling the same.

The mood in the Freer household was now volatile. One wrong word was blown out of proportion and the news that deaths and casualties, in spite of superior air power, were now coming in, fed the situation.

David was in his study when the doorbell rang. It was obviously no one for Alex and she could hear voices, but a stillness had seeped into the atmosphere, in spite of a visitor. She presumed it was a colleague or student as she heard David close the study door. She carried on with her domestic jobs, then she heard David emerge from his retreat and make his way down the hall. His steps were slow. Alex had a terrible foreboding and when she saw David's face it was confirmed. He was ashen, and he was staring at her. He said nothing until he took hold of her.

'It's Guy, isn't it, is he wounded?' she said, shaking with apprehension.

'You have to come into the study with me,' he said gently, edging her forward.

Alex was gasping, her chest was about to explode, and there was buzzing in her head. The few steps taken were like climbing Everest and once the door of the study opened Alex saw two high-ranking RAF uniforms and the two men wearing them had their heads bowed.

Convulsed sobs engulfed her as she clung to David for support; she only heard snatches of the formal announcement – 'Squadron Leader Guy Stephensen' – then the words 'Killed in action' and then, 'courage and bravery'. She blotted out further remarks; she had heard all she could endure.

'Please go now,' she heard David ask with polite authority. Then as he laid Alex into a chair the two officers sidled out and David briefly saw them to the front door then came back to his distraught wife.

The next hours were lost in the most terrible grief. By the time evening came Alex was vaguely aware of Tom's presence. He and David were taking it in turns to be at hand.

A calm moment came.

'I've run out of tears,' she told her son, who had his arm around her shoulders. She could see the enormous effort he was making to keep his sorrow at bay and she stroked his face.

David returned with a tray of tea. The phone was ringing again so he set the tray down and headed for the study.

Tom dispensed the mugs of tea, handing Alex hers which had the suspicious whiff of brandy in it.

'Has Aunt Isobel been told?' Alex asked plaintively.

Tom confirmed she had.

'I can't believe it,' she told Tom, her eyes welling up again.

David, grim-faced, returned. He was deeply concerned about his wife and he intended protecting her from well-meaning friends offering their, sometimes eloquent, condolences.

A roller-coaster of emotions beset the next days. The family were all now assembled under their parents' roof, crying, comforting and reminiscing, but Alex was aware that she had to command every cell in her body to attend Guy's homecoming. Nick was supporting Polly, David was supporting them all.

The morning that the coffin was due to return to the airbase, the family rose and dressed. Alex, in her black coat with its furry collar and black hat, looked ethereal. She pinned the gold-winged brooch that Guy had given her for Christmas into the depths of the collar, stroking it as though it was a contact to her dead son. Returning downstairs to her family she took her seat. No one spoke, frightened they would initiate a show of grief impossible to control. Each had their own private thoughts and they mustered in the sitting room staring at the carpet, avoiding eye contact.

'Would you like something to help? I have some medication with me,' Tom whispered to his mother as he sat next to her.

Alex turned and looked at him. 'Darling Tom, no thank you, I intend to be brave, just as he was, it's the least I can do.' She was clenching her hands as she spoke.

The car arrived, and the family shuffled into it. Alex could feel David and Tom on either side of her. The driver was dressed in funereal wear in respect of his passengers.

As they drove along Alex looked out of the window. Everyone was going about their daily life unaware of the tragedy her family was living through – perhaps one day she would be able to lead a reasonably normal life again, but it would never be the same without her beloved Guy.

Arriving at the airbase, Alex noted a few other relatives waiting. Guy's navigator had been killed with him; maybe his family was represented here today. She did not want to think of this. The loss of her own son was enough to bear.

Refreshments were served and the staff dealing with the families were suitably respectful and considerate. When the time came for the plane's arrival they were ushered onto the tarmac.

Alex held her head high, her teeth gripped together. Again Tom and David propped her up between them. Nick supported Polly, who was fighting back her tears.

They watched as the coffins were gently handled from the back of the plane, draped with the Union Jack. Alex squeezed her hands together until they hurt. She was not going to let Guy down. She had some irrational thought that maybe he was with Christian in some peaceful and eternal elysium.

Per ardua ad astra.

At the end of the ceremony they just wanted to leave for home. David dealt with the ongoing burial arrangements and accepted Guy's tiny bag of effects, among them the St Christopher key ring.

'He loaned his keys out to a fellow officer, they came in a separate package and we have only just received them,' David was told.

'You mean he didn't have them on him on the fatal flight?'

'That's right sir, a colleague was doubling up on cupboard space and Squadron Leader Stephensen lent them to him,' the duty officer said as delicately as possible.

David was devastated and wondered how he could relay this news to Alex. It would be the last straw for her. He would select the appropriate time to impart this fact, if ever. He rejoined the little party and they slowly made their way back to the car.

The driver stood, head bowed in respect, holding open the door. They all stood and looked back at the airbase.

'You see, I was right after all. No one gets the four aces in life,' David concluded as he led them home.